Dedications

To my darling wife Marian - though you cannot see the love in my eyes, I know you can feel the love in my heart.

To my boys, Ben and Jack – If pride is a sin then I am guilty as charged because you make me proud every time I see you.

To all at Buckie Rugby Club – It was great while it lasted but I'm sure the friendships will carry on long after the final whistle has been blown.

To all the staff, support workers and service users in the Community Support Service at The Moray Council – thanks for making each working day a joy and not a chore.

Finally, to the guys in Iron Maiden – though you don't know me from Adam, you have shown me that believing in yourself and not compromising your ideals can lead to great success. You have provided the background music to my life for the last three decades and long may it continue. Up The Irons!

Acknowledgements

To my parents, Les and Della, thank you for instilling the beauty, power and importance of the written word in me.

To Michael Molden and all at Cauliay Books – Thank you so much for taking a chance on the book and on me. I hope I can repay your faith.

Also to Mary Madden, Susan Watson, Gordon Gillies and Sean Jamieson – the privileged few who got to read it before it hit the shelves (you lucky, lucky people) – thank you for the honest feedback and the constructive criticism – you all played your part in changing it for the better.

The Crownless King

Prologue

The Holy Grail. The mythical cup of Christ. It is said to have touched His lips at the Last Supper and held His blood as He lay dying upon the cross atop Golgotha. The purity and goodness within Him are reputed to have imbued the Grail with awesome powers and rendered it anathema to those who sought to sully the world with wickedness and evil.

The Grail has been pursued across countries and across centuries. There is no doubt that it engenders a thrilling, romantic presence in the hearts of all who seek it, but as to what occurs when its magics are unleashed, well, that is knowledge that has so far escaped its pursuers.

*

The legends surrounding the Grail are multi-layered and tinged with the truth. It is likely that the Grail did come to be housed within the confines of Camelot under the stewardship of King Arthur and the Knights of the Round Table after following a circuitous route from the Holy Land. But what occurred after that happy chance?

What occurred after Galahad the Pure succeeded in his quest to find this most holy of holy artifacts? On that matter, legend is silent.

Does the Grail now preside upon the isle of Avalon, taking pride of place upon the Lady of The Lake's table?

Did it even make the journey across the Silver Lady's waters in the company of the noble King Arthur after he fell in battle?

Did Merlin, the mighty magician of Camelot, have other plans for a vessel so powerful that its like would never again grace the earth with its presence?

Did the forces of evil seize the Grail from the environs of King Arthur's stronghold in an attempt to pervert the power that was held within the Cup to their own foul ends?

Or, perhaps, the most pressing question of all should be, where does it reside now?

*

The Crownless King

By

Phil Williams

Published by

Cauliay Publishing & Distribution
PO Box 12076
Aberdeen
AB16 9AL
www.cauliaybooks.com

First Edition
ISBN 978-0-9568810-4-5
Copyright © Phil Williams 2011
Front cover: Gustave Doré's illustration of Lord Alfred Tennyson's
"Idylls of the King" (1868)

A CIP catalogue record for this book is available from the British Library.

Chapter 1

AD 30 - The Garden of Gethsemane

A pleasant breeze insinuated itself around the diners as they broke bread and partook of the robust red wine laid out for their consumption. A jovial atmosphere seemed to be the order of the day for all at the table. All bar one. One of the feasters sat in moody contemplation as the revelry went on around him. Philip, one of the twelve contented guests, attempted to engage the despondent one in conversation as he indicated the food with a sharp flick of his head.

"A most satisfying feast, is it not," he said, nodding towards the myriad platters of bread, cheese and various sweetmeats that were arrayed across the table. The man momentarily surfaced from his thoughts and nodded distractedly.

"Hmm? Yes, Philip, indeed it is." *Not bad for a last meal,* he added, in the privacy of his own head.

Philip found himself waiting for something further. He studied the normally benign features of the man's face, the face that he had come to know and love so deeply. The countenance that was normally so peaceful and calm seemed shrouded in an uncharacteristic gloom and the sparkling blue eyes were devoid of their omnipresent gleam, dulled, Philip was sure, by whatever weight his leader was bearing upon his shoulders. The gentle ever-smiling mouth was turned down at the corners, a sight so unusual that it took away the appetite of the apostle in a second. When it became clear that nothing more would be forthcoming, Philip yanked the chair next to the doleful dinner guest out from its niche under the table and sat down upon it heavily.

"What ails you, Lord? Your food remains untouched, your drink undrunk. I sense you are in turmoil."

Jesus Christ looked at his young disciple with an equal measure of irritation at the interruption of his thoughts and warmth at the fact that Philip was concerned enough to forgo his own enjoyment to try and get to the crux of whatever troubled him. He reached out and tenderly stroked the hairless chin of his follower, emerging from his own miserable thoughts to try and soothe his adherent's worries for his state of mind.

"You too would be in turmoil if you knew what I knew." Jesus gestured around the table. "One of these that we dine with, one of these so-called *friends* will betray me to the Roman legions before the sun is set."

Philip jerked back at the venom with which Jesus had spat out the word. At first he looked incredulous but when it became clear that his master was deadly serious, he could not help his gaze travelling from face to face, wondering who the perpetrator of such a heinous act could be.

Another guest sauntered over, seemingly the worst for wear. His tightly curled beard was dotted with crumbs and grease from the feast and his smock was besmirched with wine stains, yet his emerald green eyes were hooded and full of purpose, standing out in stark contrast to his suntanned skin. He smiled smarmily and placed his hands upon the shoulders of the two diners.

"What is all this hushed talk and searching eyes? Plotting to bring down Pontius Pilate?" he slurred.

Jesus and Philip leant away from each other for the man's breath reeked of wine and spicy food. "Not at all, brother," Jesus answered, "We were merely chatting. Tell me, is the food to your satisfaction?"

"Indeed it is, brother," the newcomer said, taking Philip by surprise by leaning between them and planting a kiss on Christ's cheek. "Most splendid, most splendid," he nodded.

Jesus forced a smile upon his face. "Good, I am glad it is to your liking, Judas. I hope it does not choke you."

The disciple looked slightly taken aback but disguised his unease with another toothy grin. "I hope so too, brother." He turned to Philip with a cursory nod and returned to his seat at the other end of the table.

Jesus drained a long drink from his hitherto untouched cup and banged it down upon the table.

Philip jumped like a startled rabbit. He stared intently at Jesus then to Judas.

"You think he is the one? Judas?" He could barely contain his disbelief, although now he was in possession of the traitor's identity, he began to notice little idiosyncracies in the fellow's behaviour that would have escaped him in the normal course of events, the constantly moving eyes darting all around the enclosure, glancing at but never resting on the messiah, the pink tongue darting out continuously, nervously licking lips that had been touched by copious amounts of wine but very little food, the hands forever being wiped upon the man's smock to free them of the guilty sweat with which they found themselves awash.

Jesus drew a hand over his tired face, "Aye, for thirty pieces of Roman blood money."

Philip rose aggressively to confront his fellow disciple, so aggressively in fact that he nearly knocked his chair over, which drew intrigued glances from those who witnessed it.

Laying a gentle hand on Philip's arm, Jesus shook his head. "What purpose would it serve? The deed is done." He touched his fingers to his stubbled cheek and stroked it gently, looking at his hand as if expecting to see some sort of blemish upon it as it left his face. "I have been marked out. How easily an act of love becomes an act of betrayal."

Philip could feel the tears twinkling in his eyes. In a voice that cracked with emotions barely held in check, he wailed, "Well, you must flee then."

Jesus shook his head once more, "To where? The Roman wolf will not rest until it has rent me in its jaws. No, no more hiding. It is my destiny. It is His will." Jesus pushed his chair away from the table and stood up. "Philip, know this. My death will not be in vain. My death is a beginning, not an end." He bestowed a loving gaze on eleven of his twelve disciples. "I go now to search out my fate." He patted his compatriot's shoulder, "Farewell."

Philip sat open-mouthed with tears streaming down his smooth cheeks as his mentor and friend left the garden to meet his doom. "Farewell, brother," he whispered under his breath. Turning back to the now unpalatable feast in front of him, he picked up Jesus' cup and turned it round and round in his hands.

*

Christ's youngest disciple pushed his way through the frenzied baying crowd as it wended its way up the dusty road, following the march of the condemned. The sun was merciless, beating down upon the bruises and weals that decorated the backs of the hopeless. Philip turned to the man on his left, who was also elbowing his way through the throng. "Simon," he hissed, "I am going to try and help him."

Philip's fellow disciple and attendee at Jesus' last supper looked aghast at his friend's suggestion, his deep brown eyes starting from his head. "Is there nothing else we can do? You will be crucified yourself. You know the penalty."

"Would you have me do nothing?" Philip's eyes blazed dangerously. He peered out through the crowd and past the guards as Jesus made his slow painful way up the slope, gasping in shock as he beheld the vivid scarlet cuts that had been wrought by the scourging that was always endured by the crucifixion victims to weaken them before they began the final journey to their death. Whether he felt Philip's gaze upon him or not the disciple did not know but to his surprise Jesus' eyes came up momentarily and almost imperceptibly he shook his head.

Philip turned back to his friend with despair in his eyes, an expression that Simon found all the more striking when compared to the rage that had been there scant seconds ago.

"What is it?" he asked urgently.

9

"He will not have me help him," Philip sobbed, "I tried to reason with him last evening but to no avail. His mind was made up then and it would seem that nothing has changed."

"Perhaps he has some ruse, some miracle that he will perform to save himself from this blasphemy." Simon shouted hopefully, the need to raise his voice caused by the growing intensity of the crowd's bloodlust as the execution site came into view. "After all, he is our saviour. He is God's son. Will the Holy Father stand by and let his own son die?"

Philip looked sidelong at his compatriot, "You are looking for answers to questions that I cannot even begin to understand. He said last evening that it was the Holy Father's will for this obscenity to happen."

"Letting his only son perish at the hands of the Romans? Surely you cannot be serious?" Simon snorted, tugging at his lustrous black beard as was his habit in times of stress.

"Who can say?" Philip shrugged. They both found their gazes drawn up the hill to the summit, where some crucifixes already stood, their occupants either swaying gently in the breeze as they hung, bereft of life, or screaming in pain, beseeching, pleading for an end to their torment.

Philip's gaze was wrenched back to Jesus as a stone flew from somewhere amidst the howling mob and hit him upon his abused back causing him to stumble and nearly lose his grip on the cross he bore.

As it was, it was Simon not Philip who broke free of the crowd, ducking between two Roman legionaries and racing across the arid track to lift the messiah's burden for a few seconds, knowing full well the futility of the gesture but overwhelmed by the need to do it nonetheless. He looked down at Jesus' grateful face. "It cannot end like this, Lord."

Through parched lips, Jesus whispered in a voice that somehow carried to Simon's ears above the noise of the crowd, "As I told Philip, this is a beginning, not an end. Please, rejoin the crowd. There is little sense in us both being sacrificial lambs."

Simon was grabbed by the back of his tunic and yanked to the ground. A Roman soldier levelled his spear at Simon's throat and with a face distorted by hatred and disdain, snarled, "Do you wish to join this scum upon the hill? Make no mistake, there is always room for another one of you bastard Christians up there."

"Please, he meant no harm. Let him go," Jesus implored.

The guard turned and smacked the back of his gauntlet-encased hand across Jesus' face, sending a jet of blood spattering onto the ground. "Quiet." He swung back to Simon and shook his fist. "Get out of my sight before I change my mind."

Leaving Simon slumped on the sandy trail, the Roman and his prisoner resumed the slow procession to the killing ground. Simon got up painfully, dusted himself down and walked forlornly back to Philip in the furrow scored in the dust by his mentor's crucifix. He shook his head sadly and rejoined his fellow disciple, ignoring the mocking looks and sneering laughter being directed at him.

"He means to go through with it. There is nothing on God's earth that will sway him. I saw it in his eyes, he knows his time is near."

"I suspected as much when he looked at me just now," Philip breathed, a huge sigh escaping his lips. "If that is the case then all we can do is stand vigil, pray for Him and provide comfort where we can."

They both squinted into the sun to watch Jesus as he laboured towards his own execution.

*

Night had fallen.

Philip and Simon had maintained their vigil from the moment that Jesus had been raised, naked and bloodied, upon the cross. They both huddled against each other to try and combat the growing drop in temperature as the hour grew later and the darkness grew deeper. Suspended above them was their leader, their mentor, their captain, but most of all, their friend.

"This is inhuman," Simon hissed through gritted teeth.

Philip looked up as Jesus stirred. When he was sure that he was still unconscious, he nodded at the statement. "This is but the start. I have heard of men being alive for days on these monstrosities."

"No!" Simon gaped in disbelief, "What manner of man devised such torture? It beggars belief."

Philip laughed bitterly. "Witness the product of Roman civilisation," he spat.

They both jumped as a weak voice drifted down from on high.

"Ah, my two companions. Still waiting, I see," Jesus murmured.

"We swore an oath in your name, Lord," Philip said. "Your death will not be in vain. We will spread your words and your beliefs. We will ensure that all will hear of your demise. As God is my witness, you will live on. In the stories that are told and the songs that are sung." They both dropped to their knees and hung their heads.

"And in the prayers that are offered," Simon finished. "Lord, your death will be a symbol, a source of hope to all who follow you and live by your teachings."

A smile appeared on the Son of God's face. "Even in my current situation, your sentiment is of great solace. I..."

11

A fanfare of bugles ripped the peace of the night apart and drowned out Jesus' words. Out of the gloom, an assortment of Romans appeared, made up of an equal mix of both civilian and military. In the vanguard was a grossly fat man draped in a hugely expensive cloak of finest fur. He strolled up and down, arrogantly peering from victim to victim. He glanced down at Philip and Simon and his jowls wobbled as an unprepossessing sneer flickered across his face. Without a second thought, he dismissed them as unworthy of further scrutiny. He then beckoned to one of the soldiers liberally scattered among the group which had accompanied him to the beach, "You. Come here."

The soldier jogged over smartly and ripped off a textbook salute. The fat Roman waved a languid hand in the direction of the crucified.

"Which one of these is the Nazarene?"

The legionary glanced at a couple of faces before jerking his spear towards Jesus, "This one, sir."

The Roman waddled over to the cross and circled it a couple of times, all the while not taking his eyes off Jesus' face. "So this is our messiah, is it?" he smirked. "This is the Son of God?" He turned to the two disciples and jabbed a pudgy finger upwards. "Does this scrawny little man look like a messiah now?"

Philip nodded but said nothing. Simon, on the other hand, spoke with a studied calm, though everything else about his face screamed out his inner rage. "He looks at peace. Do you see any pain upon his face? Do you see any sweat upon his brow? Do you see any sign that your barbarity is working?"

"All I see is a man dying on a cross," the Roman shrugged.

"Not just a man. The Son of God," Philip shook his head.

The Roman sneered nastily, narrowing his beady eyes and peeling his lips back in a hideous mask of hatred. "Do you Christians never cease spouting the same tired drivel? Son of God? Look at him. He is nothing. He has no power, no strength."

Philip stood up slowly, rubbing at a cramp in his freezing leg. "Yet here you are still spitting your venom against him. You know he is special. That is why he hangs, impaled upon a crucifix," he responded calmly.

"He hangs upon a crucifix for blasphemy, heresy and crimes against the state," someone in the crowd shouted.

A disgusted snort escaped Philip's lips as he swung to face the assorted onlookers, "Crimes? What crimes? He has taken no life or stolen any property." Turning back to the fat man who was standing in a catatonic state of shock at the Christian's effrontery, Philip hissed, "The only crime that this man is guilty of is not kowtowing to the fantasies of petty men who are scared of the truth."

"What truth?" the obese praetor countered. "That he is some sort of deity, some sort of heavenly creature?"

Simon and Philip both nodded. "Though he would never presume to couch it in such self-important terms," Philip said.

The Roman regarded them for a moment then yawned expansively. "I tire of this. Do you truly believe that he is your God's child?"

The pair nodded again.

An ugly grin smeared itself over the Roman's cruel face. "You will not object to me re-uniting him with his father then, will you?"

To the two disciples, it seemed that the next few seconds moved in slow motion. The Roman snatched the spear from the legionary and thrust it into Jesus' side. Jesus' eyes widened and a ragged gasp escaped him.

Philip and Simon moved quickly to go to him. The legionary, who had initially stared dispassionately at his weapon being used to skewer a defenceless man, regained his composure and moved to bar their way.

The fat Roman smirked at the two weeping men. "No, Longinus. Leave them. Let them say goodbye to their saviour."

The fanfare sounded again and the Romans retreated back into the night.

Philip cuffed away a cascade of tears and rummaged frantically in his bag. With a relieved gasp, he laid his hands on one of the cups that had been used at the feast the night before. "Simon. Water. Now."

The disciple staggered off in the direction of the houses that lay dotted around the base of the hill of crosses, leaving Philip standing helplessly at the feet of his leader, watching his life ebb away.

"Oh, dear lord," Philip wept. He began gathering up some fallen wood from decayed crosses that lay nearby.

As he was building a makeshift platform, Simon returned with the cup of water, moving as quickly as he could without spilling its contents. He stared fearfully upwards. "Is he..."

Philip clambered up the rickety structure and tried to bathe the wound. "I think not, though it cannot be long. See, the wound still weeps fresh blood."

As the water dripped into the cut, Jesus cried out, an anguished wail that pierced the hearts of both men with such agony that they felt it as an almost physical blow.

"Please be still, my lord," Philip sobbed.

Jesus' agonised writhing caused a gush of blood to erupt from the wound. In an act of instinct rather than conscious thought, Philip caught as much of it as he could in the cup. "Simon, I need more water. Fetch another cup from my bag and..." He stopped as Jesus spoke through the waves of pain wracking his body.

"No. Do not trouble yourself. It is hopeless. My life is at an end. I feel that I could have done more upon the earth to spread the good word but my father is calling me and I cannot deny His will. I have accepted my fate and you must accept it too." He tried to breathe deeply but could only manage a succession of gasps. "Now, hearken to me for I have news to impart." He fixed Philip with a gaze that somehow seemed free of pain. "Philip, the cup you hold, the cup stained with my blood and tears, you must give it to Simon."

Numbly, Philip handed the vessel over to his companion who had joined him upon the precarious dais.

"Simon, take this cup from here," Jesus continued gravely, "and guard it with your life, for it will become the object of a great quest. Both good and evil will seek it, but its mysteries will only reveal themselves to one who is pure of heart. One who is true to their faith. Only they will be able to fathom its nature. Simon, my friend, to you do I entrust the stewardship of this grail and all its glory."

Simon stared at the cup that now rested in his trembling hands. "I...I am lost for words, oh Lord, I feel humbled by your trust in me. You will not find me wanting. I will not fail you, I will..."

Philip laid a shaking hand upon Simon's shoulder. "He is gone from us."

The Steward of The Grail wept.

*

"He is dead then," Pontius Pilate, fifth prefect of Judea, murmured.

The Sadducee who stood before him nodded with the beginnings of a smile playing on his thin lips. "Yes, prefect, his seditious mouth has been silenced once and for all."

Pilate's cold grey eyes regarded the high ranking Jew with distaste, for upon his statement, an obscene light of triumph had illuminated his eyes and twisted his face horribly. However, it would not do for the prefect to be outwardly impolite to the man because, as a pre-eminent member of the Sanhedrin or Jewish High Council, the body responsible for overseeing all matters of Jewish law, he would be an unfortunate enemy to make.

Pilate shrugged, affecting an expression of boredom, resting his elbow upon his knee and his hand upon his clean shaven chin. "I am glad the outcome pleases you, Annas," he sighed. "I will send someone to Golgotha to remove the body. What would you have me do with it?"

Annas thought for a moment, fiddling with his dark-brown beard and narrowing his eyes. "If it would please the prefect to arrange for the body to

14

be delivered to the Council, we will dispose of the blasphemer in the usual manner."

Pilate nodded agreement. "It is agreed then. Expect the cadaver to arrive at your door before the sun reaches its zenith," he cleared his throat rather pointedly. "Now if you will forgive me, I have many other matters to attend to."

If the Sadducee was offended by Pilate's abrupt dismissal, he disguised it with a bow. "My thanks for your time, prefect," he said and departed through the ornate wooden doors that faced the Roman official's throne.

"By Jupiter, that man makes my skin crawl," Pilate muttered under his breath. Shaking his head, he descended the steps of the marble rostrum and crossed the intricately mosaicked floor to his desk, all the while struggling with his toga which had become entangled during his conversation with Annas.

He had been consulting the manuscripts strewn across his desk for a few minutes when a commotion sounded outside the double-doors. Tutting impatiently, he arose from his seat and strode purposefully over to the entrance to his office. Cracking open the doors slightly, he beheld his major-domo, Cennarius, gesturing abruptly with a man garbed in similar clothing to the odious Annas, a simple white tunic over which was tied a vivid red cloak inlaid with exquisite silver filigree stitching.

"I beseech you sir, moderate your tones lest the prefect takes offence at your manner and dismisses you without an audience," Cennarius was saying in a placatory tone that was underlain with the slightest hint of reproach.

Pilate hesitated in announcing his presence, for though Cennarius' diplomatic skills inevitably rose to the occasion and defused any difficult situations, there were times when the visitor took it upon themselves to try and bully him into disturbing the prefect, in which case, Pilate would wait a moment, then reveal himself dramatically and dismiss the caller without debate.

The newcomer bit back his rejoinder, smoothed down his tunic and sighed deeply. "My apologies, good sir, I let my impatience to resolve my problem override the need for good manners. If you could please announce me to the prefect as soon as humanly possible, then you would have my undying gratitude."

Cennarius bowed gracefully and said in more natural tones, "Rest assured, my lord, I will advise the prefect as soon as I can of the urgency of the matter."

Pilate delicately closed the door and retreated to his desk. He had just got comfortable upon the plush cushions of the seat when Cennarius rapped upon the door. "Come," he said.

The aged underling entered the ornately decorated room and bowed low.

"Sorry to disturb you so soon after your last visitor, my lord, but there is another member of the Sanhedrin who wishes to see you on a matter of some import."

The prefect stared at the bald pate of his minion with surpassing fondness. The man had served him loyally for more years than he could remember and did his job with such economy of effort that Pilate often found himself marvelling at the man's administrative talents. For his own part, Pilate despised the minutiae of the everyday and was eternally grateful to have such an able aide upon his staff.

Cennarius endeavoured to hold his bow for as long as it took his master to respond, as was proper, but he found his right knee was roaring with pain after a few seconds and he began to waver.

Pilate smiled slightly then shook his head at the man's dedication. "Arise, Cennarius. I apologise for my delay in replying. I was lost in thought as to why one of Annas' contemporaries would seek me out so soon after I had spoken to him?"

The unspoken question hung in the air as the prefect's assistant straightened up. Cennarius merely shrugged and said, "He would not divulge to me the exact nature of his visit but I would imagine it concerns the same matter that you discussed with Annas."

Pilate eyed his assistant mischievously. "And how are you aware of that which I discussed with Annas, Cennarius?" the prefect smirked, knowing full well the answer.

The old man smiled back, his weathered face wrinkling about the eyes and mouth, etching the multitude of lines that seemed to multiply daily upon his face into stark relief in the blazing sunshine that bathed the prefect's chamber in an ocean of gold. "Let us merely say that Annas was not as reticent about the subject matter of your meeting as his fellow councillor is."

"Very diplomatically put," Pilate murmured, his smirk becoming a full smile as he stared at his retainer. "Very well, show him in."

Cennarius bowed once more and withdrew from the room. Seconds later, the Jewish councillor entered Pilate's chambers.

The prefect, curious at the urgency of the man's manner, stared at him thoughtfully as his sandaled feet flapped upon the sunbathed floor. The slim but muscular man was in such haste to stand before the Roman that his red cloak billowed out behind him, investing him with an almost infernal look, as his face was adorned with a close-cropped beard slicked down by some sort of unguent. His hair, somewhat incongruously given the neatness of the beard, was an unruly shock of sandy blond, draped untidily over his forehead and ears.

16

He stopped before the prefect's desk and bowed rather perfunctorily, waiting for Pilate to invite him to speak.

Whilst Pilate had been keen not to overtly offend such an esteemed member of the Sanhedrin like Annas, the Jew standing before him was not a councillor that he recognised and so the Roman felt no such compunction with him. He continued to scribble at the document in front of him, seemingly studying it intently yet really testing how long the patience of his visitor would hold. When he felt his silence had reached its limit, Pilate cleared his throat and said in almost deliberately offensive tone, "What is it?"

The Sanhedrin member regarded the prefect with a calm gaze that gave no clue to the outrage he felt within at the man's rudeness. "Prefect Pilate, my name is Joseph of Arimathea and I am a member of the Sanhedrin..."

"Congratulations," Pilate interrupted him, hardly bothering to disguise the irritation in his voice. "Strangely enough, I was speaking to Annas mere moments ago. I would have thought that he would have brought up any matters of dramatic import when we met." The fifth prefect of Judea steepled his fingers and peered at his visitor over the top of them. "I must say, it is very flattering that the Sanhedrin feels the need to consult me on every small matter that arises, but it does rather impinge on my time." He smiled slickly.

Joseph stared at the smirking Roman and bit back his anger. His anger at this arrogant bureaucrat looking down his long Roman nose at him, his anger at Annas' blatant disregard for nearly half the Council's wishes, but, most of all, his anger at the events that had transpired the day before when Jesus Christ had been betrayed and murdered by the rulers of Judea, both Roman and Jewish. "It does concern the matter you discussed with Annas," he said, unable to keep the bile from his voice.

Outwardly placid, Pilate found his interest piqued as to where the conversation would lead, for he had been both shocked and intrigued at the hate with which Joseph had spat Annas' name from his mouth as if the mere use of the word was enough to leave a foul taste on his tongue. "Go on," he nodded.

"I believe you agreed with the councillor that the body of the Nazarene, Jesus Christ, would be delivered to him before noon today."

"That is correct."

"Might I ask that the body instead be released to me and I will see that it receives the treatment that it deserves," Joseph asked, his hands clasped together as if in prayer, his pale blue eyes beseechingly searching Pilate's face for any sign of agreement.

The prefect's face remained neutral whilst inside he laughed loudly. Obviously a power struggle of some sort was developing within the Sanhedrin hierarchy and Joseph was on the opposing side to Annas. The thought of contributing to the undermining of the odious Sadducee was too tempting for Pilate to resist. Slowly the prefect shrugged, "As I am sure you are well aware, the fate of the Nazarene was determined by the crowd who attended his crucifixion. The decision to crucify him was not mine." Pontius Pilate arose and strode purposefully around the other side of his desk. "I washed my hands of him in life and now it seems I must wash my hands of him in death."

The Arimathean eyed the man warily as he walked towards him. Joseph's initial thought was that Pilate was surprisingly thin for a high-ranking Roman. The usual stature of the ruling hegemony was one of rotundity bordering on obesity. However, that was where the difference ended, for Joseph had not been able to study Pilate's face closely because of the brightness of the Judean sun that had been shining into his eyes when Pilate had been sat at his desk. Now though he could see the man clearly. Pilate walked with the superiority inherent in all Romans when dealing with others not of their kind. His hair had been combed in such a way as to vainly cover a large bald spot resting in the middle of his head and was beginning to grey. His mouth was thin and cruel and rested above a practically non-existent chin, his nose was reminiscent of the top half of an eagle's beak, hooked and pointed but it was the eyes that chilled Joseph. They were mean and pitiless, sunken deep within his face like two malevolent jewels, gleaming greedily from under two fastidiously neat eyebrows.

All the while he was chewing over Pilate's words, wanting to strike him, to beat the truth from his twisted, dishonest lips. Joseph knew enough of the man's reputation to know that Pilate had known precisely what he was doing when he had engaged in the mummery of cleansing his hands upon the slopes of Golgotha. The prefect was renowned for his cruelty and ruthlessness and Jesus' death had been no exception. The Arimathean was also too well aware of Annas' hidden agenda of ascending the Sanhedrin's chain of command until he sat atop the summit and was certain that some sort of agreement existed between the two men to rid themselves of the problematic Nazarene.

"Does Annas know of your request for possession of the corpse?" the prefect inquired archly.

The moment of hesitation told the Roman all he needed to know.

"Oh well," Pilate shrugged, "far be it from me to second guess the wishes of such an eminent body of authority. Your wish is granted, Arimathean." He waved a hand dismissively. "Truth be told, I will be glad when the matter is resolved once and for all."

"My thanks," Joseph bowed and removed himself from the Roman's presence as quickly as was seemly for he felt that if he spent any longer in the company of the despicable prefect then he would be forever sullied. Suppressing a shudder, he set off for Golgotha and the site of Jesus' demise.

*

Annas stalked across the circular floor of the central chamber of the Sanhedrin and though the sun was high in the sky and drenched the marble surface with brightness, his mood was as dark as the blackest night. His sandals beat a monotonous tattoo upon the cool floor and his gaze travelled from left to right, peering across the three lines of benches that stood against the walls on either side of him and alighting on the various treasures that graced the hall with their presence.

In the normal course of events, Annas would have taken the time to contemplate the riches around him, the ornate Egyptian vases that rested in the alcoves that were carved into the tiled wall, the busts of former Sanhedrin leaders exquisitely sculpted in finest Greek alabaster, keeping their noble eyes on proceedings from atop their thick, sturdy plinths of snow-white rock. However on this occasion he heeded them not, for his mind was awhirl in a maelstrom of rage and humiliation. His face contorted into a hideous mask as he regarded the architect of his foul mood.

"How dare you!" he spat at Joseph of Arimathea. "I was the man appointed to meet the prefect. I was the man appointed by the council to deal with the aftermath of the heretic's demise. By whose authority do you presume to supercede me?"

Joseph stayed calm and composed as he weathered the gale of the Sadducee's outburst. He looked unwaveringly into Annas' hate-filled gaze and countered quietly. "You were the man appointed by a slim majority of the council to approach Pilate. It was by no means a unanimous decision." He stood up and approached the seething councillor. "You ask by whose authority I acted? I ask you by whose authority did *you* act, Annas?"

Annas' intake of breath was such that the high-ranking Jew seemed on the brink of expiring. "I acted on the holy authority of the Sanhedrin, duly appointed by God to ensure adherence to our religious laws and statutes."

Joseph made a face of disgust at the sanctimony of the statement. He jabbed a finger at the man's florid face. "And is it the will of God that his son should be unceremoniously dumped in a paupers grave?" the Arimathean bellowed. The councillor opened his mouth to shriek a reply in his accuser's face, his beard bristling and his eyes narrowed with loathing, but Joseph cut him off. "You speak of adherence to our religious laws. What about adherence to our religious beliefs? The beliefs of love and understanding and devotion to the ideals of how life should be lived." His finger moved from being inches from Annas' face to prodding itself up to the first knuckle in the ample folds of

19

flesh that encased the heavily built councillor. Joseph's voice was barely louder than a whisper, yet it seemed to carry to every single one of the Sanhedrin members present. "Look inside yourself, Annas," he murmured, "Have any of your actions of the past few days taken those into account?"

Though Annas was still seething at Joseph's intervention, something about the Arimathean's manner transcended the hostility and the volcano of his temper metamorphosed into an iceberg of disgust. "You have overstepped your bounds." He hissed and leant into his fellow councillor. With his mouth mere inches away from Joseph's ear he whispered, "And for that you will pay."

He straightened up and returned to his seat in the bottom row of the three benches that stood in a sloping rank upon the right hand side of the chamber and stood before it. "I put it to the members of the Sanhedrin here present that Joseph of Arimathea has gone against the wishes of the council and has acted in such a way as to make his continued presence upon these benches untenable," Annas proclaimed.

An excited susurration swept the room like the first gentle whispers of a summer storm before thunder roars in the heavens and lightning scorches the ground. "I therefore demand that he return the body of the Nazarene to the rightful custody of the council." Annas continued to speak, his words increasing in volume as the discord in the assembly grew. "If he does not, then I propose that he is taken from this place to contemplate his actions in one of Pilate's prison cells."

Uproar ensued. As Joseph had intimated, the fate of Jesus had only been decided by a narrow majority and many voices were raised in dissension at Annas' ultimatum. Cries of outrage echoed around the room and carried out in the streets of Judea as several supporters of Joseph placed themselves between him and Annas with implacable looks upon their faces.

For his part, Joseph sat calmly in the eye of the hurricane of his own making. He had foreseen Annas' actions and was fully prepared to endure incarceration if needs be, for he was certain in his heart of the rightness of his actions. He stood up fluidly and laid his hands upon the shoulders of two of his confederates.

"Thomas," he murmured in the ear of the bull-necked man to his right, "Andrew," he repeated to the stocky councillor on his left, "All of you. Please stay your hands. I will not be responsible for bloodshed in this holy chamber." He transferred his gaze to Annas and the Sanhedrin members who stood at his side. "I cannot accede to your demand, Annas, for even now the Son of God resides at peace in my own familial mausoleum in the place set aside for my own final rest. Now I know you are a proud man but unless you are willing to break several Jewish laws as well as several Roman laws regarding exhumation of the dead just to prove your power then that is where he will stay." As he spoke, Joseph's eyes hardened. "*If* it is the will of the council to condemn me to the prefect's cells then so be it. However, I demand it be put to the vote. Let every member here present let their feelings be known, not in the shadows of a secret ballot where loyalties and trust can be switched in the blink of an eye yet still falsely maintained in public. Let my fate be sealed in the light of the midday sun. Let all who would deny the Son of God look me in the eye as they denounce my actions in providing our saviour with a dignified resting place as befitting a man so extraordinary."

Though he had been denied his ultimate goal of recovering Christ's body, the thought of the one who thwarted him rotting in a Roman prison provided Annas with some solace. A cruel smile appeared on his lips but did not extend to his eyes. Without a word he stalked back to his seat, all the while glaring challengingly at the owlish faces that regarded him from both sides of the council chamber.

Joseph looked around the hall as Annas returned to his place on the Sanhedrin benches and in those few moments knew that he would be spending at least the next few days of his life contemplating the inside of a prison cell. With a heavy heart he watched despairingly as every man that Annas' looked at lowered their gazes to the tiled floor, unwilling to face the imposing figure that traversed the intimate mosaic that spanned the space between the two sets of benches. With a shake of his head, the Arimathean reflected upon the fact that one greedy man could cow weak men into performing shameful and unjust acts with threats and force of will, yet one pure and good man could not convince the same men to perform humane and generous acts with promises of spiritual peace and inner happiness.

Joseph stared numbly at the floor, barely aware of Annas as he proclaimed that the Sanhedrin members who wished for Joseph to be imprisoned should move to the right hand set of benches and those who wished the opposite to move to the left.

He paid no heed to the outcome of the vote for he knew what the result would be in a matter of seconds because he had seen each and every councillor whom he had looked at wither under the Sadducee's scrutiny.

Oblivious to the cries of outrage and dismay that erupted from the benches behind him, he let himself be led out of the chambers, across the baking streets filled with numerous onlookers who stared quizzically at the man in the robes of a councillor being escorted by Roman soldiery and into the compound that housed Pilate's apartments, the barracks of the legion stationed in Judea and his ultimate destination, the cells that skulked like catacombs underneath the main structure of marble and granite where Judea's prefect resided over his territory.

21

Chapter 2

Hebron

Ever since the night when Jesus' life had fled and the stewardship of the Grail had been bestowed upon him, Simon had felt a huge weight of responsibility upon his shoulders.

Though it had only been a couple of days since the honour had been given to him, to Simon it felt like a couple of years. He had not slept since the night before Jesus' demise and had barely eaten since then either. His stomach was in permanent knots as his mind alternated between the horrendous memory of his teacher and mentor perishing before his eyes and the constant fear of Jesus' murderers extending their persecution of him to encompass his followers and friends.

In his heart, Simon knew that he was unworthy of the task that Jesus had given him and his nights became the tortured stuff of nightmare as he tossed and turned relentlessly, the sheets becoming twisted and knotted around his sweating frame. He had confessed his fears to Philip, for he felt him to be a natural confidante after the pair of them had shared the intimacy of the vigil under the cross atop Golgotha.

Wringing his hands together, he accepted the goblet of wine Philip handed to him. "What am I to do? Why did he choose me? I know that my heart should swell at the privilege but instead it withers, shrinking away from responsibility like the most craven of cowards."

They sat in Philip's home, a relatively spacious abode in Hebron, one of the more prosperous areas of the Judean province. They were both seated at a wooden table set for two. Philip chewed upon the final bit of cheese on his plate and regarded his friend seriously. Simon's meal remained largely untouched though he did twist a hunk of freshly baked bread between his fingers.

Philip laid a kindly hand upon his young friend's shoulder, gazing concernedly at the depth of the shadows underneath a pair of blue eyes that should have been bright with the flush of youth, not dulled by the burdens of life. "He must have seen something in you, something that only He could apprehend." Smiling sympathetically, he supped at his own drink, smacking both lips together as the spiced liquid ran down his throat. "If the saviour thought that you were not worthy of this distinction then he would not have bestowed it upon you."

Simon nodded, conceding the point grudgingly. "That is as maybe, my friend, but what if the qualities He perceived do not manifest themselves in time for me to ensure the security of the Grail. What if it falls into the hands of the Romans or the treacherous Sanhedrin?" he wailed.

Philip was at Simon's side in an instant, gripping his forearm tightly. "Quiet your tongue, Simon, lest the Roman wolf is aprowl in the city streets and snuffs the scent of sedition." He stared nervously at the nearest window as if expecting the legions to burst through it at any moment and whisk them away to the none-too-tender mercies of Pilate's torturers. He stood abruptly and smoothed down the front of his white tunic, removing any crumbs that remained there from the meal. "You need to return to your home, Simon. You need to take stock and try to rest. Trust me, things will look better by the light of a new dawn," he said, mustering as much reassurance in his voice as he could, though he suspected that it would cut little or no ice with the troubled disciple.

Simon rose miserably from his seat, nodding resignedly. "Perhaps you are right, Philip," he sighed.

The pair said their goodbyes to each other and Simon left his friend's home, painting a sorry picture as he wended his way through the streets of Hebron, head bowed and shoulders slumped.

He turned the corner into the street where he lived, his sandaled feet raising small clouds of dust from the sun-baked road. It was smaller than Philip's, being situated in the poor quarter of the town, but it more than sufficed for the disciple's simple needs and, of course, it now housed the greatest treasure ever seen upon the earth. The young man brightened slightly at that thought as he unlocked the door and entered his home. He located the tinder and flint and lit the candle that nestled in the alcove nearest the entrance. As he struck it, it flared into life, casting the small downstairs room into a two-tone melange of pitch-black shadow and eye-watering light. He waited a moment for his eyes to adjust to the starkness of the contrast and, as had been his habit since taking charge of the Grail's care, he had gone to it the minute he had entered the house, to check on it, to study it for, despite his innumerable misgivings about Jesus' trust in him, when he was in the Grail's presence, he was hopelessly enraptured by it, entranced as one in the deepest throes of the most profound love imaginable. Breathless and awestruck, he stood frozen like a statue, save his right hand which reached out slowly, tremulously, brushing the rough cloth that he had used to secrete the artifact away from prying eyes. Finally, he gripped it and whipped the material clear of its prize. Instantly, a fractured spectrum appeared upon the stone ceiling, twinkling like a rainbow of stars upon the pitted surface as the guttering light from the candle hit the gems inset just beneath the rim of Christ's cup. Simon was transfixed by the display but managed to feel his way into a wicker chair, never once taking his eyes from the spectacular aurora of colours that sparkled over his head.

How long he sat there he did not know, but the last thing he remembered was the coruscating exhibition starting to meld into one colour, a golden hue that seemed to fill the world with serenity and calm.

With a suddenness that took him by complete surprise, Simon found himself jerking awake, bathed in glorious sunshine and nursing an agonising crick in his neck. As a shrill shriek of pain shot down his shoulder, he sat up in the chair, gritting his teeth against the stab of the muscle spasm, to stare at the wondrous goblet that had dominated his life for the past few days.

All physical pain vanished to be replaced by a mental anguish so acute that Simon could not articulate it. Instead he sat rocking back and forth, muttering unintelligibly, staring at the unladen table.

The Holy Grail was gone.

Joseph of Arimathea sat pensively in the dungeon, staring absently at a cockroach scuttling across the cold stone floor. He was perched on a wooden pallet, which served as both bed and table for him during his incarceration. He plucked numbly at a loose thread jutting from his scarlet cowl and ran dirty fingers through his long unruly mop of sandy hair.

Sighing hugely, he stood up and moved to the other side of the cell. Craning his neck, he stared at the minimal view afforded him by the square four-barred hole that was situated approximately three-quarters of the way up the rectangle of the door. A flickering torch burnt fitfully in a sconce on the wall opposite and Joseph tried to use its feeble light to see further along the corridor because the damp brickwork began to curve away to the left and the lightest of breezes caressed his face. The gentle waft of air caused him to wonder if he would ever see the sky above his head again. Would he ever feel the hot sun upon his back or the refreshing wetness of a summer storm? Myriad were the tales of the condemned being left to rot in these cells either through the incompetence of the bureaucracy that dealt with them or the prefect's casual cruelty. Offenders had even been known to have their sentences commuted or extended on the whim of Judea's ruler, though this rarely happened to the Jews imprisoned in the portion of the complex given over to those prosecuted by the Sanhedrin. That thought provided scant consolation to the Arimathean as he shuffled back to his makeshift bed and laid upon it, his right arm crooked behind his head to try to engender a little extra comfort for his troubled sleep.

He felt as if he had been asleep for mere minutes when something jerked him awake. He stared around the cell for, though there was little light, his eyes were still accustomed to the absolute darkness of sleep and his night vision had not yet been lost. An uncomfortable feeling stole over Joseph that he was not alone though logic told him that he must be. His breathing quickened to a point where he was nearly hyperventilating, the clouds of oxygen puffing from his mouth like gusts of steam from an armourer's forge. He wrapped the threadbare blanket around him and located his sandals by feel. As he came fully awake, he found himself wondering at the improbable drop in temperature. When he had first fallen asleep, the interior of the cell had been warm to the point of balminess, but now a matter of minutes, hours at the most, later he found himself enduring conditions unknown in Judea during any but the severest winters.

Slowly he became aware of a golden nimbus outwith the cell which showed the outline of the door and the barred square within it in violent contrast. With a start that made his heart race and tore all thoughts of the cold from his mind, the door swung ponderously open.

He gingerly stepped into the corridor, listening intently, expecting at any moment cries of remonstration to wreck the supercharged silence. Yet there were none. The whole place had the feel of a deserted ghost town. Indeed the quiet was so absolute that Joseph was quite prepared to believe that the whole of the palace was bereft of life.

With heart-stopping quickness, the penumbra that had bathed all before him in its golden richness winked out, leaving a shapeless blob of purple and blue dominating Joseph's vision. As his night sight reasserted itself, he began advancing again, heart in mouth, hardly daring to breathe. He had seen the door through which the omnipresent draught was blowing. Casting off the blanket so that it would not hinder his flight, he was momentarily surprised to find that the breathless temperature of the night had returned and he was sweating freely. Wiping his moistened brow with the sleeve of his smock, Joseph of Arimathea escaped into the Judean night.

As he made his stealthy way back to his home, he reflected that his assessment of the situation at the prefect's palace may, if anything, have been underestimated. He could hear neither insect scritching nor bird chirruping nor any sign of humanity whatsoever. Because of this, every step Joseph took sounded amplified in the deadened atmosphere and he was certain that he was seconds away from detection.

The all-pervading fear of discovery left him drained when he turned the corner into the street where he lived. He scuttled along, hoping that the darkness of the shadows would be enough to counteract the lightness of his garments.

He was about to set off on the final stretch of his stress-laden journey when he felt the temperature drop once more and to his right, the golden glow began to make its presence felt again. Drawn to it as a moth to a flame, Joseph let himself be deflected from the relative sanctuary of his home and began to walk towards the light, infused with a sudden determination to uncover its origin. Again, the moments that followed bore the same pattern as the events in Pilate's dungeon. The luminescence led him through the streets of Judea, yet he saw no-one. He was unaware of how long he had walked but when the light winked out again and he was jerked back to reality, he could see the sun beginning to illuminate the distant hills to the east.

Trying to ignore this worrying fact, he took stock of his surroundings and nearly staggered, for he was shocked to the core by where the light had led him. He was standing before the entrance to the resting place of his ancestors. The seal to the entrance of the mausoleum was cracked and the circular stone door had been rolled to the side, wide enough to admit a person or persons unknown. With a heinous curse directed towards Annas and his cohorts, he pushed his way into the desecrated tomb, fearful of what destruction he would find within.

To his astonishment, he found that, to all outward appearances, nothing had been touched. He scanned the cold dead room intently, taking in the inscriptions on the wall that showed the birthdays and deathdays of his family both recent and long since departed. Joseph laid a hand upon the nearest marble column, stroking the smooth surface and peering at the faces of the intricate busts that stood above each resting place like eternal sentinels staring implacably into the face of death.

Frowning deeply he began to walk among his ancestors pondering the mystery. As he passed the swaddled corpse of Jesus, he was visited by an irresistible compulsion to reach out and touch the shrouded body. As he did so, the cloth deflated with a sigh until it lay flat upon the cold slab, save for a protruberance at roughly chest height. Holding his breath, Joseph lifted the muslin, fearful yet curious in equal measure as to what he would unveil.

Of Christ's remains there were none. Neither bone, nor hair nor blood was to be seen beneath the coarse material. He was so shocked by this that he stood open-mouthed, staring nonsensically at the impossibility of what he had seen. As he reached out to snatch the material clear, a forbidding yet familiar voice boomed in his ears.

"Take the Grail and flee from this place. I name thee steward of my precious chalice, Joseph of Arimathea. Serve me well, steward. Serve me well and honour my memory. Spread the word and preach the wisdom of the Lord. For my sins I died for you, now for my sins you must live for me." The words came from everyplace, crowding Joseph, smothering him until he felt that his soul would buckle under the weight. "Go now, steward. Go. You must be upon the water before sunrise tomorrow, lest you suffer the same fate as my poor broken body upon the Roman's barren tree of torture."

With painful sobs wracking his body, Joseph wept, stumbling out of the mausoleum into the Hebron dawn. "I will not fail you, Lord," he sobbed, "I will not fail you."

Chapter 3

AD 51 - The English Channel

Joseph stood upon the deck of the Neptune and peered across the roiling waves, his gaze transferring itself from the leaden grey of the sky above to the granite grey of the sea below.

It had been a goodly number of years since the death of Christ and, as he had vowed on that fateful day when the messiah had visited him in his hour of need, he was spreading the saviour's message as far as he could. He had travelled in the company of many of Jesus' cohorts, preaching the gospel to the inhabitants of Gaul in the company of St Philip the apostle.

He had left Mary Magdalene and Lazarus in the city of Marseille in Gaul and accompanied Philip to the north of that country. Once there, knowing of Joseph's connections with the metal trade in the South-West of Britannia, the apostle had despatched him across the Mare Brittanicum to try to promote Christianity to one of the most far-flung corners of the Roman Empire.

A shout from above wrenched his gaze away from the constant movement of the water and he took in the familiar coastline of Land's End. He knew it would not be long before he was gazing upon his familiar lead mining haunts in Somerset.

His hand, as it had done so many times before, strayed to the pack that rarely left his shoulder and he found himself touching the Cup of Christ. He had carried it with him ever since that day in the burial vault of his family, taking the responsibility that Jesus had placed upon his shoulders very seriously indeed. So seriously that, in response to some unspoken unease he felt, he had not even told any of the compatriots who travelled with him across Europe the secret behind the ornate goblet he bore in his baggage.

Joseph had no idea what he was actually going to do with the Grail when he reached his destination. If he was honest with himself, he did not even know what his ultimate destination was.

Even though he viewed the stewardship of the Grail as an honour beyond imagining, the years that had passed had left him with an ever-growing feeling of isolation and loss. He felt cast adrift, alone and abandoned. He felt the need to lay down roots, to call somewhere home instead of another anonymous stop on an evangelical pilgrimage, but nowhere had felt right. He firmly believed that the end of his journey would present itself in a blinding flash of inspiration, but after such a long time on the road, after seeing so many places and so many sights, he was beginning to doubt that it would ever happen.

He stepped aside and let one of the thirty strong crew go about their nautical business of bringing the ship closer in to the Cornish coast.

One of the twelve disciples who had been chosen to travel with him to establish the first Christian mission in Britannia tapped him on the shoulder.

"How goes it, Joseph?" he asked. "You have barely left the rail since we departed Gaul."

The leader of the pilgrimage sighed and looked at the young man standing next to him. David brushed down the front of his creased off-white smock and dragged his unruly blonde hair away from his eyes as they whipped across his vision due to the increasingly powerful sea-breeze. He looked at his tutor expectantly.

"I am sorry, David." Joseph shook his head. "I have been neglectful of the eleven of you since we left Philip. You will have to excuse me. I have much on my mind and no way of unburdening myself."

David looked sidelong at his companion. "Surely you can share whatever is ailing you with one of us. A problem shared is a problem halved or so it is said."

"Not this one," Joseph laughed wearily. "No, the responsibility for this lies with me and me alone, although I do thank you for offering me your ear to bend."

The young man stared questioningly at his fellow missionary for a moment then shrugged and joined him on the rail, scanning the coastline with wide-eyed wonder. "It is beautiful," he breathed as a pair of gannets launched themselves from the chalky outcrop and dove like arrows towards the water.

Joseph nodded as he took in the varied colours of the stones of the cliffs that jutted out from the mainland. "Aye, it is that. I know this country well. There are few that can rival it in its beauty. Even when the weather is inclement, its breathtaking scenery remains undimmed."

They stood for a while in silence, drinking in the landscape and enjoying the breeze on their faces.

David followed the flight of a seagull as it bobbed and weaved on the thermals. "This will be the first time I have set foot upon these shores. What kind of country will face us? What manner of people live here?"

A crooked smile appeared on the missionary's face. He found himself remembering his younger years and the multitude of questions that had always seemed to be jostling in his mind, demanding answers and knowledge. Ah, the exuberance of youth, he sighed, when had it deserted him? His face darkened momentarily for in that instant he realised the exact moment. It was when he had been charged with the stewardship of the Grail. With an effort, he forced the memory from his mind and returned to the present and David's open honest face, politely waiting for an answer to his

29

questions. "They are a fearsome, savage looking bunch when you first set eyes upon them, but they seem, on the whole, to judge by deed rather than word. If you are honest in your dealings with them, then they are very pleasant company." Suddenly, he found his stare drawn to a pall of smoke rising above the rocky horizon. With eyebrows knitted, he shouted up to the look-out. "Ho there. What is that smoke over yonder?"

The sailor who occupied the crows nest jerked awake for he had known he would not be needed for a while and had decided to take the opportunity to have an illicit rest. He rubbed at his eyes then shielded them from the weak sun that had begun to work its way through the cloud cover. When his voice descended from atop the mast, it was fraught and tense, "Tis a village. Or, I should say, was a village. It appears to have been razed to the ground."

"Do you see any movement?" Joseph asked urgently, pushing himself off his elbows and standing bolt upright.

The answer did not take long. "I see no-one."

The holy man shook his head. "That cannot bode well."

David became agitated by his mentor's reaction. "Romans?" he asked, trying without success to keep the tell-tale quaver from his newly broken voice.

Joseph pulled at his beard and nodded slowly. "I have heard tales of Roman savagery being visited upon these lands, for the tribes who inhabit this place are proud men who will not give an inch of ground without resistance." He pulled his travel-dirtied cloak about his shoulders. "A feeling has stolen over me. This is wrong, very wrong." He shivered, despite the appearance of the hitherto obscured sun.

David followed the missionary as he made his way along the deck towards the prow of the ship. The captain was, as usual, to be found manning the wheel, nimbly manoeuvring his craft this way and that, perfectly in tune with the currents and tides that had been constant companions to him for most of his adult life. Joseph placed a hand on the man's shoulder and spun him round, asking without delay, "Where is the nearest place we can put to shore?"

David suppressed a shudder as the captain turned to face them. The seagoing ancient had one of the most lived-in faces that the youth had ever seen. His skin was tanned to a rich mahogany by decades of incessant exposure to the sun, but age had carved many deep lines and wrinkles into the man's visage, creating the look of a man hewn from trees rather than living flesh and blood. His mouth was a misshapen gash filled with black and yellow stumps that tore his face untidily in two whenever he spoke. Above that was a nose, broken in at least two places and sliced across its bridge by a livid scar that stretched across his face in a diagonal slash. And that was the reason for David's shudder, because the cut did not stop at the man's nose but

30

continued upwards straight through where his right eye should have been. Now though, there was nothing there save an angry, puckered hole of blackness, almost as if the old salt was wearing an eye-patch underneath his skin. The Captain, Jacob Watkins by name, looked disdainful at being manhandled by Joseph, but ushered the Arimathean towards his cabin. "Master McHenry, take the wheel," he said with a throaty bark. "I must have words with our esteemed passenger." They descended the stairs and turned back on themselves as the Captain's quarters were located on the floor below the foc'sle. In the absence of anyone denying him access, David joined them in the spacious room.

He found the two men poring over some hastily laid out maps. The Captain scratched at the days-old greying stubble that dotted his chin. "I estimate our position to be a number of miles south of the Sabrina Aest's mouth," pointing his finger emphatically at the map. "There appears to be a river here that cuts a fair way inland."

"Is it passable for a ship of this size?"

Watkins laughed expansively. "The map is unclear but you need have no fear, my good sir, I can navigate this old girl through the eye of a needle. As long as we are careful, I see no reason why we cannot take the path you wish." His expression turned serious. "I have seen the smoke billowing upon the headland. What perils are you taking me towards, Joseph of Arimathea?"

The grail-bearer looked slightly taken aback by the sudden change in the seaman's humour. "In all honesty, I do not know." He stroked his nose which was noble and straight, in direct contrast with the captain's. "All I can say is that I feel a strong pull, drawing me further into the land. I have an affinity with this place and its inhabitants, perhaps it is no more than that?" He walked round the table and poured himself a drink. "If you have no wish to follow us onto the mainland, then by all means, put myself and the others ashore and retire to the safety of the open sea."

David's eyes widened at that suggestion.

The Captain noted the youngster's reaction and reverted to his former jovial self. "I think that maybe your young follower is not so keen to be free of our protection."

Joseph peered over his shoulder and noticed David for the first time. "I was unaware that we had an audience. Be not afraid, David. We have our faith to protect us," he pronounced warmly.

A look of brief embarrassment passed over the disciple's face and he nodded slowly. The Arimathean walked over to him and looked deeply within his eyes. "It is only natural to have doubts every now and again," he said, as if reading the treacherous thoughts that had appeared in David's head. "If we do not face our doubts and conquer our fears, then we cannot hope to convert

31

others to our faith. Be stout of heart, my young friend." Joseph bestowed another glowing smile upon his protégé and returned to the deck.

David turned and watched him go. He too was about to return to the freshness of the open air when he became aware of the Captain's stare upon him. "He is a most charismatic man, is he not?" the seaman said.

"He certainly is," David agreed. "It is not surprising though. It is said that he was visited by our Lord Jesus Christ *after* he passed away upon a Roman crucifix." He spun round like a whip and advanced upon the grizzled commander of the ship. "Imagine, just to have been there. To have known the messiah, to have trodden the same roads and breathed the same air as Him. What a privilege."

Watkins blanched at the schizophrenic shift in the adolescent's manner. He had obviously harboured doubts about striking out across the land with Joseph, but now the mere mention of this Jesus' name had ignited a zeal in his stare that the Captain found quite unsettling in one so young. "I have also heard that story about him," the Captain nodded.

"Story!" David almost spat. "It is no story. It is the truth. Do not tell me that we are travelling with a man who is not committed to the one true faith?" The Captain's gaze hardened. "Now listen to me," he thundered, "do not dare address me in such a manner in my own cabin. Who do you think you are, you pompous little fool?" Watkins grabbed him by the front of his tunic. "Whether I have faith or not is purely my own affair. I have seen too much in my life to trust in anything other than my own wits and the capriciousness of the ocean. I have seen good friends consigned to watery graves for no reason and bastard pirates that befoul the earth by their very presence sailing away from storms that should have seen them kissing the ocean floor for eternity." He let David go and pushed him towards the door of the cabin. "So do not talk to me of your faith and your messiah. I am merely the master of this ship. I trust my crew and my instruments, nothing more, nothing less. If you wish to fritter away your life pursuing your faith then so be it, but do not expect me to join you. Now get out of my sight."

David's face had coloured during the diatribe and he hung his head in shame. "I meant no offence, sir. It is just that I feel sorry for anyone who has not had their life enriched by the words of Christ."

"Do not waste your sorrow on me, boy. Wait until you meet someone who gives a damn." The Captain jabbed a finger in the direction of the shamefaced youngster. "Now, as I said before, get out of my sight else you will feel the back of my hand."

David backed away from the fearsome old sailor and made his way back into the fresh air. A slight drop in temperature indicated that rain might be on the way and he began to walk towards the communal sleeping quarters where the majority of the Christian missionaries took their rest.

Approximately halfway across the main deck, Joseph took up station alongside him and they both walked in perfect unison back to the hammocks. The young disciple was unsure whether his leader had heard the raised voices issuing from the captain's cabin, but upon seeing the amused twinkle in Joseph's eyes and the badly suppressed smirk on his lips, he assumed that he had. "Did you know that the captain was not a Christian?" David asked plaintively, after Joseph could contain himself no longer and had burst out laughing.

The Arimathean cuffed the tears of mirth from his eyes and looked at his young charge solemnly. "Yes, I did. He takes us on this journey for Roman coin, not for his own health," he said as he stooped to enter the cramped sleeping space.

David wrinkled his nose at the rank odour of stale sweat and unwashed clothing. Joseph could see that the young man was struggling with himself. "Does it not bother you that he is an unbeliever?" he finally blurted.

A frown creased the older man's features. "I heard every word of your debate with the Captain and at no time did he proclaim himself an unbeliever."

This time it was David's turn to have a frown to darken his expression.

"He said that he thought your visitation from the messiah was a story. He said he believed in his ship, his crew and nothing else. He clearly has no truck with the teachings of our Lord," the adolescent whined. "If that is not an atheist, then I do not know what is."

Joseph waggled a finger at David as the youngster's face took on a look of righteous indignation not dissimilar to the one that had so alarmed the captain. "So what you are actually saying is that he does not believe what you and I believe," he pointed out.

"Well, yes." David replied in a bemused voice.

"And in your worldly wise opinion that makes him worthy of your pity, does it?" Joseph's voice was flat.

"But..."

"But nothing, David," Joseph shook his head and his face took on a look of sombre reflection. "The Captain's beliefs are just as valid as yours or mine. He believes that if he respects the sea and follows the tenets that he lives his life by, then he will be safe and find his just reward when he passes over. On the other hand, we believe that if we honour our God and follow the tenets that His son lived his life by, then we will receive our just reward when we pass over, yes?"

"I suppose so," David admitted grudgingly.

"So why do you find it so offensive that Watkins does not follow our faith?" Joseph asked. "We all must tread our own path. You have chosen Christianity, he has not. He has provided us with transportation, shelter and food for our journey. If he was as judgmental as you are, then we would still be stranded upon the shores of Gaul."

"With all due respect, Joseph, that is a highly bizarre outlook for a missionary to have," David gasped, unable to keep the incredulity from his voice at his mentor's reasoning.

Joseph shrugged, though his insides were writhing with the dilemma that had haunted him for many years. He sighed and ploughed on, unsure if he should divulge his thoughts, yet finding that now they had surfaced so strongly he was unable to force them from his mind without voicing them. "To be honest, David, my faith has always been, first and foremost, a personal choice. Had I not been visited by Jesus all those years ago then I doubt very much that I would be coming to these shores as a missionary. I have always been somewhat uneasy about forcing my beliefs onto others, truth be told. All I do is give people the details of the messiah's life and try to let them make up their own minds."

The moment he finished his statement, he saw the respect in which David held him melt away before his eyes. He had not even meant to disclose half of what he had said, but he had heard the zealous ardour of David's initial outburst at the Captain and it had shaken him. If the young man spoke out of turn in such a way to one of the tribal chieftains, he would be dead before he had finished his sentence.

The impetuosity of youth shone incandescently in David's eyes. "Then what in the Lord's name are you doing here, Joseph?" he hissed. "We are following you into a foreign land full of fearsome savages under the banner of Christianity and you are not even convinced that you want to spread the word?" His arms flapped wildly as anger got the better of him. "Dammit, why are you here then? Why are we here?"

Joseph stood unmoved in the gale of David's rage. "I am bound by an oath that I gave to the messiah after He died. I said that I was uncomfortable spreading his word. I did not say I would not do it."

He was painfully aware that his response cut little or no ice with the hot-headed youth. "How can you convince others to follow when you cannot even convince yourself?" David spat.

Now it was Joseph's turn for the anger to rise. He had said more than he had intended, that was true, but to have this young upstart pour such bile-filled scorn upon an honestly-given opinion was a bitter pill to swallow. "I am merely trying to stop your quick temper and slow wit from getting you and us in trouble. I am just trying to be honest with you. I am being true to the faith as I see it. I do not need your blessing to promote the faith in this manner nor do I seek it. In fact if the intolerance of the last few minutes is anything to go by, then perhaps it is you that should be questioning your place upon this mission."

If anything, David's face coloured a deeper shade of red. "Now you use your weakness to try and turn this around on me? This is the first mission I have joined to spread the word of God. You, on the other hand, have been doing this for the last two decades. How can you stand there and preach to me after living a lie for the last twenty years of your life. You are a hypocrite, Joseph. You preach the words of Jesus but you do not believe them."

The slap that Joseph swung shocked them both into silence.

David slowly brought his hand up to the red welt on his face. As tears sprung unbidden to his eyes, more from shock than pain, he pushed past Joseph and made for the sanctuary of one of the innumerable hiding places upon the main deck. The force of his passage knocked Joseph over onto the untidy pile of belongings that littered one corner of the room. Jesus' former disciple sat on his backside in shock for a few moments, ashamed beyond words at his conduct. His mind went back to the pall of smoke that he had seen above the cliffs. Ever since that dark cloud had materialised, the voyage had taken a turn for the worse. He now felt sure that he was being drawn inland inexorably. He was overwhelmed by an urge to trek across country and find out what it was that seemed to call to him so strongly.

As he often did in times of distress, he withdrew the Grail from his ever-present pack and studied it, the golden glow bathing him in its penumbra.

That was how David found him as he re-entered the room, also feeling an acute sense of embarrassment at his intemperate behaviour. "Joseph, I..." he began to apologise, but stopped dead in his tracks as he snatched a glimpse of the Grail before Joseph hurriedly smuggled it into the folds of his voluminous robes. "Joseph, I just wanted to apologise to you. It was terribly presumptuous of me to call your beliefs and methods into question. Please forgive me."

Joseph was touched by the emotional catch in the young man's voice. "Please, David, it is I who should be apologising to you. My conduct was unforgivable," he stated after expertly tucking the Grail back into his pack as he got up from his prone position.

The pair embraced as a cry from above indicated that they were about to leave the ocean and embark upon their voyage inland.

"Come," Joseph patted David on the back warmly, "let us banish what has passed between us to memory and speak no more of it."

David grinned sheepishly back. "Indeed."

They left the communal bedchamber together, David ushering the more senior man through the door first. As he stepped over the cabin's threshold, his gaze flickered to Joseph's pack and lingered there for a brief second. Then, as if coming out of a spell, he shook his head and joined his fellow disciples and the crew upon the deck.

Chapter 4

Wearyall Hill, Roman Britain

The chieftain Arviragus' double-headed axe described a scarlet rainbow as it bit through the Roman legionary's feeble defence and cleaved him from shoulder to groin.

All around him legionaries were being mercilessly slaughtered by the horde of native British Belgae tribesmen, compensating for what they lacked in battle tactics and discipline with the unbridled savagery of their attack.

The chief's second-in-command strolled over, lazily wiping his blade clean of Roman blood. "Once more we have them on the run." He hawked and spat on the blood-slicked grass as he watched the final shreds of Roman resistance evaporate. His gaze travelled from the routed soldiery, fleeing in disarray and alighted on his leader's grim face.

Arviragus' deep blue eyes stared across the battlefield trying without success to penetrate the early morning mist that shrouded the killing ground. He sighed massively, "If only it were the last of the bastards there would be a reason to celebrate, Drell." He drew a dirt-encrusted hand over his heavy beard and peered despairingly at the devastation that disfigured the landscape all around and about him. "Why must they destroy everything in their path? We were told by our leaders that Roman rule would bring better times to these shores and better lives for all who lived here, but what have we gained? Oppression and tyranny. And in the process we have lost so much more. Our crops, our independence, our identity," he kicked one of the many corpses that littered the battlefield. "That's the last time you'll destroy any Belgae land, my old son." He spat a gobbet of phlegm which landed on one of the legionary's unseeing eyes.

"Nice shot," Drell smirked mischievously. The grin soon disappeared from his face as he spotted one of his fallen comrades, nose down in the mud. He shooed an inquisitive raven from the dead man's back and turned the body over. "Ah, damn, it's Alfred." Drell ground thumb and finger into his eyes as they filled with tears at his nephew's death. He tenderly closed the lifeless eyes then returned to his feet, grunting with exertion. "You know there will be reprisals for this, Arvi."

The tribal chief shrugged. "They give no quarter, so why should we? They surrendered any chances at mercy when they massacred the tribe at Menai."

The two of them made their way to the remaining warriors of their clan who had assembled in a circle further down the battlefield. The burly men all parted as their leaders joined them. Drell and Arviragus nodded at each in turn, no words necessary as the testaments to their prowess in battle lay strewn, bloodied and broken, for all to see.

Some of the legionaries had been momentarily spared however, and now they knelt in the middle of the circle, mortally fearing what their fate would be for they could see no mercy in any of their captor's gazes. The quivering quintet stared wide-eyed and open mouthed as the two clansmen approached. Arviragus' exhausted face was smeared and filthy from his recent swordplay and the bearskin cloak that he wore as a badge of leadership was matted and damp with sweat and blood. Every centimetre of his tree-trunk legs that showed beneath the fringe of his leather kilt was covered with an unhealthy concoction of mud, grass and gore. To the snivelling Romans he was the embodiment of the archetypal British savage that they had been trained to look upon with disdain and hatred.

Drell left his commander's side and joined his comrades in the circle. Arviragus continued walking towards the weeping soldiers as they looked around wildly, praying for an escape route that they knew would never appear. From the moment of their capture they knew that, if the rumours concerning the chief of the Belgae were true, then their only escape would be the chilling embrace of death. The five captives looked at each other until one nodded and stood up. In surprisingly well-accented Anglo-Saxon, he spoke softly. Arviragus regarded the man as he faced him and even allowed himself to be a little impressed by the lack of panic in the man's voice.

The legionary's deep cultured tones carried to the ears of all those present, for the theatre of war was now deathly silent, save for the raucous calls of the crows that had materialised like black phantoms from the boiling clouds. "Chieftain, you and your tribe have bested us on the field of battle. On bended knee, we plead for our lives. We knew our time to taste the bitterness of defeat had come when we realised it was you we faced. Please, sir, we beg for mercy. You have about you the stuff of greatness, your deeds against our hitherto all-conquering legions are legend amongst the common soldiers. You have been noble and mighty in your victory. I pray that you will be noble and mighty in our defeat." With great ceremony, the Roman unbelted his sword and let it drop to the ground at Arviragus' feet.

The chief's expression was unreadable as he seemed to dwell on what the Roman had said. He found himself studying the man's features as if implanting them in his brain. Just as the tribal warrior had appeared to the defeated soldiers as a stereotypical barbarian, so this Roman appeared to the Belgae warleader as the personification of every aggressor he had faced on the field of conflict. The jutting Roman nose, the stance that came of a surety of battle prowess, the arrogant eyes that did not quite mask the innate feeling of superiority that infused the Roman race.

As their chief's lack of action seemed to stretch into minutes rather than seconds, he could sense his people becoming restive.

He opened his mouth and saw the resignation appear in the man's eyes even before he pronounced death upon him.

"I cannot." Arviragus whispered and brought his battleaxe round in an unstoppable arc.

The remaining quartet of Roman prisoners watched in horror as their comrade's head bounced to a halt on the grass.

In the blink of an eye, the tribal chief was in front of them. "Name?" Arviragus demanded of the nearest Roman.

"T-T-Tomas Arginus," he quavered, his eyes never leaving the dripping blade of the axe.

"You?" the chieftain pointed with his gory weapon.

"Quintus S-S-Sextus."

"Gerontius Augustus."

The final member of the quartet could not answer due to the fact that he was throwing up copiously on the grass.

The chieftain stared with contempt at the legionary as he crouched on all fours and emptied the contents of his stomach.

"What do you think, lads," the chief bellowed, "should we call this one Vomitus Maximus?"

The assembled tribesmen laughed heartily at their leader as he stalked round the four prisoners kneeling before him. Bending down, he grabbed a hank of hair that lay atop the beheaded legionary's head and dangled the face within inches of their own.

"Your talkative friend begged for mercy. Tell me, did the legions show mercy to the druids at Menai when they entered under a false flag of parley, slaughtered the men and children, then raped and murdered the women?"

The four legionaries held the chieftain's piercing gaze for no more than a few seconds then hung their heads.

"Well, did they?" Arviragus screamed, his spittle arcing onto the back of the legionary who had been unable to give his name. He could feel the red mist descending upon him. All of the injustices that the Romans had inflicted on the Britons, the murder, the raping, the looting, it all came crashing down upon his shoulders in an acid tide, bathing him in agony. He had lost so much in the last few years, family, lands, faith, both in his earthly leaders and in his gods. Suddenly in front of him, these four snivelling pathetic whoresons seemed to represent everything he was fighting against, everything he despised. Without another word, he swung his axe and decapitated Quintus Sextus. Before the other three could react, he spun almost balletically and slashed Gerontius Augustus across the stomach,

39

leaving the Roman screaming on the floor as his weakening fingers tried to return the slippery intestines back from whence they came.

Tomas Arginus held out his hands. "Please, no, I'm unarmed," he shrieked insanely.

Arviragus clamped both hands around the haft of the axe and continued his onslaught, lopping off one of Arginus' outstretched appendages. As the force of the blow threw the Roman off-balance, the chieftain brought his axe round and removed the other limb with another sweep. "In every sense of the word," he muttered grimly.

The unnamed legionary made a grab for a nearby sword that lay in the hand of a dead tribesman and fell upon it before anyone could prevent him.

The Belgae chieftain watched dispassionately as the light of life departed the eyes of the young soldier. With it went the rage of the berserker that had fallen upon him.

Drell padded over to where his leader stood. "Come, Arvi. Let us return home. Once again, we have a great victory to celebrate."

Chief Arviragus spat on the floor. "Celebrate? Look at him, Drell. He's barely more than a boy."

His most trusted lieutenant sighed. "Do you think if we had been captured by these scum they would have spared our lives? There's no point dwelling on things like this, Arvi. It's them or us. No quarter asked for and no quarter given, yes? Arvi?"

The chieftain did not respond. He was peering through the clouds of mist and smoke at a ship as it made its way up the river away from the devastation. "Now, what do you make of that, Drell? Did you see that ship upon the water when we descended upon these legionaries?"

The second-in-command shook his head. "It is not a vessel I recognise. Reinforcements, do you think?"

Arviragus' eyes narrowed as he scoured the landscape for any sign of an avenging band of Romans, intent on exacting reprisals for the massacre of their fellows.

Drell's eyesight was no match for his clan-leader's but he made a show of doing the same as Arviragus and looked left and right, all the while urgently casting about for a change of subject that would bring his leader out of his introspection. As it was, he had no need to distract his leader because the sight that they both spotted simultaneously was enough to banish all thoughts of despair from the Belgaic tribesman's mind.

He felt a hand on his shoulder.

"Come," the tribal chief whispered urgently.

They both, along with their tribesmen, moved to cut off the twelve that were making tortuous progress up one of the many hills that dotted the landscape.

They made no attempt to hide their passage and appeared oblivious to the proximity of the Belgae tribe, although they did seem to be making their way towards the scene of devastation. Arviragus signalled to his men that they should begin making their way towards the interlopers but indicating with a clenched fist that they should do so in silence. They circled round and ended up behind the twelve as they climbed onward to the summit.

For a few moments, Arviragus ignored the group and reconnoitred the landscape once more, just in case an unlikely ambush was to occur. Satisfying himself that no such trap had been laid, he decided to dispense with his usual caution because he found the sight before him so incongruous that his curiosity far outweighed his fear.

The travellers stopped atop the hill and stood, peering inland.

However, Arviragus had not become one of the Belgae's most successful tribal leaders for no reason, so despite every instinct telling him that all was well, he nonetheless signalled for his men to make ready their weapons.

A shout from above told him that they had finally been detected. Looking at Drell questioningly and receiving the usual non-committal shrug, he gestured his tribesmen out of concealment in the long grass and stalked up to the top of the hill.

Once there, he took to sizing up the new arrivals. Nine men and three women, young for the most part, although a couple of the men seemed more senior than the rest. There was one with an untidily cropped grey-streaked beard, leaning upon a staff, who he immediately picked out as the one they appeared to defer to and addressed his question to him.

"Who are you and what business do you have upon the lands of the Belgae?" Arviragus asked.

Joseph regarded the chieftain warily. As he had said to David on the sea voyage, he considered the Britons to be a highly agreeable race, but he could not help but note the scarlet stains on the man's clothes and weaponry. "Please sir, we are travelling missionaries and we have come to these shores to spread the word of our Lord Jesus Christ. We bear no arms and we ask for nothing, save your time to listen to our preaching."

Arviragus threw a disbelieving look at Drell then turned back to face the missionary. "Firstly, I ask something of you. Your name. I do not like the thought of strangers roaming my domain. Tell me more of your purpose and I will decide what to do with you."

Joseph bowed floridly. "Of course," the missionary hesitated, "but might I have your name first?" he asked.

"I am Chief Arviragus, leader of the Belgae, ruler of all you survey and much more besides."

41

"Chieftain Arviragus, my name is Joseph of Arimathea and my friends and I have travelled north from Gaul to bring the teachings of Christianity to these fair lands." The missionary announced rather pompously.

"What is this Christianity that you speak of?" Arviragus asked, laying his hand on the haft of his axe. "It must be very powerful to cause twelve outlanders to take it upon themselves to walk unprotected into a hostile land."

Joseph allowed himself a smile at the implied threat. "It is, chieftain. It is."

David stepped forward and before Joseph could stop him, proclaimed, "We do not go unprotected, sir. Our faith is our shield."

Drell stifled a smirk and took a few strides forward. "Well, we carry nothing more than shields and weapons. I know which I would wager upon to protect me from a Roman sword."

Joseph stepped in front of the curly-haired youth. "Please, David. Let me speak." Missing the venomous look that David shot him, he returned to his conversation. "Please chieftain, we have been on ship for many days and we are weary all." He planted his staff in the ground. "Might we be allowed to rest and prepare some food? If we can spare enough, it would be most pleasing to dine with you."

David grabbed Joseph's robe and spun him round, whispering intensely into the older man's ear. "Are you insane? Do you not see the blood on his furs? These are nothing but bloodthirsty barbarians, intent on slaughtering us at the first opportunity."

Joseph was so incensed by the young man's words that he lifted him off the ground by his robes. "Be silent, you young idiot. Talk such as that will cost us our lives," he hissed.

Suddenly Joseph became aware of the blade resting on the youngster's neck. Drell, whose eyes may not have been as sharp as his leader but whose ears certainly were had crossed the intervening space between them in the blink of an eye. He bestowed an implacable stare upon the slack-jawed disciple. "Why so scared?" He leant in and treated David to a few wafts of his ale-ridden breath. "Don't you have your faith to protect you, you insolent little fool?"

Joseph pushed David away and held up his hands placatingly. "I apologise for my fellow traveller's outburst. I hope it will not colour your judgement of us." He threw a filthy look at the horrified David.

Drell looked to his leader for guidance. "What do we do with them, Arvi?"

The chief considered this for a moment. "To murder them would be to lower ourselves to the depths of the Romans, yet as a well-respected bloodthirsty barbarian, I feel that I would damage my reputation if I didn't slaughter them at the first opportunity." He glanced at David, whose eyes dropped to the ground in embarrassment. "What to do?" Arviragus pondered. "What to…what in hell is that?" he blanched.

Both the tribesmen and the new arrivals looked alarmed as the ground underneath them began to shake and rumble. The earth around Joseph's staff began to spit and foam. The staff itself sunk into the ground until barely a foot of the wood was left in view. Arviragus took a step towards it but halted as it began to swell and engorge, sprouting branches at a frightening rate. In no time at all, Joseph's staff had gone from being a barren stick bereft of foliage to a gnarled, majestic tree, dominating the summit of the hill, its numerous boughs casting both native and newcomer in shadow.

As his tribe gathered around the trunk of the magnificent plant, touching it in disbelief, it seemed to Arviragus that Joseph and his followers were as shocked by the transformation as he was.

He gingerly approached the tree and placed his palm on the trunk, stroking the uneven surface thoughtfully. Seeking out Joseph, he stared at him intently, trying to read the words that had formed on his lips, a mantra that he seemed to be chanting over and over again. Arviragus cupped his hands around his mouth and shouted to make himself heard above the excited babble. "Ho, Arimathean, I would talk with you."

"This is the place, this is the place," Joseph whispered to himself, oblivious to everything but the tree.

"Joseph," a novice called Justin tugged upon the sleeve of his tunic, "the chieftain wishes to talk to you."

The Arimathean emerged from the catatonia he had fallen into and nodded at the chieftain. They both moved slightly away from the main group. The Belgae tribesman spoke first. "This Christianity you mentioned, it is a powerful sorcery?"

Joseph smiled wryly. "It is not sorcery, Arviragus. It is a miracle." The chief's eyebrows knotted at the unfamiliar word as Joseph continued, "As I understand it, sorcery is the casting of spells to achieve a specific end. Believe me, I am not any sort of magician. I did nothing beyond plant that staff in the ground to support my old bones."

The Briton's sceptical expression spoke volumes. "Then what happened, preacher?"

Joseph regarded the tree for some time before putting forward an explanation. "My staff was fashioned from the crown of thorns that Our Lord Jesus Christ wore upon his head as his life slipped away upon a Roman crucifix. I can only surmise that the thorns became infused with some of his wondrous powers, which were then inherited by the staff."

Arviragus raised an eyebrow, "This Jesus Christ? He perished at the hands of the Romans?"

The disciple tried hard to keep the bitterness from his eyes as he nodded. "Yes, one of his followers betrayed him to the legions. He was arrested and put to death." Joseph still found that life-changing memory all too vivid and found himself biting back tears as he revisited the events of that black day once again. "He came to me in a vision and bade me spread his word across the land. That was over twenty years ago and I have been doing his work ever since."

Arviragus considered Joseph's words as the bearded Christian excused himself and returned to the tree, once again caressing the trunk and staring in wonder at every leaf and bough. He knew that the reach of the Roman hand was in no way confined to just this little corner of the empire and supposed that there were thousands of such stories spouting from the mouths of victims in many different countries but it had never really hit home to him in such a way before. To see such similar hatred in the eyes of one so different was a poignant reminder to him that though he was beginning to detest the carnage and blood of the constant fighting with the legions, it was far preferable to the outcome that would have resulted had the Belgae simply given in.

However, it was obvious that Joseph and his party were not fighting men, so how had they managed to elude the Romans for so long?

"What did our sorcerous arrival have to say for himself then?" Drell inquired innocently.

Chief Arviragus shook his head at his deputy's apparent inability to take anything seriously. "I cannot help but feel we have a chance to redress the odds a little in our favour here, my friend." With a jerk of his thumb, he indicated Joseph. "He says that there is no magic at work here at all. He contends that his staff was made from a crown of thorns that this Jesus he speaks of wore as he died upon a Roman cross. He said that as this Jesus died some sort of power that he possessed managed to transfer itself into the wood."

Drell made an impolite noise to show what he thought of that.

"Damn it, Drell." The Belgae chief threw his hands in the air exasperatedly. "You just saw the blasted thing spring out of the ground, didn't you? Can you explain it, because I am bloody certain that I cannot?"

"True," his lieutenant conceded.

"Whether he is telling us the truth or not is irrelevant, these people obviously have some sort of power at their disposal, which I would rather be allied to than enemies with." The chief found his gaze drawn irresistibly to the tree once more. "He told me that this Jesus died on a Roman crucifix."

That made Drell's seemingly eternal expression of good-natured sarcasm turn serious. "We have never needed outsiders before to aid us in our battles. What exactly are you proposing, Arvi?"

"What is that proverb? The enemy of my enemy is my friend?" The chief answered.

Drell began to protest but his leader was not really listening. He held up his hand to stop his deputy's protests. "Enough. My mind is made up."

"I don't like it, Arviragus." Drell grimaced, using the chieftain's full name which was his usual way of showing disagreement with his chief's decisions. "That kind of wizardry is best kept at arm's length. Who is to say that they will not use it against us when it suits them, so that they might gain a foothold in these lands?" he pointed out.

Arviragus glanced at his fellow tribesman with barely concealed amusement. "Is Drell the Unflappable doubting the wisdom of his leader's actions?"

The second-in-command of the Belgae shook his head irritably, the usual ever-present smirk glaringly absent. "All I am saying is that we should be on our guard."

"What against? Someone who can make a fruitful tree appear in seconds just by planting a staff in the ground? I think that if he wanted to use that magic against us, he would have done it when we came upon them initially. Besides," Arviragus hung his head and for the first time, Drell noticed how deep the lines of sorrow were etched upon his leader's face, "as I looked around the battlefield over yonder, I felt empty, Drell. Before I have felt...I don't know, sadness for the fallen, a sense of justice that our victory was worth something but not this time. All I felt was a lust for more blood and vengeance and that scared me. What will happen now? Answer me that? The Romans will hunt us down, rape and slaughter will stalk the land once more and we will be here or somewhere like it in a few days or weeks, up to our necks in blood and guts, murdering little boys in their tin helmets."

Drell kept his counsel, he knew better than to interrupt his commander when he was in this sort of mood. The chieftain continued, "This Christianity that they mentioned, it intrigues me. I wish to learn more about it. These last few years have killed any beliefs that I used to hold. Perhaps it is time for us to walk a different path. If this tree is an example of what Christian magic can do then let us use it if we can."

Before Drell had a chance to debate further with his leader, Arviragus had walked purposefully over to Joseph and engaged him in conversation. "Ho there, Arimathean, I would talk further with you. Let us make haste to Caerleon, our hill-fort. It lies but a few miles north of here."

Joseph nodded agreement to that suggestion and the Belgae and the Christians departed from the summit of the hill.

As he walked away, Joseph could not help but look back at the majestic tree. His breath was stolen from his lungs by the sight that he beheld. The sun's rays chose that moment to break through the mist and drench the many leaves that adorned its boughs in the brightest of gold, making the tree look as if it was bathed in fire. If the missionary had not been certain before, this scene banished any lingering doubts. This was the place he had been looking for. The end of his quest for sanctuary and succour. "Chief Arviragus, what is this place called?" he asked, turning to see the tribal leader staring with a similarly enraptured face at the stunning vista.

"Glastonbury," said the chieftain quietly.

Chapter 5

Caerleon Hill-Fort

David sat at the groaning table, laden with meats, cheeses, steaming loaves of bread and mugs of ale, wine and mead, fastidiously mopping at his sauce-smeared plate with a hunk of bread, regarding his leader with baleful eyes. Joseph had not talked to him since his near fatal comment about the British tribesmen. The youngster still did not feel comfortable in the company of the Belgae warriors and was especially wary of the one called Drell who, he could not help but notice, still cast venomous glances in his direction every now and again. He did find the hill-fort quite impressive though. After years of travelling in rickety carts on dusty roads or in dirty ships on inhospitable seas, the comfort of a relaxing chair on a static stone floor came as a considerable relief.

He peered at the shields hung at intervals along the walls, escutcheons made all the more striking by the fact that they were obviously still employed on a regular basis. These emblems of battle were not merely for show because David could clearly see the notches and dents in them, each one serving as a potent indicator of their still considerable usage.

The young man's gaze was drawn towards the head of the table by a hearty laugh from the Belgae chieftain as he sat enraptured by Joseph's words and he stared with contempt at his former mentor. How could Joseph sit there and affect to be Jesus' messenger on earth when he himself did not believe one word that he was saying? Perhaps I should feel some admiration for him because he has dedicated his life to spreading the gospel, David thought to himself, but to find out that he had done so because he did not want to break his oath rather than because he actually believed the words, whilst being an admirable act in its own right, actually lessened the impact somehow.

He shook his head to try and clear it a little. He had noted a warning look from Joseph as he filled his wooden mug with the honeyed mead, but that made him all the more determined to drink it, and now, unused to the strong liquid that Arviragus served at his table, he found that it was beginning to frazzle his senses. He stood up unsteadily and mumbled a hurried "Excuse me" to the diners nearest to him.

He half-stumbled into the draughty corridor and stood with his back to the cold stone wall for a moment, eyes closed, sucking in great lungfuls of air, trying to marshal his thoughts. After a minute or two, he opened his eyes and found them soothed by the gentle light supplied by the guttering sconces dotted along the passageway. Letting out an explosive breath, he began walking as purposefully as he could towards the rooms set aside for the newcomers. Pushing his way through the door, he made straight for his bunk and, not even bothering to disrobe, slumped down on it in the comforting belief that rest would not be long in coming.

After a few minutes of tossing and turning, he cursed his lack of sleep and sat up on the edge of the bed. A headache was beginning to worm its way into his temples with a promise of becoming more severe with every second that passed. In the absence of anything else to do, he went over the window and peered through the narrow slit, hoping that the fresh air would blow away the pain. Alas for David, it did not and the pounding in his skull doubled in strength. He screwed up his eyes and tried to find his way back to the bunk without opening them. Not surprisingly, he had only walked a few steps before he tripped over a travel bag that lay at the foot of one of the other beds. The young disciple hissed a blasphemy through gritted teeth as he fell to his knees which hit the unforgiving flagstones of the floor with a painful crack. Thrusting out a hand to push the bag out of the way, his fingers brushed against something metal. To his astonishment, the agony rippling through his skull ceased for a few seconds so he turned his head to see what it was he had felt. However, as he twisted his body, he lost contact with the object and the pain came shrieking back. Blindly grasping, he discarded a couple of items before he found what he was looking for. As his fingers gripped it once more, the pain dissipated almost immediately. This time he made sure that he did not let go of the item and looked down at it. To his confusion, it was the cup that he had seen Joseph staring at just before they had landed upon the shore of Britannia. He turned it around and around in his hand, unable to take his eyes from its bewitching aura. The light from the fitfully burning torches flickered across the grimy metallic surface and sparkled hypnotically in the gems that were inset in the band just below the rim, describing a glittering rainbow upon David's face. He stood up quickly without thinking and in that instant mentally prepared himself for a fresh wave of torture to come tearing through his head. He was astounded however at how strong he felt, especially after the acute pain of a few moments before.

As he steadied himself, a memory stole into his mind of a conversation with Justin from a few months ago.

The group of Christians had been trekking across the gorgeous countryside a few miles west of Lutetia in Gaul and during those lazy days of summer, minds had taken to wandering and tongues had taken to wagging. Idle rumour found fertile fields in the minds of the young missionaries as they followed their mentors through the hamlets and villages of the Gaulish landscape.

"I wonder what it can be?" Justin tugged at a lock of his blonde hair as he stared at the blinking panorama of stars above him, whispering the thought to himself.

"What's that?" David muttered sleepily.

Justin started guiltily. He had not meant to say anything out loud even though he thought that David had been asleep. "Nothing," he pronounced airily.

The young disciple rubbed at his eyes irritably. "It was something. You woke me up with it."

Another shush emanated from off to the right somewhere making both of them drop their voices to barely audible whispers. "Now are you going to tell me what you said or not?" David jabbed a threatening finger at his blonde companion.

Justin shrunk back from the digit. He had always found David a tad intimidating as he was quick to lose his temper over not very much at all. Not wanting to risk a confrontation, Justin leant in to him and whispered, "Esther told me that she had heard from Thomas that there is something in Joseph's pack of great religious significance, something that our Lord Jesus Christ himself possessed during his time upon the earth."

David regarded his fellow missionary for a moment then tugged his blanket back over his body turning away from Justin. He looked over his shoulder and tutted, "I thought it was something important, not juvenile little stories for children who have porridge for brains."

That throwaway comment from Justin about the item of great value in Joseph's pack came crashing into his mind again. Could this be it? A mere goblet? A goblet with apparent healing powers? David shook his head. It could only be a coincidence that the pain disappeared when he touched it. Yes, that was it. Coincidence.

He placed the cup back in Joseph's belongings and made his way back over to his pallet. Lying down, all pain forgotten, he gazed up at the ceiling, eyes tracing the play of shadow of the flames from the torches across the rafters. It was not long though before his gaze was dragged back to Joseph's bag. He tried to convince himself that it was only a trick of the light, but he was sure that he could see the chalice glowing just under the fabric. Drawn to it as a moth to a flame, he rose once more and removed the cup from the bag. Closing his eyes, he shivered sensually as he felt the Grail's power flow up his arms, breezing through his veins, as if he had plunged over a waterfall and was being barrelled along a spring-fresh river. When his eyes opened again, they were ablaze with a frightening intensity. Peering greedily around the room, he pocketed the goblet and made his way to the door.

Joseph peered sympathetically at Arviragus as he recounted the details of the Menai massacre. Shaking his head, he sat unmoving as the Belgae chieftain spoke of rape, torture and brutal bloody murder.

"Alas," Joseph sighed when the chief finished his account, "the Romans are a people impossible to understand. On the one hand, they produce art, poetry and architecture that can inspire the soul. Yet on the other, they have created a war machine unprecedented in its savagery, peopled by sadists and murderers." He laid a hand on the tribesman's shoulder. "Believe me, Chief Arviragus, yours is not the only race to have been touched by the legion's cruelty." And once again, Joseph found himself reliving the pain of witnessing Christ's demise upon the cross. Even after all these years, the image of the messiah as his life began to drain away was emblazoned, bright as the morning sun, upon his memory.

Arviragus listened intently to Joseph's re-telling of the events on Golgotha and everything in between that had led him to the tribal table whilst Drell fidgeted about disinterestedly in the chair next to him.

The second-in-command of the Belgae peered around the table in an alcoholic fug, his gaze lazily drifting from face to face as tribesman and missionary stared at each other warily. The battle-hardened scowls of the clansmen watching the fresh-faced Christians from across the heaving platters made for a strange tableau, but he could not help noticing that the two sides were slightly off-kilter. An empty chair sat upon the missionary's side of the table like a gaping cavity in a mouthful of teeth. Drell sat himself up a bit straighter and realised that it was the upstart who had insulted Arviragus when they had first met. "I wonder where you have taken yourself away to, you little bastard?" he muttered under his breath.

"Sorry?" Arviragus turned to his deputy.

"Nothing, Arvi," he knuckled at his tired eyes. "I'm just going to take some air."

The chief nodded and turned back to Joseph, leaving Drell to rise and take his leave. He shook off his lethargy, taking large breaths to try and clear his head. He moved out into the corridor and peered left and right but there was no sign of the missing youngster anywhere. In the absence of any other direction, he stalked purposefully off towards the guest quarters. Throwing open the doors, he fully expected to see the young pup sleeping off the mead on one of the rickety pallets. There was still no sign however.

Drell took to wondering where the insufferable young idiot could possibly be. However, after a few moments thought fractured by the copious amount of ale that he had imbibed, he decided that maybe he was not that interested after all and went to actually do what he had told his leader he was going to do and take in some of the crisp, evening air.

50

After the warmth of the dining hall, he drew breath sharply as the coldness hit him and it took a few huge gulps of oxygen to acclimatize to it. Walking forward, he rested his elbows on the ramparts and stared up at the multitude of stars that decorated the night sky. He tugged on his beard and grinned reflectively. He knew that he was counted second only in swordsmanship and axemanship to his chief but, on nights like this, he found that somewhere underneath the blood and barbarity, there dwelt the soul of a poet, a minstrel who, every once in a while, yearned to spread his wings and sing to the heavens. He gazed into the darkness and revelled in the ageless silence of the night, a statuesque sentinel keeping watch over the lands of the Belgae. He was unaware of how long he stood like this but he knew it mattered not. Closing his eyes, he began to sing in a rich, smooth baritone, softly at first, but growing in strength with every word.

In the far and winding distance
A man, he climbs the hill
Walking ever onward
None know his name, none ever will

He's walked these lands for so long now
More years than he recalls
Conquered the mountains and seen the end
Of the rainbow's arc and the waterfalls

What wonders has he witnessed
What secrets does he know
As he strides across the landscape
Treads the cold and lonely road

The traveller will not know peace
Who knows why he walks this way
Offer him comfort, food or rest
The Traveller will not stay

Drell shook his head as he finished the traditional song. The words spoke to something deep within him for he had indeed walked most of the island before fetching up at Arviragus' stronghold at Caerleon. The Belgae chieftain had immediately spotted his potential and promoted him rapidly, much to the disgruntlement of some of the other clansmen who had been at Arviragus' side from the start of the tribal resistance to the Roman occupiers. He had had to fight many a battle to prove his loyalty and courage to the distrustful warriors, but won them over he had and now he enjoyed the exalted position of being second only to the leader of the tribe.

A mischievous twinkle appeared in his piercing sapphire eyes as he remembered the day of his appointment. The women in the tribe had been a lot more accommodating than the men and he still found himself looking back on that night with an unsurpassed fondness. He stared down at his grizzled hands, holding them clear of his body so they could be seen in the wan moonlight and the joy in his eyes faded as his memories became premonitions. He felt his shoulder and rolled it around in its socket, wincing at the bite of pain that shot down his shoulder blade. The ravages of time had not been kind to Drell recently and he knew it was only a matter of months before the joint would become too stiff to be effective with a blade, be it axe or sword.

Truth be told, that was half the reason he had found the arrival of Joseph and his cohorts so disturbing, especially the young one who had insulted the tribe. No one so young had the right to adopt such a narrow-minded attitude. What did that young pup know of the world? What did he know of fighting for his life each and every day? Drell shook his head once more and moved to go back inside. As he turned from the rampart, he caught an indistinct figure falling out of the corner of his eye, plummeting past his field of vision so fast that, for a moment, he was not sure he had seen anything at all.

He stopped dead in his tracks and ran back to where he had been standing. Steeling himself more against a fear of heights than against what he would see, he peered down the vertiginous walls, knowing with a dread certainty that the scene before him would not be pleasant.

The only reason he saw what he was looking for was that the one who had fallen had been wearing white. The starkness of the garment stood out against the dark stain of the grass below but not to the extent that Drell could make out its wearer.

Wiping away a bead of sweat that had materialised suddenly upon his forehead, he turned to run back to the feast, knowing that his news would cast an all-encompassing shadow over Arviragus' welcome to the outsiders.

With one last look at the twisted figure sprawled on the frost-kissed grass below, he left the cold night behind him knowing that his tidings would cause the temperature to drop just as much inside the warmth of the banqueting hall.

Arviragus stood at the head of the table and brought his goblet down with a crash on the pitted wood, stunning the rest of the diners into silence. "I have something to say and you all have a right to hear it. Joseph of Arimathea tells me that he and his cohorts wish to make their home here and, as chieftain of this tribe, I have decided to grant them a stretch of land to do with what they will," he paused briefly as the mutters which had erupted at his announcement died down, "my judgment has not let you down before and I feel sure that it will not fail you this time either. Joseph's words speak to me in my heart as well as my head. He too has lost too many loved ones to the Roman war machine, he watched in anguish as his leader died upon a crucifix." He pointed a finger towards the narrow window. "Yes, that is right. Like the ones that are sprouting all over this land like barren murderous forests." He could tell from the silence that his words were having the desired effect. "They wish to settle in the land that surrounds the magical tree that now crowns Wearyall Hill. Does anyone here object to my ruling?"

He peered intently round the table, intrigued as to whether anyone would dare challenge his authority. His roaming gaze fell upon the empty chair where Drell normally sat and he found himself musing that if anyone was able to talk him out of this decision, it would have been his deputy, however, he was still taking the air outside. Arviragus wondered if he should have consulted him before acceding to Joseph's request, but he was, after all, the leader of the Belgae and the ultimate choice lay with him.

There were a couple of other clansmen, both traditionalists and set in their ways, that he thought might raise an objection, but they sat impassively, betraying nothing in their outward expressions.

"Good. Therefore I ask you all to extend the hand of friendship to our new-found friends."

Drell chose that moment to come hurtling through the doors. Searching out Arviragus, he ran to his chief's side and whispered in his ear.

The colour drained from Arviragus' face and he turned to Joseph. "You had better come with us, friend."

The trio left the room at pace, as if blown by the whispering that was steadily building in volume as the diners speculated on both Arviragus' decision and also the content of Drell's tidings.

As they pounded down the corridor, Arviragus turned to the Christian and asked him, "Joseph, how many of your people were absent from the table when we left?"

They took the stairs two at a time as Joseph thought about his answer. "David was absent, I think, but other than that, I think they were all present. To be honest, Drell's entrance was so dramatic that I paid no heed. Look," he grabbed a hank of the chief's woollen shirt and pulled him to a stop, "what in the name of God is going on?"

The clan-leader looked sidelong at his deputy. The tribesman acknowledged his leader and laid a not unkindly hand upon the Arimathean's shoulder. "I

53

am afraid that I saw one of those you travel with fall from the battlements above me. He hit the ground at the base of the fort." Taking an educated guess at Joseph's response, he cut him off before he could speak. "There is no chance that anyone could have survived a fall like that. Truly I am sorry, Joseph."

Tears sprung unbidden to Joseph's eyes though his face cemented itself into a grimace of denial.

The trio set off again, picking up speed as they turned corner after corner, lit only by the dull glimmer of waning torches.

They finally came to the portcullis, which Drell lifted without apparent effort. They ran out into the freezing darkness, lit only by the moonbeams of the silver orb high above them and immediately saw the body lying scant yards away. Joseph, despite being by far the oldest of the three, was the first to make it to the corpse's side.

The dead man's smock had ended up covering the body's head and Joseph had to peel it back to reveal the identity beneath. He automatically steeled himself for the sight of David's unseeing eyes staring back at him. With a gasp, he nearly crumpled onto the wet grass next to the body. "Justin," he wept. "Justin."

The two Britons stood a little way off, discomfited by Joseph's unashamed outpouring of emotion.

"Not who he was expecting, I'm thinking," Drell observed wryly.

The chief turned to him.

"What did you see, Drell? What happened?"

"All I saw was the poor youngster plummeting past me. There was no scream, no noise. Just this lifeless body plunging downwards." Drell shook his head at the memory. "No scream, no noise," he said, half to himself.

Joseph emerged from his grief almost as quickly as he had plunged into it. "Quick, help me get him inside," he urged, struggling to move the dead weight of the corpse.

Drell suppressed a snort and said rather ungently, "Why? He's dead. No-one could survive a fall from that height. Tell him, Arvi."

Joseph's eyes were red and puffy and his beard was tufting crazily from his chin. "Please, Arviragus, help me," he beseeched.

With a sharp look at his second, as if challenging him to make a comment, the muscular chieftain easily lifted the body over his shoulders. Without waiting for Drell, they made their way back inside the warmer confines of the fort as quickly as possible. With a frustrated sigh, Drell ran in after them.

The quartet, as strictly speaking it was now, made its grim silent way to the room in which the Christian party were sleeping, mercifully managing to avoid any prying eyes along the way. Once inside, Arviragus dumped the body rather unceremoniously upon one of the bunks.

Joseph practically shoved the two tribesmen out of his way as he dived for his belongings. Casting his possessions all about the room, he came to a seemingly nondescript bag and delved frantically inside. "It is gone," he shrieked as he spun round. With narrowed eyes, he stared at the two native warriors.

Drell's hand lazily made its way down the haft of his axe. "I do not much care for the way you are looking at me, Christian," he said quietly.

The chief of the Belgae immediately placed himself between the two of them. "What is it you seek, Joseph?"

The missionary's eyes became hooded and he could not hold the chief's gaze. Without answering, he turned back to the untidy pile of belongings that now nestled at the foot of his bunk and began rooting through it once more.

Arviragus shared an intrigued look with Drell before whispering in a strangled voice, "Do you have something in your possession that can bring him back from his journey along the endless road?"

The missionary did not respond immediately, instead continuing his frenzied hunt. After a moment though, he ceased rooting through his things and his shoulders slumped. In a voice dripping with grief he blurted, "I don't know. I had..." he turned to face them, his eyes resting on Drell's axe for a second longer than necessary then continued, "...something in my baggage that might have helped. I...I just could not let him go. Not without a fight. I..." he tried to say more, but his voice became strangulated with sobs and he fell to his bed weeping.

Drell grabbed Arviragus' arm and yanked him over towards the door. "What sort of magic can bring someone back from the dead, Arvi? That cannot be right, surely." The chief shrunk back because Drell's eyes were saucer-like with fear and he made no attempt to hide the fact. "I tell you, Arvi, you cannot trust a power like that. It is not natural."

The chief peered at the inconsolable preacher but found that he could not bring himself to share Drell's point of view. He cared not for the mysterious artefact that Joseph had lost; all he could concentrate on at the moment was that his new found friend was in the throes of mourning the loss of a loved one and to him, Joseph's grief looked like the most natural thing in the world.

"I am sorry you feel that way, Drell. I had hoped for a more opportune time to bring this up but I suspect your prejudice will never allow you to see these Christians in a good light, so now is as good a time as any to tell you."

"Tell me what?" Drell's eyes narrowed.

"I have offered them some of our lands to settle in."

The deputy of the Belgae stood unmoving, staring in disbelief at what he had just heard. "Have you taken leave of your senses, Arviragus?"

The chief sighed exasperatedly. "I do not know what you have against these people, Drell, but I have seen enough of them to deem them worthy of my trust, especially Joseph."

With a shake of his head, Drell sneered, "Did you not just see what happened? You may trust him but he obviously does not reciprocate it. Who did he look at as soon as he realised that this thing that cheats death was missing? Us, that's who. He all but accused us of the theft."

Arviragus shook his head. "Who else would he look at, Drell? We are the only ones here." He started to count off on his fingers. "The man has just lost a friend. He is in shock. Just for once, can you look beyond your tunnel vision and give him the benefit of the doubt, for the gods' sake."

Drell looked at his leader as if he had never seen him before.

"I need to know you support me in this," Arviragus stated sombrely.

The words of the song that Drell had been singing came back to him and he shook his head once more. "Arvi, after the way you took me in and treated me I would follow you to the ends of the earth, but I cannot help but feel you have made a mistake letting them stay. Call it intuition, call it a hunch, whatever but someone with that kind of power needs to be kept at arm's length."

The two clansmen locked gazes for a moment before Drell sighed, "Where are these lands you have granted?"

"Twelve hides centred around Glastonbury and Wearyall Hill in particular," he shrugged. "At the site of where the tree appeared, that is where Joseph said he needed to be." As he looked back at the bereft holy man he decided to try one last time to convince Drell of the Christian's benignity. "Look hard, Drell. Do you really see a threat before you?"

Drell wanted to say so much more, he wanted to try to explain the unnamed feeling that seemed to be steadily creeping over him but he could not put it into words. Maybe it was a fear of sorcery and magic, for was it not said that if fears are to be truly conquered then they must be understood and Drell was painfully aware that he did not have the first inkling as to how Joseph had perpetrated the miracle upon the hill. Now the magician, which was the term that Drell could not help calling to mind when he looked at Joseph, was purporting to have in his custody something that could cheat the eternal frigidity of death.

Aligned with this suspicion, he knew, was a fear of rejection. There had been no new additions to the tribe since he had arrived and the chance of him being supplanted as Arviragus' favourite had not reared its ugly head.

Until now.

Drell found himself staring at Joseph with a feeling that was not very far removed from hatred. His lips twisted into a sneer as he watched Arviragus fawning over him like a sycophantic lapdog. As he did this, a thought occurred to him. Perhaps the magician had bewitched his leader. It would certainly explain the sudden decision to grant acres of tribal land to these people.

The second-in-command was still lost in thought when Arviragus and Joseph walked slowly past him. He had been so consumed with his musings that he had not seen the two of them cover the corpse and leave the room. He trailed along behind them like an errant child, entering the dining room just as Arviragus brought his goblet crashing down upon the table to gain the room's attention. The gaggle of guests quietened into silence when they beheld the chieftain's haggard face.

Without a word, Arviragus stepped back from the table and ushered Joseph into his place.

Joseph stared about the room for a minute then asked, "Where is David? I have something that you all must hear."

One of the trio of female missionaries in the party raised her hand, "He took his leave a little while ago. He said his head was spinning and he wanted to return to our chambers."

Drell regarded the woman with an unnecessarily leering look and then shifted his gaze to Joseph. "Perhaps he knows where your missing magic is?" he smirked mischievously.

Arviragus grabbed his arm and yanked him over to the wall. He leant in and hissed, "For someone who keeps saying that he is on the brink of soiling his breeches because of Joseph's incredible powers, you seem surprisingly keen to provoke him into anger."

Suitably chastened, Drell's face lost its grin and they both returned to Joseph's side.

The Belgae chieftain nodded encouragingly to his guest.

The head missionary expelled a shuddering sigh and began tremulously, "Friends, there is no easy way to say this. It is Justin..." he tried to continue but his voice cracked and tears started from his eyes.

All of the missionaries stood up but the woman who had informed Joseph of David's whereabouts flew from her position at the table to Joseph's side. "What of him, Joseph? What is wrong?" she asked, the look upon her face speaking volumes of her concern.

The Arimathean pushed her gently away and forced his voice into a high enough volume for it to carry to all of his audience. "Ruth," he addressed the woman then spoke to everyone, "all of you, I am sorry but there has been a terrible accident, a fall from the ramparts." He pulled Ruth into him as she crumpled against his side. "Justin has gone from us. He now bides with Our Lord in the Kingdom of Heaven."

He bit his lip as Ruth's wail cut through the sudden silence. Several others found their legs unable to support them and they took to their chairs in shock. Joseph's grief seemed to have run dry for the moment and he continued mechanically. "I think that out of respect for Justin we should all now retire and ponder what path we must now follow." He gestured towards the door then turned to face his host. "Chief Arviragus, we thank you for your hospitality and your more than gracious offer of the lands at Glastonbury. Please excuse us whilst we take our leave and mourn our friend's passing."

The Anglo-Saxon nodded dumbly as the Christians began to file from the room, the men shaking their heads in disbelief and the women comforting each other as best they could.

Not surprisingly, Joseph was the last to leave. As he made to move into the corridor adjacent to the banqueting hall, Arviragus called to him.

The Christian turned silently and regarded the chieftain.

"I am sorry for your loss," Arviragus said simply.

Joseph nodded acknowledgment and trudged sombrely from the room.

*

It was now the early hours and, not unsurprisingly, it had taken a long time for those bunking down in the Christians' quarters to fall to their slumbers. For a horrible moment, Joseph had forgotten that Justin's body lay upon one of the bunks in the room, but Arviragus had judiciously arranged for the corpse to be removed before anyone had seen it and so all in the group were spared that added trauma.

Joseph and Ruth had taken the longest to go to sleep, but eventually the slim blonde woman had, her head cradled in Joseph's lap as he whispered soothing utterances and stroked her shoulder length hair. All the while, his gaze flitted from the empty bag which had carried the Grail for more years than he could remember across the room to one of the two unoccupied bunks. He found it dreadfully hard to entertain the thoughts that were entering his head, but he found that he could not block them out no matter how hard he tried to think of other things.

After a brief discussion with some of the others, Joseph had learnt that David had left the feast to return to this very room which obviously led him on to the next step in the puzzle, although as far as he was aware, David had been unaware of the Grail's presence.

According to Ruth, Justin had also left the feast not long after David saying that he was going to retire to his bed.

58

Now Justin was dead after plunging from the castle walls, Drell had said in a puzzled voice that he had made no noise as he plunged to his death and David and the Grail were missing.

Though Joseph wished with all his heart that there was some other explanation, his head told him otherwise.

He sighed and stared at the wooden beams that ran parallel to the pallets across the ceiling. Was one of his, he hated to use the word but could not think of another, disciples really capable of such a cold-blooded act? His mind imagined the course of events that had played themselves out scant hours before. Justin, fatigued and exhausted, walking into the room intent on nothing other than falling to his bed, disturbing David as he rifled through Joseph's belongings. Then an argument. An unpremeditated blow in anger or possibly self-defence? Why had that thought come into his head? He fervently hoped for the latter, but then if the blow had been unintentional, why cover up the deed by hurling Justin from atop the castle? Joseph paused for thought. Would stumbling across the wonder of the Grail really have been enough to push David down this path? Could an object so pure and good have indirectly unleashed such evil? Surely not?

The Arimathean let his head loll back and rest against the stonework of the wall. He closed his eyes for no more than a few seconds but when he opened them again, he was momentarily unsettled to find himself peering up at the night sky with innumerable stars looking down upon him and a gibbous moon casting the land all about him in a cold silver ocean. Blinking rapidly in surprise, he then looked down which only added to his confusion, for his sandaled feet were surrounded by dewy grass. Lifting his head once more, he found himself atop a mist-wreathed hill in the shadows of a massive tree. After a few moments, memory asserted itself and he realised it was the wondrous plant that had sprouted from his staff a few days previously.

Reaching out to touch the miraculous growth, he was disturbed to feel his fingertips come away with a damp stickiness. Moving them into the moonlight, he saw his fingers dripping red with blood. He backed hurriedly away from the trunk then jumped as something brushed his head. Spinning round like a top, a strangled gasp escaped his lips. Disturbed by his contact, the corpse-grey body of David gently swung from a thick branch some ten feet off the ground. The bloated cadaver dangled lifelessly as Joseph fought the urge to vomit. As he stared in horror at the bloodless face, his gorge rose again as David's eyes jerked open and he gurgled, "I'm sorry."

Joseph backed into the tree trunk as the Grail fell from the hanging man's hand and was sucked into the ground, in much the same way as the staff had been. This time, however, the whole object disappeared and the ground repaired itself before the Arimathean's eyes.

Joseph jerked awake and found himself looking down at the mass of blonde hair that draped Ruth's head. He was back in the sleeping quarters, drenched in sweat and breathing heavily.

Looking around wildly and fighting for calm, he shook his head vigorously as if to rid it of the last shreds of his horrendous vision. After a few moments, he becalmed himself and pondered the nightmare, resolving to go back to the tree on the hill as rapidly as he was able.

*

The tribespeople of the Belgae stood in solemn watchfulness as they watched the Christians make ready to leave the hill-fort at Caerleon.

Joseph had talked at length with the rest of his followers and it had been decided that the offer of land from Arviragus was to be taken up as quickly as possible, hence the haste that was being made in the cold light of the new dawn. However, in the light of David and Justin's demise, Joseph had not disclosed to them the nature of his dream and the almost physical urge he now felt to see the newly-sprouted tree on top of the hill at Glastonbury again.

He had faced, with some distress, the almost angry inquiries as to why the group were leaving when David was still missing, merely assuring his followers that, should David return to the fort, Arviragus would escort him safely to Glastonbury. It was clear that this answer was not satisfactory to some of the group however and he still found himself subject to numerous questions about the youth's whereabouts.

"Where can he be, Joseph?" Ruth asked plaintively as they stood in the foreboding shadow of the Belgae's hill-fort.

The most senior member of the Christians had peered down at her pinched, tired face and forced a smile upon his lips. "I am sure he will turn up soon, my dear. He is probably sleeping off the mead somewhere." Joseph found it hard to look her in the eye as he said this, because the image of David suspended from the tree was still fresh in his mind.

Ruth looked sceptical and Joseph felt his heart breaking as her doe-like eyes moistened. "Surely all this noise would have roused him, Joseph." She leant in close to him and the pool of tears that seemed to have drained themselves dry the previous night refilled anew. "I fear he has suffered the same fate as Jus...Justin," she faltered for a moment, then continued, "I am scared, Joseph." She cast a fearful glance towards the assembled warriors who stood unmoving in the watery dawn sunlight. "Why did we have to come here, Joseph? Why?"

He sighed expansively and stared up at the lightening sky. "Ruth, you know as well as I do that we are on a mission from God to spread His word and message to people who have not had the privilege to know it before. Perhaps…" Joseph lapsed into silence as he brought his head down and met Ruth's glare. "Perhaps there is a purpose to all this, even Justin's death. He moves in mysterious ways, Ruth. Let none of us ever forget that." He was painfully aware how hollow the words sounded but he somehow managed to hold her gaze, almost challenging her to question his words.

The Christian woman stared at him for a long moment with the merest hint of doubt flickering in her eyes then she turned away and went to help the others load the horses that the tribal chieftain had supplied them with for the journey.

Joseph of Arimathea strode over to his erstwhile host and they clasped forearms. "Chief Arviragus, you have treated us with such grace and kindness that I feel compelled to thank you with some sort of gift, however I find both mine and my friends baggage bereft of any such trinket to sufficiently repay you." He dropped to one knee and lowered his head. "The only gift I can give you is an oath that, after my God, yourself and your tribe will be uppermost in my heart and my mind and if you require any help in your struggle against the Roman invader, then you have but to ask. I have nothing more to offer you and for that, I am sorry. I am also sorry that the spectre of death has seen fit to visit your house whilst we have been biding here."

Arviragus lifted Joseph to his feet with an unreadable set to his features. "With the Romans stalking these lands, death is never very far away from our gates," he sighed, then changed the subject. "But surely the sorrow should not be yours, Joseph. It is I who should be apologising to you. This tragedy has befallen your group whilst you were in my care." He found himself peering towards the top of the towering fort from where Justin had fallen.

An awkward silence followed, which neither man seemed inclined to fill. Drell, who as always, hovered at his leader's right hand, cleared his throat. "What will you do with the twelve hides of land that Arvi has so kindly donated to your party?"

If Joseph noticed the twist of sarcasm in the clansman's voice, he did not show it. "The first thing we will do is lay Justin to rest." The trio all stared at the grey steed that was to carry the grisly cargo of Justin's body to Glastonbury. "Then we will build a mission. A holy house from which we will spread the Lord's word, spread it to the four corners of the island. I trust that meets with your approval?" Joseph looked sidelong at the Belgae chief who waved the implied question away.

"Joseph, I would not have offered you the land had I thought you would use it frivolously." Arviragus nodded. "It is good to know that it will be used for such a noble cause though."

"Indeed." Drell clapped his hands together loudly. "We should not keep you from it any longer. Come, Arvi, let us help them on the first step of their spiritual journey."

Joseph regarded the second-in-command of the tribe with the beginnings of a smile playing on his lips. Though Arviragus was irritated by Drell's unending cynicism, he was cheered that it had provoked the first sign of happiness on the Arimathean's face since Justin had died.

With no further words, the Christians finished their preparations for departure. At length, they said their goodbyes and set off across the countryside.

Not surprisingly, Joseph took the lead, riding in the van of the procession, alone in his own world and, to all intents and purposes, oblivious to his travelling companions. His mind kept returning to the image of David suspended from the tree, apologising, beseeching for his forgiveness.

He was certain now that David had stolen the Grail and murdered Justin and he reflected on the spectacular fall from grace of his follower. The old missionary, and this last day he had felt every one of his forty eight years, shook his head. He disliked being judge and jury but the facts pointed to no other possibility. He was so definite in his mind, so certain that the vision in his dream was a premonition of things to come, that his brain prevented him from reaching any other conclusion.

The Christians had travelled without incident for most of the day but, as the sun began to set, a bank of clouds built up unexpectedly quickly, pregnant with the promise of rain and turning the landscape a sickly, dull yellow. Just after the sun dipped below the horizon it came, a torrential deluge that had them scurrying for the nearest cover they could see. It consisted of a group of no more than nine or ten trees clumped together in a small depression at the base of a hill that, unbeknownst to the travellers, was but a few hundred yards from their destination. However, the downpour had appeared so rapidly that visibility had been cut to a minimum and they did not realise how close they were to their ultimate objective.

Joseph stood at the edge of the copse, peering uselessly out into the curtain of water that descended from the sky, futilely hoping that he could catch a glimpse of anything familiar. His lank grey hair hung in unkempt rat-tails and deposited a goodly amount of liquid down his back, causing him to wriggle uncomfortably.

"Come in from the rain, Joseph, you will catch your death," fussed Esther, a short plump woman with warm hazel eyes and thinning dark brown curls, greying at the temples. She was the oldest woman present on the mission and, as such, had taken it upon herself to be a mother to them all.

He turned to her with an amused look, unable to resist an exaggerated roll of his eyes. "Really, Esther, you do fret so. It is only water, I will be fine."

He was about to turn back to the gloom when the air about them was ripped in two. The first lightning bolt speared into one of the trees and obliterated a bough fully six feet across. The stunning concussion threw Joseph to the soaking ground. He gingerly lifted his head as an inexplicable gust of warmth washed over him. Amazingly, despite the horrendous weather, a fire had taken hold in the little grove.

A scream reached Joseph's ears.

"Esther, your robes..." Samuel, a young shaven-headed disciple who also hailed from Arimathea, shrieked.

With a look of horror on her face, Esther looked down and saw the hem of her robe ablaze. She panicked and ran towards Joseph. "Roll, Esther, roll in the grass," the preacher yelled as the flames began to climb further up her clothes.

The blind fear meant that she did not heed his words and simply continued to run towards him. He pushed himself painfully to his feet and caught her, pushing her roughly to the floor and smothering her himself.

When the fire had been extinguished, he became aware of an orange glow above. Yet more of the branches above them were alight as a result of further lightning but despite its strength the rain was unable to keep up with their destructive progress.

Joseph tried to make himself heard in the ensuing chaos, but the hiss and crackle of the fire and constant stiletto concussion of rain together with the screams of the panicking Christians made it impossible. Nonetheless, he tried. "We must flee. Everyone. To me."

The ragged group came together and ducked out from under the trees, straight into the blinding cascades of rain that fell from above. The ten of them slipped and slid their way up the slope, desperately trying to keep their feet as the rain turned the ground into a quagmire of mud. Now though, in addition to the horrendous downpour, the smoke from the fire began blowing up the slope behind them and they soon found themselves groping blindly in a foul-smelling fog.

Somehow Joseph became separated from his companions. He ran on, trying to call to his fellow missionaries, trying to identify who was where but to no avail, the clouds of smoke were too thick and the sheets of rain too impenetrable. He kept on going, reasoning that sooner or later, he would find one of the group or that the weather would ease and he would be able to get his bearings once again.

Disorientated by the conditions, he did not realise that he had come to the crest of the hill and suddenly he found himself barrelling down the other side with his sandals unable to find any purchase on the slick grass to arrest his accelerating momentum. Losing his footing, he began bowling down the slope, falling like a fish in a river, fighting against a current that was too strong, but fighting nonetheless.

After what seemed to be an age of uncontrolled descent, he landed in a heap at the base of the slope. He lay on his back for a few seconds, discomfited by the drenched ground but frightened to get up in case he was injured. Closing his eyes, he prepared to try and move but just as he had summoned up the strength to propel himself off the saturated grass, he became aware of a light building brightly in front of him. Cautiously, he squinted through the blinding shaft that bathed him in its aurora. Dazed and confused, he unthinkingly staggered to his feet, only recognising that he was uninjured when he began to walk towards the light's source.

His mind was racing as his faltering steps took him up another incline. He knew that the light was too intense to be emanating from the moon and even if it was moonlight, the clouds from the storm would surely obscure it, but what other possible origin could it have? He ceased his unsteady trudge and looked to the sky. Or where the sky should have been. The light had become so incandescent that it disorientated him. As well as that, the rain seemed to have stopped suddenly and the ground felt dry underneath his feet.

Piecing together what he knew, he reached what should have been a comforting conclusion but one which, in actuality, filled him with a bitter trepidation. He had gone from tumbling painfully in the dark down the side of a hill in a torrential rainstorm to a place of calming peace and drenched in a brilliant light where he was in no pain and the air was as dry and breathless as a desert.

With a groan of dismay, he came to the conclusion that the plunge had killed him. Was he even now ascending towards heaven, the place that he and all other Christians had dreamt of? The final resting place that he had extolled the virtues of to so many different people in so many different places? He was not ready, he knew. He had experienced the revelation of the tree on the hill. He had then persuaded Arviragus to cede the land to his group so that they could plant the seed of Christianity and nurture it so that it could blossom and flower all over the island.

Surely, after making so much progress in His name, the Lord would not snatch the opportunity from him when it was so tantalisingly close. That thought made his 'mysterious ways' speech to Ruth sit bitterly on his tongue. How could he preach about Justin's death in that way to her when he felt so disinclined to embrace the very same afterlife that was now laid out before him?

As he stared down at his dirty, scuffed sandals, contemplating his own mortality, the light winked out so fast that a purple after-image danced across his vision and he threw out his arms to maintain his balance. Gradually, he brought his face up and his vision adjusted itself. To his astonishment, he found himself underneath the branches of the miracle tree.

The breath stuck in his throat as he beheld the bloated, discoloured visage of David swaying gently in the breeze, suspended exactly as he had seen him in the dream. As Joseph took a step towards the body, the bough snapped. It was almost as if the body of David had been waiting lifelessly for his fellow Christians to come, so that it could finally be at peace.

Where before he had been dangling in limbo, now he was at rest on the holy ground at the base of the massive trunk. Choking back tears, Joseph reached down and closed the fallen disciple's eyes for the final time.

He looked across the depression where he had fallen to the summit of the other hill from behind which an orange glow pulsed in the sky, he presumed from the burning trees, reflecting that the first task of the new mission would be to bury not one but two of his companions. Could this place really be the site that Joseph had searched for twenty years to find when it was now forever cursed by the two untimely deaths of his young charges? Would this place now be tainted from the start? Could all the years he had, he nearly thought of the word wasted but shied away from it at the last second, spent passing on the beliefs of his religion as a duty to his friend rather than as a hard, fast conviction, be building to this point? He had come so far and, with the miracle of the tree appearing from his staff, he had finally been visited by a nearly overwhelming sense of belief in his God. That had been something that he had not experienced for so long that he had nearly forgotten the wondrous sensation. Could it all have been a cruel joke played upon him by fate for living his life as a lie, preaching but not believing, sermonising but inwardly doubting?

To be so near to what he had thought was his ultimate destination in life and then be visited by feelings like this was a savage blow to Joseph, because he found himself painfully aware that whatever noble deeds were done on this island at the behest of the church, the mission would always have the spectre of Justin and David's demise casting shadows upon it like thunderclouds masking the sun.

An anguished shriek jerked him back to the present and through the dripping curtains of hair that had fallen across his face, he saw the rest of his ragged band ascending the hill towards him and David's limp unmoving body and he hauled himself wearily to his feet, preparing himself to explain yet another untimely death to his followers.

*

Two years had elapsed since David and Justin's passing and the church that Joseph and his disciples had built from the ground up was now firmly established in Glastonbury and the surrounding environs.

More often than not, a group of inquisitive tribesmen and women were to be found sitting intently in the shade provided by the canopy of the magnificent tree atop Wearyall Hill, listening in rapt silence to the words and lessons laid before them by the denizens of this remote bastion of Christendom. On more than one occasion it had been Arviragus and his fellow Belgae that had been welcomed into the religious arms of the mission and even Drell had graciously accepted that he had been wrong about Joseph's ultimate intention.

Sometimes it would be Joseph himself giving the sermon, his ageing frame being belied by the booming voice that carried easily to his audience as he spoke of the miracles that his dear departed friend and leader had performed all those years ago. Always an accomplished speaker, he did not have to work hard to impress the folk who sat open-mouthed as he spoke of a man who turned water into wine or made a basket of fish and bread feed a congregation of five thousand.

At other times it would be one of the Arimathean's charges evangelising to the attendees under the tree.

Although the church had been built with a more than comfortable interior in which to worship, the Britons still preferred to receive their teachings outside in the fresh air, even in near Arctic conditions, much to the chagrin of Joseph's underlings, who could sometimes be overheard noting their leader's sudden decline in sermonising during the winter months.

On this bright sunny day though, a day so fine that all the atheists in the world would have been hard pressed to deny the existence of God, it was Joseph of Arimathea who waxed lyrical, exhorting the tribespeople to enjoy His creation and live each day by the morals and manners expected of them by their newly adopted God.

Ironically it had been a dream, a vision in the night that had lifted Joseph's spirit so high. This time though, it had been a face from the past that had given him such joy. Not the grimacing bloated features of David hanging from the Wearyall tree, but an altogether more benign face suspended from another, more angular piece of wood on another hill, many miles and many years away.

His messiah had still been upon the hideous instrument of Roman torture, but the nails that had pierced his hands and feet were gone and he appeared to be in no discomfort. "Joseph, my friend," Jesus smiled, "how goes life in the land of the Britons?"

The leader of the Glastonbury mission smiled back, despite the bad news he knew he would have to impart. "We have established a church which has reached out to the tribespeople of the island and has brought them much needed succour and comfort in their trials against the Romans," he grinned ruefully. "As well as giving us the protection we require against them."

Jesus nodded. "That is good to hear." He paused and regarded Joseph with a penetrating stare. "However, I sense that all is not as well as it appears to be with you, Joseph. There is a sadness that lies upon your shoulders like an ill-fitting robe."

Joseph's smile faded and his eyes betrayed the grief that had travelled with him like an eternal companion for just over twenty-four months. "We have lost two of our number since we alighted on these shores. Two of my young charges are biding with you and your father in Heaven."

Despite the fact that Jesus had appeared to be pinned to the crucifix in some way, the messiah brought his hand forward and laid it on his anguished disciple's shoulder. "That must have been dreadfully hard for you, Joseph."

Joseph fidgeted dejectedly, wanting to pull away from the kindly hand but not willing to move from the comfort it gave him. "They seemed so young, my Lord. It seemed so wrong...I began to..." he sighed hugely and steeled himself to return Jesus' gaze. "I began to doubt, Jesus. I began to doubt you and your father."

To his relief, Jesus smiled acceptingly. "Who would blame you, Joseph? The path that we tread will never be entirely free of obstacles. It is how we face them and deal with them that shapes us and determines what sort of people we will be. Would it be too painful for you to tell me what became of them?" Jesus cocked his head sympathetically. "I do not wish to cause you further distress."

In that moment, Joseph of Arimathea realised that he had not in fact actually told anyone all of his suspicions regarding Justin and David's death and he took the opportunity to unburden himself. In a way, he found himself saying to Jesus, it was David's death that had hit him the hardest. The stunning fall from grace had been such a surprise, especially with the strength of feeling he had exhibited both upon Watkins' ship and in the tribal lands of Arviragus and the Belgae.

"So," Jesus appeared slightly troubled for the first time since the vision had began, "you suspect it was the Grail that was the catalyst for the deaths then?"

Joseph found himself regretting that he had voiced his suspicions because of the position bestowed upon him in the mausoleum, but now he had done, he saw no point in trying to backtrack on them. He nodded slowly. "What of the Grail now, Joseph? Where does it rest? Is it safe?" Jesus pressed, a strange light illuminating his eyes.

Joseph told Jesus of the dream he had experienced which had led him to the location of David's demise. "It rests beneath the trunk of the Wearyall tree, of that I am certain," he shrugged. "I have not physically seen it for many months but I am totally convinced of its location. There is an atmosphere, a mystique surrounding that place. It is imbued with such pleasance that there must be some sort of outside agency making it so."

The messiah of the Christian faith regarded his disciple for a moment. "You are certain of its' location?" he asked again.

Joseph nodded emphatically.

The Son of God stared intently at the Grail's keeper for a long moment then nodded gently. "Then let it bide there, my friend. It would appear to be working its magic without the need for any aid. It is safe and it is secret. You have done your job well, Steward of the Grail. You have done your job well."

Suddenly, the figure of Jesus seemed to pull away from Joseph and a blinding light, similar in luminescence to the one he had seen before he had found David but somehow more comforting, bathed him in its heat and he closed his eyes against its power. When he opened them again, he was lying on his bed, engulfed in the warming, comfortable memory of the vision.

The rest of the day followed without incident and when he finished the evening prayers, Joseph removed himself from the congregation as it meandered down to the lower slopes of Wearyall Hill and walked up to the gargantuan trunk of the magical tree.

He laid hands on the pitted wood and let the sense of well-being that emanated from it infuse his body and soul. He closed his eyes, the better to enjoy the peace and tranquillity of the moment. He did not know how long he stood there such was the ethereal solitude in which he found himself.

He was jarred from his seclusion by a gentle hand on his shoulder. It was Ruth with a look of concern hovering on her face. "Are you alright, Joseph?" she asked, taking a step back at the momentary look of aggression that passed across his face.

The Arimathean bit back a snarl. He knew, in his heart of hearts, that he would never again experience such exquisite calmness. However, the feeling of completeness he felt was quickly supplanted by mortification when he saw the look of fear that crossed Ruth's face as she beheld him. It was a face that had changed much in the past year, full of a fragile beauty before the two deaths, the brow had become lined through sorrow and the sparkle had departed the ocean-blue eyes. However, in recent weeks, hints of the old Ruth had appeared on the surface once more, infrequently at first, but becoming more pronounced every day. "I am sorry, Ruth, you startled me," he held up his hands in apology. "In answer to your question, yes, I am fine." He cast a quick glance over his shoulder to the spot where, in his dream, the Grail had been enveloped by the earth. "I am as contented as can be," he breathed, revisiting the moments of near-rapture that he had felt scant seconds before and transforming them into a dazzling smile that he flashed towards the flaxen-haired woman, "Come, let us retire to the mission." He placed a fatherly arm around her shoulder and gently propelled her towards the stone-built construction. As they approached it, enjoying the scarlet rays of the setting sun as it descended below the horizon, Joseph reflected that the church had been the first place he had dwelt in for longer than a month in twenty years.

His recent life, indeed his not-so recent life as well, had been one of transience and inconstancy but, after the visitation from his messiah, the shadow of David and Justin no longer seemed to cast a pall over the place. He stopped for a moment at the gravestones of the two fallen disciples. "You go ahead, Ruth. I will be in shortly." He watched her go and turned back to the graves. That was not to say that the spectres had entirely disappeared, he thought as he read the crudely engraved epitaphs etched inexpertly but lovingly in the off-white stone, they still remained as memories but they no longer dominated Joseph's remembrance. He now found himself recalling the way they had lived rather than the manner in which they had died.

With that thought lightening his heart, the Steward of the Grail entered the house of worship, idly wondering what he would have for his supper.

*

And so, for century upon century the Grail remained where it had fallen, investing Wearyall Hill and the surrounding tor at Glastonbury with a ghostly sense of otherworldliness and an atmosphere of inexplicable eeriness. There it rested for half a millennium, a silent and unseen witness to the birth of Britain's identity.

It lay dormant whilst the Romans invaded Caledonia in 84 A.D.

It dwelt under the hallowed ground as both the Hadrian and Antonine Walls were constructed to help cage the barbaric Picts.

It slumbered in peace before and after the Pax Romana had been made with the Caledonian tribes in the north.

It resided in isolation as the Roman invaders were removed slowly but inexorably from the island and replaced by the invading forces of the Saxons in 480 A.D.

It remained wrapped in secrecy as the Saxons were in turn defeated by the Britons in 500 A.D.

*

And there it would have stayed, undisturbed and unharried, gaining notoriety in myth and legend, but remaining intangible to the real world, had it not been for a band of men new to their calling but destined to become as renowned in fable as the vessel they sought.

Dispatched they were, dispatched on a quest by the God they worshipped to locate and resurrect the power of the Grail. They bestrode the land searching for the cup, fighting traitors within their midst and invaders from foreign lands but all the while consumed by an overwhelming yearning to find the Grail and redirect it once more onto the path of its undoubtedly glorious fate.

They were The Knights of The Round Table.

*

Chapter 6

A.D 502 - Camelot Castle

The young herald strolled through the widespread doors of the banqueting hall with a cocksure grin plastered across his face. The message that he clasped in a rolled-up parchment in his hand, he knew, would bring great joy to those arrayed around the table. As he walked through the room, he stared up at the shields that hung upon the frigid stone walls, adorned as they were with the emblems of the Round Table knights.

Pride of place was Arthur's escutcheon, three gold dragons on a field of blue. To the left of that was Gawain's, a design as complicated as its bearer, a gold band with three red dots inside it slicing in twain a field of blue above a downward pointing dagger. Then there was Sir Geraint's, a design as simple as Gawain's was complex, being a black crow on a field of royal blue. This was followed by Sir Gareth's, Gawain's brother. His shield was made up of red and grey quarters, red being in the top right and bottom left. Sir Galahad's design was that which would become known as the George Cross, just as Sir Gaheris', which was next in line was in the fashion that was to gain worldwide recognition as the saltire of St Andrew.

By this time the shields had described a semi-circle around the room and on the opposite wall to King Arthur's shield was a gaping hole. A hole caused by the removal of the disgraced emblem of Sir Lancelot, just one of the petty acts of vengeance that the King of The Britons had visited upon his cuckolder. When the shield had decorated the wall in its splendour, it had been composed of a deep blue background with three golden lions emblazoned upon it.

Continuing the circle of designs was Sir Bors' shield, drawn in the same manner as Galahad's but without the arms extending to the rim of the pitted blazon. Bedivere's emblem was similar in layout to Gawain's, save the field was red not blue and the patterns encased in the gold bands were fleur de lis. Sir Kay's was next in line, a simple design of white with a battle horn described on its rough face. This shield was brother in colour to Sir Percivale's, though his had a rather less challenging design of one single heart upon it. With the circle almost complete, there were but two shields left, Sir Lamorak and Sir Tristan's. Sir Lamorak's was blue with two ragged white stripes slashing across it but by far the most complicated design was Sir Tristan's. It was a deep blue with a harp at the top and dagger at the bottom and as well as that it had a ragged gold band in the middle with two hearts upon it pierced in an X by two arrows.

71

As well as their own personal designs, all the knights wore a necklace, given to them by King Arthur as part of the ennoblement ceremony that marked them as Knights of the Round Table. It was a weighty pendant made up of a red dragon holding a golden cross above a round table. The cross was designed to remind them that they were to live pure and sinless lives and never strive for less than perfection. The red dragon was the same beast as the one depicted on Arthur's shield and represented their allegiance to their king. The round table had a threefold purpose. It was illustrative of the eternity of God, the equality, unity and comradeship of the Order and the singleness of purpose of all the knights. Needless to say, Lancelot had been ignominiously stripped of his necklace after his dalliance with Queen Guinevere had been revealed.

The herald espied his target and made his way round the table, dodging waves of ale and mead as they splashed to the stone floor.

He waited patiently whilst his charge finished listening to the man at his right hand tell a risque joke. As the raconteur's drink pooled around the messenger's boots, the man for whom he held the missive noticed him for the first time. Licking a hem of ale from the bottom of his moustache, the man beckoned over the herald and leaned forward so he could pass on the communication.

After he had read the message, King Arthur of The Britons stood up with great ceremony, a smile of epic proportions upon his noble features.

He brought his goblet crashing down upon the table, drowning a plate of chicken in mead and stunning the room into silence.

Instantly all conversation ceased and the assembly stared at the monarch as he stepped upon his throne and jumped lightly upon the banqueting table. On the brink of fifty years of age, King Arthur Pendragon was still a vital and vigorous man, peerless with both sword and axe, though secretly his joints were beginning to feel the weight of his advancing years. He wore woollen leggings and a simple white tunic adorned with the cross of St George, an outfit that was, to all intents and purposes, a uniform for all who possessed seats at the edge of The Round Table. His emerald-green eyes narrowed as he scanned his audience, throwing the few lines of age that rested there into stark relief in the flickering torchlight. He reached up and stroked the greying stubble on his chin with a heavily bejewelled hand, decorated as it was with rings made of gold and gemstones that seemed to pulsate and glisten in the inconstant illumination. After letting his gaze perform a circuit of the banqueters, he cleared his throat and began to speak in his powerful, rumbling timbre.

"Brothers, I have just received the latest intelligence regarding my traitorous nephew, Mordred. It appears that the cowardly dog is licking his wounds in the North. Our courageous victory in fighting the forces of treachery at large in the Kingdom has left him bloodied and defeated and his bastard face will not be seen at this table again. I commend you all for your bravery and devotion to the duties that bind you to The Round Table. But for your strength and diligence, even now we would be languishing under a rule of dishonour, deceit and perfidy. I thank you all."

The gathering raucously affirmed their approval of the statement with a chorus of whoops and shouts, banging goblets and platters upon the uneven wood.

Arthur smiled lazily and gazed proprietorially around the circle of his peers. Waving slowly for silence, he continued with his speech. "However, we must be ever vigilant against the malevolent evil that stalks the land. I suspect that Mordred was but a pawn in a game far beyond his comprehension. From my experience of him, I feel that his wit is too limited to have hatched a plan to seize the Kingdom on his own. Never before would the seed of rebellion have been sown in such a barren field."

An undulation of laughter and a ripple of knowing nods washed around the table and Arthur acknowledged the response to his comment.

"Fortuitously though, thanks to the gallant efforts of our fellow knight," and at this point he nodded towards a clean-shaven pious looking young man, dressed in the same manner as the King, who remained unmoved under the scrutiny, "we now have in our possession a weapon with which to chase away the darkness. A weapon that will become a beacon in the night, driving away the shadows of evil."

His gaze left his audience and came to rest on the platform that had been placed in the exact centre of the Round Table. A platform upon which rested the Holy Grail, the sacred Cup of Christ.

The knight that Arthur had congratulated stood up gracefully and turned to face his King. Bowing low, he said, "My liege, I thank you for your gracious platitudes. However, I feel that you have misunderstood the properties of the Grail. It is not and never can be a weapon. This is the goblet from which the messiah drunk at the Last Supper in the Garden of Gethsemane. This is the vessel that held His blood after the lance of the Roman, Longinus, pierced His side as He hung dying on the cross. It can never be used to cause pain or suffering, even on treacherous curs like Mordred."

Sir Gawain jabbed a finger at Galahad. "But surely the very nature of its origin would suggest that it would resist evil and the enemies of God at every turn."

Sir Galahad conceded the point with the merest of nods. "Indeed, Sir Gawain, that is so," he continued in his deep sonorous voice, "but resistance is not the same as aggression. Make no mistake, gentlemen, there are tremendous energies present within the Grail." He began walking around the mosaic-laden floor, all the while keeping his piercing stare trained upon the golden cup. "Energies which remain untapped and hidden to all who seek to unravel them. For just as the Grail can be a barrier to all that is wicked in the world then, if it is used for evil deeds, it may become twisted and then utilised to thwart the great and the good."

King Arthur's stare took itself from the lantern-jawed Galahad and also rested on the Grail. "So what do you know of its capabilities?"

With a sigh, Galahad shook his head, "Very little, your majesty. I sometimes feel that I am on the brink of understanding certain small aspects of it but I am painfully aware that my knowledge is not up to the task."

The King looked fondly upon the earnest young man. "Please do not feel in any way ashamed or apologetic. Were it not for your sterling efforts we would not even have the Grail in our possession."

If Galahad noticed the compliment, he did not show it. Instead, he ceased his walking and leant forward, slapping both palms on the table in frustration. "But to know that within my reach lies enlightenment beyond my wildest imaginings is agonising. Such an opportunity falls at ones' feet once in a thousand lifetimes, yet I do not possess the tools to unlock the Grail's secrets."

With a suddenness that startled everyone into silence, an imposing figure stepped into view as if conjured out of the very air. Though the man was enveloped in an all-encompassing midnight-black cowl, he was immediately recognisable to all who sat at the table. The newcomer threw back the hood of his outfit and his eyes swept the table in the same way that Arthur's had scant moments before. He was slim to the point of unhealthiness and similar in years to King Arthur, yet somehow the ravages of age did not seem to have touched him. His features were without flaw, a perfectly trimmed beard that encircled a mouth framed by full, sensuous lips and above that a nose which seemed to somehow instil an impression of nobility and superiority in the man's profile. However, what was most striking about the new arrival was his eyes.

They were, at any time, both all colours and no colours at all. When his gaze fell upon you, you felt as if not only your outward appearance was being studied, but also your thoughts, your dreams, even your very soul was being laid bare and subjected to scrutiny by the depthless stare. Emotions were a stranger to this man's eyes but there was always a sense of cold pitilessness lurking just beneath the surface. His clipped tones boomed across the room and all present shuffled uncomfortably, for here was a man of power, not the noble majesty and poise of the King, but a more primal brutal power, a power that gripped spines and squeezed them into acquiescence.

"I, on the other hand, do," said Merlin, court magician of Camelot. The only man in the room, bar the King, who did not seem in any way fazed by the voice and the dramatic appearance was Sir Galahad and he did not shy away from showing it. "Ah, I wondered how long it would be before the mighty magician made an appearance."

The wizard raised an eyebrow and smirked but those closest to him noted that the smile did not seem to extend to his eyes. "Do I detect a note of sarcasm in your voice, good Sir Knight?"

Galahad fought an uneven battle against the supercilious sneer that formed on his lips, "Not at all, Merlin. Please feel free to cast your eye into the Grail's depths. Perhaps you might espy some hint as to its essence that has hitherto escaped my witless endeavours."

"Please, Sir Galahad, I would not wish to belittle your attempts at penetrating the Grail's veil of secrecy. I am convinced that you tried your utmost and strived most feverishly. Your devotion to duty does you credit." He placed his hands behind his back and strode pointedly towards the raised dais. However Galahad stepped across his path with a challenging look.

This time Merlin's smile extended to his whole face as he peered around Galahad's stony face at King Arthur. "May I?" he asked.

The King of The Britons rolled his eyes at this latest manifestation of the enmity between his finest knight and his most eminent magician. "Yes, you may," he sighed, switching his stare to Galahad as if daring him to comment. Galahad bowed with an exaggerated flourish and removed himself from Merlin's path. As he withdrew, he whispered to Sir Bors who stood off to his left, "I am sure the Grail will be honoured to have the greatest conjuror in the land gaze upon it."

Merlin stopped in his tracks and mouthed silently, "Watch your words, Galahad the Chaste. Watch your words and watch your back."

The founder of the Grail spun round at the voice that whispered in his left ear, as if spoken by someone standing just behind him. In confusion at seeing no-one there, he turned back to be met by Merlin's formidable stare.

The mystic removed his glare from Galahad and bestowed it upon the Grail. His eyes lost their ever-present cynicism as he beheld the swirling maelstrom of colours circling within the confines of the metal cup. "Tis a most breathtaking aurora," he murmured, half to himself.

After a few seconds of silence Arthur felt moved to speak. "Well, Merlin, does any indication of the vessel's properties present itself to you?"

Merlin reluctantly tore his eyes away from the Grail and bowed. "My liege, I fear that if I am to unwrap this puzzle, it will be a task of days, possibly even weeks." He paused and his face took on a pensive look. "Might I be allowed to bear the Grail back to my chambers, so that I may study it in a less distracting environment?" he asked whilst flicking a quick glance towards Galahad.

Sir Galahad, upon hearing the suggestion, threw his own look towards the King and it was one of alarm and pleading.

Arthur caught the glance and acknowledged it with the merest of nods. He pondered the question for a moment. "Merlin, your request would seem, on the surface, eminently reasonable. However, I feel that, for the Grail to do its work, first and foremost, it needs to be seen to be doing its work. It is a symbol of the light and symbols of the light should not be hidden away where their flaming auras cannot be perceived." He cast his arms wide, unconsciously imitating Jesus upon the cross. "Let the Grail remain in the room of The Round Table where it resides at this very moment. If needs be, when you wish to study it, I will order the room cleared, so you may not be so...distracted." He said the last word with a mischievous look at Galahad.

The more observant diners in the room noticed the merest flicker of irritation cross Merlin's face but the King did not appear to be among them and so no comment was made. "My humble thanks, King Arthur," he bowed.

The King continued, "I also decree that you should work in harness with Sir Galahad, as he alone of all the knights is privy to the workings of the Grail."

"My liege," The flawless knight bowed floridly once again.

Merlin nodded at the King's announcement, "As you wish, sire. As this is my first sighting of the Grail, I would like to scrutinise it further. Might I humbly ask that your Majesty clears the room, so that I may be alone with my musings?"

"Indeed," King Arthur nodded emphatically. "Let us leave Merlin and Galahad to their deliberations." He laid his hand on the shoulder of the nearest servant. "Chisnall, make sure that they are attended to at every waking minute. They will require food and drink. Ensure they do not have to wait for it." He turned back to the duo that were to attempt to solve the enigma and nodded. "Galahad, Merlin, good fortune in your undertaking."

The remaining knights and servants filed slowly out of the room until Merlin and Galahad were left alone.

The knight stared around the magnificent room, fascinated by the play of shadows on the numerous shields and weaponry that hung upon the walls, generated in equal part by the crackling fire and the magical light within the Grail. With a sigh, he strode up to Merlin and extended a hand. "As circumstances have decreed that we shall be working together, I feel that we must put our petty differences aside and turn our efforts to unravelling the mystery before us."

Merlin regarded the knight for a moment then sighed also. "Indeed, Sir Galahad, you are correct. Let us forget our squabbles and concentrate on the task before us." He gripped the proffered hand and pumped it vigorously. "Therefore, I will accept your apology." He turned away from his open-mouthed companion and slowly circled the dais, eyes never leaving the goblet. "So this is what has caused the furore about the castle for the past few days then. I can see why it is such a talking point from maidservant to monarch."

"Yes, I have to say it is breathtaking," Galahad agreed. "Might I also say that the other major talking point which has generated almost as much debate is the very fact that you have absented yourself from the Grail's presence for nearly a week since it was brought into Camelot."

"To be honest, I had no wish to become involved in the mutual back-slapping and platitudes that have no doubt been dispensed like raindrops in a storm for the past few days," Merlin stated pompously with a dismissive wave of his hand. "Now tell me, what do you know of the Grail and its sorceries?"

If the apparently well-rehearsed comment about the back-slapping had not angered Galahad then the question certainly had. His eyes hooded and he jabbed a finger at the wizard. "Sorceries? This vessel is infused with the purity and compassion of Our Lord, Jesus Christ. How can you compare the miracles He worked with the tacky deceptions of sleight-of-hand charlatans?"

Merlin held up his hands placatingly. "I do not. Perhaps it was a poor choice of words but, when all is said and done, what is a miracle? I do not wish to offend you but I would wager I could explain away any of the miracles that have been attributed to the Nazarene."

With murder in his eyes, Galahad unsheathed his sword Whitecleave and placed it within inches of Merlin's throat. "Who do you think you are to blaspheme in such a manner?" he hissed.

Merlin peered disdainfully at the weapon then pushed it away dismissively. "I see that your faith burns in you like a raging inferno, but I also see that you avoid the question. I say again, name one of the Nazarene's miracles and I will explain how I believe it could have been performed."

Galahad slid the blade back into its scabbard. "I have no wish to participate in your games, magician. Although I note you are now qualifying the question, you now say you will describe how it *could* have been done performed, in other words, admitting the possibility that they could have been achieved by miraculous means," the knight chirruped, happy with the victory, no matter how small.

Merlin shrugged disinterestedly. "Congratulations, you have outfoxed me with your mastery of semantics. Now, as I asked before, name one. Name a miracle."

Galahad wished that he could have stifled himself but there was something about Merlin that made him want to lay about him with his weapon, "The turning of water into wine at Cena."

A condescending smirk appeared immediately upon the wizard's face, "A mere parlour trick. All that would be required would be the adding of a few barrels of wine to the water system. Whilst everyone is peering perplexedly at the fountains pouring forth, the remaining water is switched for wine."

Galahad made an indelicate sound. "I think not."

Merlin made a complicated pass with his hands in front of his face. "The quickness of the hand often deceives the eye." He rolled his arm over and and held it up again for Galahad's inspection. "Apple?" he asked, offering the knight the shiny red fruit that now lay in the palm of his hand.

The knight waved him away then asked, "What about the feeding of the five thousand with but one basket of fish and bread? How do you explain that away?"

Merlin began pacing the room. "If memory serves me correctly, Jesus produced the food from atop a sand dune in the desert and fed the followers who stood below him, yes?"

Galahad nodded. "That is how the Bible has it."

Merlin tried to stop a grin appearing on his face but failed. "My dear gullible Galahad, tell me, does the holy bible mention if anyone was standing on the other side of the sand dune behind Jesus?"

"Not that I recall."

"Hmm. One wonders why?"

Galahad stared at the wizard in outraged disbelief, "Enough of this sacrilege. You may think yourself clever, Merlin. You may think it amusing to pick holes in the wondrous acts performed by our Lord, but let me ask you this. How do you explain the wondrous prize that proudly stands upon the rostrum before you?" He gestured enthusiastically at the Grail.

Merlin chewed upon his lip. "Ah, Sir Galahad, you have found the weak spot in my theory. The short answer is I cannot explain it. But, if it takes me a lifetime, I will unravel the conundrum." He leant forward and stared at the Grail almost threateningly, "Even if it takes me a lifetime."

Three days later, the pair of them were still to be found, prowling the room of the Round Table like caged tigers, frustrated by both their self-imposed captivity and their lack of progress.

Galahad removed himself from the Grail's presence and made his tired way to a narrow window which looked out over the beauteous vista of one of the castle's ornamental gardens, though his mood did not allow him to appreciate it as he normally would have.

"Another sunset," he sighed. "Another day passes without any progress worth speaking of."

Merlin shook his head irritably without taking his eyes from Christ's cup. "Perhaps we would make more headway if you ceased your trite announcements and stopped disturbing my contemplation," he sneered.

Galahad stormed over to the magician, face reddening like the evening sky. "Well, you have been staring at it for hour upon hour. Yet despite *your* contemplations I fail to see any addition to our pitiful amount of knowledge."

Merlin let the sarcasm pass. "Sir Knight, I really must ask you to desist your babbling whilst I concentrate."

Galahad was about to deliver another verbal riposte when the massive double doors at the end of the hall swung open to admit the King. He strode purposefully across the patterned floor and gestured for them to rise from their bowing. "So, gentlemen, how goes it? Anything of interest to impart?" he said, eyeing the Grail warily.

Merlin stepped forward before the King's champion could speak, "Unfortunately not, your majesty. The veil of mystery that surrounds the Grail is as impenetrable and thick as my chivalrous companion here."

King Arthur's hand flew to his mouth as he tried to stifle the guffaw that nearly escaped him.

If anything, Galahad's face became even redder than the sunset that blazed through the window, setting the room afire with its vivid scarlet. He pushed Merlin out of the way and strode to within inches of Arthur. "Sire, I really must protest at my treatment at the hands of this…this illusionist. I am incapable of achieving anything of value whilst he stalks the room incanting spells and reciting mantras."

That comment struck home and Merlin's face flushed in anger. "Have a care, Sir Galahad, or…"

The smile on Arthur's face dissolved as quickly as it had arrived and he cast about for a way to bring them both to their senses. He espied a glass of wine upon the table and grabbed it, hurling it against the wall, shattering it into a thousand pieces. "You will do nothing!" he bellowed. "Look at the pair of you. On the one hand, I have the most puissant spell-caster in these lands, capable of the most astounding feats of mysticism and magic than any man alive and on the other, I have my most trusted knight, second to none in valour and honour, yet you are both behaving like quarrelsome children." He strode over to the Grail and jerked his finger at it but could not quite bring himself to touch it. "We have here, in our possession, the most awesome vessel of power known to man. And you two are the men counted most likely to comprehend its constituents. If you love your country and your King then this pathetic display of one-upmanship must cease. You have the

79

power to pull us forward into an age of wonder. You have the power to insert the key into the lock and throw the doors of knowledge open wide." His voice lowered to a whisper as he peered intently at the cup. "Who knows what marvels will be visited upon the world when the door is ajar?" Reluctantly, he tore his gaze away and resumed the lecture. "Will you really let your pitiful rivalries come at the price of the good of the country? Hell, maybe even the good of the world?" He shook his head in contempt as Merlin and Galahad studiously avoided his stare. When they did finally bring themselves to face the irate King they shrunk back from the two pools of ice that Arthur's eyes had become. "I command you both to banish this ill feeling from your minds. There cannot be distractions. You must walk side by side down the path of knowledge or you will never reach your final destination."

Galahad seemed about to burst into tears, but instead dropped to his knees dramatically. "My liege, I am truly sorry. From now on, I can assure you that, for my part at least, I will restrain my temper from this moment forth and will concentrate all my endeavours only on solving the puzzle of the Grail."

Arthur looked quizzically towards his court magician. "What of you, Merlin? Will you cast aside your differences and strive in concert with Galahad?"

The magician nodded quickly. "If I may be so bold, majesty, whilst I would be happy to continue studying the Grail with my earnest companion, I feel that the manner in which we have been confined is not conducive to unravelling the problem. I feel that I need to return to my chambers to take stock and ponder what little has been deduced before I am ready to tackle it again."

The King stared at him for a few seconds then shrugged, "As you wish." He dismissed Merlin from their presence. "Return to your rooms and consider what you know. Then come back refreshed and inspired, for your work here is by no means at an end."

Merlin acknowledged the King's words with a florid bow and departed the room.

After he had gone, Arthur sat down and beckoned for Galahad to do likewise. "Sometimes I feel that Merlin is as complex and mysterious as the Grail itself."

"Indeed, sire." Galahad sniffed, scratching at his forehead, just below the line of his severe, uneven fringe.

King Arthur burst out laughing. "Tell me, Galahad, what is it that you find so irritating about him? I have known you for years and you seldom let your emotions get the better of your devotion to duty, yet in Merlin's case I feel that you are constantly fighting down the urge to run him through with your sword."

80

Galahad tried to remain serious, but he too dissolved into fits of laughter. "Tis true, I must confess I find the man insufferable. He is blasphemous, rude and possesses an opinion of himself so large that Camelot resides always in its shadow."

Arthur's expression became sober. "He is a man of many talents, Galahad. I might venture to say that his opinion of himself is matched in size by his skills in his magic arts. The feats I have seen him accomplish, well, they are beyond the wildest imaginings of you and I."

Galahad nodded. "I concede that he is unsurpassed in his practice of the black arts, but I still..."

"Ah, my dear pious Galahad, your language betrays your misgivings." Arthur interrupted, "There is no doubt that some of his...activities tread the border between light and dark, but unfortunately needs must as circumstances dictate. And let us not forget, he was instrumental in prising that nasty little insect Mordred from this very castle."

King Arthur's foremost knight arose from his seat and began pacing the room. "I am aware of the great deeds he has done in your service, my liege, it is just that I find it difficult to deal with a man such as him."

"As I said, Galahad, needs must. Do you wish to comprehend the Grail and its' powers?" the King shrugged.

The knight's eyebrows creased at the unexpected question. "Of course, sire."

"Then you must work alongside Merlin."

Galahad returned to his seat, slumped down and drew a tired hand across his eyes, "Yes, your majesty," he sighed.

A low chuckle escaped Arthur's lips. "Now you make it sound as if I am chiding you like a recalcitrant child."

"My apologies, sire."

"Let us talk of it no more. Compared to what lies in front of us, it is a matter of little importance." He clapped his hands together. "So, truthfully, how goes it? Does your research near fruition?"

Galahad rolled his eyes ceilingward, "Far from it. I have stared into the rainbow whirlpool for so long that I feel I am on the brink of toppling in, never to return. We have explored every avenue open to us. We have touched it with other holy objects, yet it does not react. Merlin has incanted spells and enchantments in many languages and dialects, but it remains unchanged. There is a way, my King, I know there is a way, but at this moment in time neither myself nor Merlin can apprehend it."

Arthur looked troubled but held his counsel.

"Sire," Galahad blurted suddenly, "could I ask that we cease discussing the Grail for a few moments. Bar Merlin, it has been my sole companion for these past three days and nights and while it is infinitely better company than the wizard, I feel the need to talk of other matters for a while. What has occurred beyond these four walls in the past few days? Anything of interest? News of Mordred? What of our comrades who share the seats at the Round Table? How do they fare?"

Arthur went over to a drinks table and poured them both a goblet of wine. He placed them on the floor between the two chairs and resumed his seat. "Well, there have been reports of banditry hereabouts and I have dispatched Bors and Gareth to deal with it before it becomes widespread."

"Damn your bastard nephew. There was not even a hint of such things when you sat upon the throne previously," Galahad seethed. "Have you received any news as to their success?"

"Not yet," Arthur shook his head. "But they were only sent out last evening, so there is no need for undue concern."

"What of the worm Mordred? Is there any intelligence as to his whereabouts?" The Knight of The Round Table leant forward eagerly.

The King's face hardened at the mention of his perfidious nephew. "He seems to have gone to ground. Whether or not that is for good or ill remains to be seen."

Galahad regarded his leader dubiously. "Where was he last sighted?"

A look of pain crawled slowly across the King's face and he found he could not hold Galahad's gaze. He looked down at his slippered feet. "He was last seen about to set foot on the road to Joyous Garde," King Arthur muttered.

"Joyous Garde! But surely that is…"

"Aye, Lancelot's domain."

For a long moment, both men were silent. Arthur stared unseeing into the fire, unconsciously following the play of the flames as they licked luxuriantly at the borders of the surround.

Galahad cleared his throat self-consciously. He had no wish to force his King to revisit such painful memories, so he skirted around the subject of Arthur's adulterous wife and her betrayal of him with Sir Lancelot by switching the conversation back to Mordred. "Surely your nephew does not believe he will receive succour there, does he?"

King Arthur shook his head, all the while staring intently into the crackling blaze. "No, Galahad. Lancelot has done me great harm with his actions, but on matters like this, he would not betray his King."

"Trustworthy in affairs of state but treacherous in affairs of the heart," Galahad murmured in a louder voice than intended.

Arthur's head whipped round at that.

Galahad started back from the expression on the King's face, sending himself sprawling off his chair and onto the floor with a painful sounding crack. "I'm sorry, my Lord. I meant no offence, I..." he babbled before stumbling back to his feet.

King Arthur waved away his knight's discomfort. "He stole my Guinevere's heart, that is true. But there is no doubt in my mind that she loves me first and foremost. Whether it is the love of a wife for a husband or the love of a subject for her King," he shrugged and suddenly looked every one of his forty-nine years, "who knows?"

Sir Galahad felt a huge sympathy well up inside him and, in a breach of royal protocol, placed a comforting hand upon the monarch's shoulder. "Have you had any word from your beloved since she...departed?"

Arthur knuckled his eyes vigorously, stood up and strode over to the window. "No, I have not and I am not sure that I would wish to. Though my mind screams at me for my stupidity, I still have a deep abiding love for my Guinevere, but it is a love conjured by memories. I am not a man who dwells in the past, but by all that's holy, I will cling onto my reminiscences of Guinny for the rest of my days."

Galahad felt awful that he had raked up such agonising recollections. "I am sorry, my King, I have no wish to cause you pain."

"No-one can change what has happened, Galahad. What's done is done," he said dully.

"Aye, but the wounds inflicted on you will take a lifetime to heal. That much is clear."

Arthur nodded and looked pensively across the table at his champion. "Why is it that you have never taken a wife, Galahad? There is certainly no shortage of maidens beating a path to your door."

Galahad coloured at the directness of the question. He pondered it for a minute, before shrugging, "I have chosen the chaste life. I have kept myself pure and unsullied so that all my energy can be channelled into my devotion to God and in my duties as a Knight of The Round Table. I believe that my purity is the reason I was able to perceive the Grail and bear it here to Camelot. Unfortunately, as of yet, it has not helped me resolve the enigma before us."

"I admire your single-mindedness," Arthur observed with a wry smile. He stopped, for the knight was staring open-mouthed at the golden goblet upon the table. "Galahad?" he asked.

The knight stood transfixed, staring at the Grail. "Behold!" he breathed.

Arthur followed his gaze and was immediately hypnotised by a red glow pulsing from the Grail. Without warning, a concussion rocked the room and smoke began billowing from the vessel. Arthur remembered himself enough to begin calling for help but Galahad signalled for him not to do so. "See, it has frozen, sire."

Indeed, as Arthur looked back, the smoke had solidified into a cloudy screen. Gradually it began to clear until there was a picture in the centre of the cloud. With a suddenness that took them both by surprise, the flags fluttering in the sky began to billow and the indistinct figures began walking jerkily.

The standards oscillating in the wind were immediately recognisable and both leant over the table to better comprehend the scene before them, momentarily forgetting the miraculous medium by which they viewed it.

"Tis the bastard high traitor himself," Arthur hissed.

"Gone to ground no longer then," Galahad surveyed the emblems bulging and flapping in the grainy sky. "How many men do you count?" he asked the King.

"Too many for comfort, that is for sure," he responded.

They jumped as Merlin came hurtling through the massive doors, skidding to a halt as he took in the impossible sight of the Grail working its magic. "It would seem that the lock has finally been picked." He stared at Galahad with a modicum of respect. "How did you activate it?"

The knight tried his best to look nonchalant. "I did nothing, Merlin. This display is not of my doing. It would appear that the Grail reacts as and when it sees fit."

Merlin nodded curtly. "Tell me then, was there any change in its appearance prior to this spectacle?" He gestured towards the unmoving cloud.

"It glowed red, a cloud arose and became solid, then this," Arthur supplied, looking over towards Galahad for confirmation. The knight nodded once and returned to his scrutiny of the moving pictures before him.

Merlin pulled gently at his beard and appeared to be pondering something. "Red, you say?"

Arthur placed both hands on the table. "What is it, Merlin? You suspect something?"

"Please understand that I do not wish to cause fear and panic where there need be none, but red is the colour of danger, is it not? Couple this with the appearance of Mordred and I would suggest that there is a more than likely explanation for the Grail's behaviour."

"You think the Grail seeks to warn us that he wishes to return to Camelot?" Arthur snorted incredulously.

"Where was he last seen?"

"Heading north on the road to Lancelot's estates."

"How long ago?"

"Two days."

"No word since then?"

"Merlin, the man is a pitiful coward. He would not dare to try and sneak back inside these walls," King Arthur scoffed.

Merlin nodded emphatically. "I would wholeheartedly agree with your summation of that observation, your majesty, were it not for the evidence of my own eyes. The man has the makings of an army at his back and is on the march. Would you wager your kingdom that he does not seek to return?"

Sir Galahad stepped forward. "Pained though I am to agree with Merlin, he does make a very pressing case, sire."

Arthur's gaze roamed from face to face before it returned to the silent marchers tramping from one intangible side of the cloud to the other. "If we could only establish where he skulks."

Merlin began walking round the table, pursing his lips and muttering to himself. At length he stopped and faced the King. "Sire, I may have, at my disposal, the means to locate him."

Arthur practically pushed Merlin out of the door, "If such a thing is possible, then god-speed to you, man. Go about your business and flush the devil out."

The mage bowed deeply, took one last look at the Grail then flew from the room.

King Arthur turned back to the insubstantial fog. "I will have your guts upon my blade, Mordred. You will not escape Excalibur's bite a second time."

Merlin stalked down one of the numerous tapestry-lined corridors that criss-crossed the castle. He stopped at a wall that looked very much like its fellow on the opposite side of the passageway. However, after a quick check to ensure that he was not being watched, he pressed a stone panel and a whole section of the wall slid across, admitting him to a flight of stairs that led to the very top of one of the highest towers of Camelot.

After negotiating the multitude of steps, he arrived in a room that appeared, at first sight, to be nothing more than a deserted cell. After describing a complicated pattern in the air, the room transformed into a roofless circular chamber that was rich with bizarre flora that could not be found in any other place upon the island. Once he reached the pentagram that had been scratched in the floor of the room, he wasted no time incanting the spell.

In the dead centre of the chamber he stood, rolling unfamiliar words and phrases around his tongue.

The first to arrive was a raven, its black feathers covered with an oily glisten. The raven was then followed by the majestic form of a golden eagle, its noble profile peering down upon the wizard with apparent disdain at being summoned in such a way. After a few moments, as many as twenty different species of birds were perched upon various eyries in the room, sparrows fluttered next to kestrels and robins chirruped under the beady gaze of falcons yet there was no suggestion that the normal hierarchy of the food chain would be observed. Instead there was a raucous cacophony of chattering and squawking that Merlin ceased with a snapped command.

"Be still," the magician hissed. "Attend!" He threw some herbs into a cup that was very reminiscent in appearance to the Holy Grail and a similar cloud of smoke belched forth, solidifying and showing Mordred's rat-like face. "Find him," he said simply.

In a flurry of feathers, crows, finches, raptors and numerous other species took to the skies above the castle, filled with an unexplained urge to find the temporary usurper to the throne of Camelot.

Chapter 7

The border of England and Wales

In a thickly wooded forest, many miles from Camelot, an unshaven guard stood in front of a dirty, threadbare tent and probed an aching cavity with his tongue whilst he disinterestedly scanned the immediate vicinity. He knew that the rest of the area was being swept by his comrades and really could not see the point of his duty other than to massage the hugely oversized ego of his leader. There was no possible chance that an enemy could breach the outer boundaries of their camp without creating enough of a disturbance to alert all who patrolled nearby. Shaking his head, he hawked and spat and began what seemed like his hundredth circuit of the tent's diameter.

As he was about halfway round, the flutter of wings and the raucous caw of a crow startled him with its nearness and he dropped his pike to the floor. Cursing, he scooped his weapon up from the leaf litter as well as a medium sized pebble. With an angry snarl, he cast it at the bird, causing it to take flight and land on another branch out of range of the irate soldier. From its perch, it kept its beady eye upon him as he vanished out of sight around the curve of the tent.

Unseen by the ill-tempered sentry, a robin hopped inside the tent and landed upon one of the trestles underneath the table nearest the entrance flap. Its tiny black eyes focussed on the group of men who milled around inside, some armoured, some not, poring over a map splayed across a table dotted with drinks and half-eaten food.

One of the men, a slim unprepossessing fellow dressed from head to toe in black, jabbed a thin finger at the parchment and said in an irritating squawk of a voice, "That is the plan I propose. We shall take stock here in the woods, biding our time, regaining our strength. Then, when the moment is right, I shall return to Camelot. And when I return, it will be in a manner befitting a conquering monarch welcomed back into the bosom of his subjects. My uncle robbed me of my rightful place atop the dais in Camelot's throne room. When I return, he will pay for that insult with his life. He will kneel before me and beg to die."

One of the armoured men removed his gauntlets and ran his fingers through a mop of greasy blond hair. "It is without doubt a bold and breathtaking plan, sire," he fawned.

"Thank you, Guy," Mordred accepted the compliment graciously.

A hitherto silent knight stepped forward and asked, "How long do you propose we bide here, your majesty?"

The blond-haired knight's face took on a crooked smile. "Is the climate troubling your delicate constitution, William?"

William Baldwin snorted and glared at his comrade-in-arms, "Hardly. I merely wished to point out that the longer we stay in one place, the more likely we are to be discovered."

"The guards on the perimeter will dispose of any visitors who become too inquisitive." Mordred shrugged.

"My liege, I do not refer to the serfs and peasants hereabouts. It is common knowledge that Arthur is more than happy to make use of Merlin and his magic when he sees fit."

The pretender to the throne nodded. "Your point is well made, William. However, do not be afeared. I have taken steps to ensure that we are not located by sorcerous means."

Baldwin bowed obeisance to his leader, but he did not look convinced.

"If that is all, gentlemen, I bid you retire to your bedrolls for night is upon us."

The incumbents of the tent all filed out, including the unseen feathered observer. Mordred ran a tired hand over his greedy face and placed a mug of ale on the map, carelessly spilling some of it across a distant range of mountains. Whilst he was engrossed in the placement of his troops, he became aware of a chill wind and shivered. Wrapping his sable cloak about his shoulders, he whipped round, scanning the tent warily, in response to a creeping uneasiness that was slowly stealing over him. Sensing a presence but seeing no-one, he turned back to the table and gaped in surprise at the man who sat opposite him, settled in a comfortable position as if he had been there all the time. Perhaps he had, Mordred reflected grimly, as he took in the close-cropped goatee beard, piercing sapphire-blue eyes and immaculately backswept black hair of his magician.

"Damn and blast, Montagu. Do you think yourself amusing, creeping unseen like a phantom, scaring people out of their wits?"

Montagu just continued sitting there staring at Mordred, the hint of a suppressed smile playing on his lips. He found it hard to keep the contempt from his gaze as he looked upon the shifty features of his 'leader'. The beady grey eyes, the cruel slash of the mouth, the irregular patches of facial hair that the wearer presumably thought constituted a beard. Still, Montagu inwardly shrugged, he had his uses.

Mordred bit back on more heated words and instead shifted uncomfortably under the prolonged scrutiny. To escape it, he spun round and strode as confidently as he could muster across the tent to the wine table. "Drink?" he asked the new arrival.

Montagu leant forward and peered over the map.

"You did not answer Baldwin's question," he said, in a cold, lifeless voice. Mordred took a long draught from his refilled goblet, as much to calm his nerves as anything else. "I did not see the need."

Resuming his languorous position, Montagu steepled his fingers, "You need to watch yourself, Mordred. Your sycophants may appear to hang on your every word when they are in your presence, but the whispers in the wind speak of treachery and desertion."

"Nonsense," Mordred blustered. "True, conditions are not hospitable hereabouts, but when we retake Camelot, they will know comfort beyond their wildest fantasies."

Montagu could contain his amusement no longer and a huge chortle erupted from his thin-lipped mouth. He shot out of his seat and advanced on the pretender, his contempt increasing as Mordred retreated before him. "You really think your feeble-minded plan has any hope of success?" he spat, his snarl hideous to behold. "Camelot is the best defended stronghold on this island. Do you really propose to overrun it with your ramshackle bunch of hooligans?"

From somewhere, Mordred found a rock of self-esteem in the ocean of scorn that he found himself floundering in. "I believe it can be done. As long as we remain resolute and committed. With my inside knowledge of Camelot," he nodded, more certain of himself now, "yes, I believe it can be done."

"Your inside knowledge of Camelot consists of nothing bar where the wine cellar is and which maids are prepared to offer up their favours to you for your money. Your inside knowledge is of use to neither man nor beast." The dark wizard sneered.

"Have a care, Montagu." Mordred somehow found the strength to take a faltering step or two towards the spellweaver.

Montagu seemed to grow in height and Mordred's resolve found itself eroding as quickly as it had appeared. "You do not frighten me, pretender. I could snuff out your life as easily as the flame of a candle."

Mordred stood unmoving for a moment then sighed hugely, knowing he was powerless in the thrall of the sorcerer. "Alright, Montagu, fighting will get us nowhere. What do you want of me? Why are you here?"

"I bring you news of what occurs within the four walls of Camelot."

Mordred took his seat eagerly, "Really? Go on," he nodded, his tongue flicking out unpleasantly.

Montagu also retook his chair, resting his elbows on the table and pursing his lips. "Arthur knows you have not continued north. Even now, Merlin has dispatched his spies to locate this camp. They may even be in our midst as we speak."

Mordred's eyes widened and his face twitched. He stared agitatedly into all four corners of the squalid marquee then turned back to the wizard. "You assured me that your powers were the equal of Merlin's," he snivelled. "You assured me that you would be able to deflect any magic away from the camp. Do you say now that you lied? Are you a match for his sorcery or not?"

"Everyone must sleep," Montagu shrugged. "I erected a shield above the camp that would hide us and allow me to detect any attempt at magical intrusion."

"And?"

"And several minutes ago, I felt a jolt of energy hit the shield. I endeavoured to muster my defences in time to heal the rift, but I suspect something made it through." Suddenly he jumped up and with a swirl of his cloak he was past Mordred and standing outside in the coolness of the night. "Come, Mordred," he beckoned the would-be usurper of Camelot out of the tent.

Reluctantly, Mordred skulked into the darkness, eyes frantically flickering left and right, seeking out any threat that may have been lying unseen beyond the penumbra of firelight. He whispered, "You said something rather than someone. Do you mean that Merlin's spies may not be human?"

"I could not fathom the nature of the disturbance. It entered and then was still. As if..." Montagu tailed off and his head turned upwards towards the sky.

"As if what?" Mordred breathed, grabbing the wizard's robe.

Montagu stared with disdain at Mordred's hand and he quickly removed it from the material, "Quiet, you dullard. Can you not feel it?"

Dumbly, Mordred shook his head.

"We are being watched." Montagu's head returned to its scrutiny of the sky.

"Are we in peril?" Mordred hissed hysterically through gritted teeth.

Montagu shook his head tersely. "I doubt it. Merlin's power may be great but he would be unwise to risk an outright attack. No, this has the feel of a scouting mission rather than a raiding party."

They both stood tensely, Montagu straining every ounce of his intuitiveness to detect the origin of his unease, Mordred fighting against every instinct in his body to run away and hide.

Eventually, the feeling of cowardice was replaced with one of irritation. Mordred tutted though a tell-tale tremor in his voice betrayed how fraught his nerves were. "I am in no mood for this. You exaggerate Merlin's powers too much."

With no warning, Montagu sent a bolt of white-hot energy sizzling past Mordred's ear into the canopy above. "It is the birds," the magician roared, "He uses the birds to find us." He sent more bolts of energy hurtling through the darkness, streaks of blinding incandescence that obliterated the black of the night. Some of the guards dropped their weapons and clawed at their eyes in pain, whilst others, who had greater presence of mind and had looked away when the first bolt had been unleashed, nocked arrows to their bows and fired haphazardly into the trees.

"Cease, you idiots," the black wizard bellowed. "Can you see the birds in the twilight? I can perceive them but I need my sight free of other distractions."

In the trees, a flock of hugely varied birds took flight at the sudden blaze of fury and heat that illuminated the forest for miles around. On blessed wings they flew, eager to return to Camelot and impart their tidings to Merlin.

The room of the Round Table was heaving with knights, manservants, serving girls and the King's personal retinue, these being uniformed slightly differently to the other servants to enable the more intoxicated diners at the feast to identify them.

The banquet was in honour of Arthur's fiftieth birthday and every inhabitant of the Camelot estate was invited, aside from a few luckless guards who had drawn sentry duty for the evening.

There was a multitude of fantastic dishes on offer, spit roast boar killed earlier in the day and still fresh from the hunt, numerous plump chickens roasted to perfection as well as large steaming loaves of bread baked in the gargantuan kitchens situated in the lower levels of the castle before the various cooks and workers had joined the revellers.

The air was rich with the babble of conversation. Jokes and anecdotes flowed as freely as the fine wines that had been brought up from the cellars which skulked one level down from the kitchen.

All in all, it was one of the happiest times Camelot had seen for many a year, probably in fact, the happiest since the aftermath of Queen Guinevere's elopement with Lancelot Du Lac.

Arthur slapped Gawain on the back, sending the young knight's chicken leg racing across the table into someone else's goblet. The two men looked at each other then fell about in hilarity.

Arthur's eyes moved to each diner's face in turn, noting the joy and happiness on one and all. At length, his eyes fell upon what he felt was the catalyst for the sudden lightening of all their spirits. Even though he knew Mordred marched somewhere in the lands with an army at his back, at this particular time and place, he would not have cared if his pathetic nephew had arrived at the other end of the drawbridge demanding entry to the festivities.

He was certain that these feelings were down to the presence of the Grail. He got up a little unsteadily, eyes never leaving the Cup of Christ. In his route around the table, he passed Sir Galahad who was politely but firmly declining the favours of a particularly persistent chambermaid and Sir Bedivere who was impolitely and firmly accepting the favours of another.

He stopped when he got within reach of the Grail. He had yearned to reach out and touch it from the second he had seen it in Galahad's gauntleted hand, but had hitherto resisted the urge. Now though, with the giddy mixture of a companionable atmosphere and a large quantity of alcohol melting away his inhibitions, he decided that the moment had come for him to lift it to the sky and toast the wonderful people of Camelot.

His fingers were about to close around the delicate stem when Merlin came hurtling through the double doors that had been propped open to allow easy access to the partygoers. He wasted no time in grabbing the King's arm and propelling him into the torch-lit corridor.

Even in his alcohol-fugged state, Arthur sensed the urgency in his court magician. "What news?" he asked immediately.

"The little worm lurks in the woods, scant miles from the border of Wales. As I first suspected, he plans insurrection. He thinks that you have robbed him of his rightful place upon Camelot's throne," Merlin confirmed.

Galahad, who had joined them uninvited in the passage, asked, "Do you know of his exact location?"

Merlin waved his hand vaguely. "Not accurately, no. My means of locating him is not a precise art, but I can pinpoint it closely enough that he may be found with ease."

"Then the time for waiting is over." Arthur looked from one to the other then spun on his heel and in five long strides made it to the edge of the Round Table. Placing his foot on the arm of an unoccupied chair, he propelled himself onto the most famous piece of furniture in the land. He held out his hands at right angles from his body, inhaled deeply, then bellowed, "I will have silence!"

The raucousness ceased almost instantly and all eyes flew to Arthur, who stood, still with arms outspread, peering down upon his audience like Moses on the slopes of Mount Sinai.

"Scant moments ago, I have received tidings of my treacherous nephew. He has been sighted in the West near the border of Wales, skulking in woodland, with an army of cut-throats and pirates at his back and the throne of Camelot in his sights." A few eyes left Arthur momentarily to look at the ornate seat that the King usually occupied at the Table, but when he resumed speaking, he held every one of them in the palm of his hand once more. "I say that we will not wait for Mordred to attack us. Let us strike the first blow. Let us find him and put the miserable whoreson to the sword. People of Camelot, I will not rest until Mordred lies before me impaled like a stuck pig upon the blade of Excalibur, on this you have my word." At the mention of his celebrated weapon, he withdrew it from its scabbard and flourished it above his head, silently exulting as the Grail's internal illumination caught the blade to perfection and described a rainbow across the ceiling, high above the feasters. "To victory!" he yelled.

The response from the assembled throng to Arthur's entreaty sounded like nothing more than a thunderstorm rumbling through the sky ready to rain down death and destruction upon Mordred and his cohorts.

The King held up his hands for silence. "It pains me to cease the festivities, but we must make ready. Begone from here and prepare for the journey ahead. We ride at dawn."

With that he descended from the table and patted each Round Table knight upon the back as they left the room. The last in line was Sir Galahad. Arthur grasped him by the shoulder and indicated with a jerk of his head that they should go back into the chamber. "I would talk with you, Sir Galahad," the King said and instantly a sense of disquiet stole over the champion of Camelot at the formality of the statement.

They both seated themselves in the suddenly empty room, Galahad watching the King warily for the monarch seemed to be wrestling with a great struggle within himself. Suddenly, the King looked up and said, "I find myself in a dilemma, good Sir Knight. I fear the Grail cannot be left unguarded whilst the knights of Camelot are absent. As you can appreciate, though you without doubt possess bravery, swordsmanship and valour in equal measure to any of the knights who break bread at this table, you are also the only one of us who has any sort of rapport with the Grail. It weighs heavily on my heart to make this pronouncement but I am afraid I must ask you to stay behind and protect it from peril." The King's eyes took on both a distressed and quizzical look as he waited for a response.

Sir Galahad had suspected that this was what the King was going to ask and responded immediately with an unprepossessing whine in his voice. "Could it not be of use to us in the coming conflict, my liege? To heal the wounded and ease the pain of the dying. I will stow it in my possessions so that it will not come to harm."

"And if your horse bolts? What if you are injured, laid low by a lucky strike of sword or flight of arrow? Do you propose to carry it into battle with you?" Arthur shot back.

Galahad wrung his hands. "But, my liege…"

"Please, Sir Galahad. I do not wish to command you to remain, but if the occasion demands it, I will. The only other possible candidate to stand guard over it is Merlin. Would you have me turn the Grail's stewardship over to him?"

"No, my liege," the knight of the Round Table sighed and hung his head.

Arthur lifted Galahad's face up by his chin. "Come now, do not be downhearted. This is not a punishment, it is an honour."

"As my King commands," Galahad arose from his seat and bowed stiffly.

Arthur said no more, but he acknowledged the bow then left the room to prepare for departure in the morning.

Galahad turned back to the Grail and stared at it intently. "I had thought that you would be a treasure beyond worth. Instead you are a burden beyond endurance. Why will you not divulge your secrets to me? I am your saviour, yet I am also your servant. Help me to understand you, give me a sign," he whispered beseechingly, dropping to his knees and hanging his head dolefully. "Please just give me a sign."

From behind one of the tapestries liberally dotted around the walls, Merlin emerged silently and with an unreadable expression upon his face exited the room without Galahad ever knowing he had been there.

A blustery autumn wind swept across the stone frontage of Camelot as the assembled knights and their retinues sat, under the dullness of a dark grey sky, stretching from horizon to horizon with gloomy rain-laden clouds.

Proud and erect were the knights of Camelot upon their mounts, each one watching their King riding back and forth upon his magnificent white stallion, Gryphon. The steed's muscles wriggled gracefully under its smooth ivory skin as it trotted haughtily from left to right, requiring no more than a flick of the reins to obey Arthur's commands.

When his army stood ready and poised, Arthur ceased his to-ing and fro-ing and stood high in his stirrups, so that his voice carried as far as possible. He had found himself instantly sobered by Merlin's intelligence of Mordred and consequently felt no ill-effects from the banquet of the previous night. He had a mission before him and nothing was going to deflect him from it. His deep booming voice rang out over the throng before him.

"Today we march forth to rid these lands of a cankerous sore that has visited much misery and turmoil upon this castle. My nephew Mordred attempted to sow the seeds of rebellion in your hearts whilst I was away fighting our enemies. He sought to steal my home and my throne, yet he could not. And the reason he could not stands before me now. It was your loyalty that prevented Mordred achieving his goal. It was your bravery and your courage that thwarted his ultimate aim. You stood firm and you held your ground. You fought hard and you fought long and you won. You won for your King, your country and above all, you won for yourselves. You have every reason to feel pride and satisfaction at your accomplishment. However, whilst that task was performed with such valiant gallantry, at that moment in time it could not have been followed through to its natural conclusion. Now though, that moment has come. We must now finish what was so bravely started. Here, on your home ground, you did not yield and you forced the army of perfidy into retreat. Now we must march into the lions den and slay the wounded beast. You did not have the wherewithal before to attempt a raid on Mordred's forces." He swept his arm across the panorama of standards flickering in the stiff breeze. "Now you do."

He resumed his trotting across the front of the massed ranks as a great cheer arose from the gathering before him. He held his gauntleted hand up to quell the seemingly never-ending tumult just as the sun chose to miraculously appear from behind the clouds. It reflected off the ringed mail surface of Arthur's metal glove dramatically and to the onlookers took on the appearance of a beacon emerging from the dark of the deepest winter's night.

"As your King, I solemnly make this promise to you, my faithful and courageous kinsmen. You will not see me sit upon the throne of Camelot again until my bastard nephew lies unmoving in the cold embrace of death. I thank you all for defending your King's honour. Now, as your King, I am honoured to defend you."

He thrust Excalibur towards the rapidly dispersing clouds scudding overhead. "Onward!" he roared, "Onward to victory!"

He spurred his steed into motion, Gryphon's legs bunching underneath him before he launched forward at a thunderous gallop.

The knights who had been sat motionless atop their own magnificent beasts, hanging on their King's every word, let out a great cry as one and followed him to meet the usurper.

After the initial burst engineered by Arthur's inspirational oration, the march settled down to a more stately pace as the various entourages fell into step with their masters and the food wagons regained lost ground.

While Arthur would not hear a word against Camelot which, after all, was his spiritual home, this was the aspect of ruling his kingdom that fired his heart the most. Not sitting upon a throne between four walls issuing proclamations and declarations that once spoken created consequences unseen. This was where the blood pumped harder, the chest swelled prouder and the heart and spirit rose higher. He was aware of the proverb that pride came before a fall but, as he surveyed his noble forces marching through the glorious Wessex countryside in perfectly synchronised step like a well-oiled machine, he could not help but feel as if he was bursting with honour to be leading such a revered band of men. He was also honest enough with himself to acknowledge that there was an element of intoxication intrinsic with the knowledge that he had so much power at his beck and call, but he had always found himself able to resist the temptation of employing it for his own ends and had only ever deployed it for the good of his people. As he was now. He was all too aware of the misery and gloom that would settle on the population if they were to become the subjects of the selfish and unjust king that Mordred would no doubt prove himself to be, so he did indeed feel that this was not just a revenge mission against his deceitful kinsman, but it was also his duty as king to his subjects.

He was interrupted in his thoughts by Sir Bors riding up to him, a grim look smeared across his ruddy jowls. The muscular knight fiddled with the upturned ends of his moustache, a trait of his that always became more pronounced when he was in the presence of the King. Whilst Bors gave the appearance of an outwardly confident man, King Arthur found himself idly wondering if the twiddling of his facial hair was a product of nervousness or merely an unconscious habit.

The King's party had happened upon Sir Bors and Sir Gareth, out bandit-hunting in the picturesque countryside as they had been sent to do. They were just about to confront a gang of robbers with more bravado than sense. The two Round Table knights were handling themselves easily against the brigands, their swords deflecting the wild blows against them with the minimum of effort, when Arthur's army had crested the hill.

Suddenly Bors and Gareth had taken a few steps back and fallen upon one knee. The bandits had advanced eagerly, ignoring the strange behaviour and raising their swords ready for the killing strike.

"Ho there." Arthur had hailed them as the front line of knights rammed their lances down upon the dusty road, causing a sound not unlike an army taking a step forward.

The robbers had stopped, frozen in their tracks, frightened to turn round for fear of what they would see. Sir Bors had returned to his feet, unsuccessfully preventing a massive grin from creasing his face.

"It is not your lucky day is it, my friends?" he had laughed heartily.

The thieves had long since been taken back, bound and shaking, to face the justice of Camelot, whilst the army continued upon its mission.

The humour on Sir Bors' face at that moment was now replaced by a look of such grim sobriety that Arthur pulled up his mount and waited for his fellow warrior to fall in step beside him. The florid knight gestured towards the northern horizon. "My liege, another army approaches."

Arthur's head whipped round and he squinted against the sun which had fully melted through the cloud cover and bathed the rolling fields in a golden haze. "Sir Bors, do you…" he turned back to see the knight studiously avoiding his gaze. "Bors?" he asked suspiciously.

"I imagine that the good Sir Knight is agonising over how to tell you under whose banner they march."

Arthur blinked in surprise, for Merlin had appeared to the left, walking nonchalantly out from a stand of trees as if he had been waiting for them all the time. He sat atop Gryphon open-mouthed as Merlin continued calmly, "The army rides under the banner of Lancelot Du Lac."

The King tried to speak, but the words seemed to stick in his throat. He frowned and, with teeth audibly grinding together, turned to face the advancing soldiery once again.

Within seconds of the identity of the approaching force being established, preparations had begun to make camp. So it was that Arthur sat, perched on a hastily constructed dais of wood collected from the stand of trees from whence Merlin had appeared, haphazardly yet sturdily lashed together, looking down upon the entrance to his command tent as the former knight of the Round Table was ushered into his presence.

The man who had stolen away the love of Arthur's life fell upon one knee immediately and bowed his head, "My liege," he said simply.

The King sat in silence, studying the features of the man who had inflicted such emotional damage upon him. The face haunted his dreams, forever colouring his memories of the queen. The monarch studied every aspect of the fellow before him, flickering from the mass of blond curls atop his head that Guinevere would have run her fingers through, down to the unblinking blue eyes that had stared upon his wife's naked body, past the angular noble nose to the full-lipped mouth that had whispered words into his beloved's ears and kissed her into submission. He felt his eyes moistening and bit his bottom lip in an attempt to stem the flow of tears that he felt he could not hold back. Somehow though, he managed to bring his emotions under control. "Give me one good reason why I should not strike you dead where you kneel," he spat.

Lancelot got stiffly to his feet and stared at the King, meeting the icy gaze unswervingly. "Sire, I know that I have done you a great disservice by my conduct, but I beg you to try and understand my predicament. I was torn between my King and my heart. I went through agonies searching for the right path to take, as did Guinevere. Our intention was never to cause you pain, King Arthur."

The monarch bit back a response, unsure that his voice would hold steady because of the wave of emotion that the mention of Guinevere's name had triggered.

Sir Lancelot took the King's silence to mean that he could continue. "Make no mistake though, my liege," Lancelot spoke respectfully yet challengingly, "what Guinevere and I feel for each other is love. There is no other way to describe it. You could run me through with Excalibur, you could drag me over hot coals for mile upon mile, but it would not change the way we feel about each other. We are in love, nothing more, nothing less."

The King's fingers curled around the haft of his weapon and all who saw it tensed, unsure what would occur if the King were to unsheath his blade. They knew Arthur to be a man of impeccably high morals and virtue but they also knew how much he had doted on his wife and how black his mood had been when she had deserted his side. The King bit upon his bottom lip once more, outwardly calm but inwardly roiling like a storm-wracked ocean. He so wanted to do what Lancelot had suggested and skewer his cuckolder like a pig, but he was resigned to the fact that it would achieve nothing. Eventually, he managed to say, "Is she here?"

Lancelot shook his head, "No, my liege. We both felt that her presence here would cause you too much pain. She is safely ensconced at Joyous Garde."

Arthur leant forward and sneered, "Could you not have afforded me that same favour by ensuring that you did not come into my presence either?"

Lancelot's face hardened but he merely said, "I am only doing my duty in aiding my King in his quest to apprehend his villainous nephew."

Arthur's eyes narrowed. "What do you mean? What do you know of Mordred's whereabouts?"

Lancelot's eyes flickered between the King and his magician. "I received news that he planned to journey north into Lothian to escape your attentions. My army headed him off and turned him around. He now skulks in Wales awaiting his fate, though for some reason his exact location still remains a mystery to my scouts."

Arthur, who had noted the brief glance that Lancelot had shot towards Merlin, raised an eyebrow and murmured coldly, "You say you received news?"

Lancelot shrugged, "Aye, from Merlin."

Arthur's icy glare transferred itself from the knight to the wizard.

Merlin seemed unaffected by the King's hostility, blithely saying, "Affairs of state take precedence over your enmity, Arthur. If Mordred had managed to escape to Lothian, he would even now be sweeping south with an army of Picts at his back before you could blink. He had to be prevented from passing Hadrian's Wall and Lancelot was best placed to do it. I acted as I saw fit for the good of the country and the good of your monarchy."

Arthur was forced to concede the logic. "I applaud your initiative, if not your presumption. Do we have any other surprises in store when we resume our journey?"

The magician's face quirked into something approaching a smile, "No, my liege. Lancelot's appearance here was a necessity. I apologise for my rashness, but my motive was beyond reproach."

"Indeed," Arthur nodded dismissively. "Well, it seems that Lancelot has done as he was bid. Now that Mordred has been driven into Wales, he has nowhere to go. He is trapped. Therefore, it would be ungracious of me to separate Lancelot from his love for any longer than necessary." He turned back towards his former second-in-command. "Lancelot, your King thanks you for your service. Return to Joyous Garde and dwell in the loving embrace that awaits you."

"But, sire, I..." Lancelot protested.

"You have something to say?"

Lancelot stared down at his greaves. "Well, I was hoping to conclude the task that I undertook and join forces with you in your pursuit of Mordred."

"But surely you have your sweetheart to return to. I could not, in all good conscience, keep you apart." Arthur smiled nastily.

"Sire, I beg you..."

"Return to Joyous Garde, Lancelot. Never forget that I will forever see you as a liar and a betrayer. Your actions are beyond forgiveness." He leaned forward and hissed with an unsettling spite. "You stabbed me in the back in the most heinous of ways. If someone had hurt you in such a way, would you invite them to stand beside you again?"

Lancelot's mouth gaped, but no words were spoken.

Arthur drew a tired hand across his face and half-closed his eyes as if on the brink of exhaustion. "Begone, Lancelot. Begone."

The former knight turned on his heel and marched as quickly as formality permitted from the King's presence. Arthur stared around the tent grimly, as if challenging anyone to say something. He waved his hand dismissively. "All of you, go. Go on, get out."

As the various onlookers left, Arthur dismounted the throne and poured himself a drink. Staring at it for a time, he lifted it halfway to his lips before shaking his head and hurling it to the floor.

In another encampment, not too many miles away, the mood was even darker.

The three occupants of the grimy command tent stood poring over the maps once more along with a multitude of scrolls that were untidily strewn across a large table.

"How many?" Mordred hissed, fussily sipping at his goblet of wine, whilst his beady eyes regarded his subordinate with a healthless mixture of impatience and contempt.

William Baldwin sighed heavily and ran a filthy hand through his thinning brown hair. "We lost upwards of fifty men in the last skirmish."

"More like thirty, actually," a deep resonant voice cut across the conversation closely followed by its owner.

The knight turned to the new speaker. "Do the numbers really matter, magician? Be it thirty or fifty, if we keep losing men at this rate, we will all be dead within the month anyway." He looked amused as he stared at the other two men present. "I am surprised you presume to be so accurate about the number of casualties anyway."

Montagu's azure eyes deadened as he asked, "Your meaning?"

Baldwin blanched at the wizard's glare and swallowed loudly. He refused to be cowed however and continued to speak. "My meaning is that your only behaviour of note today was the conspicuousness of your absence from the battlefield."

Montagu advanced slowly. "I am the only practitioner of magic in this whole ramshackle army. Would you take the chance of me being taken by a stray arrow or lucky sword thrust?"

"If you are as mighty a magician as you say, surely you would be able to protect yourself." Mordred's lieutenant snorted then looked for support from Mordred and the other knight who stood impassively watching the exchange. When he saw none, he sniffed and returned his stare to the spell-weaver. "I do say if..." he left the statement hanging.

Montagu chuckled though there was little humour in the sound, "If, you say? Well, never let it be said that I will step away from a challenge. Close your eyes, William, and let us see how mighty I really am, shall we?"

Baldwin licked his lips nervously, wondering if he had overstepped the mark, and his eyes swivelled in their sockets like trapped rodents. He looked again at Mordred and his fellow knight, Guy Dubois, but there was no help forthcoming.

"Come, William," Montagu hissed, "it does not do to keep a magician waiting, even if he is only of humble talent."

With a last beseeching glance at his leader, Baldwin cleared his throat and closed his eyes.

Montagu stretched out his palm and slowly closed it into a fist. Both Mordred and Guy gasped in shock at the magician, for when he opened his hand, two floating orbs of light could clearly be seen floating above his palm. "Open your eyes, William Baldwin. Open your eyes and tell me what you see."

Baldwin's face contorted into a mask of fear as he did as he was bid and he spluttered incoherently. Guy and his leader both shifted uneasily as they found themselves looking at eyes that did not look back. Instead, they merely consisted of two eyeballs, both milky white and completely devoid of colour.

William overcame his initial shock and found his voice again, shrieking in a yell so loud that it brought ten of Mordred's soldiers running into the command tent. "You bastard!" he screamed, "You bastard!"

Lashing out hopelessly, Baldwin staggered around the tent, knocking into the table and sending the maps and parchments flying into an untidy pile on the floor, futilely searching for his tormentor's throat. "Where are you? Where are you?" he howled.

"Desist," Montagu flipped a lazy hand towards the incandescent soldier and the man who had so recently been robbed of sight now found himself robbed of movement. "Let me free, you bastard. Let me free," he sobbed pitifully.

"Do you wish to see again, Baldwin?" Montagu chuckled impishly.

The fearful knight continued to struggle against the mystical bonds which held him and did not respond to the question.

"Do you wish to see again?" Montagu bellowed, stopping the blinded man's efforts in an instant.

With a shuddering sigh, William wept shamelessly, "Yes, of course."

"Are you sure?" the black hearted magician asked again with a wink at Mordred.

William could only nod, as when he tried to speak, all that came out was a series of painful sobs.

"Damn it, Montagu, give him back his sight," Mordred fidgeted uncomfortably as he gave the order.

Rolling his eyes exaggeratedly, Montagu said calmly, "Close your eyes again then, William."

Still sobbing like an infant ripped from the teat, Baldwin did as he was told.

Montagu closed his palm once more, but this time when he opened it, the lights were gone. "Open your eyes and tell me what you see now."

Baldwin gingerly lifted his eyelids and breathed a massive groan of relief. However, when he had recovered his composure, he sought out his persecutor with murder in his newly-restored eyes.

The black magician raised his eyebrow challengingly.

Looking round at the others assembled and still unable to find any support, Baldwin stormed out of the tent.

Mordred, who had watched Montagu's display with mounting horror, cleared his throat pointedly and returned to his perusal of the map. "We have to make a stand. We cannot retreat much longer else we will end up in the sea."

Guy Dubois looked sidelong at his leader. A slight man who was cursed with a harelip and broken nose which was the legacy of many taproom brawls, he was a man who during peacetime would probably have picked a fight with his own shadow, yet he was also possessed of a strength of purpose in battle that had brought him to Mordred's notice on innumerable occasions throughout the campaign. Arthur's nephew was enough of a realist to know that a good deal of his force was made up of untrustworthy ne'er-do-wells who would probably turn tail and flee if King Arthur actually appeared on the horizon, but lieutenants like Guy were the spine of his army, a rod of constancy running through the centre of it, making sense of the chaos, keeping it vital and manipulating its every move. "But where, sire?" Dubois asked in a voice that was surprisingly gruff and no-nonsense for a man of his build.

With a sigh, Mordred gestured at the map. "There is nowhere obvious."

Behind their backs, Montagu's fingers flickered momentarily and he swept out an arm as if throwing something.

Suddenly, Mordred stiffened.

Guy was at his side in an instant, "My liege?"

The would-be King shook himself as if emerging from a trance. "Here is where we stand." He pointed to a nondescript area of the map.

Guy glanced quizzically at Montagu for a moment but the magician ignored him and so he turned back to Mordred and followed the trajectory of the digit. "Why there, sire?"

Mordred stared coldly at his deputy, "Because that is my order. Do you require another reason?"

Guy saluted crisply. "No, sire." Magic and mysticism he did not understand but he knew the importance of obeying orders.

"Then let us retire and enjoy a good night's rest, for tomorrow we ride to Camlann."

A gathering had been summoned to King Arthur's command tent by Merlin the magician.

The ten knights of the Round Table stood in a rough circle around the wizard as he chanted and murmured in an unsettling tongue. Chilling voices seemed to chitter and whisper on the cusp of hearing and the air within the canvas enclosure became dark and still.

In the midst of this uneasy atmosphere, Merlin stood, arms outstretched and eyes screwed tightly shut, bending his will to the task at hand.

Suddenly, as the thaumaturge opened his eyes, the oppressive air seemed to lighten and the guttering torches blazed anew. "They will make a stand at a place called Camlann," he said.

Immediately Arthur and the others flew to the map, which was spread out upon a hastily pushed together pair of tables.

A bout of whispering broke out as Camlann was sought and located.

"Camlann?" Sir Gareth exclaimed. "Why there? It is not easily defensible. It appears to give him no particular strategic advantage."

"Nonetheless, Sir Gareth, that is the place that the magician has placed in his head."

Arthur looked sharply at his court magicker, "His magician?"

Merlin looked grave and lowered his eyes for a moment. "Aye, King Arthur, a monster birthed by Satan himself by the name of Montagu."

Arthur looked surprised at the ferocity of Merlin's snarl as he spat the name. "This Montagu is familiar to you?" the King asked.

"I have only heard the name recently." The wizard took himself over to one of the many makeshift seats arrayed around the tent and slumped down upon it dejectedly. "I first began hearing reports from the North of long-forbidden rituals being resurrected. These rites were so barbaric, so blood-soaked and evil that they were outlawed many decades ago and any caught practising them were instantly condemned to death. Whole villages were being robbed of their women and children in the name of these ceremonies. Evil such as that cannot remain secret for long. A man from one such village staggered into the castle one night," he waved a hand as Arthur began to speak, "it was mere days before you returned to Camelot with Galahad and the Grail. In actual fact, it was why you saw so little of me for days after you re-entered your castle. But anyway, as he lay dying..."

Arthur's eyes widened at this. "How casually you talk of those no longer with us."

"As he lay dying," Merlin continued, ignoring the king's implied reproach, "he told me of crucifixions, bloodletting and other similar atrocities. His wife and children had been amongst the victims of a raid upon his village." The magician finished his statement so quietly that Arthur struggled to hear him. He then let out a huge sigh and stared into the flame of the nearest torch, remembering the night as if it had happened scant moments ago.

"And this Montagu was the culprit?" Arthur hissed through gritted teeth. The sight of Merlin looking so shaken was disturbing in the extreme.

"It would appear so, sire."

Arthur thought for a moment then turned to the assembly, all of whom were standing dumbstruck with horror at Merlin's story. "Then, gentlemen, it would appear that our mission is now two-fold. That Mordred attempted to ascend my throne by traitorous means is bad enough, but to throw in his lot with this abomination beggars belief. We shall not rest until both lie dead at our feet."

His speech was treated to a ragged cheer. However the exultation was quickly quashed by Merlin's ominous tones. "I warn you, Arthur. Killing Montagu will not be easy."

"Your meaning?" the King inquired, choosing to ignore the informality.

"The ancient ceremonies that Montagu has revived."

"What of them?"

"If they are as reported, then it means that he has sold his soul to the Dark Lord," Merlin said in a flat voice.

"He serves the Devil himself?" Arthur physically recoiled.

Merlin simply nodded confirmation.

The King's face took on a steely resolve. "Then we must redouble our efforts to rid the land of this demon magician."

Sir Gareth tentatively stepped forward. "My liege, if I may speak. As I said before, Camlann is not easily defensible, nor is it strategic. Could it possibly be that there is something there that may be of use to this Montagu? Something to aid Mordred in his fight against us?"

Arthur nodded pensively, "Merlin, your thoughts?"

"Nothing springs to mind that could be of any use to him. Not against so many of us." The wizard shrugged.

The monarch of Wessex began pacing up and down the tent. "I am beginning to wish I had acceded to Galahad's request and let him accompany us with the Grail. If there is some sort of devilish weapon that Montagu can lay his hands on, the Grail will be invaluable."

Merlin's eyes widened. "The Grail!" he exclaimed. All eyes turned to the wizard as his face went ashen. "Surely he does not...he cannot..." the sorcerer gaped.

Arthur shared confused looks with the group as each pondered the reason for Merlin's consternation.

Though he was sure it was a trick of the light, the tent suddenly seemed darker and the shadows twisted into eldritch threatening shapes as Merlin began to speak. "There is one such item of evil. Evil enough that it might challenge the Grail," he whispered.

"Go on," Arthur cajoled.

"But it is a myth. A legend mentioned in nothing but the most obscure of occult texts."

"What is its nature, Merlin?" Sir Gareth pressed.

"It is a sealed goblet similar in design to the Holy Grail. It is said to contain all the evils of the world. If supped from, it will bring absolute dominion to the drinker and all who dwell upon the earth will perish," Merlin answered.

"What is its name?" Sir Gareth asked haltingly.

"The Judas Cup. Its infamy is twin with that which surrounds the tale of Pandora's Box. When Pandora opened the box, so it is said, she instantly realised that she had done wrong and closed it quickly, thus keeping hope from escaping. If Montagu is actively seeking the cup, he can only be doing it for one reason and one reason only."

"Surely he does not mean to drink from it?" Arthur gasped.

Merlin shrugged helplessly.

"Surely you said that all upon the face of the earth would die." Gareth's voice squeaked.

Merlin's face suddenly seemed draped in shadow as he intoned, "Not if they are in league with the devil and his minions." He got up so quickly that the knights nearest to him jumped in fright. In three bounds he ascended the platform on which Arthur's chair stood. "Gentlemen, hearken to me. If our surmisings are correct, then we cannot fail. We must not fail. If Montagu finds the cup and drinks from it, we are done for. He will not falter at the last and shut the box as Pandora did. He will let hope escape." He paused and looked from face to face. "And without hope, there is nothing."

Arthur joined him and gazed upon his subjects from on high. "Then let us make sure that he does not find it. Send word back to Camelot. I want Sir Galahad to join us as soon as humanly possible."

Sir Bors bowed and murmured "My liege"as he ran from the tent.

As Arthur watched him go, he muttered under his breath, "Let us pray we are not too late."

*

The traitors army marched raggedly along, under a granite-grey sky, made heavy with clouds promising a deluge of rain.

Mordred rode at its head, trying desperately to look noble, puffing out his thin chest and straightening his back. His magician rode alongside him, shaking his head and smirking at his leader's vanity.

The usurper's eyes caught the mocking sneer and he clenched his teeth, wanting to say something to bring Montagu up short, to prick his ego and deflate it, but at the last, his resolve fled and he pretended not to see it.

"Halt," he held up his hand, "we camp here tonight."

As the knights made ready at the base of the wooded hill, Mordred took his spell-weaver to one side and asked, "Can you detect whether our enemies are near?"

Montagu peered around the trees, then shut his eyes and sent forth his consciousness into the ether. After a minute or so, he shook his head and opened them once more. "I detect nothing."

With a sigh of relief, Mordred began stalking around the small clearing, circling the magician, who followed his walk disinterestedly. "I cannot believe that it has come to this. Scant months ago, I was sitting atop the

105

throne of Camelot, king of all I surveyed. Now, look at me, dank and dirty and pursued across the country like a common renegade. Why did Arthur have to return when he did?" he sneered, punching a mailed fist into his palm.

Montagu waved a finger at him. "You are not just a common renegade though, are you? You have been named traitor. Traitor to the crown. Arthur will not rest until Excalibur has removed your head from its shoulders. It will not be long before the clammy hands of death circle your throat and squeeze the very life out of you."

The pretender to the throne took a step back at the vehemence of Montagu's voice. "No," he shook his head, "no, we will stand and we will win. Damn and blast, Montagu, whose side are you on?"

The magician's eyes bored into him, twin windows gazing into hell itself. "Arthur will come to Camlann and crush you," he sneered.

"If you are so sure of our imminent defeat, then why do you still remain? Why have you not used your talents to spirit yourself away?" Mordred shot back as his backbone momentarily hardened.

Montagu held Mordred's gaze for some time, then he began circling the clearing too, in near perfect mirror image to Mordred, "Because I am not sure. I am certain your army will be defeated but, if luck is on our side, then we will emerge triumphant."

King Arthur's nephew's eyes rolled. "Now you talk in riddles. How can an army be defeated yet still emerge victorious?"

"If my plan comes to fruition, then while we may lose the battle, we may yet win the war."

Mordred's face took on an even more confused look. "I feel war is a rather grand title for this conflict. It is my army against Arthur's and Lancelot's, not nation pitted against nation."

The magician placed his arm around Mordred's shoulder, "Oh Mordred. Poor simple Mordred. This has never been about you and Arthur. You play at kings but, in reality, you are mere pawns to be sacrificed when the need arises."

Mordred pulled himself away from Montagu's embrace with a distasteful look. "What do you mean?"

"Do you really wish to know whom you fight side by side with?" Montagu turned his back on him and stood perfectly still.

When he remained statuesque, Mordred stepped towards him. "Montagu?" he whispered.

The usurper gasped as Montagu turned to face him. The wizard's face had turned scarlet red, his teeth had become pointed fangs and from them dripped acid saliva. The worst aspect of him though was his eyes. Where they had been a pitiless sapphire-blue before, they were now black as pitch with not a hint of white to be seen. They glistened like black pearls and were surfaced like mirrors, showing Mordred the pitiful gibbering wreck that Montagu's transformation had reduced him to. When he spoke, his voice was the clanging of doors in a mausoleum, the echo of falling rubble in the deepest pit in the darkest recesses of the earth. "With you as the King I would have had no trouble fulfilling my plans. I could have turned the country upside down and no-one would have dared raise a finger against me. But now with Arthur back, I have to tread with great care. Waiting, waiting, always waiting. I have waited for eternity, but now my prize is so near, I feel I can almost reach out and touch it."

Mordred had tripped over an errant root that sprung out from the bottom of a gnarled oak and was sprawled upon the dank forest floor. "P-prize?"

His eyes grew wider as he saw that Montagu's hands had changed into claws and he shrank back as the demon magician jabbed a talon at him, "Yes, Mordred. My prize. The Judas Cup. Once I have it in my grasp, I will be master of everything and everyone. I will have dominion."

Mordred had regained his feet and sidled over to Montagu, every fibre of his body screaming at him that he should flee and try to put as much space between himself and this travesty. However, the most overriding aspect of his character, his greed, won through and he steeled himself to stay. "What manner of cup is it that has so much power?"

"It is the ultimate weapon. It is mercy to no-one. It is death to all," the sorcerer intoned.

Mordred cowered as Montagu advanced upon him. With an upward jerk of his hand, he gestured and Mordred felt his feet lifted off the ground. In horror he looked down to see that he was hovering three feet in the air with no more control over his body than a puppet dangling on its strings.

"Behold," Montagu breathed and extended his hand. The traitor's eyes widened as it bore relentlessly on, first fingertips, then knuckle joints, then the whole hand disappeared inside Mordred's jerkin yet he felt nothing. Suddenly, the weaver of magic withdrew his clenched fist and Mordred found himself reaching for a breath that would not come. His saucer-wide eyes sought out the sorcerers'. "What have you done to me?" he shrieked.

Montagu unclenched his scarlet-drenched fist to reveal a heart, wobbling yet vital. "Your task is to hold back Arthur's army whilst I search for the cup. It lies here somewhere on the field of Camlann or so I have been told. If you hold off Arthur long enough, you may have this back. If not, well..."

Mordred's waxen visage contorted in fear as he strove for the non-existent breath again out of force of habit. With one last scowl at the magician, he scuttled back to his army.

Montagu returned to his human form with a sickening series of wrenching sinews and snapping muscle. He stared long and hard across the swaying meadow, wondering what the future would hold for him as he sought his trophy upon the field of Camlann.

Arthur's army had made good progress en route to their destination. The pressing nature of the mission had demanded that the horses be rode harder than normal and it was only at Merlin's insistence that they saved their steeds so they would be fit for battle, otherwise the army would be facing Mordred's forces on foot, leaving them at a considerable disadvantage.

So it was, around noon on the third day since they had left the security of Camelot, they crested a hill and the field of Camlann lay before them.

"Behold, sire. This is the place we seek," Merlin gestured dramatically.

Arthur stared across the expanse of shimmering grass, undulating gracefully to and fro in the light breeze that wafted in from the west. He reserved special attention to a stand of trees skirting the far corner of the field. Staring intensely, his instinct for battle told him it was peopled with Mordred's soldiers, weapons at the ready, poised to descend upon his knights with a battery of crossbow bolts and arrows. "Do you espy anyone?" he whispered tersely to his magician, who was stood unmoving at his side.

"A moment," Merlin closed his eyes and passed his hands over one another, describing complicated patterns in the air. Suddenly his right hand snaked out and grasped a crossbow bolt that was heading straight for Arthur's forehead. "Over there," Merlin pointed, "the trees and long grass. They are swarming with Montagu's men."

"Surely you mean Mordred's men," Sir Gawain, a fresh-faced young knight with blond shoulder-length hair pointed out.

Merlin smiled with his mouth, although his eyes remained distant. "Montagu is a leader, not a follower. You can be sure that Mordred is under the thrall of Montagu, not the other way about."

Arthur conceded the point. "If this abomination does indeed possess the powers you say, it does seem unlikely that he would submit to the wishes of that odious little worm." He paused and stared back over the battlefield, squinting to see the far side now as they had moved out of range of their opponent's weapons. "Are you sure there is no enchantment at work here? This seems overly easy. He has barely bothered to conceal his men and he knows we march with superior numbers. Are we walking into a trap?"

"There is nothing of a magical nature at work here, Arthur." Merlin shrugged then chewed his bottom lip vigorously. "What is slightly worrying however is that I detect no sign of Montagu either. It makes no sense. If he does seek the Judas Cup and believes it to be here, why has he apparently quit the field of conflict?"

Gawain stepped forward once more. Although he was a mere stripling compared to Merlin or Arthur, on previous occasions, he had demonstrated considerable tactical acumen and both men listened intently to what he had to say. "Perhaps this is a distraction, my liege. Having heard what Merlin has said about this Montagu, I am sure he would not think twice about sending hundreds of his men to their deaths just to obscure his real purpose."

Camelot's magician signalled his agreement with Gawain's premise but all he could do was repeat what he had said. "There is certainly no trickery at work here so perhaps Gawain has hit the mark."

"So what do we do, sire?" Gaheris stepped forward. "Are we to attack or hold position until Merlin locates this demon spell-weaver?"

The King threw a vicious stare towards the trees and grass in which his enemies lurked. "That cowardly scum out there have thrown in their lot with my nephew. They may not be aware of this Montagu's magic but they are certainly aware of Mordred's treachery." He wheeled Gryphon and beckoned his knights towards him. "We prepare for battle."

As Arthur and the rest of his armoured warriors readied themselves for conflict, a small force led by Sir Galahad galloped its way down an uneven track that wended gently through the Wessex hills, desperate to join with their comrades for the imminent attack.

The message had arrived early that morning. Galahad, who had fallen asleep in the company of the Grail once again, was stirred from his slumbers by the agitated messenger. Without hesitation, he had snatched the Grail from its lofty pedestal and scoured the castle for as many able-bodied men as he could muster. Whatever misgivings he had about setting out with such a woefully unprepared force were outweighed by his eagerness to join with his King in battling the traitor.

He was made to reflect on his recklessness and lack of numbers as the party rode around a bend in the track and along a dusty avenue that cut through bunches of gnarled and crooked trees, all of which stood on both sides of the indistinct trail.

The unfortunate warrior who rode in the van was the first to fall victim.

Without warning, a massive black shape dropped from the canopy and grasped the man in its vicious claws. Its powerfully muscled legs crushed him like a fly as it wrenched and tore at him, trying to prise him free from his saddle. The man's right foot was firmly wedged in its stirrup, however, and the creature's efforts were in vain. It finally gave up trying to pull him free and instead used the man's shoulders as a platform on which it stood. It then stretched out two huge leathery wings and screeched imprecations at the sky. If the appearance of the massive bird-like monster had not been enough to freeze the blood, then its call certainly was. The horses had been petrified in fear by the beast's appearance but its shriek sent them into a blind panic. They began kicking and bucking, trying to rid themselves of the extra weight of the riders so that they could make good their escape.

Most of Galahad's party were unseated and the fiend descended upon them, ripping at them with a razor sharp beak and impaling them on its piercing claws.

The screams of Galahad's men increased yet further. Most had retreated in disarray, dashing for their lives into the trees, but it was clear that the creature's call had summoned some of its fellows and the forest by the roadside soon became awash with agonised howls as the demonic beasts fell upon the knights.

The steward of the Grail had lain about him as best he could, slicing at the evil monsters with Whitecleave, a blade nearly as famous as Arthur's Excalibur. He had managed to seriously injure two of them, including the one that had first attacked the troop, but he could see that it was not enough. Keeping an eye on the creatures as they circled and wheeled over the remnants of the group, he rummaged in his pack frantically, looking for the only thing that he could think of that might swing the balance back to the side of good. Locating it, his hand closed around its stem and he withdrew the Grail from its pouch, holding it high in the air as far as his arm would extend.

"By all that is holy," he shrieked, "do your work now or reside in the hands of evil forever." His left hand, which was still wielding Whitecleave, flicked out the sword and barely managed to deflect another swoop from one of the birds. Unfortunately though, the concussion as it flapped its wings was enough to unhorse him and he fell to the dusty road, losing his grip on the sword but still clinging for his life to the Grail. "For God's sake, weave your magic."

In desperation, he thrust it upwards once more and threw his other arm across his face in preparation for the bloody death that he felt sure he was about to fall victim to.

Instead he felt a white-hot sensation stream up his arm and loose itself into the sky. His eyes snapped open as the moans and screams of his men were drowned out by the piercing screams of the demon birds. He found himself staring in disbelief as bolt after bolt of fire shot out from the Grail and washed over the flying foes above. In no time, the flame burned through their thick leathery hides and wings and even seemed to be incinerating their bones. The light from the rapidly perishing creatures became too much for Galahad and he had to shield his eyes once more. When he sensed that the incandescence had ceased, he gingerly eased his eyelids apart and gaped at the scene before him.

Blood and gore was spattered all over the leaf-littered floor, making the surface slick and dangerous underfoot. He spotted five or six of his comrades, groaning and writhing in the muck, but of the bird-like travesties, there was no sign. He guessed that they had all been obliterated by the power of Christ's cup, but he still regained his feet warily, at any moment expecting a maelstrom of pointed claws and shrieking madness to descend upon him.

After a few moments spent finding out who had perished and who still lived, Galahad and the survivors began the grisly task of giving their fallen companions as decent a burial as they could in the circumstances.

They went about the duty like men possessed, acutely aware of the respect they needed to show to the dead, but also conscious of the fact that they had an urgent assignation with their King.

After barely more than an hour, they left the devastated forest and resumed their journey.

One of the surviving knights rode alongside the steward. "What were they, Sir Galahad?"

The champion of Camelot answered through gritted teeth, "The spawn of Satan. Creatures forsaken by God and risen from the pit. Call them what you will."

"Do they seek the Grail?" the knight asked nervously, casting a glance at Galahad's travelling pack.

He shot the inquisitive knight a vicious look. "I know not, Sir Franklin. I do not tend to consort with Beelzebub's minions. Nevertheless, the Grail repelled them and that is all we need to concern ourselves with."

"But..."

"Please, I wish to be alone with my thoughts." Galahad raised his gauntleted hand.

The knight nodded and retreated from his leader's side.

The Grail-keeper stared grimly at the road ahead as they rode on, ever nearer to the field of Camlann and whatever destiny held for them.

In a near mirror image of his speech in the front of the walls of Camelot, King Arthur of the Britons rode from left to right in front of his warriors, exalting them to further deeds of chivalry and valour.

"You have fought for your King and country before now, so I know that you are as brave an army of men that has ever set foot upon this land. But now I ask you to fight once more. I ask you to fight against a most heinous evil. I

111

ask you to fight against the most hideous disease that has ever afflicted the world. I ask you to fight for your God, your King and your country, but above all, once more I ask you to fight for yourselves. For, make no mistake, if we are vanquished this day, generations as yet unborn will languish under a most terrible tyranny. A tyranny built on the foundations of a million corpses, cemented together with the blood of centuries. A tyranny bred in hell and birthed by the Devil. A tyranny that must be stopped, right here and right now. We must prevail." Arthur hung his head momentarily, drained by the passion and emotion that had coursed through him as he had spoken the words. Then, raising Excalibur to the skies once more, he bellowed at the top of his voice. "Let us bring them before the judgement of Heaven." He wheeled Gryphon to face the enemy, "Attack!"

A great atavistic roar erupted from the throats of Arthur's host as they followed hot on the heels of their leader as he galloped onto the killing field of Camlann.

It was answered by a bestial clamour from Mordred's forces as they too drew their weapons and went to meet their foes.

The struggle that followed was brutal and vicious, both sides knowing that no mercy would be afforded them should they fall. Swords and axes were swung with such strength that much of the armour could not withstand them and it split as easily as the skin of ripe fruit, sending eruptions of blood splashing to the grass.

The initial charge had enabled Arthur's men to cut a large swathe through Mordred's ranks, but they had now regrouped and were trying to surround the Camelot knights in the middle of the meadow.

Excalibur was drenched from tip to shaft in blood and Arthur had to keep swapping hands to wipe the oily cloying liquid off his gauntlets lest he lose grip of it. He ran it through the stomach of an unlucky knight, who had been propelled into his path by the flank of another horse. He avoided looking into the man's eyes as he withdrew the razor sharp blade from his intestines, for fear of humanising the enemy who, until battle had been joined, he had been able to imagine as soulless demons intent on the extinction of life. Now though, as he looked at the devastation and tried desperately but unsuccessfully to blot out the screams of the dying, he was all too aware that he would spend the day slaying men who, if he looked deep inside his soul, were not much different from himself.

He mentally shook himself, trying to free his mind of the melancholia that had suddenly engulfed him. As he stared from face to face, he saw the torture of his thoughts mirrored in every one of his comrades.

Suddenly, so suddenly in fact that he nearly dropped Excalibur to the grass, Merlin's voice whispered eerily across his mind.

"It is Montagu playing with your senses. Look to yonder hill and you will see."

Arthur's head whipped round and he peered up to the border of the trees as they began to scale the upslope of one of the hills nearby. There were two figures there, silhouettes on the edge of the trees, standing immobile like sentinels, watching the progress of the battle from afar.

Gripping Excalibur like it was the only real thing on earth, King Arthur raised it to the heavens, then brought it down and thrust it forward, as if attempting to impale the pair of shadows that stood so impassively mere yards away. "To me, Knights of The Round Table," he bellowed.

Mordred jumped like a startled rabbit when he heard the cry, which seemed to carry over the battlefield and arrive straight in his head. Quavering, he turned to the magician who stood unmoved at his shoulder. "How long have we to hold?" he asked, trying to muster enough strength to quash the shudder in his voice.

He was answered with a contemptuous look. "You will hold until I say otherwise. Battle is joined for little longer than it would take you to piss your britches and already you are bleating like a frightened lamb. The size of your cowardice is only matched by the size of your incompetence." With a complicated gesture and a small cloud of smoke, he disappeared, leaving Mordred isolated and vulnerable on the side of the hill.

"Montagu?" Mordred whimpered, spinning around in a frenzy, looking in vain for an indication of where the spell-weaver had gone.

In an unconscious reflection of Merlin's trick of a few moments ago, an eldritch voice insinuated itself into Mordred's head.

"If you fail me, you die."

Like an automaton, Mordred's hand drooped down to his sword and he went to join his men on the field of battle.

The decimated band of Sir Galahad was continuing its breakneck journey across country in an attempt to join up with King Arthur.

The steward of the Grail led from the front, hair streaming behind him and Whitecleave, securely fastened in a loop on his saddle, a very reassuring presence at his side. They had just scaled a rather steep hill and the horses were heavily lathered in sweat. Galahad would have kept going, were it not for the hairs on the back of his neck standing up and his mount whinnying pitifully, clearly unwilling to ride onward.

He raised his left hand, struggling to keep the Destrier steed under control. "Be alert," he called back, "I have a sense that things are not as they should be up ahead."

They trotted on, all the riders forced to use their equestrian skills to the utmost to stop their horses from bolting.

A raven's boisterous caw cut through the gilt-edged silence. As one, they watched it land on a wall that was haphazardly stacked at the side of the path. The horses became even more jumpy and one of them nearly unseated its rider. After the confusion that followed had been sorted out and the horses soothed back into obedience, the company of six found its number increased by one.

As they had been trained to, in perfect unison Galahad's men all went for their weapons and the newcomer found himself threatened on all sides by crossbows and swords.

"Please, I mean you no harm," he said.

Sir Galahad, who had noticed that the raven had disappeared, advanced towards the stranger. "Who are you?"

"So mistrustful, Sir Galahad?"

The knight's eyes instantly hooded. "How do you know my name?"

"Come now, good Sir Knight, everyone knows who you are. The knight who located the Cup of Christ? The only person able to sit upon the Siege Perilous at Camelot. You underestimate your achievements."

"Well, you have me at a disadvantage then. You know my name, yet I have no idea as to your identity."

The stranger pulled a face. "My name is not important. I am a mere conjuror, a trickster who lives by fleetness of foot and sleight of hand."

"Indeed," Galahad regarded him dubiously. "Well, do not let us keep you from your journey."

Ignoring him, the man walked forward and said airily, "I note that you have more horses than riders."

Galahad's face darkened as he said, "We had trouble on the road a few miles back."

Laughing heartily, the stranger said, "Come now, surely you jest, what manner of enemy could possibly trouble the great Sir Galahad and his men?"

One of Galahad's companions breathed, "Creatures from hell itself, good Sir."

Another snort of derision emanated from the stranger.

"Great bat-like things they were," Sir Franklin put in. "I've never been so frightened in all my days."

"Aaaahh!" the new man nodded.

"You know of them?" Franklin asked in a startled voice, leaning forward in his saddle.

"Know of them?" Montagu replied. "I am one of them," he laughed once more as he gripped the knight's head and twisted it round in a circle to the accompaniment of a multitude of cracking bones. His laugh grew into a

114

hideous bellow as the skin on his face stretched and contorted before peeling back to reveal a skull of vivid scarlet with eyes of blackest pitch. Fanged teeth that protruded over his bottom lip sunk into another one of Galahad's men's necks before the others had time to react.

The mage's robe was wrenched from his body as monstrous wings erupted from his shoulder blades and he took to the air, hovering over the group, slashing and ripping with the talons that had sprouted where his feet had been. The knights below yelled resistance and presented arms to the beast above, however, the shock of losing two of their comrades so swiftly and brutally after the slaughter in the avenue affected them too much. The first to die overstretched with his swing and Montagu managed to get his talons clasped around the extended limb, ripping it mercilessly from its socket in a gush of gore, then as the man fell back screaming in abject horror at his injury, the avian fiend swooped in and tore his head from his shoulders.

Galahad, who had been knocked to the ground in the melee and had narrowly avoided being trampled by a panic stricken horse, shook his head to try and clear his vision, but he found it blurred and so was unable to lend his considerable swordsmanship to the struggle. To his despair, he saw one of the remaining two knights slip on the severed arm of the second knight to perish and then lose his footing.

From a purely dispassionate point of view, the killing machine that Montagu had become was a terrible and cruel study of brute force. Unfortunately for those in the way of the creature, it was allied with an appallingly effective grace that allowed him to pick off his victims in a viciously swift manner.

So it was with the fallen rider. Before the other knight could react to protect his companion, Montagu was upon him, rending him to pieces, cutting his shrieks off pitilessly with a talon through the heart.

Even on the ground the winged creature was able to fight off the one remaining soldier of Camelot. Once again, the slickness of the gore upon the ground proved the warrior's undoing and he too soon fell under the gaping maw of the demon.

Weeping and bellowing incoherently, Galahad tried to make his way over to the blood-drenched monster, intent on wiping it from the face of the earth, but his concussion would not allow him to gain his feet and he half crawled, half stumbled over the carnage, barely able to keep Whitecleave raised high enough to protect himself.

Closing his eyes momentarily to try and clear his vision, he opened them again to find that Montagu had resumed his human form. The black magician held out a blood-spattered hand and calmly advanced, "The Grail, Sir Galahad, if you please," he said.

The steward of the Grail stopped his erratic progress and retreated drunkenly to his baggage that lay strewn about the path. "What use would it be to one as you?" he snarled. "The Grail is a source of good. It would not allow itself to be used for your evil purposes."

Montagu snorted derisively. "The Grail is a vessel, Galahad. It is the wielder of it who determines which path it follows." He breathed heavily. "Now, I say again, the Grail, if you please." The last three words were spoken in clipped angry tones.

The champion of Camelot reached down to one of his bags and found the goblet nestling inside. He gripped it and the giddy feeling that had accompanied his every movement since falling from his saddle evaporated like mist on a summer's day. Thinking clearly now, he decided to continue acting as if on the brink of unconsciousness. "Over my dead body," he slurred.

"If that is what you wish." Montagu shrugged. With a contemptuous flick of his wrist, he sent a bolt of fire hurtling towards Galahad. The knight took it full in the chest and was slammed against a tree, his life saved only by the strength of his armour. Feeling sick and giddy, he could only watch helplessly as Montagu reached past him and clasped his fingers around the stem of the cup with an ecstatic sigh. Steeling himself for the fatal blow, he closed his eyes and began praying.

When he opened them again, he saw Montagu still standing over him, a disdainful look twisting his face into a hideous mask. He hawked and spat on Galahad's face then began strolling up and down in front of him, gesticulating wildly at the bloodshed he had wrought. "You have just witnessed the slaughter of all your men and yet you still spout your hollow words to your weak and feeble god. I would kill you where you sit, but..." he turned his back on Galahad and began to transform once more into the winged beast that had wreaked such havoc, in preparation to fly from the scene of his victory.

Whether it was the thought of the Grail falling into Montagu's hands or simply the desire to avenge the deaths of his fallen comrades he did not know, but suddenly Galahad found a force of will flowing through his veins and he rose up, Whitecleave unsheathed and ready, and slashed down at Montagu's left wing.

The steel blade bit through the musculature and Montagu screamed in agony as he rose into the air, whirling and flapping wildly, trying to gain and then maintain height.

Galahad watched him open-mouthed as the beat of the fiend's wings began to settle into a less irregular rhythm. Snapping out of his trance, he leapt onto his steed, which had mercifully not ridden too far away, and began to follow the creature's path as it flew on the strengthening wind.

Galloping along underneath the hideous apparition, Galahad saw with mounting horror, that the landscape ahead had a distinctly cut-off look about it. As he drew closer, he saw that his quarry had flown over the lip of a steep incline that dropped away to the shores of a huge lake and was now plummeting towards the waters in an unstoppable descent.

With a cry of despair, Montagu hit the water and both he and the Grail disappeared from view.

A low whimper escaped Galahad's lips as he peered out across the rippling lagoon, hoping against hope that the Grail would somehow float to the surface so he could retrieve it and resume his stewardship. The wind whipped at him and he blinked his fringe away from his eyes but though his gaze swept the constantly moving surface for movement, he could see no trace of either the Grail or its temporary custodian.

Hanging his head, he sank to the damp grass and offered repentance to God at his failure to ensure the safety of His son's goblet. "Forgive me, Lord. I have failed you. I have failed in the responsibility bestowed upon me when I brought the Grail back to Camelot Castle. I was charged to protect it with my life and I have been found wanting. With this act, I submit myself to your judgement."

Slowly and methodically, he pushed the hilt of Whitecleave into the sodden ground, leaving the wickedly sharp blade angled towards him. He undid the straps on his travel-stained breastplate and flung it to one side of him, watching it until it rolled to a halt.

Taking a deep breath, he stared fixedly at the point of the sword, then closed his eyes and fell forward, flinging his arms to the side in an approximation of Jesus upon the cross. Seconds later, he was lying face down on the ground, puzzled as to why he was not ascending to heaven to face his God. He awkwardly shifted his position and stared to the left, suddenly aware of a shadow looming over him. His gaze took in the instantly recognisable boots, long midnight-black robe and the blade of Whitecleave that was planted in the ground next to the feet. Shaking his head, he got to his feet, finally plucking up the courage to look into the man's eyes.

"Come to gloat over my failure, Merlin?" he laughed bitterly. "It seems yours and Arthur's estimation of me was correct. I was unable to protect the Grail."

To his surprise, the look on Merlin's face was not one of triumphal arrogance but one of great sympathy. "You are wrong, Sir Galahad. You have not failed in your duty. You prevented the most powerful practitioner of dark magic in the land from possessing the Holy Grail."

117

Galahad's eyes left Merlin's face and swept the now glass-calm surface of the lake for any sign of the magician's reappearance. "You mean it was a human in demon form rather than the other way about?" he gasped incredulously. "But what it...he did, it was sickening."

Merlin nodded gently, "Aye, his name is Montagu and he has allied himself with the King's bastard cousin. He is a magician of the blackest of black spells. Now, please," he strode forward and handed Galahad's weapon back to him, "this sword has performed services to your God and your King of immeasurable value and courage. Do not let its final deed be the waste of your life."

The Knight of The Round Table held Merlin's gaze for a moment. Taking Whitecleave in his grasp, he stroked its length then re-sheathed it. Looking up, he nodded gratitude to King Arthur's magician and breathed deeply. "Thank you, Merlin," he said simply and they clasped forearms. They each took one last look at the lake then Galahad turned to him, "I took you to be with King Arthur," the knight said. "How did you come to be here so quickly?"

A look of momentary annoyance passed across Merlin's face for he initially took the inquiry as an inference that his motives were suspicious. However, Galahad's gaze contained nothing but honesty and candour so he let it pass. "I felt...I don't know...a wrongness. I simply knew the Grail was in peril. I presume the bond that I have with it is stronger than I first appreciated. Now tell me, is Montagu vanquished?"

"I have seen neither hide nor hair of the demon-spawn since he hit the water," Galahad confirmed.

"I wish there was some way to confirm his demise." Merlin sighed hugely. Then he tutted impatiently and shrugged, "Oh well, it cannot be helped now. Galahad, take my hand. We must away and quickly. Even now, Arthur and Mordred do battle upon the field of Camlann."

Merlin spoke words under his breath and they both vanished.

Sir Galahad forced his eyes open to find himself soaring across the sky, the landscape a mere blur underneath his rushing flight.

"Spectacular, is it not?"

The voice jerked Galahad out of his awestruck silence. His eyes teared as he stared through the tumultuous wind and saw Merlin flying alongside him, seemingly impervious to the buffeting gusts. The Knight of The Round Table could only nod at the wizard's wry observation. It was not long before Merlin snaked out a slim finger and indicated where they were heading.

From the vertiginous height it was hard to make out details. The noise, however, carried up to them as they hovered over the battlefield.

As they looked down, the troops seemed to split into two groups and two ant-like figures detached themselves and began circling each other.

King Arthur flicked out Excalibur, causing his adversary to lunge backwards.

"So it ends, traitor."

Mordred hawked and spat at him. "Nothing is decided yet, my dear uncle."

Arthur's face hardened at the familiarity. "Do not remind me that I am related to you, you bastard. Unless your swordsmanship has vastly improved since we last met, there will only be one outcome." He pointed at Mordred's throat with the point of his sword, "Your death."

Mordred laid his sword down and stepped back, arms spread. "Surely you would not slay an unarmed man. Where is the honour in that?"

"You have the gall to stand there and speak to me of honour? You who have joined forces with the foulest creature ever to have walked these islands."

Mordred placed his hands on his hips. "Montagu? Yes, it is true. I needed magic to combat Merlin's trickery and he came to me. I knew nothing of what he really was until about a month ago," he shrugged, "By then, it was too late."

Arthur could not contain a snort of disgust. "You have spoken lies on so many occasions before, why should I believe you now? You are lying just to save your own miserable skin."

"Believe what you will, Arthur. But I am speaking the truth." Mordred sighed resignedly.

The King searched his nephew's face for deception but found none which disconcerted him slightly but nevertheless he spoke on, "There seems little point in repenting now, Mordred. Your life was forfeit the moment you tried to ascend to the throne."

Mordred held the King's gaze for a long moment then dropped to one knee as Arthur strode towards him.

Merlin and Galahad swooped downwards, the knight speechless with fear and with stomach lurching, partly because of the speed at which the field of Camlann was ascending to meet them but mainly because Merlin was screaming above the sound of the gale generated by their passage, "Arthur, stay your hand, it is a trap. It is a trap."

Arthur raised Excalibur to the heavens in preparation for the final blow. As he began the killing stroke, he became aware of a succession of gasps and exclamations creeping through the crowd that were steadily gaining in volume. He looked down into Mordred's saucer-wide eyes and all of a sudden, found himself in two minds. This was his kinsman after all. Could he really bring himself to extinguish it in such a cold-blooded manner?

A shrill screech was beginning to separate itself from the general murmur of the assembled soldiery and he managed to pick out his name being hailed but little else. He stared left and right, trying to find the source. Noting the upturned heads of the crowd, he too found his gaze dragged skywards until he spotted the two figures hurtling towards him.

By now, Galahad had been caught up in the moment and had leant his voice to Merlin's beseeching cry. "My liege, it is a trap!" he yelled, willing the words across the divide between himself and his King.

Mordred had closed his eyes as Arthur began to bring Excalibur down, expecting the cold slash of steel to bring an abrupt bloody end to his life. He began to sob, thinking back to when the first seeds of sedition had been planted in his head by the accursed wizard. Despite what Arthur obviously thought, he had been telling the truth about his relationship with the black magician. When he had first met Montagu, the mage had been lying, bruised and battered, by the side of the road half-dead and savagely beaten. Thinking him to be a waylaid traveller, brought low by bandits, Mordred had allowed his entourage to tend to him and bring him back to his luxurious house where he was nursed back to health. Looking back, that act in itself had been suspicious. Mordred was self-aware enough to know that he was not the sort of person to put himself out for strangers, no matter how badly injured they were.

As he knelt in the damp grass of this distant field preparing to meet his maker, he pondered whether he had been under Montagu's thrall from that moment on. Seeing little point in pursuing the thought, he shivered and braced himself for Excalibur's bite.

Nothing happened. A strange keening came to his ears and his face scrunched itself up in confusion until a thought came to him. Montagu! At the last he has come to save me, he thought. Opening his eyes, he risked a look upwards.

Arthur was standing in front of him, covering him in his massive shadow, but not paying him any attention. Taking advantage of this, he peered about, longing to see the face of his unlikely saviour but of Montagu, there was no sign. Cursing in frustration, his gaze also found itself irresistibly drawn towards the two plummeting figures.

He instantly recognised Merlin and his nerve fled him once again. His situation had been bad enough when he was merely at Arthur's mercy but now he knew he would be subject to the ministrations of Merlin and all the magic at his disposal and having spent time in the company of Montagu, he was all too aware of what tortures the weaving of spells could inflict.

From somewhere deep in the abyss of his despair, a sudden burst of steely resolve struck out for the surface. The appearance of Merlin brought into sharp focus the fact that he was damned whatever he did, be it die at the hands of Arthur, Merlin or Montagu, so he took the only course of action open to him and tried to remove at least one of his three nemesises from the equation. In an almost trance-like state, he fluidly grabbed the hilt of his sword which mercifully was still within his reach upon the trampled grass. He gripped it and brought it up in one smooth sweep.

Arthur sensed the movement because he began to turn, but he was too late. Mordred brought the blade up and ran Arthur's side through.

Gasping at the sudden screaming agony that rippled through him, Arthur brought Excalibur round in a vicious hacking swing and decapitated Mordred. He stared in disbelief as Mordred's headless corpse crumpled to the floor. Then his horrified gaze transferred itself to the copious amount of blood that was draining out of the wound in his hip and with it, his strength and vitality.

In one movement, Arthur fell face down into the wavering grass that carpeted the field of Camlann.

Merlin rushed to the King's side whilst everyone else stood transfixed, shocked into petrification by the events unfolding in front of them. Galahad was the first to free himself from the trauma. He staggered over and gasped, "Is he..."

"Not yet," the magician's clipped tones cut the question short before the Knight of The Round Table could finish, "but he will be if I do not get him to a place of safety." Before anyone else could react, Merlin and Arthur's body disappeared from sight.

Galahad's eyes gave forth a cascade of tears that splashed to the blood-soaked grass of the battlefield. He felt a great well of emptiness opening inside him, hollowing out his insides and leaving a void of nothingness where his emotions should have been.

Then the tears dried and a slow trickle of emotion began to fill the hole and the emotion was anger. The trickle became a torrent which became a flood. Then the well was full and the rage exploded in a tsunami of violence. Spinning round like a whip, Galahad advanced on the headless corpse of Mordred shrieking incoherently. He planted a kick into the lifeless chest and stamped down viciously on one of the legs. Spying the head a little way away, Galahad leapt off the body and went to aim a kick at Mordred's unseeing face.

As his foot swung towards its target, the head vanished into thin air. The kick that he had attempted to land was powerful enough to cause the knight to nearly lose his balance. Blinking in shock, his stare swept the field for Mordred's body but it too had disappeared without a trace.

Chapter 8

Montagu's lair

Dark candles flickered and guttered across the ceiling of the dank cave, the fumes that rose from them giving off a sickly sweet smell that was both unsettling and alluring in equal measure.

Montagu stalked purposefully around a marble bier upon which rested the body and head of Mordred. Every few seconds he stopped and spoke an incantation over the grey-skinned corpse, the mystical tongue in which he talked becoming harsher and more guttural as the spell wore on.

Eventually the magician of the black arts ceased his restless pacing and sat down, drained by both the length and the complexity of the spell. He was already tired beyond endurance by the magic he had employed to repair his blistered skin after its contact with the water in the lake. Still, it was just another potent symbol of his power that he was able to mend his broken skin so swiftly and then have the presence of mind to rescue Mordred's decapitated body from Camlann.

That thought made him lift his head up wearily and stare at the unmoving cadaver. Cursing, he spat and flung a fireball at the far wall, shattering numerous glass containers to the floor which oozed strange liquids and gave off rancid odours as they fell.

His head whipped round at a horrendous wheezing sound that emanated from the dais. Mordred was sitting up, clawing at his throat and struggling for breath.

Montagu was at his side in a second. "Calm yourself, Mordred. The stuff of life will come to you."

Indeed, as the wizard predicted, Mordred felt the oxygen flowing into his lungs like the sweetest drink he had ever swallowed. After the initial shock at finding himself whole again, Mordred began to take in his surroundings. He stared in dismay at the damp, dark walls and eyed the mess on the cold flagstones distastefully. "What is this place?" He sniffed then scrunched his nose up. "And what is that god-awful smell? And what is wrong with your arm?"

Montagu ignored the last two questions and instead bowed sarcastically as he answered the first. "Welcome to my humble home."

The would-be usurper of Camelot rounded on his host, "You? Where were you? Battle was joined and you were nowhere to be seen. Where did you skulk off to, you miserable swine?"

Montagu smiled lazily and waggled a warning finger. "Watch your words, Mordred." He advanced upon his retreating guest seemingly intent on causing him harm, but at the last, he placed a companionable arm around his shoulders. "Come now, is that really the right way to talk to the man who ensured that you would survive Arthur's attentions on the field of Camlann?"

"What?" Mordred spat.

Montagu prodded a finger into Mordred's skinny chest. "My dear Mordred, what does the heart do?"

"Sorry?"

"It pumps the blood around your body and when I, shall we say, extracted it, I made you invulnerable."

The former Prince of the Realm raised a sceptical eyebrow. "I do not understand?"

"When you were out on the battlefield, you were, to all intents and purposes, dead. You were a spectre, a ghost made flesh. No blood pumped in your veins, no air inflated your lungs."

Mordred's hand flew to his neck. "But my head was..."

"You're not listening, Mordred. You were already dead. Excalibur could no more have harmed you than a thousand crossbow bolts to your brain."

"So I owe you my life then?" He said sceptically.

"Indeed you do." He laughed heartily. "Perhaps you should kneel before me?"

"I think not. The last time I knelt before anyone, I ended up being beheaded."

Montagu folded his arms, wincing slightly, but recovered himself enough to laugh heartily. "I am hardly going to go through the trouble of re-attaching your head to your body just to remove it again. No, you should kneel before me because I am like a god to you. I took your life away and then returned it. Drink?"

Out of nowhere, a goblet appeared in Montagu's hand. Mordred snuffed in the aroma of it and smacked his lips together. Grabbing it from the mage, he swilled the dark red liquid around a couple of times before draining it in one swig. "Forgive me, I am finding all this rather hard to take in. Now my life rests in the hands of one of Satan's minions?"

"It could be so much worse, Mordred. Would you like me to return you to Camlann? I am sure your corpse would make a veritable banquet for the ravens and the worms."

The pretender went pale then shook his head resignedly. "Did you find it? The Judas Cup, I mean." He murmured, glad to change the subject.

Montagu shook his head and scowled. "No, I did not. I had believed the task of obtaining it would be relatively easy but I was mistaken. No, the cup remains tantalisingly close yet still so far out of reach." The sneer disappeared and was replaced by a wicked smile. "Have no fear though. We will find it."

Mordred's brow wrinkled. "We?" he asked quizzically.

If Mordred had thought that Montagu's smile had been evil before then it was nothing compared to the look that had planted itself on the magician's face now. "Oh yes, Mordred. You will not be rid of me for a few years yet. Tell me, have you finished your potion?"

The King's nephew's eyes widened and he threw his cup to the ground as if he had been stung, "Potion?" He stared in horror at the cup before hissing at Mordred. "What have you done?" he demanded.

"Do not look at me like that." Montagu sniffed. "Once again, I have extended your lifespan beyond its natural course. You have much to thank me for."

Spitting out the little amount of liquid that he had not swallowed, Mordred sank to the uncomfortable stone floor and began moaning pitifully.

Montagu pulled him roughly to his feet. "Come now, there is no need for such a pathetic display. Longevity potions are harmless. They merely increase ones life according to the strength of the dose."

With a sinking feeling, Mordred quavered, "How strong is this one?"

"Hmm," Montagu wiggled his hand up and down, "it is one of the weaker ones I have concocted, to be honest with you."

Desperation gave Mordred enough courage to advance on the sniggering wizard. "Montagu, do you ever give a straight answer?"

"You will live for five hundred years longer than normal, give or take a decade."

Mordred stared at him for a few seconds, then his face creased up and he dissolved into a fit of laughter. He had been expecting fifty or maybe a hundred years, somehow five hundred seemed impossible to envisage.

Montagu continued, "Once again, you owe me your life. Once the Judas Cup has been located and drunk from, you and I will be among the elite few to still alive to rule the world. Such power," he breathed, "Such power."

"I will live for half a millennium?" Mordred asked after regaining a modicum of composure.

"Unless the fates are against you, yes." Montagu confirmed simply.

Mordred's eyes hooded. "Meaning what exactly?"

"Meaning no spell of this nature is infallible. There is a way that you may still be slain but it is unlikely to happen." The wizard sniffed dismissively.

"How unlikely?" Mordred pressed.

"If your heart is completely removed from your body and exposed to the open air then you will die but, as I said, it is not very likely, is it?"

"Is that not what you did to me at Camlann, though?"

125

Again, the arm snaked out and Mordred found himself being companiably walked about the dank cave by the wizard. "Ah yes, but now we understand each other a little better, do we not? So I shouldn't think that I would need to do that again, will I?"

Mordred gazed into the deep green eyes and saw no mercy within them. "No" he said sadly.

"Ah yes, if memory serves, you cannot survive in direct sunlight either."

Mordred threw his hands up in despair. "If memory serves?!?" he spat. "Do you think you could dredge your memory and let me know of any other fatal flaws in your magic?"

Montagu grabbed the resurrected man by the throat and propelled him effortlessly against one of the walls of the cave. "Just because you are, for want of a better word, immortal, it does not mean you can't still feel pain, so do not presume to talk to me in such a manner again." Montagu's other hand snaked out and bent the little finger on Mordred's right hand back until, with a shudder of pleasure, he felt it break. He dropped his unfortunate servant to the floor and raised his voice slightly to drown out the wails of pain. "Beware though, Mordred, for as I said, you can still feel pain. The catalysts that trigger the worst agony seem to be that without which life cannot live. Water and sunlight. Avoid them and you should live to see your five hundred and thirty-fifth birthday."

Mordred cradled his abused right hand in his left as he stumbled to his feet. "So now you tell me that I may not drink or enjoy the warmth of the sun upon my face?"

This entreaty was met by another shrug, a habit of Montagu's that Mordred was beginning to find extremely irritating.

"Dammit, Montagu, it is not much of a life that you have saved for me, is it, if I may not drink or bask in the summer sun."

"The cold embrace of death is but a mere flick of my fingers away, Mordred." Montagu warned. "If you do not wish to join with me in my quest for dominion, then go and throw yourself in a lake." With that, the black magician turned to one of the tables arrayed around the cavern and began fiddling with various bottles and crucibles. After a few moments he turned round once more. "Still here, Mordred?"

The Prince held his gaze for as long as he could, until he sighed hopelessly and peered down at his boots. "Do you have any idea where the cup might be?"

Montagu shook his head. "No, at the current time I do not know exactly where it resides, but now we have a good part of eternity at our disposal, I am sure we will be able to lay our hands on it." He smiled.

Chapter 9

The shores of The Silver Lake

The sky itself appeared to be weeping as the litter transporting the body of Arthur, King of The Britons, made its stately way to the boat which gently bobbed on the tide of the Lake of the Silver Lady.

The King's corpse travelled slowly under the tunnel of blades created in his honour by the swords of the assembled Round Table Knights.

It ceased its eerily smooth movement as it reached the small craft. In an unusual show of emotion, Merlin reached out and tenderly laid his hand upon Arthur's.

"Goodbye, my King." He whispered, the words barely audible.

Galahad moved to his side as Arthur's body was laid to rest in the boat. "You did all you could, Merlin. But it was a mortal wound. Mordred's blade had cut him too deeply, no one would have survived it, even one as strong and vital as the king."

When the magician turned to Sir Galahad, the knight had to stop himself stepping back in shock at the haggard appearance of the wizard. "Your words are kind, good Sir Knight, but I find no solace in them. There is nothing you can do or say that would make this..." he gestured towards the boat which had begun to drift away from the shore, "... any easier."

Galahad nodded in sympathy before turning and feeling the breath stolen from him by what he saw. "Behold, the lady comes to claim him."

The wizard glanced over his shoulder at the ethereal figure that was slowly ascending from the water's embrace.

From nowhere, a mist began to form. Wispy at first, then growing in thickness, it was not long before it had enveloped both the boat and the Lady. Seconds before the King was lost from sight, Galahad thought he saw Merlin signing some sort of message across the lapping water to the Lady, who seemed to acknowledge it with the merest of nods. However, before he had a chance to inquire about it, the mist began to disperse. When the final tendrils dissipated, both the Lady of The Lake and the boat upon which her tragic cargo travelled had vanished.

"Take good care of him, Lady." Galahad murmured. He then turned from the scene and cocked an eyebrow at Merlin. "What were you..." he began to ask before the spell-weaver cut him short.

"I cannot stomach any more of this. If you will excuse me, Sir Galahad, I would be alone with my thoughts."

The knight was still intrigued by the exchange between the two but felt that this was neither the time nor place to pursue it. He nodded and placed his hand on the magician's shoulder, "Of course, Merlin, of course."

Merlin landed lightly upon the ramparts of the castle. He had just enjoyed an invigorating flight through the crisp night air and he felt refreshed after the harrowing events of the King's funeral, but then he had good reason to. He made his way to the room from which he had despatched the birds to hunt Mordred and marched purposefully into it.

He was halfway through the door when a sword blade appeared at his throat. Brushing it away as if it was nothing more than an inquisitive bluebottle he tutted, "Do you really feel that there is any need for that, sire? You and I are the only ones in the whole of the island who know of this room's existence."

King Arthur re-sheathed Excalibur and smirked at his magician. "Did it go as planned?"

"Indeed. No-one suspects a thing." Merlin's grin was positively mischievous.

For a moment the King's matched it but then the humour dissolved from his face and he became serious. "Let us make sure it stays that way."

Merlin nodded agreement. "You know it was touch and go for a while, Arthur. I had to haul you back from the brink on more than one occasion."

In an unconscious mirroring of Galahad's last gesture to the mage, Arthur laid his hand on Merlin's shoulder. "I know and I thank you for it."

The wizard waved away the platitude as he began to pace up and down the floor. "It is of no moment, my liege. I did what I had to do."

Arthur nodded and retired to sit on the edge of one of several sofas, upholstered in plush velvet. He watched Merlin for a long moment as he stared out of the window. "You seem distracted."

The wizard continued to gaze out over the darkness of the Wessex countryside until he suddenly turned round and looked piercingly at the King. "I am, sire. I find it hard to believe that a mere injury to one of his limbs and a fall into a lake would be enough to kill as powerful a wizard as Montagu."

"You think him still alive?"

An emphatic nod answered that question, "Especially after the way Mordred's corpse disappeared from the battlefield."

King Arthur's face hardened at the mention of his nephew. "Mordred vanishing off the face of the earth is no great loss."

Merlin allowed himself the briefest of smiles. "Nevertheless, he was the servant of Montagu. Perhaps he needs him alive to aid his search for the Judas Cup?"

"If that is what they are seeking?" Arthur pointed out.

"I cannot believe that it is anything else." Merlin sighed.

"But I decapitated the bastard, Merlin. How can he still be alive?" Arthur shook his head.

Merlin shifted uneasily. "There are certain spells available to those who are willing to take the risk of using them."

"They cheat death?" Arthur hissed incredulously.

"For a time, yes, and at a great cost."

"But one that Montagu is no doubt prepared to pay."

Once again, Merlin nodded agreement. "And now we have lost the Grail, we are especially vulnerable."

"At least Galahad prevented Montagu from getting it though." Arthur observed.

"That is the only good thing to come out of this. He has neither the Cup nor the Grail. With either of them at his beck and call, I feel he would be virtually unstoppable."

Arthur winced as the wound in his side pulled at him. "We must do all we can to stop him obtaining either of them then."

At that moment, Arthur shrank back as Merlin turned the most intense look that he had ever seen upon him, a look that hinted at the hidden depths of power that the wizard had at his disposal. "Do you really mean that, Arthur? Really and truthfully?"

"Of course I do." King Arthur nodded immediately. "I could not live with myself knowing that I had some means to stop him and not used it."

Merlin began pacing up and down again. "The thing is that Montagu will go on searching long after we are no more."

"What do you mean?" Arthur asked, his brow furrowing.

Merlin stopped and ran a hand through his greying beard. "This is an educated guess, but if he has invoked the spell to cheat death, then it is likely he will have utilised other dark magic as well."

"Other spells?"

"Immortality," Merlin whispered hoarsely.

The King's eyes rolled heavenwards. "Now you are telling me that he has eternity to search for that which he seeks."

"I may be wrong, but it is likely I am not. There are spells that allow the caster to live for approximately five hundred years."

Arthur's mouth dropped open and he stared numbly at the opposite wall. "So all he has to do is lay low for fifty or so years and then resume his search."

"Indeed, sire, unless..." Merlin left the sentence hanging.

"Unless what?" The King asked, worried by what he sensed was coming.

"The spell that was available to him..." Merlin took a deep breath before plunging on, "... is also available to us."

This time it was Arthur's turn to bestow a penetrating stare upon Merlin. "What are you saying?"

Merlin dragged a stool over and sat in front of the King. "Were you serious about what you said, Arthur, because if you were, then I would have thought that the answer was rather obvious?"

"Merlin, I am not sure that I am prepared to live for another five centuries." Arthur sank back into his seat.

"Be clear on this, sire. If Montagu obtains possession of the Cup, all of the world will be turned into a wasteland. No-one will be exempt from his demonic reach. If Montagu retrieves the Judas Cup, his master will rule the world. Would you have the human race subjugated by the demon hordes of Satan?"

Arthur had never felt less royal, less majestic than he did at this moment. He had not known such fear as this before and it chilled him to the bone. He looked down at the floor and mumbled, "If he is immortal, how can he be stopped?"

"There are ways and means of ending the spell, Arthur." Merlin placed a hand under his chin and raised his face towards him. "There can be no ifs or buts, sire. Can you not feel the hand of fate upon your shoulder, slowly propelling you towards your destiny? This is what you were born for, my liege. I have nurtured you from a babe-in-arms to the King you have become and this is why. You are as powerful a mortal as you can possibly be at this moment in time. But if Montagu drinks from that Cup, it will all be for naught. No-one to respect you, no-one to honour you, no-one to serve you, no-one to remember you," Merlin smiled inwardly as he saw that his appeal to Arthur's vanity may have had the desired effect. His face remained neutral however.

"How did such an evil come to be?" The King asked, shaking his head despondently.

Merlin shrugged. "Who knows? Perhaps it is to maintain equilibrium. The Grail is infused with infinite goodness, so perhaps there has to be something that is so steeped in wickedness that it is capable of doing unspeakable harm to the world as we know it. But the fact is Montagu believes it to exist. And we cannot take the chance that it is a myth. Let us not forget, we thought the Grail a legend until Galahad returned with it. We must assume the Judas Cup exists." He looked at Arthur again, the intensity in his stare returning. "Well, Arthur, will you join me? Will you drink the potion and give mankind a chance?"

The King's eyes fell on two ornate goblets resting on the table in the centre of the room, "Why me, Merlin? Why not Galahad? He has more affinity with the Grail than I."

The magician's gaze hardened. "Would you argue with destiny, Arthur? You are special. Your fate has been writ large in the stars since the day of your birth. It was you who pulled the sword from the stone. It was you who brought justice and harmony to the Kingdom when it threatened to disintegrate into myriad little baronies squabbling over lands and titles. You have the mark of greatness upon you and Montagu knows that. That is why he engineered the confrontation at Camlann. He placed an enchantment on Mordred's sword. Had the blade plunged but one inch deeper than it did then you would now be an eternal guest at the Silver Lady's banqueting table. Montagu knows you will come after him. He could see that you would not shrink from your appointed task. That is why he tried to kill you."

"I have no choice but to drink the drink then, do I." Arthur sighed resignedly.

Merlin handed him the cup. "It was pre-ordained from the moment you took your first breath."

Arthur Pendragon, King of The Britons, grasped the goblet in his hand, swilled the dark liquid around a few times, took a deep breath, then swallowed it all in one go. He shuddered as he felt the tasteless fluid slide down his throat then watched as Merlin drained his cup.

"It is done." The wizard stated sombrely.

Chapter 10

AD 652 – The border between England and Scotland

For year upon year, decade upon decade, Arthur and Merlin stalked the land, hunting relentlessly for signs of Montagu and Mordred's re-emergence. Through blazing hot summers and freezing cold winters, across rain-starved fields and swollen rivers, they walked.

They lived on their wits and slept on the ground, two road-weary travellers on a never-ending quest, the purpose of which was known only to them. So it was that, a century and a half to the year from when they had drunk the longevity potion, they found themselves walking along a northern road, tired and hungry, in need of shelter and succour.

"Just once, Merlin," Arthur wheedled in an unbecoming voice.

The magician let out an exasperated sigh and threw his hands in the air. "Arthur, I have told you before. I will not use my magic to find us food. It is too damned risky. Montagu could have spies anywhere and everywhere. Thanks to the ruse at Camlann, we have become the stuff of legend. King Arthur residing within the Silver Lady's chambers at Avalon and Merlin, the once mighty court magician of Camelot, inconsolable in grief for his lost monarch, disappearing into thin air and not seen again since the day his King was lost. You would risk all that for a morsel of food?"

When Merlin put it into those words, Arthur felt an overwhelming sense of shame. He shook his head silently.

Merlin's voice lost its harshness and he placed a hand on both of Arthur's shoulders and shook him gently. "I realise this is hard for you, Arthur. Gods, man, you were the king. You had luxury and privilege everywhere you turned. To go from that opulence to living unwashed and unfed on the road is a fall of epic proportions. I sympathise, I really do, but do not forget why we are really here. We cannot allow ourselves to become distracted from our ultimate goal. We must find Montagu and Mordred before they find that cup."

Arthur pushed the hands off petulantly. "Dammit, Merlin, it has been so many years, so many roads, so many false alarms. Has it occurred to you that he may actually have died when Galahad cut him and he fell into the lake? A century and a half is a damned long time to go about undetected."

"Yet we have managed it, have we not, Arthur?"

The King pushed past Merlin, angry at the magician's indifferent reaction to his complaints. What made him even angrier was that he knew Merlin was correct. For a long time he had felt like he was under hostile scrutiny but despite his constant warnings to Merlin, just as tonight, the grizzled old wizard had refused to send out even a weak spell, in case it was a trap, designed to make the two of them break their cover.

His booted feet scuffed the ground and he wrapped his ever-present cloak closer to him. Despite the itchy rough fabric, it had been a positive boon to the King. It had kept him warm on the long, seemingly interminable winter nights spent huddled in caves or deserted out-buildings but also protected him from the austere rays of the sun that, due to the longevity potion, would have meant pain beyond enduring.

An urgent rustling in the bushes by the side of the track jerked him into the present day and he stood as still as a statue, waiting to see if anything emerged.

As he eyed the bushes intently, he became aware of flickering splashes of colour playing over the foliage. He found his gaze dragged upwards to the sky above where a landscape-spanning spectrum glimmered and twinkled over the land. Without taking his eyes off the panorama overhead, he breathed in awed wonder, "A small spell would have sufficed, Merlin."

He heard footsteps coming closer. The magician's voice was no less awestruck than his own. "This is not my doing, Arthur."

For the first time since the display had begun, Arthur's eyes left the sky and rested on his companion. "Then what is it?"

"I have heard of this. It is called the Northern Lights. I never imagined, well, it is the most fantastic thing I have ever seen." Merlin breathed.

They stood for what seemed like ages, lost in the coruscations above, oblivious to the biting cold, oblivious to the sleet that began sweeping across the bleak countryside, oblivious to everything but the blazing tints and shades that decorated the darkness.

As the lights began to dissipate, they became aware of one colour more than any other, lighting up the sky to the northwest. A fluttering orange glow grew stronger in brightness and the two footsore travellers felt the ground beginning to vibrate underneath them.

Suddenly, over the hillside, they came. A mob of villagers brandishing torches and pitchforks descended towards them but because their senses were still so captivated by the Northern Lights, they failed to react until the crowd was nearly upon them.

The spell now broken, they blinked furiously in the guttering flamelight as they stood in the middle of a circle of fearsome looking men, all with murder blazing in their eyes.

Merlin drew himself up to his full impressive height and cast a baleful stare over the throng. To a man, they all shrank back from it, though they did not retreat.

Arthur stepped forward. "May we pass?" he asked warily.

One of the men detached himself from his fellows and reluctantly faced them. "N-No you may not." He quavered. "What is your business here?"

Despite the seriousness of the situation, Arthur and Merlin cast an amused glance at each other.

"What business is it of yours? This is the King's highway. As far as I was aware, my companion and I have as much right as any man here to walk it." Arthur hissed angrily.

The man, who had lowered his weapon, raised it once more and thrust the tines at Arthur. "I am Wilfred Baker, the village elder of our little hamlet and I'll not see it destroyed. We have lost so much already." He spat.

Arthur and Merlin exchanged bemused looks. "I am sorry, Mr Baker, but I feel as if I have fallen asleep and missed half of this conversation," the King said. "What in God's name makes you think that we mean harm to either your good self or your village?"

"When the rainbow appears in the night, they will come"
"The doom of your village is nigh"
"When the flames light the sky in the dark, they will come"
"The doom of your village is nigh"
"Two there will be, from the south they will roam"
"The doom of your village is nigh"
"One weaver of magic, one king with no throne"
"The doom of your village is nigh"

The entire mob chorused the mantra in a sinister monotone. Merlin leant in and whispered in Arthur's ear. "This is too much of a convenient coincidence. We must have been close to Montagu's trail, unless he is prepared to go to every village throughout the land and light up the sky for miles around. He must have sensed us following him."

Arthur nodded grimly, "If he knew we were so near in our pursuit, why did he not attack us?" The King shouted above the chanting which was growing louder as the mood turned uglier.

Merlin shrugged and shook his head then spread his hands wide and forced a smile onto his face. "Come now, what nonsense is this? A king with no throne? A weaver of magic? Where on earth did you hear such an uninspiring piece of doggerel?"

Wilfred Baker hissed, "From the mouth of an angel, sent to our poor village to turn back the tide of death and sadness that has visited us all."

The two travellers remained unmoved as the mob closed in all around them.

"An angel that visited us last twilight. An angel that descended from Heaven and brought us succour." For a moment, Baker hung his head, forced to remember a memory that he would rather have forgotten, "An angel that saved my life but was moments too late for my daughter and my grandson. They were struck down, as were so many others, by your..." At the last, Baker's voice cracked and he turned away from the two of them, breathing deeply and willing himself to calm down. When he turned back, he had the look of a man who had been to both heaven and hell in the space of a few short hours. With tears in his eyes, he advanced on Merlin and Arthur, pitchfork upraised. "The angel warned us of you. You are a curse, a hex, a pox upon this land. Wherever you walk, plague and misery lay the way for you."

The two travellers looked at each other, nonplussed.

"What gibberish is this?" the wizard began.

Baker stopped Merlin short. "The angel said that we were to send word to Achvaich, a village twenty miles or so to the south."

Merlin and Arthur shifted uncomfortably, waiting for what was to come. They had passed through Achvaich in the early hours of the evening on the previous day.

"The angel told us to ask after Godwin Williamson, the landlord of the Plough Inn."

The two captors nodded slowly, their lips dry as they remembered the simple but pleasant meal of cheese and bread they had enjoyed there the night before.

"The poor man is dead now, thanks to you two demons. He was struck down by your pestilence. First boils, then a fever, then vomiting until he bled, then merciful death. His wife said that he was crying out to die in the end, he was in so much pain. When she had wept out her loss, she also related other stories that she had heard from patrons of her establishment. The same sort of deaths, isolated to be certain, but exactly the same symptoms. There was a farmer in Kincardine, another innkeeper in Edderton, a whole family struck down in Ballchraggan."

As he continued with his litany, Merlin and Arthur's eyes widened in disbelief. The village elder may as well have been reading from an itinerary of their passage through the North. It was now obvious to them that they had been closer to finding Montagu than they had ever imagined. The black magician had been following them and slaying anyone who had extended them aid on their quest, even a gesture as little as giving them a bed for the night. For some reason though, he had not attacked them directly, a fact that Arthur at least was eternally grateful for.

As it was plain that Montagu was aware of their pursuit, Merlin dropped any objections he had to using his powers. He threw back his cloak and extended a hand, voice even and measured but positively dripping with menace.

135

"Enough!" he bellowed, "Enough of this charade." With a sweep of his arm, the front line of villagers fell like wheat harvested by a scythe.

Baker stumbled back to his feet and stared at Merlin haughtily then slowly, beckoning his fellows to follow him, he made his way to the verge at the side of the track.

"We may not be able to stop you passing on the road but we will fight to the death before we let you set foot in our village. Begone from us, magician. You are not welcome here nor will you ever be." Baker's proud demeanour slithered off his face as Merlin advanced towards him. His eyes rolled upwards as Merlin slapped a hand upon his forehead.

Arthur withdrew Excalibur from under his cloak and circled around Merlin, flicking it out whenever anyone edged forwards, holding off the villagers, praying that their fear of Merlin would outweigh their yearning to protect their leader.

The court magician of Camelot felt the power surge up his arm, building, building, until it broke through the barriers and entered the old man's memory, probing, searching, rummaging through the recent hours of the elder's life. It did not take long for the sneering face of Montagu to rear into view. There he was, never to the fore, but always in the background, murmuring, cajoling, insinuating himself into the old man's favour, filling his head with visions of the supposed victims of Merlin and Arthur's pestilence as they writhed in the final throes of death, then joining Baker as he sat vigil, unblinkingly watching his daughter and her son slip away from him, all the while continuing with his relentless mantra of scaremongering and doomsaying. Merlin saw that the elder's loved ones were about to pass on and broke the connection. There were some things that deserved to remain private.

As Baker peered up, awestruck and tearful, the wizard whispered in Arthur's ear. "We will find no comfort here, Arthur. Montagu has planted the seed of suspicion far too deep for me to unearth. We will be forced to fight every man here if we do not move on."

King Arthur ceased his swordplay for a moment to gain confirmation of what Merlin was saying. "There is no hope of persuading them otherwise?" he asked, surprised at the undeniable note of pleading in his voice.

Merlin shook his head.

Arthur shrugged helplessly then turned back to Wilfred Baker. "At least let us leave with no further harassment."

Baker held his counsel for a moment, staring from face to face of the villagers that looked to him for leadership. Then he turned back and before he had said anything, Merlin tensed and Arthur dropped into his battle stance.

"No, we cannot," snarled the old man. "Get them."

Excalibur snaked out instantaneously and opened a thin wound on the elder's forearm. Baker's snarl turned into a yelp of pain as he drew back out of Arthur's range.

After the initial shock of the injury to their leader, the people of Bakerstown advanced in unison and in seconds the two weary travellers could see they were hopelessly outnumbered.

"For Gods sake Merlin, use your magic or we are lost." Arthur gasped as the two of them beat a hasty retreat.

The magician risked a look back over his shoulder before turning a sharp glance towards his King. "I will not raise my hand to these people, Arthur. They are victims of Montagu's misinformation and malignance. I will not see them suffer further."

Arthur thought that Merlin could have picked a more suitable time to show his nobility but held his counsel. "Well, damn it all, fly us out of here then. They already know who we are. A demonstration of the full extent of your powers would not go amiss, Merlin. Merlin?" Arthur cast a nervous glance at their pursuers for the magician had halted in his tracks. "Merlin?" he hissed urgently.

"No, this is not right." The wizard murmured. "Not right at all."

Without preparing Arthur for their ascent, he grabbed the King's arm and they took to the air, much to the chagrin of their hunters. A few pitchforks were thrown in their direction but Merlin absently deflected them aside with the merest flick of his arm, still muttering under his breath.

Arthur closed his eyes and tried to believe that the ground was within touching distance when, in actual fact, it was many feet below. This was only the second time that he had joined Merlin in flight and he found the experience as acutely distressing as he had the first time. Risking a glance downwards, he saw, with rising panic, that they seemed to be flying straight over the upturned faces of the mob.

Merlin was taking them into the village of their assailants.

Mere minutes later, they alighted gently on the ground in the middle of a rustic square. A few scattered huts were dotted liberally around intermingling with, amongst other things, a tannery, stables and a shabby looking inn that proclaimed itself to be The Wheatsheaf.

It seemed that all the villagers had been in pursuit of the two of them, for the plaza was deserted. The night itself seemed unnaturally still and Arthur found himself looking at Merlin expectantly.

Then, on the cusp of hearing, a mournful whisper of pain, so slight that Arthur and Merlin were not sure that they had heard it.

Angling off towards the inn, the wail came again, louder this time, loud enough for the wizard and the King to establish its origin. Tentatively advancing, the two of them peered around the edge of a half-opened door in one of the stables to the right of the tavern.

Their eyes fell on a woman, no more than twenty years old, cradling a bundle of rags in her arms. There was no need for closer scrutiny of her burden as her agonised whimpers were eloquent enough.

As the pair moved quietly into the warm stable, the woman ceased her sobbing and stared at them both with eyes that suggested she had seen far more than she should have for one of such a tender age. She hugged the bundle closer to her and stared wildly from side to side, obviously seeking a means of escape.

Arthur stepped forward cautiously, anxious not to scare the poor waif. "Please, lady, we mean you no harm." He said in a sing-song voice.

Still she remained silent as she scrambled to her feet, nearly dropping the babe that she clasped to her breast.

Arthur looked at Merlin, who had strode back to the stable door and was peering out into the murky night, searching for signs that the villagers were returning, but the wizard merely shrugged.

"Can you help my son, he's very sick." A timid voice jerked Arthur's head round and the King found himself staring into a pair of doe-like hazel eyes, rapidly filling with tears.

Despite himself, Arthur reached out and gently brushed away a tear that had escaped down the girl's cheek, "Merlin," he hissed tersely.

The magician took one last glance out of the doors then came into the warm musty gloom of the stable. Without saying a word, he took the child from the young woman and retired to another corner of the barn.

The girl stood, gently swaying, next to Arthur, who was at a loss as to what to do. The child was unnaturally still and silent and he had no doubt that the unfortunate infant was dead. She had obviously known something was wrong with her child, judging by the state she had been in when they had first happened upon her, but when Merlin confirmed the baby's condition, what would the poor woman do?

He stared at her out of the corner of his eye. She had ceased her movement and was now plainly wrestling with herself, wanting to go over to Merlin's side and be with her child but scared to death of what she would see.

Arthur's eyes were scanning Merlin's back, hunting for any indication of the baby's health.

He was also aware that he was selfishly worrying about the villagers, who would be returning to their homes very soon. Would this poor woman's anguish betray them to the blood-lustful mob that was surely only moments away?

Arthur watched numbly as she left his side and walked over to the magician. He then scrunched his eyes up and bolted for the door as a piercing squeal ripped through the night.

Luckily the square was still deserted. Arthur breathed a sigh of relief and then immediately chided himself for such a self-interested reaction when the woman they had just met was going through such pain and misery. He went to move to her to comfort her when another cry broke through the supercharged air. To the King's disbelief, it was the baby. Merlin had worked a miracle.

The woman gaped in incredulity, firstly at her newly revived child, then at the tall silent magician as he rose to his feet.

With a whoop of delight, she threw her arms around him, burying her head on his shoulder.

At first, Merlin was taken aback by the raw emotion of the gesture but he regained his composure and embraced the trembling figure back, the faintest hint of a satisfied smile playing on his lips.

Arthur's eyes were drawn to a vivid gash on Merlin's arm which, upon noticing the King's scrutiny, he swiftly covered up with the sleeve of his robe.

By this time, the woman had released Merlin from her grip and was cooing over the baby. She picked him up, swirling recklessly around the room with the bairn held at arm's length above her head. Eventually she ceased her joyous dance and placed the baby over her shoulder, whispering words of love into his ear and gently caressing his back and head.

Arthur made his way over to her and placed his hand on the woman's unoccupied shoulder. "I am so pleased for you," he said and took a moment to stare at the baby's cherubic face. Leaning in closer, he noticed a couple of red spots on the infant's cheek. "What the..." he murmured, brushing them away. He noted, with distress, that it seemed to be blood staining his fingertip. He cast a scathing look at Merlin, who merely raised an eyebrow in response. "What did you do?" he whispered urgently, dragging the wizard out of the woman's earshot. "How did you rejuvenate him?"

The way Merlin's hand flew to the area of the cut on his arm was answer enough.

Arthur gripped Merlin's arm in exactly the same place as the wound and twisted it viciously. "You fed him your blood?" he spat.

Merlin's eyes blazed but he resisted the urge to lash out at his King. "It worked, did it not, sire." He drawled. "We both have the stuff of immortality flowing through us. I thought the risk of expending a few drops of my blood was worth the price of a baby's life or was I wrong? Should I have let him die, Arthur, because he surely would have had I not intervened? If you had the wherewithal at your disposal to spare him but did not use it, would you be able to live with yourself because I could not."

Arthur's gaze fell on the baby once again but was wrenched back when Merlin resumed talking.

"His blood was rotten with the residue of Montagu's witchery. I could not kneel there and watch him slip away from me."

Arthur heaved a huge sigh and relinquished his grasp of Merlin's arm. "Enough." He shook his head and went over to the woman, who was now murmuring a lullaby into her son's ear. "Tell me, what is his name?" the King asked. Whether it was the woman's reply or the first cries of the returning mob that froze Arthur's blood cold he was not sure, but before he could respond to her answer, Merlin cast an invisibility spell upon the four of them, masking them from the impending violence that would surely follow if they were discovered. Unable to voice his thoughts for fear of giving away their location, Arthur found himself staring intently at the babe-in-arms. Surely this is more than coincidence, he thought as he gazed warily upon the now slumbering form of little Montagu.

Wilfrid Baker stalked into the village square as if an inferno of emotion was blazing through his mind. The villagers watched nervously, holding back from him in case the volcanic wrath that so obviously raged within him erupted. They knew that his failure to defend the hamlet from the plague-carrying monsters would prey upon his mind and though he was quite a frail man, his temper was renowned as being vindictive and spiteful.

The angel had been quite explicit about what would occur if the two travellers gained entrance to the community. He had said that those hitherto untouched by the plague would be dead within hours.

Baker stopped in front of the throng that had followed him and raised his hands. He waited momentarily for the people at the back to join up with the rest of their fellows then began to address them.

"Friends, we all know what the angel said and we can all imagine those two fiends even now spreading their pestilence through our homes." He stared around the frightened faces before him. "If the monstrosities that he warned us about gained ingress into our midst, he said we would not last the night. Unfortunately that is what has come to pass. They are here somewhere upon our land. For us there is no going back." He hung his head as his voice began to crack but when he raised it again, his eyes shone with an obscene ardour. "So I say we must fire the village and burn the demons in the flames of hell. Save whom and what we can and then burn this place to the ground. Let the flames be the light that will show us the way to salvation."

A burly farmer muscled his way to the front of the crowd and thrust his pitchfork at the elder. "Are you out of your bloody mind, Baker? What are you saying?"

"He is doing my bidding." An ominous voice echoed across the rooftops.

As one, the heads of the crowd rose upwards as if dragged by invisible strings. Montagu descended serenely into the centre of the unsettled crowd and strode up to the villager who raised an objection. With a contemptuous flick of his wrist, he snaked out a thin-fingered hand in a slashing motion. With that he turned back to Wilfrid Baker and shook his head as, behind him, the farmer collapsed to the floor in one movement, his head falling free of his neck in a gush of blood and rolling to a halt a couple of inches from the magician's ankle.

Suddenly mayhem reigned. The mob began to run left and right, determined to put as much distance between themselves and Montagu as they could. They ran from the unchecked power emanating from the magician, they ran from the horror of what had happened to their friend, but most of all, they ran to save themselves.

Montagu's stare remained fixed on the old man who cowered under the scrutiny. "One thing, one damn thing I ask you to do and still I find you wanting. Honestly, Mordred, you really are the most obscene waste of breath upon this earth." Again, the slim hand extended swiftly but instead of the head parting company with the body, the whole shell of the village elder split and Mordred emerged, bloody and filthy, like a newborn lizard hatching from its mother's egg.

A brief flicker of defiance broke the surface of Mordred's obeisance. "They are here, are they not?" he muttered sullenly. "I was brave enough to let Merlin touch me and read the false memories that you implanted in my head, was I not? Where were you?"

Montagu nodded slightly as he regarded his besmirched vassal. "Yes, that is true, I suppose." He turned and stared from building to building. "I sense that they have also found the baby and its harlot mother." He stared about the chaos that reigned in the square. "Even now they are cowering in one of the stables over there, huddling under an invisibility spell."

"Which one?" Mordred asked, casting a fearful eye over the numerous outbuildings that surrounded the square.

Montagu cast a thunderous fireball at the thatch of Merlin and Arthur's hideout. "The one that is on fire," he answered.

Merlin's head jerked up. "We must flee."

141

"Why?" Arthur asked just as a concussion hit the roof of the wooden building. There was no need for Merlin to answer the question because smoke began to billow around them and the musty darkness began to glow orange. The wizard went carefully but quickly to the half-open door and chanced a glance outside. He turned back to them with a look of alarm on his face. "I think we have located Montagu."

Arthur shielded the babe and his mother as a beam crashed to the floor next to them. "He is outside? This is his doing?" the King swatted ineffectually at a large ember that was gently wending its way down to the hay-strewn floor.

A shriek from behind stopped their conversation dead in its tracks. The woman was batting at the back of her head with one hand, while the baby wriggled precariously in the other. Wisps of smoke were floating up to the ceiling from her hair and she was whimpering with pain.

In a couple of bounds, Arthur was there. He took the baby from her and engulfed her in an all-enveloping hug which smothered the fires that were singeing her.

By now the baby was screaming in distress, having been woken up by the chaos that had erupted all around because of Montagu's attack.

The four of them retired to the farthest corner of the stable and scanned the building for a way out. Merlin gathered himself and drew back his arms in preparation for casting a spell to splinter a hole in the side of the barn when a section of the roof fell in, burying him in a maelstrom of blazing wood.

"Merlin!" Arthur screamed.

The woman had taken her baby back but was nonetheless wrenching at the debris that had collapsed on top of the mage. "We must rescue him. He saved my son," she moaned.

In an instant, Arthur pulled her clear of the flames. "Please, lady, keep you and your baby safe and I will free him." He began dragging at the mountain of wood, throwing the beams clear like a man possessed.

He spotted Merlin's leg, unmoving and rigid. "I have him." He yelled and set about the mass of lumber with a renewed vigour. He found the wizard lying dazed under the rubble with a raw gash slashing across his forehead. Arthur leant in and was relieved to feel a ragged breath soughing through his close cropped beard.

"Is he alive?" the woman whispered urgently.

Arthur nodded abruptly and continued unearthing Merlin from the floor. "Yes, he is, but ..." He stopped short and gaped at the door.

The woman turned and saw a figure silhouetted in the doorway. She flew to her feet and let out a shriek. To Arthur's astonishment, she ran over to the figure and threw an arm around him. "Look, look, our baby, our baby." She

142

capered joyously, oblivious to the heat and flame that licked and flourished around her.

The figure wrapped her and the baby in his cloak and began to propel them towards the door. "Come," he commanded.

"But..." she unwrapped herself from him and gestured towards Merlin and Arthur, the latter returning to the onerous task of unearthing the magician from the floor, with the occasional glance at the two shadows in the rectangle of light afforded by the open doorway.

Unseen by the woman, her companion flicked out a hand towards the roof and a cascade of wood and thatch crashed in between them, violently ripping them from each other's line of sight.

There was no time for Arthur to think, he began kicking, punching, raging at the boards nailed across the back end of the barn, snarling incoherently, spittle dribbling through his beard, desperately trying to forge an escape route with his bare hands. His gauntlets and boots raised splinters and cracks but not much else. Unconsciously, his hand strayed to the shaft of Excalibur and he drew it out in one fluid movement. In one brutal hack, he cleaved a three-foot long split across the pitted planks. Again and again, he swung at the wall of timber and in a matter of seconds he had hewn a jagged gash in the wooden barrier that stood between life and death.

With an enormous effort of will, he extricated Merlin from the debris and dragged him bodily through the narrow opening to the relative safety of the open air. After checking the wizard's condition, he flopped to the floor and stared up at the sky, breathing in great lungfuls of the acrid air as if it was the very scent of heaven.

After feeling some semblance of fitness return, Arthur sat up and scanned the immediate area. It did not take him long to realise that he and Merlin were stranded. They were out in the open with nowhere to hide. They could not move far as the magician appeared to have been knocked insensible by the falling rafters. They were safe at the current moment, having moved out of the shadow of the blazing stable, but the King knew it would not be long before they were discovered by the fleeing villagers and if they were, he was painfully aware that he would have to fight them alone.

Sure enough, he had just begun struggling to move Merlin to a more concealed location when shouts erupted in unison from his left and right. Cursing quietly, he let the dead weight of Merlin slide from his grasp and straightened up. Slowly and deliberately, he slid Excalibur from its leather haven and brandished it at the sky.

He could see the hatred in the villagers' eyes and knew that he would be unable to reason with them.

The crowd moved towards him, closing in on both sides.

143

"They are the ones," he heard someone bellow.

"It is as the angel prophesied." Another yelled. "They came into our midst and now look at us. Wilfrid is dead and so will we be unless we appease the angel's wrath and kill these demons."

Arthur hawked and spat on the floor. He hefted Excalibur, swinging it lazily from left to right in a horizontal figure of eight, ready for the first foolhardy one to stray within its murderous arc. "I warn you," he hissed, pitching his voice just loud enough for the front row of the throng to hear. "We are no demons. But, by god, I will kill each and every one of you if you take one step closer to my companion and I. This 'angel' that you speak of is the demon in your midst. He is a magician of the blackest arts. He is the one who has unleashed this plague that has blighted your village. He has you under his thrall, mesmerising you with his weasel words and evil deeds."

Even though several of the villagers looked sceptical, they all heeded the threat and not one of them advanced any further.

Arthur's eyes scanned the crowd for a sign of whether his words had had any effect, but almost immediately he felt as if he was staring at a hundred Montagus and he licked his lips nervously, tensing for the first man to attempt the initial assault that he felt sure was to come.

Whether it was the loss of eye contact that triggered the first attack, Arthur could not be certain, but it came just after Merlin groaned feebly, causing Arthur to turn round at the sound. His immediate instinct was to drop to his companion's side and tend to him but fortunately his warrior sense kicked in within a split second.

He felt the movement behind him and instantly swivelled round, thrusting upwards awkwardly. His assailant, not anticipating the move, gaped at the blade that had skewered him through his stomach. With a sigh, he fell from the sword as the King withdrew it from his gut.

Arthur straightened, the initial guilty frisson that always accompanied a killing being tempered by the realisation that he had dispatched one of the innocent townspeople. "I warned you. I warned you all." He tried to snarl, but a telltale quiver in his voice betrayed his true feelings. He had just killed someone, albeit in self defence, but his memory kept returning to Merlin's words as they had run from the villagers for the first time. These people were the victims of Montagu's malign influence, yet how was he able to protect himself without hurting them.

"Please, I beg you," he heard himself beseeching, "we are not evil. Moments ago I saw him save the life of a newborn babe in the barn over there." He gestured towards Merlin, still prostrate on the dusty ground.

"Lies," screeched a scrawny man, who detached himself from the crowd and began walking around Arthur, eyes constantly flickering between the King's face and his bloodied sword. "Newborn babe?" he scoffed. "Where is this magical infant? Perhaps it is inside the inferno attempting to put out the flames with its dribble?"

"There was a lady, a lady of no more than twenty. Brown hair, brown eyes. She was cradling the child in her arms when we sought refuge in the barn." The skinny man turned to the crowd then back to the ever-watchful King, waving his arms through the air as if conducting an orchestra. "What, pray tell, was her name?" he sneered.

Arthur stood agape for a moment before he mumbled, "She did not tell us her name."

The obnoxious man nodded knowingly as if he had scored some sort of victory over Arthur. "Yet she entrusted the two of you with the welfare of her baby even though she had never met you before."

Arthur could only nod back. Even he could see that his version of events sounded unlikely.

"Lies!" the man snarled.

Then, as if the sun had appeared from behind a cloud, Arthur's memory stirred and he blurted out the only thing he could think of that might help verify his story. "She said the boy's name was Montagu."

Any noise that was susurrating through the crowd immediately ceased.

"What?" The thin man's voice was so full of venom and bile that Arthur nearly took a step back.

"The woman..." he stuttered, unable to understand what had triggered the sudden upsurge in hostility, "...she said the boy's name was Mont..."

"Montagu was the name of Wilfred Baker's grandson. He was killed by the..." he hesitated then shook his head, "no, let me get it right, he was killed by *your* plague. Along with his daughter. His nineteen year-old daughter."

Arthur shook his head. "No, no, we saw..."

"Enough of these filthy lies," The man's arm slashed downwards through the air. "Let's kill these bastards," he yelled.

As the King's eyes widened, he saw the skinny man's eyes change and he knew for a certainty that it was Montagu staring back at him. The man winked and a tidal wave of rage broke inside the King. He threw himself towards the man who had begun retreating through the press of villagers. A pitchfork skidded across his ribs and he fell back, gasping painfully, the injury disseminating the red mist in an instant. He tripped over Merlin and lost his hold on Excalibur.

The crowd saw him lose his only means of defence and advanced upon him with murder in their eyes and hearts.

Out of the sight of the howling mob, the man transformed back into Montagu and the magician turned to someone standing in the lee of one of the few

145

buildings as yet unravaged by the fire, which had now taken hold of the square and was raging unchecked.

"See, Mordred, that is how you manipulate a crowd into doing your bidding. Now let us leave this forsaken place." They began to make their way over to a covered cart that was large enough to sleep four people in its rear. A gurgle escaped from the cover and Montagu's face twisted into a smile. He reached inside and picked up the baby, who cooed and babbled at his father. "Shh, my son, we will soon be gone from here and you will see your new home. Now, sleep, for we have a long journey ahead of us." He passed his hands over the child's face and the infant was instantly at peace.

As they left the village, Mordred reined in the horses and Montagu retired to the back of the wagon and emerged with the woman whom Arthur and Merlin had found so frightened and scared in the stable. He dragged her by her hair, kicking and screaming into one of the huts situated to the left hand side of the road.

He re-appeared several minutes later, relieved of his burden.

King Arthur kicked, bit and punched as the crowd rained blows of their own upon him. His chain mail was able to repel most of the thrusts from the villager's arsenal but he was already beginning to tire and he knew he could not keep up his resistance for much longer.

Then, with a heart-stopping suddenness, the nearest attacker froze and fell silently to the floor, closely followed by all the others who had fallen upon the King.

He felt a hand on his shoulder and a flood of relief washed over him as Merlin's voice came to his ears.

"How did we end up here, Arthur?" he asked.

With a booming laugh, Arthur threw his arms around the wizard and tears of joy came to his eyes. "By God, you like to leave it late, do you not? If you had not woken when you did, then I suspect you would not have woken at all." In front of what remained of the wide-eyed crowd who had all ceased their attacks when Merlin had begun to unleash his magic and were now standing frozen to the spot with fear, the King cheerfully related the story of the rescue from the blazing stable, however, he could not stop his face clouding momentarily as he recounted how the woman had run into the arms of the enigmatic figure who had appeared in the doorway. The figure that he now felt sure was Montagu.

A look of pain passed over Merlin's momentarily grey face and he swayed where he stood, using Arthur for support. When the dizziness had passed, he snarled at the remaining villagers who had not been affected by his spell.

146

"Begone!" he hissed, "or feel my power as you die. You have survived it once, do not presume that you will be as lucky a second time."

The threat was enough for them to disperse, running back to the chaos in the main square, some pausing to contemplate the destruction of all they held dear, others continuing past the village and out into the surrounding fields, determined to put as much distance between themselves and the pair of strangers as they could.

Arthur darted forward and grabbed Merlin's arm to steady him as his stance wavered slightly once more. The wizard blinked and knuckled at his eyes then transferred his hand to the back of his head, wincing as he explored the numerous lumps and bumps that decorated his skull. "Are you alright, my friend?" he asked concernedly.

Merlin nodded then immediately regretted it. "It will pass," he waved away the King's ministrations. "Please, Arthur, do not fuss so."

The King withdrew his hands with an exasperated look, "So what now?"

"Did you see which way that whoreson went?" he asked. "There is nothing for us here. We have to leave so we might as well keep the scum in sight if we can."

The former monarch shook his head. "No, he set the village folk upon me and retreated back into the square. From there," he shrugged, "well, he could have gone any number of ways."

"The square it is then." Merlin propelled the King back towards the place where they had first arrived in the village. Despite the obvious discomfort and dizziness that beset him as he bent towards the ground, Merlin peered intently at the dust, searching for the tell-tale sign of Montagu's passing. "There." He pointed excitedly.

Sure enough, the only set of regular footprints that led away from the square joined with another pair, which in turn went in the direction of two wavy lines that led to the main gate of the village.

Arthur raised an eyebrow, "A wagon? Why use a wagon? Why not fly?"

Merlin pondered the question as they walked between the two furrows leading away from the devastation that had been wrought upon the unfortunate community of Bakerstown. "Perhaps he was overburdened with what he was taking with him? Or maybe he had too many companions with him who could not fly." Merlin nodded meaningfully.

Arthur indicated his agreement, "Aye, the babe, the mother." He nudged Merlin gently in the ribs. "He is obviously not as powerful a mage as he purports." Arthur continued walking towards the gate for a few more paces until he realised that his travelling companion had stopped. He turned to see Merlin gazing pensively at the ground. He walked back to the wizard. "What is it?" he asked, trying to guess what the magician found so fascinating on the gritty path.

Then he saw the footprints leading to and from one of the crudely built huts to the left of the gate. Feeling an almost overwhelming urge to follow them, he began tracing their path but Merlin extended a surprisingly strong arm and stopped him. "It may be a trap. Let me go first." With that, the magician stalked towards the hovel, eyes closed and arms extended, sending forth every sense available to him in an effort to ascertain an ambush of magical origin. Just as he was about to cross the threshold into the house, he turned to Arthur and shrugged, "I detect nothing," he whispered and pushed open the door which, rather disconcertingly, was already open. "I..." Merlin began to say, but the sentence was never finished as he beheld the sight in front of him. Arthur pushed past him only to stop dead in his tracks as well. "Dear God," he breathed.

The young woman they had rescued was lying in the middle of the room, drenched in blood, sweat and vomit, sightless eyes gazing at the ceiling, arms and legs arranged in such a way as to call to mind a star or, given that Arthur and Merlin knew whom the perpetrator of the murder was, a pentagram. Indeed, as they plucked up the courage to move further into the room, they saw that tattoos had been daubed on her forehead, hands and feet. Although crude in design, there was no mistaking the jagged shapes of the mark of Satan.

The only aspect of the gory scene that could be taken in any way optimistically was the fact that the unfortunate woman's son was nowhere to be seen.

Arthur fought against the nauseous feeling that was climbing inexorably up his body. "That poor girl," he breathed, aware of how inadequate the words sounded weighed against the enormity of the horror before them. "Do you think he has taken the child with him?" he managed to say before retching.

Merlin nodded grimly and turned to the King. Arthur took a step back, such was the intensity of loathing in the wizard's eyes. "It is his progeny, the continuation of his line." He sighed hugely and looked to the ceiling. "I fear he has made me look a fool once more."

Arthur spun Merlin round, ostensibly to talk to him, but more to shield the scene from his eyes. "What do you mean?"

"He tricked me, duped me like I was born yesterday."

"Merlin," the King gripped his shoulders. "I do not understand."

"Now he has an heir."

Arthur still shook his head. "But he will long outlive him anyway. What is the use of having an heir if he is going to live for four hundred more years?"

"In four hundred years, think how many bastards he can father? How many children could he spawn? All growing into adulthood, all coming after us or aiding their dear father in his search? He has it in his power to give them riches even beyond your wildest dreams. What is there to stop him?"

"There is us." Arthur gripped the handle of Excalibur and stared intently at the young woman who had been robbed of her life so savagely. "I will take him before the judgement of heaven and make him realise he is as nothing in front of God."

Merlin rolled his eyes. "All very noble, sire, but the fact is at the moment he is foiling us at every turn. For God's sake, Arthur, he just deceived me into saving his son's life. He was obviously unable to do it himself, so he contrived to make me do it." Merlin shook his head. "Perhaps he has the best of me." He mumbled, casting a despondent glance at the woman whose face had been so full of joy barely an hour ago.

Arthur placed his hand on the spellweaver's shoulder and gently but firmly removed him from the room back out onto the path. "Do you think he still has Mordred with him?" the former King asked, more to try to lift Merlin's mind from its melancholia than out of any real interest in the answer.

The magician merely shook his head and continued walking out of the village without looking back. The King watched him go helplessly. He had never seen the arch-mage so disconsolate. He glanced back over his shoulder, knowing what he should do, but also acutely aware that he had no time to do it.

Spinning around for some way to solve his problem, his eyes alighted on a pair of villagers cowering just inside one of the houses opposite. He bounded across the intervening space and hammered on the door, "You in there. Come out else I shall tear the door from its hinges." He bellowed.

Whispered voices emanated through the window, until a clearly reluctant man opened the door gingerly. "Y-yes?" he quavered.

"That house over there. There is a woman inside it. She has been murdered by your so-called angel." He sneered.

"The Bakers?" the man gasped.

"I have no idea." Arthur shrugged, then withdrew Excalibur slowly and deliberately, bringing it round in a slow arc until its tip was pointing directly at the house where the murder had taken place. "It is that one. You will ensure that she receives a proper Christian burial. Is that understood?"

The man nodded fearfully, though his expression made it clear that, whatever Arthur said, he did not believe it was the angel who had committed the crime.

The King brought Excalibur round to rest scant inches from the man's stomach. "Be clear on this. I will return to this place. It may not be for months, it may not be for years, hell, it may not even be for decades, but I will return and upon my return, if I find that you have not performed this one act, I will hunt you and your kin down and have my vengeance. Is that clear?"

The man's mouth opened and closed but no sounds would come out. He merely nodded his head.

"Good." Arthur cast a final glance at the house. He nodded again, "That is good."

With that, he walked out of Bakerstown, praying that his threat had been powerful enough to make the man and his family honour his wishes and nullify the effect of any satanic ritual that Montagu had performed upon the woman. She had only had a short life and she did not deserve to spend her afterlife in Hell because of whatever foul practices Montagu had perpetrated with her body.

He began to hurry after Merlin, whom he could just make out scaling a hill that lay just outside the village. As he slowly made up the ground between them, he found himself pondering the fact that he and Merlin had walked the earth longer than any other mortal men. How many more needless deaths would occur as a direct result of their pursuit of Montagu? The black magician had already amply demonstrated that he had no qualms about slaughtering any who offered the pair of them any sort of assistance, be it food or shelter. They had walked the island for over a century and a half, yet were no nearer their goal, no nearer their twin goals, in fact. They had still not located the Grail and they had still not stopped Montagu in his quest for the Judas Cup.

How much longer would they have to remain alone together?

Arthur crested the hill and stared across the landscape before him. It seemed to stretch away like the remaining three and a half centuries of his life, bleak and with no visible end in sight. With a shake of his head, he began to jog down the slope towards his companion, feeling as depressed as Merlin had been when discussing the ease with which Montagu had outwitted them. He hoped that he could find the words to convince Merlin, whilst being unsure that he could find the words to convince himself.

Chapter 11

A.D 794 – Beal (Northumbrian Coast)

Arthur Pendragon, displaced King of the Britons, pulled his cloak closer about his shoulders and gazed across the granite-grey sea, his eyes following the undulating white tips of the breakers as they gained the beach and retreated back out into the ocean.

He slumped down on a rock and knuckled at his eyes. He felt like he had not slept in weeks, his body and spirit drained by the endless nomadic nature of his and Merlin's current life.

He glanced across at his older companion but, to his slight chagrin, he saw that the magician seemed to be faring a good deal better. Mind you, Arthur reflected with a hint of a grim smile playing on his lips, if he had the kind of magic at his disposal that his associate had, then he would certainly not be above using it to tweak his condition into being better than it actually was. He cleared his throat to attract the other's attention. "I am glad they did as I demanded," he said.

Merlin nodded. "Aye, it was a noble thought, sire. It is good to see that they carried out your instructions to the letter." For the first time in a while, the magician looked up and held Arthur's gaze. "Would you really have hunted down that man's family?"

Arthur raised his eyebrows, surprised at the question. "Of course not, I would have thought that you knew me well enough to know that I would not menace innocent people." He itched at his scruffy beard and peered out over the sea again, irritated at the intimation.

"What if they had not carried out your wishes?" Merlin persisted.

The King cast a stone angrily over the cliff and stood up. "The question is immaterial, is it not? The fact is that they buried her in the grounds of their church as I requested."

Merlin shrugged at his companion's irascible response. "They even resurrected the village," he said. "They obviously did not heed the angel's warning," he sniffed sarcastically.

The allusion to Montagu did not go unnoticed by the King and he found his thoughts dragged back once more to the bane of their existence. They had now sought him for nearly three centuries and were still chasing shadows. A vague sighting here, a possible clue there but never anything more solid than that.

"Merlin," he bit down his anger and pretended that the last conversation had not happened, "would our time not be better served by searching the lake for the Grail? If we had it in our possession, then the next time we run into the esteemed high bastard himself, we would stand a chance of at least incapacitating him."

Merlin sighed. "That is possible, yes, but I feel safer if I can keep him where I can see him. That way if he does locate the Judas Cup, I will be there to do my damnedest to stop him drinking from it."

"Easy to say when you are able to use magic to salve your aching feet and thirsty throat." The King murmured.

"Oh, grow up." Merlin snapped. "If I was doing that for myself I would do it for you also. You are of no use to me dead. As I keep telling you, I will only cast spells in the moments of our greatest need. Anything of a mystical nature that I undertake will shine like a beacon in the darkest cave to him and he will fall upon us with all his might and fury. Is that what you want, Arthur?"

The King shook his head. "No," he mumbled quietly, even now unused to being spoken to in such a disdainful manner.

"Exactly," the magician sneered. "The only reason that I appear more composed than you is that I see no point in complaining about that which cannot be changed."

King Arthur stared at the ground for a long, long time, ashamed at the implied criticism. "Perhaps it is time for us to dissolve our partnership then," he said.

Merlin shot up from his sitting position and nearly ran over to the King. "That is a mistake, Arthur. We are at our strongest if we are united. If we split up, then our ability to strike at Montagu is halved. You will be no match for him should he assail you with magic, just as I will be no use if he mounts a two-pronged attack against me. I can deal with his magic or I can deal with his foot-soldiers, but I cannot deal with both at once. You are the arrow in my bow and the sword in my scabbard."

The King removed himself from his cold, hard perch and inched his way forward to peer at the jagged ground that skirted the base of the cliff. "What would happen if I was to jump off here now? Would I die, I wonder?" he murmured, half to himself.

"Do not even think it, Arthur." Merlin warned.

"Look, my friend," Arthur began, "we have been chasing this blaggard for what seems like an eternity. Us always behind, him always ahead. I just think it is time that we try to steal a march on him. I am tired, Merlin. Tired of trailing in his wake, tired of not knowing where we will find ourselves from one day to the next." He knelt down on the brink of the precipice. "I am just tired of it all, Merlin."

"Arthur, turn that thought upon its head. What if he locates his prize before we locate ours?"

The King stood up and spun round, prodding a finger in Merlin's aquiline face. "What if, what if…Dammit, Merlin, what if I throw myself off this cliff right here, right now? What if that?"

The magician conjured a brittle smile. "Then I would suggest that the next two centuries will be rather uncomfortable for you."

Arthur's eyes narrowed. "You find this amusing? What if I were to cast my cloak off and let the sunlight burn me to ashes?"

The mage's mirthful expression turned sombre once more. "Could you really do that, Arthur? Condemn the world to a torment of never-ending darkness and evil just because you are having a bad time of it?"

The passion disappeared from the King's voice and he sighed deeply. When he spoke again, his utterance was that of a man resigned to whatever fate held for him. "And there's the rub. You and I both know I would not, could not, do that."

"Destiny is a harsh mistress, is she not?" Merlin stated pompously.

"Huh!" Arthur sniffed and transferred his gaze back to the cloud-smeared horizon. "Why are we in this god-forsaken corner of the kingdom, anyway?"

Merlin turned and waved a cowled arm seaward. "Lindisfarne Abbey lies barely one mile away across the sea. We are to visit the monks who bide there?"

Arthur's face screwed up in dismay but he held his counsel. "How are we to get there if it lies beyond the shore?"

"There is a causeway over yonder that allows entry to anyone who wishes to seek out the monks' wisdom." They began walking once more in the direction of the path to the abbey as Merlin continued, "The monks have many, many callers beating a path to their door. It is my hope that one of these pilgrims will have some information as to Montagu's whereabouts."

Arthur turned back to the leaden water and shook his head. Three hundred years passed and this was as far as they had progressed. Relying on hearsay and gossip from a group of religious hermits. As he was pondering this, his face became pensive and he extended a hand towards the waves, "Ships," he pointed.

Merlin grunted non-committally and continued to walk down the uneven stones that had been trodden by the passage of innumerable men down the cliffside on their journey to the monastery.

Arthur's hand dropped back to his sides and he fell into step behind Merlin, occasionally glancing back at the dark silhouettes on the horizon as the shapes resolved themselves into masts and sail.

They were mere yards across the causeway leading to the Abbey when a tenuous fog began to form, growing in strength with every step they took. A chill slowly began to seep through the spines of the two travellers which had nothing to do with the fog, but was rather the product of a nameless dread that seemed to increase the nearer they got to the house of the holy.

Every now and again, the tendrils of cloud dispersed sufficiently for them to look out over the sea once more. Arthur gripped Merlin's arm and wordlessly extended a finger towards the horizon. The number of visible ships had increased five-fold.

In the breathless silence, they could make out the pounding of the drums and the creak of oars as they sliced through the water. The King turned to look at Merlin and saw that he was incanting, eyes closed, lips shaping words of mystery. Slowly but inexorably, the fog began to clear, revealing the smoking ruins of the abbey. Merlin let out a huge cry of distress and began barrelling down the pathway, oblivious to the dangers of running at such a pace on such a slick surface.

"Merlin!" Arthur called. He made to go after his companion, but found his gaze wheeling back to the flotilla that was making its stately way across the water towards what he still thought of as his kingdom, even though during his reign he had never been within hundreds of miles of the place he now stood. He reasoned that to take to the waves with such a large amount of ships could only mean one thing. Invasion.

He took a few faltering steps down the stone walkway, clearly torn between what dangers lurked inside the ruined monastery and what peril was carving its way noiselessly towards this bleak coast of North-east England.

Then the fog cleared completely and the breath was stolen from his lungs.

There, bobbing gently in the water, was anchored a huge ship. Hewn from the thickest trunks of the Scandinavian forests, the Viking longship reared up like a waiting predator, as if it was preparing to pounce over the walls of stone.

With all thoughts of the approaching enemy banished, Arthur joined Merlin in the headlong rush towards the doors of the abbey that lay splintered and broken in the entrance, scared to death of what he would see once he gained the threshold.

It did not take long for the sounds of conflict to reach his ears. He stumbled over the remains of the doors and found himself staring into a large courtyard, drenched in a chill shadow that had more to do with the atmosphere than the weather. There was a terrible sense of desolation here, a sense of a place that had been built by love and devotion but torn down by hatred and violence.

The shouts of struggle were coming from a pair of open doors to the left of the entrance courtyard. Wrenching Excalibur free from his belt, Arthur strode purposefully towards the room. As he came closer, he became aware that the raised voices were in a tongue that he did not recognise. He crept forward, barely breathing, lest the sound warn those inside of his approach. The first thing he noticed was a shadow being cast by someone standing to the right of the door. Before entering, he chanced a glance further inside and saw at least four others standing, weapons drawn, facing something or someone on the far side of the room.

Guessing that it was Merlin keeping them occupied, he calmed himself, offered a quick prayer to God and barged into the room, sending the man to the right of the door crashing to the floor and breaching the circle of warriors who had their backs to him.

He skidded to a halt and nearly fell backwards as he found himself face to face with a ravening, rabid hound, snarling and growling, the animalistic noise acting as a pointed reminder of the daily dangers of a more primeval time.

The hound advanced, saliva dripping from its savage maw. The former King looked into its pitiless eyes and for one of the first times in his life, knew true fear. Completely forgetting the massive weight of Excalibur resting in his hand, he tensed himself for the attack and raised an arm across his face, preparing for the worst.

He felt rather than saw a huge shadow leap over him and the guttural words behind him turned to shrieks of pain as the beast attacked with a ferocity and speed that belied its enormous size.

The warriors fell back, axes slicing the air in front of them in a vain attempt to halt the hulking brute's onslaught but it was to no avail. The hound had ripped off one man's leg as if it was made of nothing more than paper, shaking its head vigorously and spattering the other men with the blood of their fellow axeman.

Realising that he was now free of the beast's attention, Arthur stumbled to his feet and swept up Excalibur from the blood-slicked floor, awed at the sight of the magnificent dog despatching its attackers swiftly and mercilessly.

Of the five foes that he had seen on entering the room, only three now remained. They had spread out and were circling the beast, one bravely facing the muzzle and the other two positioning themselves on the animal's flanks, poised to hamstring it if and when it pounced.

In the chaos of the creature's attack, they paid little mind to Arthur. The former King, now certain that the huge dog was Merlin in one of his myriad guises, slashed out at the muscular warrior covering the left hind leg of the dog. The blond hulk must have seen Arthur's feint out of the corner of his eye, for he brought his axe round in a desperate attempt to halt Excalibur's momentum. That he did, but at great cost.

In his anxiety to block Arthur's stroke, he was not gripping the axe firmly enough and the jarring concussion snapped back his wrist with a sickening crack.

As the weapon clattered to the floor, Arthur brought the hilt of his sword down upon the man's helmet and he slumped unconscious to the floor.

The one that was facing down the monster muttered something to his remaining countryman, who cast a quick glance in Arthur's direction, but shook his head and resumed his scrutiny of the dog.

Arthur began stalking towards the man, a battle-scarred stocky bruiser with a shock of red hair, sprouting out from underneath his conical helmet. He was not used to being dismissed so easily and decided to force the warrior's hand into acknowledging him as a threat.

Now the redhead was swapping his stare from Arthur to the dog and back, the motion of his head making his braids fly out horizontally from the sides of his face.

The final event that cemented the true identity of the beast in the King's mind was the way it timed its attack on the Norseman for surely no mere animal would have the wherewithal to time its assault upon its enemy with such effortless precision.

It had retreated slightly after Arthur's successful assault on the blond soldier on its left flank, the better to watch the two that remained. It stepped forward as if to attack the warrior in front just as the redheaded one swung round to face Arthur, only to check its step and launch itself sideways at the warrior's throat. He realised too late what was happening and fell screaming under the gaping jaws of the beast.

It was all over in less than ten seconds, leaving Arthur breathless at the creature's ferocity, certain that no ordinary animal would possess such intelligence, but also slightly disconcerted by the bloodlust that was apparent in the creature's eyes. He had never seen Merlin possessed by such violence and anger before.

Breathing hard, he stepped up to take station by the left shoulder of the massive hound, holding Excalibur in both hands and pointing it at the last man standing.

Even against these odds, the final combatant looked no more than slightly concerned, his bearing suggesting that the scene before him held no great fear. Suddenly he stepped forward and swung his bloodstained axe, causing man and beast to take a step back. He then spun on his heel and made a break for the open door.

The beast let out a bone-chilling growl and bounded after him, oblivious to its new-found ally, who it cannoned into, sending Arthur bowling to the floor.

Arthur sat for a second, regaining the wind that had been knocked from him by Merlin's thirst for the chase. He looked up and saw the magician standing in the frame of the door, looking drawn and pale.

He was up in an instant, worried by the obvious distress that the wizard was in. He ushered him into the one chair that had miraculously escaped the mayhem of moments before. Arthur concluded that seeing the effects of his brutish incarnation through his now human eyes had shaken him as much as it had Arthur.

"So many killed, so much destroyed," Merlin gabbled after taking a long draught from a jug of water that Arthur had uncovered from the top of a table in a distant corner of the room.

The King surveyed the destruction that had been wrought in the room. "Indeed. Still, we repelled them, did we not?" He smirked.

Merlin looked blankly at his long-lived travelling companion. "What do you mean?"

Arthur gestured at the carnage that littered the room, both human and material. Perhaps Merlin had no memory of what acts he had committed whilst in the mind of an animal, he supposed. "I have never seen you change into that monster before," he said. "Though I must be honest, it was exhilarating to watch you despatch the enemy so clinically."

Merlin stood up a little unsteadily and jabbed a finger at the King. "What are you blathering about, Arthur? What monster?"

"How do you feel when you are in the guise of such a beast? Is it a swift change or does the body take a while to adapt?"

The magician stared at the King as if he was mentally unsound. "Arthur, I have absolutely no idea what you are referring to?"

At that moment, the huge hound padded back into the room like a faithful beast returning to its master's hearth, licking the gore from its whiskers and smacking its lips together as if it had just enjoyed a hearty meal.

Arthur stared at the new arrival with absolute horror. He had stood shoulder to shoulder with the brute, thinking it was Merlin when, in actual fact, it really *was* just a gargantuan dog.

Merlin looked from the creature to Arthur's terror-stricken face and when realisation hit him, he burst out laughing. He approached the animal directly but cautiously, holding out his hand gingerly, so that it could breathe his scent.

The former King's hand flew to the haft of Excalibur as the massive mouth opened and the teeth bared but, instead of Merlin losing his hand, a rough pink tongue snaked out and the dog licked his fingers vigorously. After a few seconds of this, Merlin knelt down and began scratching the hound behind each of its ears, "So, my liege, you have met Kelson then."

157

Arthur merely stood there, open-mouthed and dumbstruck as Kelson mewled contentedly and flopped at Merlin's feet.

The wizard wiped his eyes clear of tears of laughter that were streaming down his face. He stared down fondly at the top of the massive beast's head and his expression became serious. "He belonged to the monks who live...," at this point he hesitated with a tell-tale catch in his voice, "who used to live in this abbey. He was a guard dog."

Arthur's face screwed up in thought. What could possibly be worth guarding in a monastery, cut off from the mainland by a causeway that flooded every time the tide came in?

Seemingly in answer to Arthur's unspoken question, Merlin suddenly jumped up and beckoned the King through the door. "Come, we do not have much time. I fear that this was no more than an advance party. The rest of the armada is but a few whims of the current away from here. If we do not salvage some of the treasures housed in this place then it will be sacked and burnt to the ground along with everything inside. We cannot let that happen, Arthur." With that, he exited the room.

The King began to follow his magician, but skidded to a halt as Kelson roused himself and also took his leave.

Seconds after the dog followed him out of the door, Merlin's head reappeared round the edge of the door-frame. "Coming?" he asked, with a mischievous twinkle in his eye.

Chief Helveg Arnessen, head of the Wjissengarde clan, found his stare dragged irresistibly from the restless surface of the North Sea to the brooding presence of the abbey, rearing up in front of his anchored longship. "Any word from Jandahl and the advance party?" he asked his lieutenant, a one-eyed shaven-headed barbarian by the name of Tonmaug Helgusson.

The clan-chief's second-in-command half-turned, causing his leader no small discomfort, feeling as he always did that the puckered eye socket was watching him.

Tonmaug spat over the side of the ship. "No," he leant over the side, the better to see the shore beneath the overhang of the bow. "Not a word, not a sign." He sighed, clearly suspecting that all was not well but keeping his counsel.

The chief dismissed his underling's unspoken concerns with a snort of derision. "Jandahl can look after himself. For the god's sakes, Tonmaug, that is one of their holy buildings." He thumped his chest pompously. "What trouble could a group of monks give to warriors like us?"

Helgusson nodded emphatically. "Forgive my overly cautious nature, Helveg," he waved a hand in the vague direction of his eye, "the last time I rushed into a situation that I was ill-equipped to deal with, this happened."

Nodding disinterestedly, having heard the story a hundred times before, the chief changed the subject, gesturing towards the mainland. "I see our approach has not gone totally unnoticed. They have lit their little warning lights."

Indeed, as they watched, a couple more fires erupted from the summits of the distant hills, sending their silent messages inland that death was approaching from across the sea.

"Pah!" Tonmaug hawked another huge gobbet over the side of the ship, a habit that Arnessen was beginning to find annoying. "They can bring a whole army to this shore but they will not defeat us."

Helveg regarded his comrade with a raised eyebrow. "You were the one who suggested this little excursion. You were the one who said that these islands were ripe for the plucking. If you are so sure of your prowess in battle, then why are you so fretful about Jandahl? You are so jumpy that, if it was not for the fact I know you are hairless from head to foot, I would think you infested with fleas."

Helgusson threw a look of disgust at the captain. "I just thought that he would be back by now, that is all." He pointed towards the clouds of smoke still rising from the unchecked fires that were raging within the building. "Those flames have been blazing for half a turn of the hourglass and still there is no sign of them. The orders were to gather whatever was of value and fire the place. Either Jandahl is disobeying a direct order or there is something within there that is delaying his exit."

For the first time, Chief Arnessen actually pondered what his deputy was saying. After a few moments, he conceded that maybe the bald man had a point. Having come to that conclusion however, he was not about to let Tonmaug see that his counsel had swayed him so he waved a dismissive hand. "Honestly, you cluck like a mother hen. If you are really so sure that something is amiss then take some men and go have a look. I, on the other hand, am going to retire to my cabin. Be sure to let me know if the monks have converted Jandahl," he finished with a snigger.

With that said, the chief wrapped his fur cloak around himself with an unnecessary flourish and retreated below decks.

Helgusson watched him go with murder in his eyes. "Idiot," he muttered under his breath. Then, turning his attentions back to the task at hand, he bellowed across the wave-splashed deck to the crew, "Hoy, I need seven men to go with me to the abbey and find that cretin Jandahl. Who is with me?"

159

This elicited little or no response from the assorted soldiers within earshot. Tonmaug sniffed and spat at the nearest man, causing him to square up menacingly. "Ah, there is something I can do to get you mongrels to pay attention to me, is there? You want that I should come and spit over all of you until you acknowledge me?" he sneered with a raised eyebrow.

Inexplicably, the crew shrunk back from the implied threat. "Good. Now, I will say it again, who is with me?"

At the second time of asking, Tonmaug found himself staring at six raised hands. "That's a bit better," he crowed, "Still one short though. Not keen for a battle, Dermdor?"

The man that Tonmaug addressed sighed resignedly, shook his head then raised his hand.

"Wonderful." The bald man laughed heartily. "Let us go then."

The seven located some rope, slung it overboard, paid it out until it tickled the rocks below and descended it to take their first steps on the soil of Britain.

Merlin, Arthur and Kelson made their way through the devastation of the abbey, averting their eyes from the more hideous killings perpetrated by the invaders.

Every now and again, Merlin would shake his head as he happened upon various books and tapestries that had been damaged beyond repair.

His distress paled into insignificance alongside Kelson's, however. They had to keep urging the dog on because, with every corner they turned, they found bodies. The monks had been pitilessly slaughtered and it seemed that all of them must have been involved in Kelson's care, for the hound stalked through the carnage with head bowed and a continuous mournful whining escaping his lips.

Arthur's heart ached, for a bottomless well of pity had opened up inside him as he beheld the murdered residents of this holy place. They must have been hopelessly ill-equipped to face such a merciless foe. He pondered how he would feel if he had seen all he held dear destroyed and been powerless to prevent it. Kelson had probably been their only means of defending themselves and now here he was, feeling that he had failed them all. The King moved to the beast's side and stroked him gently. He was gratified to hear the whine change pitch and become an almost quizzical sound. However, as he looked down, it became clear that his ministrations had nothing to do with the change in Kelson's voice.

One of the monks was still moving, his movements causing the puddle of blood that he was lying in to ooze obscenely. As quickly as he could, Arthur knelt by the man's side and cradled his head. "Merlin!" he called, halting the magician in his tracks. "This one still lives."

Within seconds it became clear that this would only be a temporary state of affairs because, as the man tried to speak, he coughed and sent a dark gush of arterial blood splashing over his robes.

Merlin looked at the King's face and shook his head sadly. Indeed, it was only a matter of seconds later when the last breath appeared to flee the man's lungs.

As they began to rise to take their leave, with a suddenness that scared the life out of Arthur, the man's right hand snaked out, grabbed the King by the collar and yanked his ear down to within millimetres of his mouth. "Save the Gospels," he croaked.

"I..." Arthur began to reply, but the grip loosened and the hand fell to the floor. Kelson nuzzled against the dead man's face for a few seconds, then returned to Merlin's side.

"What did he say?" the magician asked.

Arthur reached down and gently closed the man's eyelids. "He asked me to save the Gospels. Does that mean anything to you?"

The wizard nodded. "He speaks of the Lindisfarne Gospels. The words of Matthew, Mark, Luke and John, the Four Evangelists of Christ."

Arthur felt his breath quicken. "They are here?" he breathed.

"Yes." Merlin said simply but his eyes seemed to be lit from inside with a zeal that Arthur had not seen in his companion for many a year. "There are many and varied items housed within these walls, parchments from Roman times, ancient gifts brought by the pilgrims who flocked here, other articles of antiquity that..."

He stopped speaking abruptly, for Kelson was staring down the corridor intently. A low rumbling growl started to come from the dog and it was obvious that he yearned to bound away and challenge whoever it was that was about to cross their path.

The mage crept over to the dog's side and began to calm him, stroking his massive head and whispering in his ear. The three of them entered a room just to the right of where they stood and waited breathlessly, Arthur unsheathing Excalibur with vegetable slowness and Merlin tugging edgily at his close-cropped beard.

In the distance, they heard the same guttural accents that had been spoken by the men that Kelson had fought off moments before. The closer they came to the room that the trio had secreted themselves in, the harder it was for Merlin to restrain the hound as they retreated further back from the door.

From behind an upturned table, they peeked over and saw the eight newcomers stalk past. Arthur and Merlin looked at each other in trepidation as they took in the blood-spattered patchwork furs, the wicked assortment of weaponry and the air of irresistible menace that seemed to cloud the group.

These were clearly men who would kill you the instant their malevolent gazes fell upon you.

As the last of the warriors disappeared from view and were safely out of earshot, Arthur let out a huge sigh and gently laid Excalibur down on the floor. With his other hand, he massaged some life back into his sword hand because during the Vikings' passage, he had been gripping the haft so tightly that his palm had been indented with the pattern fashioned on the handle.

When they were sure that the fur-draped barbarians had gone from the immediate vicinity, Merlin stroked Kelson's head and murmured praise into his ear. Then they got up from behind their wooden shield and made their way from the room, the two men nervously glancing behind them in case the warriors reappeared.

They were about to turn the corner when a bellow of anger and anguish erupted from the far end of the corridor.

In unspoken unison, the party of three took to their heels, recklessly fleeing before the Vikings returned. The new arrivals had, presumably, happened upon the scene of Kelson's grisly rampage and would now be hell-bent on discovering and exacting revenge upon the perpetrators.

The harsh imprecations increased in volume as the Norsemen heard the flight of the trio. Arthur was only too aware of the sound of the pursuing footsteps coming ever closer as they searched in vain for a place to retreat and regroup.

They turned the corner of yet another corridor, one decorated spectacularly with rich tapestries and ornate scriptures draped on the walls. The splendid sight was so unexpected that Arthur actually stopped momentarily, so breath-taken was he.

A dissonant screech from behind broke the spell and he spun round to face a grimacing Viking, his lank hair lifelessly cloaking his shoulders, wafting a hideously sharp axe in front of him.

To the King's surprise, the warrior spoke Anglo-Saxon like a native. "You killed our scouts," he snarled.

Kelson snapped at the blade swinging to and fro before him, however, it was clear to Merlin and Arthur that the weapon's reach was more than enough to terminally halt any attack that the beast could launch so Merlin barked a clipped command at him and he grudgingly subsided, though a low growl still vibrated in his throat.

A nagging feeling crept over Arthur as he studied the savage's face. The confirmation came seconds later.

"Now, now Dermdor, there is no need to be discourteous. You know what we came here for. Let us not get distracted."

The other Vikings, who by now had joined their fellow warrior in confronting the fleeing group, were looking at each other, muttering perplexedly and

162

Arthur could see the confusion writ large on their faces. They had come out of a room which was drenched with the blood of their comrades, then within minutes located the probable killers, but now, suddenly, two of their crew-mates were talking fluently to their captives in a foreign tongue.

One massive red-headed warrior prodded the one called Dermdor and raised his sword threateningly towards the other. "Tonmaug?" he hissed threateningly. "What is this sorcery?"

Tonmaug raised an eyebrow, regarding the speaker coolly. "Oh damn," he huffed, "I had hoped to avoid this." He flicked out a hand and the warrior folded up like a rag doll. He then snapped his fingers and Arthur heard a crash behind him. Spinning round, he saw Kelson whining and pawing at Merlin, who lay prostrate on the floor.

The one called Tonmaug smacked the Viking that Arthur had first encountered on the back of his head. "In the name of God, Mordred, could you not keep your mouth shut until we had found the Gospels. They would not have had an inkling otherwise." He snapped his fingers again and the remainder of the raiding crew collapsed to the intricately mosaicked ground.

Arthur stood, mouth agape, staring from Merlin to Mordred and back again. Almost without thinking, he unsheathed Excalibur and lunged at his treacherous nephew. If he had taken the time to think about his actions, he would have attacked Montagu first as he was clearly the main threat, but hearing the name of his nephew and recognising the face of the man who had nearly killed him upon the plain of Camlann all those decades ago, awoke in him such a rage that all rational thought fled his mind.

Mordred shrank back from the primal howl of his attacker and he half-heartedly raised his weapon to try and ward off the seemingly inevitable blow that was coming. He glanced pleadingly at Montagu and squealed, "Do something. Put a hex on him. Stop him, dammit."

The look of contempt that Montagu bestowed upon him was so withering that Mordred all but forgot about Arthur's advance and hung his head.

The dark magician snapped his fingers again and the murderous swing of Arthur's blade slowed then stopped as if turned to stone. To his distress, the King found that his whole body had been petrified. The only thing that he was able to move was his eyes and they swivelled frantically in their sockets, trying to keep watch on Montagu as he stalked past him.

He wept with the effort of trying to break free from the invisible bonds that held him in place. He knew he was helpless. He knew true fear once more. He knew that he had failed in his quest.

His ears strained to make out what was occurring behind him, yet there was silence. He was sure that it was due to the spell that he found himself subject

163

to, because he could not bring himself to believe that Montagu would forsake this opportunity to dispatch Merlin as he lay helpless on the patterned tiles. With a suddenness that sent his head spinning, sound came flooding back to his ears.

He heard Mordred cursing and saw that he too was also frozen in place, presumably caught in the effects of his master's magickry.

Then he heard Kelson barking but that savage sound was cut off seconds later by the whispering velvet voice of Montagu that came at him from all sides and engulfed his senses. If he could have staggered he would have done, for the sound was so overwhelming.

"Kill him, Arthur, kill him. He is your true enemy. He stuck you like a pig and left you seconds from death. He usurped your throne whilst you were absent fighting the enemies of your land. He betrayed you, your family, your subjects. He is the one who brings the world to the brink of darkness, not I. I am merely a puppet in his thrall, subject to his whim with no more power over my destiny than an autumn leaf in the September breeze. He is the true enemy. Kill him and you save us all. Spare him and you condemn us all."

The former King of England felt warmth spreading through his body and he found himself able to walk forward towards his nemesis, although his legs still felt leaden and cumbersome. His mind was barren, save for one thought, dominating his brain to such an extent that it seemed to be echoing around his skull. He hefted Excalibur in both hands and bore down upon his desperate nephew.

"What did you say to him, you bastard?" Mordred screeched, his weaselly eyes flaring wide and staring at Montagu. "What have you done?"

The dark magician's laughter bounced off the walls at Mordred's distress.

King Arthur raised the famed blade above his head and prepared to bring it down, all the while with Montagu's speech coruscating through his subconscious.

He tensed and prepared to swing.

It was as if there was nothing else in the world but himself, Mordred, Excalibur and the voice. The all-encompassing, omnipotent voice that proclaimed what the future would hold. It would have been easier to disobey the law of gravity than it would to disobey this voice.

"Kill him, Arthur. Slaughter him like the dog he is. Give in to your innermost feelings. Kill him, kill…"

The King found himself holding his breath, waiting for the next word, unable to do anything without the guidance of the voice.

But nothing was forthcoming and Arthur shook his head, slowly surfacing from the suffocating grasp of Montagu's words.

The magician was prostrate on the floor, one arm clamped in Kelson's jaws, the other punching, slapping, fighting off the dog's attack.

Before Arthur had a chance to take advantage of the situation, he glanced at Mordred, because he had noticed that the statuesque shadow of the treacherous prince had begun to move.

The fighting that followed was lumbering and painfully slow for the effects of Montagu's hex were slow to wane. Arthur deflected a sweeping stroke from Mordred's axe and turned it into a counter-thrust that his nephew barely blocked. The effort of swinging their weapons through what felt like treacle left them struggling for breath and they backed away from each other, circling, testing their limbs for increased responsiveness.

As Mordred retreated out of Excalibur's range, Arthur chanced a glance at the two floored magicians. Montagu was still wrestling with Kelson but Merlin remained disconcertingly still. The black magician was desperately trying to bring his magic to bear but Kelson's frenzied assault was keeping him at bay for the time being.

A noise from over his shoulder dragged the King back into his own personal conflict and he stepped to the side, ready to face his nephew once again. They stalked warily round each other, Arthur thrusting weakly with his blade and finding his sword arm renewed in vigour and Mordred mirroring the action with his double-headed axe.

Naked fear was in Mordred's eyes and he attempted a desperate swing that was woefully misplaced but was enough to send Arthur dancing backwards. Unfortunately he trapped his heel upon the edge of one of the tapestries that was draped on either side of the passageway. The destruction visited upon the abbey must have loosened its fittings because although Arthur only brushed against it, the heavy cloth fell from its fittings and engulfed him in its rich fabric, rendering him totally incapable of defending himself in any way shape or form. He began to struggle frantically, certain that he was seconds from death at the hands of his hated relative.

"Leave him," came a strangled voice, "and get this bloody dog off me. See, Merlin awakens."

Arthur increased the strength of his thrashing, wanting to be free so that he might aid his friend of centuries.

"If he is roused before I am free of this hound's attentions, all is lost." Montagu screeched.

Arthur heard one more faltering step, then running, a shrill bestial yelp, then the sound of further running. He fought with the priceless tapestry, eventually loosening up his arms enough to be able to slash his way to freedom. He staggered upright and stumbled over to Merlin, who was kneeling and murmuring an incantation over the bloodied form of Kelson.

165

The King began to say something but was hushed by the magician. He watched in awed silence as the gaping gash that had torn into Kelson's side began healing itself, the loose flaps of flesh and skin knitting together as if sewn by an invisible needle. To his relief, the mighty hound whined then got to its feet unsteadily as it tried to lick Merlin's face.

In Arthur's experience, a successful casting such as this would normally have had the magician smiling lazily and awaiting plaudits from his audience. It was a measure of the seriousness of the situation that he firmly but gently pushed the dog's muzzle away and began scurrying down the corridor in pursuit of their foes. "Come, Arthur," he bellowed as the King began walking after him, "we must find the Gospels before them."

"Why?" Arthur asked as he reached the wizard's shoulder. "You think they mean to destroy them?"

Merlin gave Arthur a look of contempt that the King found quite offensive. "Sire, do you really think that Montagu would come all this way to this tiny island that houses naught but the abbey, if there was no purpose to it? You heard what Montagu said, he explicitly stated they had come for the Gospels."

King Arthur bit down his displeasure at being spoken to in such a way. It was clear that Merlin was beside himself with worry, for although the wizard had often spoken to him as an adult would to a dull-witted child, he had never been quite so withering in all their years traversing the country. He grabbed Merlin's arm. "I am sorry, I still do not understand. Those Gospels are the words of the quartet of disciples whom Jesus Christ counted his closest confidantes. Why would a monster under the rule of Satan wish to lay his hands upon such a holy object?"

Merlin yanked his arm away and galloped off down the passage, acting as if he had not heard the question. He darted in and out of the rooms that lined either side of the corridor, signalling for Arthur to go into the ones that he missed. After a few minutes of this, he beckoned to the King. "Stay close by. We must not allow ourselves to be separated. If we do, it will be our doom." Arthur nodded grimly and resumed the search.

They both emerged from their respective rooms at the same time and the King heard Merlin curse, "Dammit, this place is like a rabbit warren."

"What are we to do if there are rooms leading off the rooms that we are entering?" The King asked plaintively. "You said we were not to separate."

Merlin looked like he was about to launch another diatribe at the King but instead sighed hugely and laid a hand upon Arthur's shoulder. "We will have to cross that bridge when we come to it. Trust me, Arthur, it is imperative we find the Gospels before Montagu does."

166

He knew that Merlin was not telling him everything but recognised that this was not the time for petulance, so he wheeled away and kicked open the next door.

Merlin watched him go then turned and, with a flick of his wrist, opened the next barrier to his progress. As he emerged, he caught a look of suspicion from Arthur before the King disappeared into the next room.

As they met again in the corridor, Arthur stopped and jabbed an accusing finger at his companion. "What are you not telling me, Merlin? You obviously know something with regard to these Gospels. I cannot believe you are making so much fuss over them because they are pretty and you have certainly never been much of a dedicated worshipper of Our Lord, so what is the reason you are so concerned? What is housed within the manuscript that agitates you so? Dammit, I have a right to know. I have travelled with you for nearly three centuries on this quest but I tell you now, I am not moving one step further until you tell me all that you know." With that, he sheathed Excalibur then crossed his arms.

Instead of the usual arrogance that never seemed far from the magician's face, a look of near pleading appeared on it. "Arthur, I swear to you, I will tell you all that I know regarding the Gospels once they are in our possession, but I beseech you, we must not tarry."

The former King of Wessex placed his hands upon his hips and looked heavenward. After a seemingly interminable time which was, in reality, mere seconds he looked down again, exhaled a seething breath and ran into the next room, ignoring Merlin as he emerged from it and moved off down the corridor once more.

The hunt continued in complete silence with even Kelson detecting the change in atmosphere between his two newfound companions which meant that every now and again he would whimper quizzically at one or both of them.

The King emerged from what seemed like the thousandth room that he had explored to find Merlin standing at the threshold of another room with a grimace of despair on his face.

"What is it?" the King asked quietly.

The spellweaver shook his head despondently and wordlessly ushered the King into the chamber.

The moment he walked through the door, Arthur could see that this room was unlike any of the others that he had explored. The walls were draped with jet black hangings which deadened any extraneous light. In fact, aside from the light of the corridor there was no other illumination, save a hole in the ceiling which allowed an ethereal silvery light to wash over an ornate lectern which occupied a plinth in the exact centre of the room. Breathlessly, the King knelt down to examine the base. It was four-sided with a depiction of what appeared to be a figure kneeling at the feet of a man on a hill. The carving was so exquisite that he could make out the beard upon the man's face and even somehow feel the sense of serenity and wisdom that came from him.

The seed of suspicion that had appeared as he stepped into the chamber blossomed forth and he got to his feet gracefully. Laying a hand atop the pedestal, he turned to Merlin. "This is the place, is it not? This is where the Gospels were housed."

The magician nodded sombrely.

Arthur's finger absent-mindedly traced a line in the thin film of dust that had collected on the stand, another legacy of the Viking's destruction. A large rectangular shape lay in the middle of the dust on top of the wooden stand, clearly showing that something which had lain there was now gone.

Merlin spoke for the first time since they entered the room. "Aye, this is where the Gospels resided. I think we have to assume that they are now in the hands of our enemy. The monks would not have the will to commit this blasphemy, certainly not in their own abbey."

Arthur toyed gently with the rounded end of Excalibur's pommel. He looked up into the magician's eyes and muttered quietly, "Will you tell me now? Will you tell me what has you so afeared?"

Merlin took a massive breath and gestured for the King to move out of the room and into the corridor. They seated themselves upon a pair of plush upholstered chairs that had remained relatively unscathed in the chaos. Kelson laid his head on Arthur's lap and the King gently caressed the hound's massive skull as Merlin began to speak.

"The Gospels are part of a prophecy, a prophecy that encompasses you, me, Mordred, Montagu," and here he took another deep breath, "and the Grail and Judas Cup."

At that, Arthur's eyes hooded and the reason for Merlin's thunderous face when he had emerged from the Gospel's chamber became all too clear, "A prophecy? Detailing what, exactly? Our destiny, the outcome of our quest?"

Merlin shrugged. "I have never been privy to their exact contents, but I understand that if you are able to decipher them, then they contain hints as to the whereabouts of the Grail."

Arthur shifted position, causing Kelson to murmur his disapproval at being disrupted from his comfortable position. "So what you are saying is that if Montagu unravels the contents of the Gospels, he will be able to locate his prize and we will be left floundering like hooked fishes?"

Merlin hung his head and nodded.

168

Arthur stood up, eyes blazing, ignoring Kelson's irritated growl. "Why are you only telling me this now? You said that you knew about these monks. You are not seriously telling me that in all the correspondence that you have shared with them, they omitted to mention the fact that they had these Gospels within these walls."

Merlin sprang to his feet and jabbed a finger at the King. "These monks were specially trained to protect the book. There was no enemy, no magic, no power in the whole of the land that could have breached their defences." He wailed.

With an angry gesture, Arthur swept his arm towards the devastation that pock-marked the corridor, "Really?"

"Or so we thought." Merlin muttered in a small voice. "We never for a moment believed that..." He waved a despairing hand in the same direction as Arthur's arm and his voice withered away to silence.

"So once again, Montagu runs rings around us." The King wanted to rage at the magician, yearning to scream his disgust at the complacency and arrogance that had caused this state of affairs but seeing this normally powerful man hunched over and distressed beyond words caused an overwhelming sense of pity to rise up within him and the flames of anger flickered and died aborning.

"Look, my friend," Arthur began, laying a hand upon Merlin's shoulder, "what's done is done. There is nothing we can do, so let us take stock of the implications of this theft and see what we may do to limit the damage that it has caused." The King resumed his seat. "So what knowledge is Montagu privy to now that is denied to us?"

A brief look of gratitude passed across the sorcerer's face. He sat forward and peered intently at his companion. "It is probably better to think of the Gospels as a journal to better understand what lies within them. They constitute a diary of what was, what is and what will be. It was scribed by the four disciples of Christ throughout the years that He walked the earth. It is a document of His thoughts, His visions, His predictions for the future," Merlin sighed hugely. "And we are part of it." He said simply, sitting back and seeing if Arthur fully comprehended the significance of his statement.

The King's face took on a look of great scepticism. "You are saying that we were in our Lord's thoughts all those years ago when he walked among the people healing the sick and comforting the needy?"

The magician nodded sombrely. "Far-fetched though it sounds, yes, that is what I have been told is in them. I have been in regular communication with the monks of this parish from the moment this discovery came to light." He raised his hands as Arthur began to protest, "I know that we have barely been apart for the last three hundred years but I have certain ways and means by which I can impart tidings and receive news. Ways all but undetectable in the magical ether," he shrugged and continued speaking before Arthur could get a word in. "I can only assume that the circumstances of our quest caused resonances that reached further than even we foresaw. We have created ripples in the ocean that are still expanding. The Nazarene knew that our destinies would become inextricably entwined with the Grail, or so it says in the Gospels. According to the text, as His life ebbed away on a crucifix, he vouchsafed to those who attended him that the Grail would become the subject of a great battle between good and evil. And I can only presume that because he beheld us both bathing in its penumbra, we were accorded a special place within the manuscript."

Arthur still looked doubtful. "So does this prophecy mention what happens at the conclusion of all that we face? Are we to be successful in our search or fall short in our endeavours?"

The magician thrust himself out of his chair and began stalking up and down the corridor. "I know not, Arthur, I know not. Though the Gospels came to light many, many years ago, the language was so obscure and prosodic that the process of translation was painstakingly slow and there is still roughly one third of the book to decipher but now," he gestured helplessly towards the placid room from which the Gospels had been removed, "we may never know."

The King's face tilted up towards the ceiling and he closed his eyes. "One thing is certain. If Montagu did not have the upper hand before, he surely has it now."

Merlin slumped back into his chair and held his head in his hands. "I know." He whispered in a hoarse voice that Arthur could barely hear. "I know."

Kelson loped over to the mage and nuzzled at the distraught man until he pushed the hound away and rose suddenly, catapulting his seat to the floor with an almighty clatter. "He has made a fool of me for the last time. I will hunt him to the ends of the earth until I have my vengeance." Merlin shrieked.

Arthur shrank back from the fury in his voice and held up his hands. "Hold hard, Merlin. Now is not the time for blind pursuit. Like it or not, he is too powerful a sorcerer to risk attacking without plan or stratagem. We must…"

To Arthur's shock, Merlin turned on him, pinning him against the wall and thrusting his face to within inches of the King's, blithely ignoring Kelson's cacophonous barking. "Oh, so now it is we, is it?" He snarled. "What of our conversation mere hours ago? Montagu always ahead, ourselves always behind? Well, my liege, for once I will heed your advice. I will find that cold-eyed bastard and by all the power I have, I will make him pay for what he has done."

Just as quickly as it had appeared, the tide of rage ebbed away and Merlin let Arthur slip from his grasp. Tentatively, the King extended a hand and placed it on the wizard's shoulder. "You must try to distance yourself from all this. You are too wound up in the devastation you see before you to think clearly." The rage erupted once more and Merlin pushed the King to the ground although, as Arthur caught a glimpse of his eyes, it became clear that Merlin was directing the anger towards himself rather than the King. "Is it any wonder I am wound up, Arthur? This destruction, this chaos is a product of my arrogance, my pride. We could have held the manuscripts at Camelot, I could have protected them personally but, oh no, I thought myself clever beyond all others and allowed them to remain in the halls of this secluded monastery, thinking my guile in doing so would be enough to fool any who sought the Gospels for their own selfish ends. No, Arthur, I will not, hell...I cannot distance myself from this atrocity."

Arthur regained his feet and squared up to the magician. "Will you listen to yourself? If you find your arrogance so distressing, then you have a damned funny way of showing it. This is not your fault, man. When the monks began translating the Gospels, they must have gleaned some sort of knowledge as to their contents. They must have known that the book's secrets would one day place them in some sort of peril." His voice softened. "Do not let your misguided feelings of shame be your undoing."

Merlin clenched and unclenched his fists, breathing heavily. "Maybe you are right and I am not as blameworthy as I feel I should be but that does not alter the fact that my decision to allow the Gospels to abide here made Montagu's theft all the easier."

Arthur shook his head. "Those ships out there were an invasion fleet. He has probably wormed his way into those warriors' ranks intent on laying waste to these islands and masking another attempt to find the Cup or the Grail. He probably was not even coming here to steal the book, he just happened upon it."

Merlin moaned. "So now you are saying that you think he was coming here to raze the whole of the country to the ground to try and find what he seeks?"

Arthur shrugged, "Possibly."

"And now he has a book that, if the rumours are true, will help him locate the very thing we sought to deprive him of," Merlin pointed out.

The half-smile on Arthur's face disappeared abruptly.

"Thank you, Arthur. You have made my decision all too clear. Go south, my liege. Seek out the Grail in the waters of the lake. I have other tasks before me."

As the King watched in open-mouthed despair, Merlin the magician, the man who had been at his side for such a long time, waved his hands in a complicated series of gestures and dissolved into wisps of nothingness.

Chapter 12

Aboard the Skarvlang

Chief Helveg Arnessen pulled pensively on his blonde moustache as he saw the other ships in the Viking armada grind into the shore and disgorge their muscular crews onto the gritty beach.

He turned to one of the Viking warriors who remained upon the deck and was moving some ropes around in a desultory way. "You there, Dermdor, is it?"

The beardless Viking walked over in a sycophantic half-crouch as if he was not sure whether he should be bowing or not, "Yes, Chief?"

"Where is Tonmaug?" he asked, whilst looking distastefully down his nose at the craven fool in front of him. "I wish to speak to him."

"I...I will go and see if I can locate him. I think he is in his cabin." Mordred backed away from the Viking war-chief, tripped over the coil of rope that he had been moving and sprawled to the sodden deck.

Helveg snorted at the pathetic display and turned his attention back to the other longships.

Presently, he returned with Helveg's hairless lieutenant in tow. His second in command seemed distracted as he leant on the railing next to his chief and joined him in the scrutiny of the rest of the fleet. Arnessen pulled his cloak closer about his shoulders as a biting wind blustered across the North Sea. After a few moments of silence, he gestured vaguely in the direction of the shore. "Why are we still wallowing like a whale out here on the tide when the rest of the clans are staking their claims right under our noses?"

Helgusson inhaled deeply and rolled his eyes towards the rain-bloated clouds above them, just as they began to empty themselves of their watery burden. "I told you, Helveg. They may be exciting themselves over a few rocks and a pile of mud but the treasure that I have found within that abbey is far and away more valuable than anything they will get their filthy hands on."

Arnessen pushed himself away from the rail and threw his hands up in an over-dramatic flourish. "A book?" he spat. "I did not bring the Skarvlang all this way with its hull emptied in preparation for receiving the spoils of war, just for us to turn back with nothing more than a pretty painted book to show for our endeavours."

Tonmaug stared deliberately at the captain and spat on the deck directly between the chief's booted feet.

In shock, the Viking warleader stepped back momentarily before recovering himself and loosening his axe from its leather thong, "Who in the nine worlds of Hel do you think you are to treat me like this upon my own ship?" He snarled, raising his axe and swinging it to and fro in front of his deputy's face. He stopped the movement and turned it, resting one of the wickedly sharp edges inches from the man's good eye. "You will lose the other eye for this disgrace, Helgusson."

"Will I, Helveg?" Tonmaug grinned as he passed his hand over the angry puckered socket that had disfigured his face for longer than the chief could remember.

Arnessen lost his grip on the axe in shock, not even flinching when one of the butterfly blades of the weapon shaved a sliver of his boot as it bit into the wooden deck.

"Impressed, Helveg?" Tonmaug smirked, winking at the bemused war-chief with an eye that had newly appeared where nothing had been before. "What about now?" The bald Viking asked as he stroked his head from forehead to neck resulting in immaculately coiffured hair appearing atop his skull.

When Arnessen still could not bring himself to answer, Tonmaug flicked his finger and the axe rose from its location in the deck between the chief's legs and began to hover in the air, the haft weaving in front of the horrified Viking's eyes.

Tonmaug glared meaningfully at Chief Helveg Arnessen and for one of the first times in his life the leader of the Wjissengarde clan was frozen in fear. His blood chilled as he comprehended what was to happen and he began to plead, "No, Tonmaug, n...."

He was cut off in mid-sentence by the axe slicing down and bifurcating his skull in a gush of scarlet horror. The stroke was taken with such force that it exited the chief's groin and the two halves of his body fell to the deck in near-perfect unison.

Montagu stared at the mess for a second before hissing, "You are the disgrace, Helveg," under his breath before one more mystical pass of his hands saw the two pieces of the chief's corpse fly from the blood-sodden wood and over the side of the ship.

Without waiting for the splash, he went below decks and ordered the oarsmen to begin their work. To a man they had seen what Montagu had done to their chief and none were willing to question the man's authority.

Grunting disinterestedly at Mordred's snivelling congratulations, he left the bastard prince on the top deck and retired to his quarters, eager to resume his perusal of the newly acquired Gospels. His anticipation was, however, tempered by the frustratingly florid language of the tome and with a sigh which contained both irritation and excitement in equal measure, he returned to the page that he had last been reading before being summoned by the unfortunate clan-chief.

He began picking his way through the thees and thous and verilys that were liberally dotted throughout the text and had just begun poring over a particularly descriptive passage which, in actual fact, did not describe anything very much, when he became aware of a change on the air. A feeling of tangible hatred gripped him and he dropped the book to the floor, scrabbling to his feet hurriedly to try and identify its source. Hastily, he pushed the Gospels under his bunk and began muttering a protection spell to cast upon himself.

The sense of loathing was so oppressive that it seemed to choke the air from his throat and he was unable to finish the spell. He yearned for nothing more than to burst forth from the room and scramble on to the rain-soaked deck mere feet above him but he found he could do nothing, petrified as he was by the claustrophobic foreboding that held him in its power.

The air in front of him shimmered unpleasantly and suddenly he found himself staring into the cold, unforgiving eyes of his nemesis.

Unfortunately for King Arthur's magician, the appearance of such a familiar face after such feelings of dislocation and uncertainty was enough to wrench Montagu from his fear and back to reality. He instinctively lashed out and sent a bolt of energy rippling through the air. Merlin smiled lazily and swayed backwards, letting the spell pass harmlessly over his shoulder where it crashed into the wall of the cabin, leaving a blackened smoking hole in the wood.

Merlin stepped forward, as unstoppable as the tide and grabbed Montagu by the throat, lifting him easily off the ground although the dark magician was only a couple of inches shorter in stature. "You have made a fool of me once too often. It ends here." He increased the pressure on Montagu's windpipe and the dark mystic felt himself begin to pass out. He had been so shocked at being manhandled in such a way that he had forgotten his hands were free, free to cast spells that, at this range, would have quite devastating potency.

However, before he could react, Merlin dropped him to the floor, kneeing him on the way down and winding him, which broke his concentration and prevented the completion of the magic. Merlin then kicked him savagely in the ribs and landed a brutal punch on the back of his head.

The former magician of Camelot cast about the cabin for something with which to bind Montagu's hands. In the end, he ripped some of the sheeting from the bed. Once the magician was securely tied, he leant over him, sneering inches from his face, spittle arcing from his mouth onto Montagu's head. "I could easily kill you now, but the knowledge that I have bested you is enough. I will merely bind your powers and turn your body into a hollow shell, so that you may not pollute the earth with your malignancy any more," Merlin pinched his index finger and thumb together, "but I will leave a

175

minute piece of your mind intact, so that you will be aware of every waking second, as you dribble your food down your clothes and soil yourself in your bed. Your former glories will parade themselves in front of your eyes but you will be naught but an empty husk," Merlin laughed evilly. "I hope that the next few centuries pass slowly, Montagu, so that they might act as a recompense for the heinous acts that you have committed across this land. You have been taught a lesson today, you son of a mongrel. Learn it well for I do not like to repeat myself." The magician glowered arrogantly as he began describing occult patterns in the air.

The breath turned to stone in Montagu's throat. Merlin had been right in his assumption that the feeling of defeat at the hand of his nemesis would score a raw wound across his mind for centuries to come and the master of the dark arts found himself staring over the edge of a precipice of despair.

Merlin laughed as he neared the end of his conjuration and he brought his hands back in preparation for dispensing his own special brand of justice.

Montagu gaped stupidly at King Arthur's court magician as he brought his hands down.

Arthur Pendragon gawped at where Merlin had stood moments before. Kelson growled quizzically and walked around the patch of floor where the magician had been, snuffling and snorting at the cold flagstones.

The King slumped down upon the chair nearest him, unwilling to accept the enormity of what had just unfolded.

He held his head in his hands, trying desperately to curb the swirling feeling of giddiness that had swamped him, but he knew it would take more than that to still the maelstrom. His world had been knocked off its axis, possibly permanently, and he did not have any sort of idea what his next move was. His mind cast itself back to the conversation on the cliff where he had leant over the lip and contemplated jumping.

Then, his words had been borne of frustration at trailing in Montagu's wake and petulance at Merlin's condescending manner, but now he found himself wishing that he had never uttered them. In an unconscious mirror of Montagu aboard the Skarvlang, it was now Arthur who sat bereft of hope, staring into a dismal pit of oblivion.

He was so wrapped up in his melancholia that the deep throaty growl of Kelson took a few seconds to permeate his consciousness. He shook his head and painfully hauled himself to his feet. "What is it, boy?" he asked quietly, scratching at the massive hound behind his ears in a way that normally reduced him to a drooling puppy. This time however, the menacing snarl did not change one iota.

176

That was enough to bring Arthur's mind fully into the here and now and he unsheathed Excalibur, standing poised to defend himself.

Soon the objects of Kelson's hostility came into view.

The Vikings that Montagu had rendered insensible in the corridor plus two of men from the room where Arthur had met Kelson had regained consciousness and were now seeking out their betrayer.

With a suddenness that surprised him, a red mist descended upon Arthur. The frustration and setbacks of the past three hundred years all welled up inside him, ready to burst forth in blistering savagery.

As he stared through the scarlet fog, to his confusion, he saw eight Montagus standing before him, all sneering and mocking him. He opened his mouth, threw back his head and spat out an atavistic shriek of fury which was so fierce that even Kelson whined and took a step back.

Whilst the Vikings milled about, unsure what to do, Arthur advanced. The adrenalin of the berserker leant his attack such speed that he had despatched two of the eight before the others could raise their axes, one decapitated, the other run through the eye.

Seeing this, the other six hung back, unwilling to put themselves within the murderous arc of Excalibur but aware of the overwhelming odds they had in their favour. They soon found themselves with no option but to fight because the cloaked maniac had manoeuvred them into a corner and they had nowhere to retreat to.

With feints and attempted strikes, they managed to encircle Arthur, each tentatively snaking out their weapons in an attempt to injure their attacker without coming in range of his blade. Unfortunately for the Norsemen, two more warriors over-reached themselves and Arthur flung himself round in a full three-hundred and sixty degree spin, shearing both of their weaponned hands cleanly off at the elbow.

The ornate butterfly axes that the severed hands were clasping skittered away across the floor, causing one of the remaining four Norsemen to jump out of its way, straight into the unstoppable path of Arthur's sword. The former monarch of the realm grabbed a fistful of one of the man's braids, yanked them upwards then drew Excalibur across his exposed neck. The man was dead before he hit the floor.

The raw rage was beginning to subside somewhat and Arthur found himself thinking more clearly. He stared wildly at the three remaining Vikings, who returned the gaze with murder in his eyes.

He momentarily settled his stare upon the one to the left.

The fearsome warrior was nonplussed to see Arthur nod then turn his back. The insult of being dismissed so casually was enough to overcome his fear of the berserker and he roared a challenge at the blood-soaked swordsman before him. However, the feeling of indignation was quickly replaced by one of dread as he realised that Arthur had not nodded at him but at someone behind him. He tried to turn but it was too late. Kelson leapt at him and sunk his jaws into the man's forearm, tearing through the flesh and bone as if it was no more than a swatch of the sheerest silk.

The duo that now faced Arthur stared across the space between them and in unspoken unison launched their assault simultaneously.

The King blocked one sweep but the other got through. He gasped in pain as the metal blade miraculously slid down his ribs rather than shattering them and he lashed out desperately as he fell backward.

Luckily for him, his stroke hit home and the Viking fell back, screeching in agony as the sword of Camelot bit into his thigh. The amount of dark-red blood that began spurting to the floor confirmed that Excalibur had severed an artery. Indeed, as the warrior tried to put his weight on the leg, it folded up beneath him and he collapsed to the floor, his face a picture of bemusement as to why he suddenly felt so weak.

The King's remaining adversary, having seen his companion's blade come within an ace of landing a killing blow, attempted to press his advantage and slashed down, raising sparks from the stonework as Arthur rolled out of the way.

The heavily-bearded blonde warrior snarled something in his guttural language and gestured at the dead or wounded clansmen that lay strewn about the length of the corridor.

Arthur stood up straight and pointed his sword to the floor, lowering his head slightly though not enough to lose sight of the man before him.

The warrior's brows knitted in confusion at the change in the madman's demeanour. He stood unmoving for a long moment, trying to make some sort of sense of Arthur's intentions. When there was no sign of Arthur's aggression returning, he glanced away momentarily to see how his afflicted fellows were faring.

The one closest to him was twitching in a vast puddle of blood that had gushed from the wound in his thigh. His eyes were rolling in his head but they managed to focus on his compatriot for a moment. A barely audible sigh issued from his lips and then he was no longer moving. The warrior reached down and closed the man's eyes.

Seeing the poignancy in the massive man's gaze meant that Arthur suddenly felt compelled to justify his barbarous assault even though he knew the man understood nothing of what he was saying. "I do not know…what to say," he began hesitantly, "…the man you stood with, he is the most evil foul creature ever to walk the earth, he is the devil himself, he is…" The King sought more insults with which to describe Montagu but stopped when he saw the Viking's eyes upon him. Was there a flicker of understanding there? The Viking spoke one word. "Tonmaug?" he asked.

Arthur nodded slowly, remembering the name that Montagu had been called just before he had used his magic upon his erstwhile countrymen.

The Viking seemed to ponder this then nodded again.

Before he could react, Arthur strode forward purposefully. "Let me help your countrymen," he said as he began slashing at the tapestries and trying to fashion it into a makeshift bandage. As he stepped towards one of the warriors that clutched a bloodied stump rather than an arm, the man staggered to his feet, screaming imprecations both at Arthur and the unharmed Viking who stood passively by, watching owlishly.

"What in the hells are you doing, Friedrik? This bastard has just killed four of us and cut mine and Vigord's arms off. Kill him, you cowardly bastard, kill him!"

Arthur licked suddenly dry lips as he heard the huge Viking move behind him but as he turned all he saw was the man laying down his axe.

A look of misery flickered upon his face as his erstwhile compatriot spat at him and stumbled off down the corridor. He was joined by Vigord who followed him in the same clumsy manner. They stopped as they reached the corner of the passageway. "Arnessen will hear of your deeds today, traitor. Your head will be separated from your shoulders before you gain the deck." With that threat hanging in the air, the two wounded clansmen departed the carnage.

That left Arthur, Friedrik, Kelson and the warrior that the hound had mauled, frozen in a grisly tableau, surrounded by gore and death on all sides.

"Kelson," Arthur hissed. The dog looked up and obediently dropped the man's sleeve before padding over to Arthur's side.

Friedrik ran over to the prostrate warrior's side but it was clear there was no hope for him. Kelson's powerful jaws had caused hideous damage to the man. His arms were torn to ribbons where he had tried to stop the onslaught then, when his resistance had been too weak, the hound had savaged his face, leaving him blinded and without a nose.

The massive Viking lowered his head and heaved a shuddering sigh.

Arthur's hand slowly snaked down to the pommel of Excalibur once more and he tensed himself for the explosion of anger that was sure to come. The recent eruption of rage unchecked that had engulfed him when the Vikings had first appeared was such that he found himself praying that Friedrik would not be visited by the same madness, for Arthur knew that if he was, he would not stand a chance.

179

Instead, the Norse warrior got to his feet, hooked his axe in his belt and walked off down the corridor with neither a word nor glance at the King. Heaving a sigh of relief, Arthur looked down at the massive hound next to him. Kelson returned the gaze whilst happily licking the Viking's blood from his whiskers and jowls. The King could not believe that this was the same slavering beast that he had first seen laying waste to a room of pillaging Norsemen. Where Arthur's first impressions had been that Kelson was some sort of hellhound, he now found himself not hesitating to reach down and pet him as he was doing now. Kelson almost purred at Arthur's stroking and leant against the King's legs, threatening to overbalance him. "Get off, you daft hound," he smirked.

The grin fled from his mouth as a scream from ahead reached his ears. Kelson was off before Arthur could stop him, his four long legs easily outpacing the King. "Kelson, stop, damn you," he bellowed, but the hound ignored his order and ran round the corner.

A yelp caused him to redouble his pace and as he turned left into the next corridor, the breath caught in his throat.

Kelson lay in a pool of blood, though whether it was his or not was unclear, as he was slumped next to a freshly decapitated corpse.

A gobbet of phlegm launched itself from behind a pillar. "We told the snivelling cur he would lose his head," Vigord sneered, "Now you will lose yours." The other one-armed Viking appeared and they both took up station in the middle of the corridor, swaying from rage and blood loss. To the King's confounded senses, it appeared as if he was facing a single adversary who was standing next to a mirror. The pair hefted their weapons in perfect synchronicity, the only difference being the hands in which they held their blades.

The King brought Excalibur into the arena of battle with a silken swish, but this time found that there was no red mist descending, instead he was engulfed by more of an icy blue calm that had concentrated his anger into the hardness of a diamond.

The Vikings continued to bawl curses at the inflicter of their dreadful wounds, but Arthur remained silent. Aside from the fact that he could not understand a word that they spat at him, the detached part of his mind where his consciousness now dwelt seemed to be telling him that this situation was beyond speech. To respond to the curses would be to acknowledge his part in the slaughter that he had perpetrated on his foes not twenty yards away from where he now stood. He knew what the Vikings had done to the denizens of Lindisfarne Abbey, how they had torn through the cloisters and courtyards like a howling typhoon, obliterating all in their path, but had they done it of their own free will or had they too fallen under the spell of

Montagu and his profane powers? Had they too been rendered mindless by that seductive voice, just as he had been when on the point of killing Mordred?

If so, were their actions any worse than his when, moments before, his humanity had fled him and the animalistic bloodlust had consumed him?

These thoughts did not sit well with Arthur as he slowly retreated from his one-armed assailants.

His final sight of the blood-slick passageway before he backed around the corner was of Kelson, limp and lifeless, tongue lolling from the side of his mouth, staring at the wall with sightless eyes.

As the hound disappeared from Arthur's view, he felt the slightest of ripples begin in the tranquil lake of his psyche. With Kelson gone, he was now alone. Alone and isolated in a world from which he should have departed many moons ago.

In a matter of minutes, not only had he lost Kelson, a newfound ally that had saved his life on more than one occasion, but he had also lost the only person in the world who could possibly empathise with his situation. Merlin had deserted him, hell-bent on a mission of vengeance that would probably see him killed.

And here was he, facing two men that he did not know, intent on despatching them to their own personal Valhallas, whilst the promise of ultimate rest was denied to him for another two centuries at least.

As he retreated from his adversaries, the weighty feelings of loss for Merlin and Kelson plus the brutal memory of the savagery that he had inflicted on the Vikings sent his mind into a plummeting depression that wrenched his concentration away from the fight before him and into a gushing river of remembrance, swamping him in memories from the last three centuries when Merlin and he had walked the earth as men alone, set apart from the rest of humanity, on a quest of epic scale, unable to share the burden of knowledge with anyone else for they knew not who they could trust.

They found themselves eyeing all that crossed their path with suspicion, just as the people they met regarded them.

In that minute isolated world, the only constant had been his court magician, always there, commanding or cajoling, casting an immense shadow over Arthur's existence like an ever present shelter against the wiles of the world. Now though that omnipresent shield was gone and the harshness of reality was battering down the barriers of the King's mind, barrelling through them as if they were made of balsa wood, leaving him bruised and naked in an emotional desert under an unforgiving sun.

Arthur clasped his head, suddenly feeling as if it was on the brink of explosion and screamed and screamed and screamed.

His shrieks were enough for the two warriors confronting him to share a wary look of apprehension. Was their opponent about to transform into the unstoppable berserker of moments before?

The former King of England dropped to his knees with a pitiful whimper, losing his grip on Excalibur as he did so, sending it clattering to the floor, the noise a cacophony in the breathless silence.

The Vikings took this as confirmation that their enemy was bereft of the stomach for conflict and found their confidence again.

Vigord strode towards the diminished figure, whirling his axe in intricate patterns over his head in preparation for the kill. His laugh echoed around the corridor as the wicked weapon began its downward sweep and he closed his eyes with a satisfied sigh, marvelling at how easy it had been to avenge his compatriots.

He felt the blade hit home and a frisson shivered down his spine as the glory of his deed engulfed him. He stared over at his fellow tribesman with an exhilarated smile, waiting for the acknowledgement of a clean slaying. Instead the smile dissolved on his mouth so quickly that it appeared to have been blown off by a gale.

His compatriot stared back at him in disbelief, spending the last few seconds of his life silently asking his friend why he had nearly split him in half with his axe.

Vigord stared at his hand in total bemusement. How had his weapon found its way from the back of Arthur's neck to the middle of his countryman's ribs? "Breegan, I..." he began to say but words failed him as he found his gaze wrenched inexorably to the snivelling heap at his feet. What manner of enchantment did this man possess that he could outfight a group of eight Wjissengarders without receiving so much as a scratch?

Vigord knew that he could not hope to challenge such magic and swiftly decided that the prize of this mystic warrior's head could be claimed by another. He nearly tripped over his feet as he retreated with indecent haste back to the sanctuary of the Skarvlang.

Arthur had begun to surface from the depths of his agony and painfully lifted his head at the sound of the Norseman's scuffling feet when suddenly his nightmare became a dream of the sweetest piquancy.

He saw Vigord skid to a halt as he was about to round the corner.

He saw him hold out his hands in supplication and begin to back towards the King.

Against all logic, he saw Kelson bound around the corner with all the energy of a pup and launch himself at the Viking, opening a fatal wound in his jugular.

Then the dog was on him, pawing and licking at him, smearing the blood of his latest victim all over the King but Arthur could not have cared less. Until the massive hound had knocked him to the ground and winded him, he had assumed that the Viking had in fact killed him and he was in a dream, waiting to ascend the stairway to heaven, but now he found his spirit renewed once more as the miracle of Kelson's return to life overwhelmed him. He clasped the dog roughly and nuzzled his head against the tight fur of the animal's head, sobbing unashamedly.

"Come now," a deep voice chuckled, "is that any way for a former monarch of the realm to behave?"

Arthur's grip relaxed on Kelson's neck as he found himself staring into a face that he thought he would never see again. "M-Merlin?" he managed to blurt. The wizard of Camelot smiled at his leader and extended a hand. Kelson grunted indignantly as Arthur was heaved to his feet by his long-lived companion.

"Praise be to God that you have returned," Arthur breathed and threw his arms round the mage, "but what of Montagu? What of the Gospels?"

The benign countenance clouded and Merlin extracted himself from the King's bear hug. "That unholy son of a whore has hidden the book but I know not where. I searched the ship from deck to bilges but I could not find it." The magician hawked and spat on the back of the Viking warrior that he had compelled Vigord to unwittingly skewer upon his axe. "He laughed at me and said he had destroyed it, but I did not believe that for a second." Suddenly, Merlin's face lit up with a mischievous smile. "Still, if my suspicions are correct and he has hidden it, he is no longer in any position to find it."

Arthur's breath caught in his throat as he picked up on Merlin's use of the past tense. "Do you mean you..." he began.

Merlin nodded before the King could finish his sentence, a gaze of frightening intensity belying the casual smirk that was smeared across his mouth. "Yes, Arthur. I killed the bastard. I have single-handedly removed the biggest obstacle that stood between us and the Grail's discovery. My deeds now mean we have over two centuries to search for it, unharried and unharassed."

Arthur felt a peculiar numbness creep over him as the magician's words sunk in. They were now free to pursue their quest, no more fearful glances over their shoulders, no more nervous waiting for the dread hand of Montagu to blight their lives. He knew that their hunt was by no means over but Merlin's courageous slaying of the black magician was such a huge step towards their ultimate goal that Arthur could not contain himself and he capered about the blood-splashed passageway like a jester as Merlin looked on, a faint sense of disdain present in his gaze.

When the King had ceased his merriment, he let out a huge sigh and laughed, "Come, let us quit this place and head south. Let us find the Grail and bring happiness and purity to the world."

Merlin clapped Arthur roughly on the back. "A capital idea, sire," he chuckled.

As they strode purposefully down the corridors, so quickly that Kelson had to trot to keep up, Arthur turned to the wizard and asked, "So how did you do it? How did you kill a man who still had two centuries of his life left to live?"

The adulation in Arthur's voice was such that the mage's cheeks began to colour. "Please, sire, we have many miles ahead of us. I promise I will tell you of it on the way, but do you mind if we do not talk of it now. I had to perform some rather dark magic to eat away at his resistance and even now the spells leave a foul taste in my mouth. Let me compose myself then I will tell you all."

King Arthur's mouth gaped stupidly at the response and he found a surge of admiration welling up inside him. He had thought that Merlin's vanquishing of Montagu would be the only topic of conversation for the next few weeks, such was the magnitude of the magician's ego so for him to shy away from discussing it was a pleasant if unexpected surprise. Not that Arthur begrudged his companion his triumph in any way shape or form, but he concluded that whatever Merlin had done to slay Montagu must have been so distressing, so similar to the dark arts that Montagu had practised, that it had left a deep scar upon him, one that would take an indeterminate time to heal. To that end, he decided to leave the topic alone and only speak of it if Merlin broached the subject.

He cast about for some other topic of conversation. He looked down at Kelson, who was happily bounding along beside them. He reached down and ruffled the coarse fur on the dog's back. "You have much to be thankful for, boy. That is the second time he has saved your skin," Arthur grinned, jerking his head at Merlin, who rolled his eyes and pointedly pretended to ignore the comment.

Kelson, on the other hand, seemed keen to acknowledge the debt and loped over to lick the imposing figure's hand, which raised a smile on Arthur's face as Merlin withdrew his hand quickly and tutted at the beast's attention. He was poised to leap at Merlin and pin him against the wall with his massive paws, but one warning look from his saviour was enough to caution him against it.

Instead he decided to use some of the boundless energy that his miraculous recovery had instilled in him and contented himself with dashing manically between his two new companions. At times, he became subdued as they passed some of the murdered monks but he could not contain his joy for long.

Whether the dog sensed how close he had been to death before Merlin had revived him Arthur did not know, but he found himself fighting back laughter at the gargantuan hound's puppy-like behaviour.

They turned another corner and found themselves at the far end of the courtyard that had, for centuries, greeted all the pilgrims and visitors who had made their way to the abbey's threshold in search of knowledge, succour or both.

Now it skulked in dust-laden ruin, a formidable testament to the awesome marauding power of the Vikings. The two men hung their heads in despair at the havoc that had been wreaked upon it.

"Merlin," Arthur whispered, feeling that to raise his voice in this holy place after it had been destroyed in such a manner would be an unnecessary insult. "I have a question for you."

The mage continued walking but indicated that the King should go on.

"I found myself pondering the possibility that maybe Montagu had possessed these warriors into committing this blasphemy in the house of God. Would these men have acted in this way of their own volition?"

"Kelson," Merlin snarled, "cease your infernal gambolling."

As the dog retreated behind Arthur with a hurt look on his face, Merlin stepped forward and climbed over the rubble that had fallen in front of the main door. When he drew near to the top, he crouched to his haunches and beckoned for the King to join him. When Arthur had taken up station next to him, Merlin gestured to the headland that they had so recently walked upon.

There were hundreds of Viking tribesmen sitting, dancing and carousing around large fires dotted at irregular intervals under the shadow of the cliff. Those were not the only blazes that the two of them could see however. Entire sections of the heather and gorse had been set aflame, sending billowing clouds of black smoke into the air.

"There is your answer, I think. Such wanton destruction performed after the fiend's passing. His hand used to reach far but I think that the lowliest depths of hell may be too distant for him to exert an influence," Merlin sighed with a peculiarly regretful look on his face.

"Please, Merlin," Arthur said, "I did not wish to cause you pain. The memories of your struggle with Montagu are obviously still too raw to talk about. I am sorry." He affected a look of concern whilst secretly hoping that his implication that Merlin was still upset by his slaying of Montagu would be enough to prick his pride and goad him into explaining exactly what had transpired aboard the Viking vessel.

If Arthur was honest, after so many years of trying and so many setbacks along the way, it irked the King that he had not been there to assist or at least witness the demise of the most heinous travesty of human flesh ever to befoul the earth.

"Thank you for your concern, Arthur." Merlin nodded and made his way carefully down the other side of the hill of debris, ensuring that he stayed out of sight of the revelry on the beach.

Arthur bit back his disappointment at the failure of his ploy, beckoned Kelson to his side then followed the magician down the jagged stone bank.

Chapter 13

A.D. 798 – near the Avon/Somerset border

Arthur Pendragon, erstwhile King of the Britons, sat upon the shore of the lake where Merlin assured him the Grail had been dropped all those years ago by a gravely wounded Montagu as he fell before the might of Whitecleave, the blade of Sir Galahad of Camelot.

The journey south to the lakeside, where they now sat, had been a grim and depressing one across a ravaged country, blighted by the incurable plague of the Vikings.

They found themselves witness to atrocity upon atrocity perpetrated by the Norsemen. Slaughter, rape, cruelty beyond enduring, all seemed to hold no fears for the all-conquering invaders.

Merlin had been forced to stay the hand of the King on innumerable occasions. There had been so many times when Arthur had felt his heart would burst in anger at the evil visited upon those he still thought of as his subjects, but the magician had always managed to talk him back from the precipice, reasoning that if they were to locate the Grail, they really would be able to do something about what was happening to the land rather than making a token gesture which could only ultimately end in defeat.

Arthur grimly reflected on how hollow those words sounded now as he thought back over the last two years that had been spent walking the perimeter of the god-forsaken body of water where Galahad had performed the deed which had saved the world from being plunged into eternal darkness.

What made it even worse was that he yearned with every fibre of his being to aid Merlin in his search of the lake's floor for the goblet of Christ, but he knew he could not. When the meadow grass had begun to thin out into a gritty shore of pebbles and stone, Arthur had been so elated at Merlin's confirmation that this was indeed the Grail Lake that he had momentarily forgotten the constrictions of the spell that he laboured under and had run into the brackish water before Merlin's warning cry could penetrate his excitement.

The pain that had seared up his legs was still fresh in his mind all these months later. Unconsciously, his hands reached down to the scars that now decorated his legs from toe to knee. The injuries had been such that the first few days at their destination had been spent by Merlin applying salves and poultices to Arthur's ravaged legs. The pain had taken weeks to disappear but he had learned his lesson. He could still wash by splashing a minimal

187

amount of water on his skin and mixing it with certain herbs but total immersion was out of the question.

He sometimes contemplated jumping into the lake and trusting the healing power of the Grail to soothe his agony but he could not bring himself to do it. Instead, he was forced into the role of protector to the inert form of Merlin, who sat cross-legged on the shore in the same place as he had done every morning for what seemed like time immemorial but was, in reality, just a couple of years. Merlin had charged him to stay alert whilst he probed the murky depths of the Grail Lake, as they had christened it, with his mind. It was an immensely tortuous process with Merlin warping the minds of the assorted creatures of the lake into combing the pebbly bottom of the water for the cup.

"I am afraid it is rather an inexact science, my liege," the wizard had explained, "and requires the full extent of my attention. Therefore I have to rely on you to guard me as I search. I will sit here on the shore and send my consciousness forth into the waters but, as with you, I may not enter the water myself."

And that had been it. Arthur had been condemned to patrolling the lake against an intangible enemy whilst the wizard sat motionless, eyes closed, to all intents and purposes, dead to the world. With Montagu gone, Arthur could not really understand Merlin's concerns. The evil magician had long passed over, even though, to Arthur's continuing chagrin, Merlin refused to disclose exactly what had happened below decks aboard the Skarvlang.

On top of the absence of Merlin's companionship, he had no-one else to share the responsibility of watching over the catatonic wizard with, for Kelson had long ago departed the earth. The King's depression momentarily lifted as he remembered the huge hound, his bright eyes and lolling tongue, the massive shoulders and menacing jaws that had struck fear into many but conjured up nothing but love in Arthur's heart.

They had lost him early on during the journey south. They had stumbled into an ambush set up by a group of Norsemen who had obviously noticed their progress not far behind them.

Even though, Merlin had healed the dog twice before, the trio had become separated and by the time Merlin had gathered himself enough to despatch the aggressors with magic, Kelson had walked too long in the infinite darkness for Merlin to revive him.

Arthur had insisted on burying the faithful hound where he had fallen. The fact that they were in forests swarming with Norse warriors had not escaped him however and although there had been loud protestations from Merlin, he had taken his time, marking the spot with an immaculately constructed cairn of stones.

188

Shaking his head, he sighed as the happy memories of Kelson dissipated and he descended into an attack of melancholia as he stared across the limpid waters of the lake. He gazed up at the headland and imagined the demon plummeting into the waters, injured grievously by the slash of Whitecleave. Thinking of the famed sword, second only in renown to the King's own blade, conjured the face of Galahad in his mind and he imagined the flame of faith igniting the passion in Galahad's arm and inspiring him to land the disabling stroke on the fiend from hell.

He stared for long moments, his eyes following the scudding clouds as they made their sedate way across the sky. A slight movement in the scrubby bushes on the steep rock face caught his eye. It was as if a head had popped up out of one of the plants about halfway up the bank then disappeared again just as quickly.

His gauntleted hand was instantly on Excalibur and he drew the weapon, shocked at the close proximity of the intruder but secretly gladdened that there might be a temporary alleviation to his boredom.

"Ho there," he bellowed, "show yourself or I will come up there and drag you out by the scruff of your filthy neck."

Nothing moved, apart from a violent ripple of the undergrowth as a chill breeze suddenly appeared behind Arthur and swept past him with a mournful sough.

The King advanced purposefully towards the swaying brush where the observer had secreted himself. With an evil grimace on his face, he began slashing through the greenery in front of him with his sword, carving a path towards the place that he had last seen the head. To his mild surprise, there was no eruption of leaves as the concealed onlooker took flight. In fact, the lack of movement was so disconcerting that Arthur began to doubt what he had seen. However, he decided to plunge on, reasoning that even if his eyes had been playing tricks on him, the trip halfway up the incline would be a welcome if minor change in his routine.

It was the work of a few moments for the King to find himself standing in front of the bush where he had seen the head. In a voice as cold as the wind that was now whipping up the slope, he spat out the threat again. "Show yourself or feel Excalibur's fury."

He held out the blade for a few seconds longer but the threat did not have the desired effect and no-one emerged. The King grew impatient and hissed out another warning. "I take your silence as an admission that your presence here is one of sinister purpose. I will give you to the count of three then Excalibur will slit you from throat to groin."

Silence remained the only forthcoming response.

"One," he snarled.

Arthur nearly found himself admiring the intruder's courage but stopped just short of it, instead concentrating on the years that he had spent walking the earth, fearing every stranger that had crossed his path lest they were a minion of Montagu.

"Two," he shouted, enraged by the continuing lack of response.

He took a huge breath and sneered, "Enough of this charade. Three!" With a vicious thrust, he jabbed Excalibur into the thorns. "Show yourself, dammit." He stabbed again but to no avail. Whoever had been there had gone. Or had there ever been anyone there? Was the loneliness of the last two years distorting his mind?

He shoved Excalibur back into its sheath roughly and ground his thumb and forefinger into his eyes as a sudden wave of fatigue swept over him. He looked up at the clouds and realised that the sun was well on its way to relinquishing its position in the sky to the moon so he took one last look behind the bush where he thought he had seen someone watching him and turned to go back to the shore.

What he saw stole the breath from his lungs. There, as clear as day, was a cowled figure striding towards an unguarded, unmoving Merlin.

"Gods, no," he moaned, breaking into a run but knowing he would never cover the ground in time. "Merlin!" he shrieked. "Awaken, awaken!"

The wizard remained as placidly still as the surface of the lake that stretched out before him, blissfully unaware of the stranger that approached him across the gritty shoreline.

King Arthur wrestled to free Excalibur once more as he bolted down the slope. He tried to yell another warning but the breath was knocked out of him as he hit the level ground awkwardly and nearly fell to his knees. Regaining his balance, he continued the race towards Merlin, suddenly daring to entertain a slim hope that he would in fact be able to gain the territory between the magician and the newcomer.

The stranger, for his part, seemed quite unconcerned by the imposing figure rampaging across the ground towards him like a big cat chasing down a gazelle. Instead, without breaking stride, he extended his left hand with the palm facing towards Arthur and murmured, "Be still."

The King felt as if he had run into a wall. The wind was wrenched painfully from his lungs and he fought for a breath that he was not sure would ever come. As the lack of air began to overwhelm him and he felt himself to be on the brink of passing out, a bright light seemed to expand above him and he reached for it, reached with every fibre of his being, because he could feel the chill of a seductive darkness behind him and he knew in his soul that if he allowed himself to be consumed by it, he would never breathe again.

Suddenly he touched it and the light shimmered. He felt it envelop his outstretched hand and pull him upwards. In the blink of an eye, his hand was completely immersed by it and he felt a sickening sensation of speed as the light winked out.

Just as suddenly the sky was above him again and he could feel the breeze on his face. He went to raise himself from the ground only to realise there was no ground to raise himself up from. He was floating in the air as insubstantial as a ghost. Fighting down a rising sense of panic, he managed to spin around so he was looking down at the stony shore of the Grail Lake. His gorge rose as he found himself looking down at his own spread-eagled body, petrified in an agonising pose on the damp pebbles.

He strived to get closer to his, he shuddered at the word, corpse but he could not. As he wept with fear and frustration, a movement caught his eye and he dragged his stare away from the distressing scene before him.

The stranger had reached Merlin.

Momentarily forgetting that he was, to all intents and purposes, a spectre, Arthur frantically propelled himself towards the newcomer, determined to exact some sort of revenge upon his murderer. Using an action not dissimilar to a swimming stroke, the King inched towards them both.

As Arthur concentrated his whole being on getting nearer to the two of them, he was gripped by gut-wrenching alarm as he tried to warn the magician but could find no breath with which to do it.

The newcomer ceased his stride with a terrible smile twisting his face into a grotesque mask. He hunkered down in front of Merlin, eyeing him with a strange intensity. He passed a hand across the magician's face to make sure that the entranced wizard had not been roused by Arthur's shouts of moments earlier. Satisfied that his quarry remained totally oblivious to his presence, he stood upright and twisted his hand in a circle. A ball of fire flamed into existence in the palm of his hand and he stared at it for a few seconds, entranced by the white-hot flames that lapped over his hand without burning. He took a deep breath, threw the ball into the air, caught it, drew his arm back and let fly at the unmoving figure in front of him.

He threw himself to the ground as the fireball hit some sort of invisible shield and rebounded straight back at him.

King Arthur also ended up flat on his back as a result of the blow. As he sat himself up, shaking his head to clear it, he held the spectral Excalibur up, blade pointing to the sky. To his utter astonishment, there was not a mark on it, not even where the folded steel of the weapon had deflected the fireball. Feeling a little more comforted by his thwarting of the hooded man, he lurched upright and went to stand in between Merlin and his would-be killer.

Gaping at the smoking circle that had been scorched in the sand behind him where the fiery projectile had struck the earth, the stranger scrambled to his feet and edged closer to Merlin before dropping to his haunches once more. For the first time since his arrival, the newcomer threw back his cowl. His jaw was finely chiselled and his tanned face was sculpted by classically high cheekbones. His hair was blond, lustrous and shoulder length. As Arthur was struck by an inexplicable feeling of deja-vu, the stranger flicked an errant ringlet from his eyes with a practised swipe of his hand. The man's eyebrows knitted together and he gingerly began to probe the air around Merlin, as if expecting to receive some sort of shock. After he was satisfied that the mage was not protecting himself, he stood back with his hands on his hips and an unmistakable air of bemusement about him. He walked forward until he was mere inches from the magician. As he did so, an unexpected shiver rippled through him for it was a balmy night, and he found himself staring about nervously. His eyes fell upon the twisted body of the King and for a long moment he gazed at it. Then suddenly the sun of understanding shone upon his face like a beacon and his emerald eyes flickered with recognition. "Of course," he sighed, rolling his eyes in embarrassment that he had not puzzled out the conundrum sooner.

The words jerked Arthur out of his contemplation of Excalibur. He had crept up behind the man as he had been studying Merlin, waited for the right moment then swept his blade round in an unstoppable arc, perfectly slicing across his shoulders and severing head from neck. At least that is what he expected to happen. Instead, the only noticeable change in the man had been a huge shiver unsettling him and causing him to stare at the King's corpse.

Arthur jumped as a deep booming laugh sounded in his ears.

The stranger was pacing up and down the shore, hands clasped behind his back in the manner of one giving a lecture, "Very impressive, Arthur. Such a shame that, whilst your enchanted toothpick can deflect magic while you walk in the shadowlands, it cannot harm living flesh and blood." He thumped a hand upon his chest. "Flesh and blood, on the other hand, can do great harm to shadows." The stranger sauntered over to where Arthur's body lay and placed a foot upon its windpipe.

The phantom king clawed at his neck in a desperate effort to stop the awful feeling of suffocation engulfing him. This was the exact sensation that he had experienced when the first spell had been cast and he had been transported into this other state of being. He dropped to his knees and hoped that the light would appear again to offer him salvation from the pain. This time though, there was no light. Just a black hole unravelling in front of him, calling him forth, inviting him into its eternal embrace. With an almost grateful sigh, Arthur collapsed forwards into the abyss.

The stranger increased the pressure on the King's neck, readying himself for the sweet sound of shattering bone.

"I really wouldn't do that if I were you," came a voice across the stones.

The newcomer spun round so fast at the unexpected interruption that he lost his balance and sprawled to the ground. Fortunately for him, the tumble saved his life because Merlin had cast a fireball which would have caught him squarely in the chest had he remained upright.

However the magician did not have time to cast another one for, in the blink of an eye, the new arrival had magicked himself from the scene.

"Damn and blast," Merlin spat. He put his irritation aside and flew to Arthur's side, cursing hugely at the condition his companion had been left in.

The king was plummeting forward, his senses assailed on all sides by stomach churning fear. He tumbled over and over, throwing his arms out frantically in a bid to catch hold of something, anything that would arrest his downward plunge. His fingers brushed tantalisingly against possible handholds but they were gone too quickly for him to grip them.

His eyes had filled with water, although whether that had to do with the fetid fumes emanating from below or him weeping with terror, he neither knew nor cared.

Insubstantial somethings brushed his body and, on the cusp of hearing, his name was being repeated over and over again.

...Arthur...Arthur

Although he had no sense of time and no reference points to relate to, he felt that his plummet was gathering speed. Then a dot of light winked into existence before him. He could not be sure how near or far it was from him, so he swiped a hand across his face to try and gauge the distance. As his arm arced in front of him, the momentum of his swing sent his body into an uncontrollable spin and he lost sight of the pinpoint of brightness that had appeared seconds before...

...Arthur...Arthur

He glimpsed it again for an all too brief time before it was gone from his vision once more but, for the first time since the nightmare plunge had begun, he started to become aware of a sensation. Hitherto he had been conscious of nothing more than the air whipping at his face and clothing, but now he could feel a warmth that caressed his body in a blissful cloak...

...Arthur...Arthur

With a suddenness that surprised the King as much as the radiance from below, the voice that had been whispering for him became filled with a distressing urgency and, if such a thing were possible, added another level to his terror...

...Arthur...Arthur

As he turned his head once again to try and identify the speaker, he noticed that the heat was becoming more concentrated and the cold sweat that drenched him was evaporating and being replaced by its more usual counterpart...

...Arthur...Arthur

The king's eyes widened as the light below resolved itself into a chaotic ocean of fire and flame. Even more frantic now, he struck out on all sides, praying for some sort of miracle salvation to appear and arrest his descent into the raging volcano below...

...Arthur...Arthur...Arthur...Arthur

The voice increased in volume to such an extent that it felt like an invisible yet tangible force pounding upon his brain. He screamed and screamed but no sound came.

When the concussion hit, it ripped the air from his lungs. His whole body found itself wrenched to the right and the orange maelstrom disappeared so quickly that it was almost as if it had been a product of Arthur's imagination.

He laid still, his lungs desperately gasping for the air that had been stolen so abruptly from them. He had come to rest on cold, unyielding stone although after what had just occurred, it felt to Arthur like the most luxurious carpet imaginable.

Once the world ceased swirling about him and equilibrium reasserted itself, he propped himself up on his elbows and began to take note of his surroundings. The little details that he could see lurked in a sickly greenish light that gave everything it touched a diseased demeanour. He staggered to his feet and made his way to the nearest wall. Before he touched it, he peered intently at the stone for it was caked in a fluorescent slime that Arthur surmised to be the source of the feeble illumination.

Gingerly, he brushed his fingertips across the rock, grimacing slightly at the unpleasant texture. The residue had no smell but it made the ends of his fingers tingle uncomfortably and he smeared his hand down his tunic quickly.

Steeling himself, he stood as erect as he could, withdrew Excalibur from its scabbard and struck out for he knew not where.

As he crept along, he became aware of whispers in his ears, nothing more than the ghosts of words but words nonetheless. He strained his senses to the utmost to locate their origin but as he did so, a rank wind introduced itself to his nostrils and seemed to blow the insubstantial sounds away. He wrinkled his face in disgust at the odour and edged forward. An unexplained change in the half-darkness ahead suggested that the narrow passage was about to resolve itself into something more expansive.

And so it was that, as Arthur rounded the corner, he found himself staring into a massive cavern which gave the impression that it went on forever.

Another rancid gust of air assailed him and he staggered back against the wall. His left hand fell upon the pitted surface where his fingers lingered despite the unedifying feel of the sludge on the cold stone. He peered closely at the wall because the ridges that he was feeling seemed too angular to be natural. Cursing quietly because his eyes were unable to distinguish them, he slowly lowered his eyelids and let his fingers become his eyes.

A chill slowly started to seep down his spine as he deciphered the words. A couple of passes over the first words were enough to unravel their nature. They also offered a bleak foreboding as to the place that the King now found himself in. He was certain what the final two words would be as he continued to touch the wall but experience told him that he had to be sure.

As his fingers left the frigid surface, he hung his head in despair. He had thought that the diversion from the headlong descent into the fire had been one of salvation but instead it appeared to have only been delaying the inevitable.

With all the nobility and bearing that he could muster, King Arthur Pendragon strode forth into The Halls of Reckoning.

The Halls of Reckoning were, as pagan legend had it, the last staging post before one reached the afterlife and, in their massive environs, the soul would sit before the judgement of the Arbiters.

The Arbiters were said to be seven great heroes from the myths of Arthur's ancestors, whom were deemed so immaculate in thought and deed that they were considered incorruptible. Therefore, when it was their time to make the journey into the afterlife, they were not admitted any further but instead honoured and appointed as the ultimate judges who would determine whether the billions of deceased souls that passed through the Halls would end up in the eternal bliss of paradise or the everlasting torment of damnation.

Their decisions were final, their verdicts absolute.

Arthur wove his way through the multitude of spectres that roamed the Halls. There appeared to be no particular order to the souls being judged, one moment a pale shade would be standing nearby then a beam of light would pierce the crepuscular cave and the soul would disappear in the blink of an eye, apparently sucked into the shaft of brightness, which emanated from a place on the far side of the cave well beyond Arthur's sight.

Whether the other phantoms were aware of him or not was unclear. The King fancied that some of them paid him heed, whilst others continued with their seemingly aimless rambling.

At a loss as to what to do, Arthur ceased his motion and simply stood where he was, perfectly aware of what he was seeing but trying as resolutely as he could not to believe it.

Surely it could not really end like this. He had walked the earth for more years than any man, yet had nothing to show for his efforts. It was not fair and not right. He had thought that good was on his side for all this time and yet, it had ended like this. Slain by a mysterious stranger on a bleak shoreline, miles from anywhere, whilst protecting....his hand flew to his mouth...Merlin!

A new despair now rested upon him. He had failed in his duty to protect the mage as he searched for the Grail. Knowing it was futile but doing it anyway, his gaze swept the Halls, hoping against hope that he would see his friend and companion of centuries and be able to throw himself on his mercy and plead forgiveness for his abject failure.

The more Arthur looked, the more he realised just how vast the Halls were and how useless his actions seemed. The odds against him finding Merlin in the throng were immeasurable. With a shake of his head, he began to weep. He wept for the loss of his friend and wept for the failure of the quest. He had been given the opportunity to send the world forward into a new golden age, to achieve immortality by his deeds, yet he had fallen woefully short and, in the process, buried countless of his companions in the earth. His vanity in thinking that he had been capable of such a deed now sat bitterly on his mind. He raised his head and through a veil of tears, begged to be taken, to be judged by the Arbiters so that his torment would be at an end, but the beam of light would not come.

As he sunk to the ground despondently, he realised that his current predicament, as well as being the last step on the path of his life, had also caused irrevocable damage to another foundation of his life, his faith.

As a committed Christian, the fact that his final breath was to be taken here, in a place that was only meant to exist in the long forgotten myths of his antecedents tasted like ashes in his mouth.

Did that mean that there was to be no judgement of heaven to face when his time was ended? If that were so, then what else that had been preached to the knights and servants in the grand surroundings of the chapel at Camelot was wrong? Had it all been lies?

He jumped slightly as a brilliant spear of light uplifted one of the whey-faced denizens ambling nearby to whatever her short future held. He managed to get the general idea of which direction she had rocketed away towards but the ultimate destination was still denied to him by the massive nature of the Halls.

As the beam disappeared, another blazed into existence and earthed itself a goodly way to Arthur's right. With it, a light flared in the King's eyes. If he could intercept the light before the shaft hit its target then perhaps he could replace them and challenge the Arbiters to judge him before his time.

He had never felt so bereft in all his days and now found himself friendless, faithless and just wanting to be spared further torment.

Now, with a new purpose driving him on, albeit a morbid one, Arthur began to make his way back into the heart of the crowd again, pushing past the wraiths who were ignorant of his presence, eyes paying no heed to where he walked, simply fixing themselves on the horizon awaiting the next burst of brightness. His passage cut a swathe through the souls and he simply shouldered his way past anyone who stood in his path. The fearsome set to his jaw would have been enough to move the living, let alone the massed ranks of undead but, as it was, the souls simply swayed to the side and treated this ungracious interloper with absolute indifference.

There! The beam struck agonisingly close to the King's right but he had not been prepared for its speed and missed the opportunity. Shrugging off the missed chance, Arthur rolled his head around and loosened his muscles in preparation for his next attempt. He took a huge breath and adopted the classic battle stance that had stood him in such good stead when conflict had reared its ugly head during his life in Camelot.

Excalibur felt as light as a feather as he swapped hands back and forth, back and forth, poised to anticipate the next shaft of light.

Then he was off! The unerring arrow of brightness hit its target like a bolt of lightning and Arthur flung himself toward the one who had been chosen. His left hand closed around the hem of the man's robe but the wind was knocked from him as he hit the unyielding ground and he could not maintain his grip. Cursing effusively, the King regained his feet and resumed his patrol.

Whether it was by design or a twist of fate, the next five victims were standing nowhere near Arthur's chosen spot and so he was forced to watch impotently as one after the other disappeared into the ether.

In all, twenty-five of the denizens of the Halls had been called to judgement in the time that Arthur had been trying to execute his idea and the nearest he had come to success was the fleeting brush of the coarse material of the first man's robes.

He was drenched in sweat from his exertions and breathing heavily. Perhaps a change of tactic was required? Arthur sheathed Excalibur and dropped to his haunches but did not sit down just in case the light fell on a person near to him and he was unable to lay his hands on them in time.

As he saw it, he had two courses of action open to him. He could either begin walking towards the origin of the light, which could take days to find, or he could pick out one of the unfortunates arrayed around him and simply stand with them, hand grasping their shoulder, and wait until they were chosen.

He knew that both could take an infinite amount of time, so which should he opt for? Whichever path he chose, he knew it would not be a quick solution to his torture.

Shaking his head, he straightened up and arched his aching back. He caught himself thinking that he was getting too old for this and, for the first time in a long time, a smile cracked his face. Getting too old to die? Now there was an interesting thought.

He elected to choose one of the throng that was dotted around him. He laid Excalibur on the cold floor and spun it around, the metal haft scraping unpleasantly on the stone as it wheeled to a stop. The blade finished up pointing at a young boy of no more than ten years old. His long lank hair dribbled down his shoulders unpleasantly and his tunic bore the claw marks of some sort of beast across its back. By the amount of scratches and the severity of damage to the garment, it was clear that the boy had been mauled to death and sent to the Halls by the creature that had attacked him. One look at the remains of the boy's face was enough to confirm Arthur's supposition. The poor child's face lacked a left eye and most of the nose, these two organs being replaced by a gaping, jagged wound. Shaking his head in pity for the unfortunate boy, Arthur took up station on the boy's right, ready to cling to him with his left hand and hefting Excalibur in the other. He stood and waited, mentally preparing himself for whatever the future held.

Arthur did not know for how long he stood there. The beams came and went, sometimes in bursts of five or six in quick succession or sometimes as little as two in an hour. A few had landed within close proximity to the man and boy, but Arthur had remained resolute and not flinched from his chosen plan.

Though he had been, for want of a better word, awake for an extremely long time, he did not feel fatigued and that had been one of his chief worries. He imagined himself falling asleep just at the crucial moment and releasing contact with the boy then waking up to find him gone and himself back to square one.

He shrugged and shuffled his feet a little to avoid any stiffness seeping into his limbs. As he did so, he found himself thinking that perhaps that was how existence was in the Halls of Reckoning, no state of awareness and no state of sleep, just an impassive waiting game until the time for ultimate justice arrived. With that thought, something stirred in the King's mind and a candle of hope flared in his heart. He continued the thought process slowly in the manner of a hunter stalking a particularly elusive quarry. Why was it that he remained alert and aware whilst the others simply stood, dull of eye and vacant of thought? He found himself shying away from the next notion that came to him lest his rising optimism be dashed once more. Could it be that because he had arrived in the Halls via such a circuitous route, he was not, in actual fact, dead? Could it be that by some extreme chance, he was an intruder in a place that he had no business being in?

He found his eye drawn once more to the vicious cuts that raked down the back of the child he had selected. Gingerly, he sheathed his blade and felt at his neck, reasoning that if he was indeed dead, then that is where the fatal blow would have been struck. In as much as he knew of such things, his throat felt fine. He chewed upon his lip. Surely if his windpipe had been crushed or his neck broken, he would be able to feel some sort of irregularity in the structure of his neck but there was none.

Again, he had come within an ace of plunging headlong into a lake of flame but, at the last second, he had been catapulted sideways into the Halls and not injured at all. Not fatally, anyway.

The more Arthur put together his thoughts, the brighter the flame within him burned and his eyes began to flicker about the room in a quickening frenzy. There was a man standing roughly three lines along to his left, scarred hideously by some sort of burn that reached from the top of his head, down his face and into his tunic which had melted in the heat and clung obscenely to his withered frame.

To his right, there was a woman of proud bearing, her noble nose pointing like an arrow towards the direction of the beams. However, as he looked at her, Arthur saw that her head did not sit quite correctly upon her shoulders. He clamped his hand on the boy's shoulder and dragged him across the divide between them so that he might study her more closely. As Arthur faced her, he could not help a smile breaking out upon his features. The woman had indeed broken her neck, for it was bruised and a bone jutted cruelly against her porcelain skin, seemingly set to puncture it at any moment and break forth from within.

Almost immediately, Arthur chided himself for his reaction to the poor woman's injury but as he looked around and saw more and more of the souls and their fatal injuries, he found he had to smother a whoop of joy. It was such a heady feeling to find some hope so soon after feeling so low and depressed. He took a deep breath and collected himself. Whether or not he was simply deluding himself into thinking that there was a way to fight the darkness or not, he did not know nor did he really care, all he knew now was that he had something to fight for. He had been granted a second chance to complete the quest that had been placed upon his broad shoulders and he would not be found wanting.

Finally, his emotions began to wane and his head started to raise a few caveats to try and smother the blooming optimism slightly. If, by some miracle, he had been transported to the Halls in error then how would he be able to leave them without facing one or all of the Arbiters? The King reasoned that it was unlikely they would simply let him depart without any sort of recompense. Would they even let him depart at all? What if he had experienced some sort of seizure brought on by the stress of the situation that he was in when he left his earthly body? Could he really be sure that he was alive? After spending some time pondering the myriad of questions that had exploded in his head, he decided that he had no way of knowing one way or the other so he would just have to take his chances and pray that salvation would come on swift wings.

Stroking his beard, he began looking about for some sort of alternative means of escape rather than trusting his luck with the Arbiters. That was strictly for the final roll of the dice. He knew that the way he had entered the Halls was of no use because that was just a tunnel leading to a huge expanse of fire but perhaps, just perhaps, there were other tunnels that led away from there. Upwards, he decided, upwards was the way he needed to go. However, for now, he would just settle for anywhere. Anywhere away from the thousands of stark reminders of his mortality that stood, impassively waiting for the ethereal shaft of light to come. Mortality! The word sung in Arthur's head and he stood perfectly still for a moment, in case his movement caused the word to take flight from his mind and never return. He could not be dead. He was enchanted to live for at least another hundred years, unless his heart was removed from his body. His left hand flew to his chest, gently caressing it for any sign of marks or weals. There were none. All that his fingers felt as they brushed the wiry hair upon his breast was the steady rhythm of his heart, pumping the stuff of life through his veins.

Convinced of his continuing life now, he ran to the side of the Halls and began examining it, pushing, prodding, smacking anything that looked slightly out of place. He set about his task like a man possessed, scrutinising every nook and cranny for hidden levers or keys or anything that would set him free.

After another fruitless examination of a peculiarly shaped gap that yawned between two massive edifices of stone, Arthur ground his teeth together and sank to the floor. He was beginning to suffer for his exertions now. He ached from head to toe which, in one way, was a good thing as it showed that he was indeed still vital but, in another way, was hideously frustrating, for he yearned to be free of this place as soon as he was able. He slumped to the ground to catch his breath, head bowed towards the granite floor in exhaustion. As had often been the way in his battles as knight and monarch, he found that when the tiredness did eventually hit, it was like a relentless ocean, pounding him insensible with wave upon wave until he succumbed to its dark depths.

He knew he had to fight against it, to continue his search for a way of escaping the impossible situation he was in, but his arms felt like lengths of wet rope. He was about to stand back up when a strange thing happened. He fancied that one of the souls had been staring at him, yet when he looked, the head appeared to turn away thus obscuring the onlooker's face.

He watched for a while longer but the figure did not move again and he simply put it down to his mind playing tricks on him in response to the long isolation from human company that he found himself enduring.

Arthur staggered to his feet and resumed his search of the rock wall, stopping at various intervals to probe the consistency of the stone. It was getting progressively harder to lift his arms above shoulder height and, on more than one occasion, he nearly fell to the unforgiving stone of the floor but always when he felt his legs begin to buckle, the flame that fuelled his thirst for life would reignite his resolve and he would fumble onwards.

As his exhaustion began to reach unmanageable proportions, he found himself noticing little things that had hitherto escaped his attention. The way that some of the souls appeared to be almost luminous whilst others skulked amidst cloaks as black as pitch. The way that some of the beams were of different strengths, some blazing like a new sun, others dull and washed-out like a fog-shrouded morning. The way that his footsteps echoed eerily around the near silent Halls. It did not seem right to Arthur that there was no sound to accompany all these wandering spirits, indeed, the only noise that broke the uncanny stillness was the sigh that accompanied the departure of each soul as it was called to account. Shaking his head as the wonderment of his predicament assailed him once again, he resumed his attempt to escape.

As the beams had been fairly constant since the King had entered the Halls, it was not until they had ceased for a moment and he continued on his search that he became aware of a subtle wrongness.

As he walked, the echo of his footsteps appeared to be reverberating strangely as if they were overlain with a reply. Arthur desperately tried to puzzle out the phenomenon, wondering whether it meant that he was nearing another wall or that it was just a trick of the echo but he found the fatigue overwhelming him once more and he struggled to stand. Now his ears were definitely playing tricks on him for, even though he was standing still, he could hear footsteps, running footsteps. He frantically tried to maintain his balance but as he turned his head towards the phantom noise, his poise deserted him and he fell into a couple of lost shades.

It saved his life.

Blinking furiously, he watched in disbelief as the soul that he had suspected of watching him detached itself from the throng and ran at him, sword at the ready, poised to run him through.

Acting on pure instinct, Arthur hurriedly unsheathed Excalibur and just about parried the blow. He dug his heels into the ground and pushed himself backwards just as the blade of his attacker's weapon slashed onto the stones, raising a shower of sparks. The adrenaline rush had been such that it had given the King a second wind and he regained his feet within seconds. Excalibur described a figure of eight as Arthur vainly tried to identify his assailant. However, the man was enveloped in one of the dark clouds that Arthur had noticed earlier and he could not be clearly seen.

"Show yourself, cur," Arthur sneered, his debilitating weariness all but vanished and his monarchical nobility and bearing restored. "Do not hide behind that shroud of smoke. Come into the light or are you so foul that you do not wish to corrupt it with your ugliness?"

The challenge did not cause the swordsman to emerge, it merely served to bring on a fresh attack. Now that Arthur had regained his feet though, he was easily able to keep the spectral wraith at bay.

The lack of a face at which to direct his anger was becoming an irritation to the King so he went on the offensive, determined to unmask his would-be killer in the quickest possible time.

The shadow retreated slowly but inexorably, barely able to keep pace with the King's lightning strokes. After a particularly brutal set of two handed swipes at his attacker, Arthur broke through the man's defence. He feinted an overhead swing but, at the last second, changed its trajectory so that his blade swept under his attacker's and hit home with a satisfying sound.

An excruciating shriek shattered the silence and the black cloud began to disperse as the man slumped to the ground. Despite Arthur being confident that he had inflicted a mortal injury, he still kept the point of Excalibur trained on his victim as the last tendrils of the fog cleared. He leant in to get the best possible look at the swordsman's face.

He stood dumbfounded at the features he gazed upon. He had not known whom he had expected to see but of all the possible suspects, this one was one of the most unlikely.

Breathing raggedly, the man stared up at his killer. "It looks like you have finally got your wish, Arthur," Mordred sighed as a thin trickle of blood dribbled from his lips and began to stain his tunic.

Although the King was completely thrown by the face that gazed back up at him, he stared at his nephew as dispassionately as he could. What Mordred had said was true, he had wished him dead on more than one occasion but now, to have actually committed the deed, in this of all places, left Arthur feeling somehow sullied. He could not bring himself to forgive Mordred for throwing in his lot with Montagu but, despite his best efforts, he knew that a tinge of pity was evident in his eyes.

"You brought my enmity for you upon yourself, nephew," he sighed. "To have tried to usurp my throne and kingdom whilst I was fighting the French was hateful enough, but to employ that hell-spawn as your lieutenant, that is beyond pardon."

Mordred tried to shift his position but the pain of his death-wound seared his body and he was forced to remain where he had fallen. Arthur was surprised, however, by the look of defiance that flared in Mordred's eyes. "I have scant seconds left alive, yet you force me to repeat myself. As I said to you on the field of Camlann, it is I that is under his spell, Arthur. Do you honestly think that Montagu would allow himself to be led by anyone, let alone the bastard nephew of his worst enemy?" A racking cough shuddered Mordred's broken body and a gout of dark clotted blood erupted from his mouth.

Arthur frowned at this. Surely it was Merlin that was Montagu's nemesis, not him. Shrugging, he wrote off the statement as the confused ramblings of a man knocking upon death's door. "Whether you were under his enchantment or not, he could not watch you day and night. If you had really wished to escape his attentions, I am sure a slippery snake such as yourself could have done so."

Mordred tried to smile but the pain was too great. "I did escape him for a time," he sighed, eyes staring at some distant point in his memory. "But at such a price, such a price." The usurper's eyes glazed momentarily and Arthur thought he was about to pass on but suddenly the intensity grew anew in his eyes and he glared at the King. "How long have you been here, Arthur? A week? A month?"

The King pondered the question, staring off into the darkness that stretched into the distance. How did you measure time here? With no sunlight or moonlight, it was impossible to gauge the passing of the hours. "I know not," he answered after a while, "I feel that it has not been very long, a few days maybe, but without the warmth of the sun or the cold light of the moon," his voice trailed off, "I could not say."

"Four years," Montagu wailed. "I have been condemned to walk this place for four years."

Arthur's eyes widened at the thought. Four years with no human contact, four years of being reminded at every turn of death and mortality. "You have walked the Halls for all that time, yet you have still not been chosen?" the King gaped incredulously as another beam of light coruscated through the air in the distance.

Mordred shook his head and his face took on a look of bitterness. "It is not my time, uncle. Montagu sent me here for he had foreseen that you would arrive here one day, he just did not know when. This is my punishment for trying to please him and thus free myself of his wickedness."

Something was setting warning bells off in Arthur's head but the tide of weariness had ebbed back into his mind and his head was swimming once more. "Are you not immortal as I am? Your heart must be removed before you die, must it not?"

Mordred's eyes shifted nervously from side to side but the King was so tired that he barely heard the answer. "I may have nearly two more centuries promised to me by Montagu's potion but I can still feel pain. Dammit, Arthur, you have nearly cut me in two. I cannot move. I might as well be dead."

Despite himself, tears welled in the King's eyes at Mordred's agony. His mind recalled the old saying, 'The mouth may lie but the eyes may not'. Arthur studied the injured man's stare and could not see any evidence of deceit, only pain, fear and despair. He stood unsteadily, unsure if he was taking the correct course of action, but determined to ask the question nonetheless. "I know that you were sent here to kill me and have tried to kill me on more than one occasion but, as I stand here and see you writhe, my heart fills with sorrow, not joy. I have no wish to see my kinsman in such anguish. If you have spoken truly then there will only be one answer to this question, but I feel I must give you the choice. Do you wish to live out your days like this or do you want me to hasten your path to the afterlife so that you may accept whatever judgement is bestowed upon you by the Arbiters."

Mordred did not hesitate. "You would do that for me? Despite all the things that I have done to both you and your companions? You would set me free from Montagu?"

Arthur could not bring himself to speak, merely nodding his affirmation. He did not have the heart to tell Mordred that he had been free of Montagu's terrorism ever since Merlin had bested him aboard the Viking ship off the shore of Lindisfarne.

Arthur's nephew ceased trying to lift himself from the floor and slumped back to the cold granite with an almost beatific look upon his ghastly grey face. "Thank you, Arthur, thank you."

Not for the first time, Arthur found himself wondering what foul deeds Mordred had committed or witnessed by Montagu's hand that caused him to want to embrace the Reaper so readily. He calmly acknowledged his nephew's gratitude and placed Excalibur in both hands, the tip of his blade resting on Mordred's torso. "You are sure of this?" he repeated.

The fatally injured man nodded almost eagerly. He laughed madly and shouted at the top of his voice. "Do you hear that, you black-hearted bastard. I am to be free of you. No more voices in my head. No more dark visions haunting my dreams. I am to be free."

"You do not fear what awaits you when you move from this life to the next? After all you have done?" Arthur asked as he adjusted his grip slightly on the pommel of his sword.

Mordred fixed him with the most forbidding glare he had ever seen from his nephew. "Arthur, I have been living in hell ever since Montagu wormed his way into my life. I have lost the will to care about what happens to me after I die. I just want to escape his clutches. I am tired of the constant commands, the constant insults, the constant gloating. He has treated me like the lowest piece of filth from the first day we met and he will continue to do so until I can release myself from this prison."

Again a clarion of warning rang but this time Arthur was able to pinpoint exactly what troubled him. It was Mordred's continuous use of Montagu's name in the present tense that grated upon him. He stepped back from the stance which towered over his nephew and forced a laugh. "You talk of it as if it was only yesterday since the two of you spoke."

Mordred stopped his diatribe against Montagu and wrinkled his brow. "It was, uncle. What of it?"

An icy feeling began to creep down the King's spine and his face hardened. "Even in the face of death, you continue to spout your lies. Montagu has been dead years past. Merlin slew him aboard a Viking longship after he had stolen the Lindisfarne Gospels."

Mordred blinked owlishly at his uncle. "I am sorry, Arthur, but you are mistaken. It..." the would-be usurper of the throne of Wessex stopped speaking abruptly. His eyes rolled around in his head and he whimpered, "Please, no, no, nooooooo..." Despite his injury, Mordred's hands shot up to his ears and he screamed and screamed and screamed.

The King's mind was willing him forward to try and help his nephew but his body would not respond. The last thing he saw before he passed out was Mordred's heart erupting through his ribs, grasped tightly in the death grip of an unseen hand.

Though he was exhausted by the events that had just passed, Arthur did not sleep for long. His slumber was troubled by nightmare upon nightmare. It was true that he had often been visited by horrendous night terrors before but these had a vividness and clarity that had startled him into wakefulness more than once during his rest. He shivered and pulled his cloak about him. The moment his eyes adjusted to the feeble green light, he stared to the place where Mordred had been slain, bloodied and broken after the swordfight. He was not surprised to see that the corpse had gone, after all, his heart had been separated from his body and now he was entirely justified in occupying a place in the Halls.

He stared dumbly at the site of Mordred's death, turning over and over what Mordred had said in their final conversation. With the benefit of rest, his mind felt clearer and he found himself able to analyse Mordred's final words. There were numerous hints contained within them that Montagu remained alive. Arthur's mind shrunk back from thinking about that. Merlin had said that he had killed him and, as far as the King was concerned, though Merlin could be called any number of unflattering names, liar was not one of them.

Yet if Montagu was dead, how had his words come to torment Mordred for so long? The manner of his nephew's death was not to be dismissed lightly either, bloody and violent as it was. Was it possible that Montagu's power was such that he was able to command others to do his will from beyond the veil?

All these questions reeled around the King's head, demanding answers but obtaining none.

He was so lost in his contemplation that he did not notice the change in atmosphere behind him. He did not notice the cessation of the beams of light. He did not notice the slow steady increase in the brightness of the cavern. He did not even notice that, due to the brightening of the chamber, a shadow was starting to form from the base of his feet, patiently moulding itself into a clear silhouette that stood with one hand up at the face, stroking a beard, and the other resting on the pommel of a sword.

Finally he emerged from his trance and blinked at the stark relief of his profile on the floor in front of him. The breath caught in his throat but he forced himself to turn round and face whatever it was that stood behind him, bathing him in its light.

The being that stood before him was impossible to distinguish, for the incandescence was such that Arthur had to squint to bear it but he did not need the full use of his eyes to see that it bulked a good head higher than him. He stared to his left and to his right, but the light was all-encompassing. He had nowhere to go because somehow he had become backed up against one of the walls of the vast cavern. In the absence of any other ideas, he drew Excalibur from its scabbard and described an arc that took in the two edges of the light and everything else in between. Fear and the interminable silence made the King speak although his voice was shaky and dripping with nervousness, "If you wish to attack me then attack. I do not fear you," he hissed, the lie in his statement being revealed by a telltale squeak in the final word. In truth, Arthur could feel the massive nature of the presence before him and he had never felt so scared in all his days.

The move did not create any hostility from the being, however. Indeed, a whisper on the cusp of hearing seemed to spread through it and to Arthur's ears, which strove to pick up any hint of the being's nature, it appeared to contain one or two snatches of what sounded like mocking laughter.

Gradually, as the King's eyes started to accustom themselves to the light and the brightness began to fade, Arthur found himself able to see clearly that which stood before him.

Arrayed in front of him were seven huge beings, none shorter than ten feet tall, each robed in exactly the same garment, a simple piece of white cloth, clasped around their necks by an ornate brooch and reaching to the floor. Arthur found his gaze drawn like a magnet to the set of scales embroidered on the cloth above the left breast.

"Who dares spill living blood in the Halls of the Dead?" intoned the nearest. Arthur immediately sheathed his blade and bowed at the newcomers. "I am Arthur Pendragon," he stammered, "former King of the Britons and leader of The Knights of The Round Table. And I..."

The one who had spoken held up his hand and Arthur's voice lapsed into silence. He stood uncomfortably, painfully aware of his complete defencelessness in the face of these giants.

All seven closed their eyes at the same instant and Arthur guessed that some sort of unspoken communion was occurring between the septet. In a matter of seconds, the beings were all regarding him again, some indifferently, others with glares bordering on hostility.

It appeared to Arthur that the one who stood nearest to him was the leader, or at least the spokesman, for it was he who continued the dialogue, *"Arthur Pendragon, we have overseen these Halls for time immemorial. All whom have perished upon the earth above have been subjected to our scrutiny and judgement and none have taken issue with the verdicts we have pronounced. There have been many whom have sought to outwit us, some have even tried to best us through strength of arms, yet in the final reckoning all have submitted to our decision. In all that time, however, none have stained our chambers with the taint of blood, none have ever been robbed of life, no sins have been committed and no miracles performed, but most pertinently to you, we suspect, none have ever returned to the earth above from this chamber. Make no mistake, Arthur Pendragon, this is a place of death. Life cannot flourish here, for here there is no food, no water, no air. Here there is no hope."*

The words seemed to be arriving directly into Arthur's mind. There was no flexibility evident in the Arbiter's voice, just simply the ultimate knowledge that what was being said was what would come to pass. They crashed down upon the King's shoulders like lead weights, breaking his spirit and destroying his resolve. He wanted to speak, to explain, to plead but he could not find the words.

The Arbiter continued his monotone. Arthur clamped his hands over his ears but still the voice droned on, unyielding and relentless. *"We are aware that it was not your blade that sent Mordred to our chamber but it was your blade that spilt his blood upon the stones. As this is such an unprecedented occurrence, we feel we have no choice but to meet it with an unprecedented response."*

Arthur released his hands from his ears and his arms flopped down by his sides.

The Arbiter spoke once more, this time using his voice. "Arthur Pendragon, you are an interloper in our world. To compound this most unusual set of circumstances, you have also spilt the stuff of life in a place of death, a place that has not seen such an act in its entire existence. In light of this inexcusable deed, we must forgo the usual practices and call you to account before your time. You are to be returned to our chamber and judged forthwith."

One by one, the Arbiters extended their right hands and a beam of light similar to the one that had dotted the halls for as long as time could remember erupted from each. The only difference was that instead of the arrow of brightness flying straight and true, the bolts snapped out like whips and bit at Arthur's body where they fell.

The King shrieked at the burning sensation that enveloped him from head to foot. Through the pain, he managed to look down at his ethereal shackles. There was one upon each of his legs, one upon each of his wrists and the final one, the one held by the Arbiter who had done all the speaking, was lashed around his neck, a collar of simple beauty but complicated pain.

And so it was that the Arbiters of The Halls of Reckoning led King Arthur through their domain like a dog, chained and restrained, the first soul to be judged before its time.

As the procession meandered its way through the endless ranks of patiently waiting souls, Arthur found the pain of his fetters dulled somewhat and after a while he was no longer viewing events through the bitter sting of his tears. The despair that had evaporated when he realised that he still lived had quickly returned with a venomous vengeance when the manacles had been attached to him. How could he possibly entertain hope in a place where there was none? He had tried on more than one occasion to engage one of the Arbiters in conversation but they all remained silent. Arthur was aware that they seemed to commune with each other on a frequent basis, for on those occasions when he had spoken to them, he had noticed that their eyes were shut, yet one or two of them could clearly be seen mouthing words that were beyond the edge of his hearing though he strained with all his might to pick up their thread.

As the agony of the shackles dissipated, so the despair began to give way to anger. He felt like he was being paraded like a common criminal through the streets of a ghost town. For whose benefit was this charade? Surely they could simply transport him to the place of judgement via one of the light beams rather than this endless ramble through the Halls? Tentatively, the former King of Britain tried to tease at his bonds but there was not an inch of purchase to be found upon them, they were skin-tight and inescapable. In frustration, he blurted, "Dammit, will this walk take much longer?"

The spokesman for the Arbiters turned with an amused expression on his face. "Did we not say you would be tried within the hour?"

Arthur spun round for he had not really been expecting a response. "Yes, you did." The King replied, his rage diminishing. "But surely we have been trudging for more than an hour?"

The Arbiter shook his head. "You are mistaken, Arthur Pendragon. We have walked for no more than a few minutes."

Arthur's brow creased in distress. He had no cause to doubt the Arbiter's word, after all, a being as legendarily incorruptible as this would have no reason to lie, but without any point of reference to relate to, he had no way of distinguishing the time anyway. "Can you not simply summon one of your lights to convey us to our destination?" he asked.

"Can you not simply accept your fate and await your judgement with dignity rather than mewling like a child?" the Arbiter countered.

Cheeks flaming with embarrassment, Arthur shut his mouth and resigned himself to a long walk, the end of which would result in the final walk that he would ever take.

The Arbiter continued, "There are things that you must see, Arthur Pendragon. Faces that you thought you would never behold again."

With that enigmatic statement floating in the air, the Arbiter closed his eyes and began the unspoken communion between himself and his fellows once again.

In the absence of anything else to do, Arthur began studying his surroundings again. The green luminescence was still evident but not quite so widespread. It was steadily being replaced by a brightness of a different hue, this one a softer, more welcoming light. Also, the endless ranks of the deceased seemed to be forming into distinct lines rather than being arrayed in the haphazard manner that he had seen previously.

Suddenly, the breath caught in the King's throat. There, before him, stood one of his closest confidantes from his days at Camelot, yet also the man who had, albeit unwittingly, brought about the King's near demise. "Galahad?" he whispered hoarsely.

The cherubic face did not respond in any way, it simply remained staring towards infinity.

"Please stop." Arthur tried to pull against the implacable strength of the Arbiters' bonds, but to no avail, they merely continued walking, oblivious to his struggles. "Please, I would talk with my friend," the King pleaded, the urge for human contact once again on the brink of overwhelming him.

"He would not hear you, Arthur Pendragon. His consciousness inhabits a different realm now."

Straining to turn his head so that he could gaze upon the familiar features once more, the King watched despairingly as Galahad's face disappeared amidst the multitude. When his neck could bear no more, he spun round and shook his head sadly. He held his arms up and shook them in the vague direction of the nearest Arbiter. "Can we dispense with these chains? I have nowhere to flee to, should I even attempt an escape."

Again, the silent intercourse ensued. "No, we may not," said one of the Arbiters to Arthur's left, after a few moments. "The time of your judgement has been set and any differentiation from it would have repercussions that would spread through the Halls and maybe even ripple upwards onto the Earth above. You see, Arthur Pendragon, everyone is pre-ordained to come under our scrutiny at their appointed time. We sense that you do mean to try and flee despite your words. This would be unacceptable to both ourselves and the ones you see all around you, patiently awaiting our judgement."

King Arthur seethed at this reply and began yanking at his shackles once more. "If that is the case, then how are you able to judge me before my time? I was not pre-ordained to even be in this benighted place at this time, let alone come before your judgement. Galahad must have been dead for centuries yet he is still waiting to be judged? Why am I so special that you feel you can pronounce verdict upon me before these others?"

The Arbiter who had done most of the talking previously, flashed a look of undisguised anger at his counterpart who had spoken to Arthur. "That is none of your concern," he stated flatly.

"On the contrary, I would say it is very much my concern," the King pressed. "If I am to be tried before my time, how am I to know that I will receive a fair trial? How do I know that you are not just using me to be made an example of?"

That stopped the procession in its tracks. The septet of Arbiters turned to face the former monarch of Britain. It seemed to Arthur that they grew in size, suddenly looming over him, obliterating the pleasant light that had begun to outshine the sickly green glow.

"You enter our chamber by underhand means. You spill blood on a floor unstained since time immemorial and now you call our integrity into question? Who do you think you are, Pendragon?" The Arbiter raised a hand as if to strike the King and he instinctively backed away. There was no need however, for the first Arbiter stepped between them, facing down his colleague. "You forget yourself, Gregor. He must be judged properly. By striking him down here, you will only make matters worse."

"As if they could be worse already," Gregor muttered.

"*Cease this! You will say too much,*" the first Arbiter spat aggressively at Gregor via the communal mind.

By the same means, Gregor shot back, "*It is you who forgets yourself, Raemund. Since when did you presume to order us to do anything? We are the seven, we preside as seven, we judge as seven. You are not a first among equals, you are an equal among equals and you would do well to remember that fact,*" Gregor countered with a calmness that belied the fearsome expression which had flown onto his face.

Raemund turned stiffly and the walk resumed. The Arbiters' strides were now longer and more defined as if they were in great haste to begin the trial.

Although he kept alert, eyes darting from face to face, Arthur failed to pick up any more signs to suggest that the Arbiters were in conversation with each other. The King also judged that something had occurred between the one called Gregor and the unnamed one who seemed to do most of the talking. The looks on their faces were like thunder and Arthur wondered if that could perhaps be used to his advantage.

He had no time to ponder this however, for the procession turned a corner and found itself facing a forbidding door that stretched from the floor to a point so high above that Arthur could not see where it stopped. Without a sound, the massive doors swung open and he found himself gazing upon that which no other living man had ever seen. The Chamber of the Arbiters. Arthur stood agape at the visual feast before him. He had thought that some of the larger rooms at Camelot had been rather ostentatious but they were nothing compared to this.

The ceiling was painted to resemble the deep blue sky of a summer's morn with a few delicate wisps of cloud dotted liberally throughout. Upon closer examination, Arthur spotted numerous flocks of birds sprinkled at various intervals across the panorama. Sighing in wonder, he reluctantly tore his gaze from the ceiling and let his eyes roam the walls.

There was a seascape on the one to Arthur's left, a vast limpid pool of azure, stretching away to the horizon.

To his right, a winter scene of stunning detail, so vivid in fact that Arthur yearned to shrug off his bonds and feel the snow melt under his fingertips.

Chancing a quick glance behind him, he was able to see that the door split the wall in two. To the left, there was a single tree standing upon a hill, adorned with leaves of many colours. Every now and again, one would part company with the branch and fall to the ground, there to wither away. Making sure that the Arbiters were not about to start the proceedings, Arthur turned more fully towards the tree. He watched a couple more leaves fall off, which left a solitary frond clinging to its branch. When this one finally fell, the instant it hit the ground, the carpet of leaves around the trunk vanished and re-appeared back in their rightful place, turning the tree from a wrinkled, gnarled deformity into a lush verdant piece of flora.

To the right of the door was a single red rose not quite ready to bud. After the other three designs, Arthur found this one to be a bit disappointing and not at all in keeping with the other spectacular friezes that decorated the room. However, it soon became clear why the flower had been included in the room's design for, as he watched, the flower swelled and burst forth into full bloom.

A pointed cough jerked Arthur from his contemplation and he turned to face his fate. As he stared, he saw that the wall behind where the Arbiters sat was also split into two tableaux. One side was the stuff of absolute nightmare, fire and smoke surrounding a door of horrific design. An evil looking throne was depicted there with the occupant shrouded in shadow and only the occasional lick of flame giving any hint of the seated being's appearance.

The other side was simply an amalgam of the designs on the other three walls. It was distinctly divided into four squares, the flower occupying the top left segment with the seascape next to it. The picture in the bottom right hand corner was of the tree, practically denuded of foliage but ready to grow again. The final portion was filled by the wintry scene which Arthur again

212

found himself marvelling at in wonderment, his breath taken from him by the amazing detail instilled in the picture.

"Arthur Pendragon," one of the Arbiters barked from behind the table at which all seven now sat.

The King jumped at the sudden return to reality and apologised profusely. "I am sorry, it is just that this room is unlike anything I have ever seen before. It humbles me."

Gregor found Arthur's enthusiasm to be bordering on the sycophantic and could not hide the disdain in his eyes. "It suffices." He dismissed Arthur's praise with a diffident shrug. "Raemund," he nodded at the Arbiter who sat in the middle of the septet.

Standing up, Raemund began to speak. "Arthur Pendragon, by your deeds shall you be known and by your deeds shall you be judged. I, Raemund, say it is so."

This chant then went around the table. The Arbiters announced themselves one by one starting at the left hand side of the table and proceeding through Raemund to finish on the right. The leftmost Arbiter was called Flammel, his red hair resting luxuriantly upon his shoulders. Next to him sat Leonid, whose poker face and ice blue eyes gave away nothing. He was in turn flanked by Fabian, who appeared to be the yin to Leonid's yang, for there was nothing but openness in his youthful countenance. To the right of Raemund sat the only female Arbiter, Kirsten, an unspoilt rose among thorns. For a moment her beauty brought Guinevere to Arthur's mind and he sighed longingly at the memory.

To Kirsten's right was Gregor, whose gigantic size was highlighted even further by his presence next to the slighter build of Kirsten. The final occupant at the table of the Arbiters announced himself as Perceval, a name that provoked a flicker of shock from Arthur as it had also been one of the names of his fellow knights at the Round Table.

Raemund stood up with his arms outstretched. "With the oath complete, I now call this trial to order." He pronounced pompously. "Arthur Pendragon, today you take the first steps upon a new path. A path upon which you may only proceed in one direction," Raemund paused and glanced over his shoulder. "You will no doubt have seen the doors situated in the wall behind us. I am sure you have apprehended their destinations by the designs painted upon them. We shall see today which one permits you ingress and which one will be forever closed to you. Let the trial commence."

Suddenly, a screen popped into existence halfway between the Arbiters and Arthur. It was, in appearance, startlingly similar to the one that had appeared above the Grail when Mordred was advancing upon Camelot. Puzzled,

Arthur leant in to study the pictures more closely. There he was, holding court in his castle, surrounded by his knights and retinue.

Kirsten arose from her seat and walked past Arthur. To his astonishment, he saw that one of the pictures on either side of the door behind him had changed. Instead of a vibrant healthy rose, there was now a picture of a stalk, barren of petals and colour. As he watched, Kirsten extended a finger and described a pattern in the air. Gradually a shape emerged from the end of the stalk. It did not take long for Arthur to decipher its nature. It was a bud. Intrigued by this, Arthur watched Kirsten gracefully resume her seat.

A frown creased the King's features as the next scene from his life was replayed in front of him. Here he was seen raging atop his throne, spitting venom and anger at two people kneeling before him. The breath caught in his throat for it was Guinevere and Sir Lancelot. He choked a strong surge of tears as he saw himself raise his hand and viciously swipe his lady to the floor. Numb with shame, he watched Fabian rise from his position at the table and walk to the picture of the verdant tree. The Arbiter's hand seemed to meld with the picture. His fingers closed around one of the branches and shook it until all the leaves had fallen to the ground.

The King hung his head and only heard Fabian return to his seat.

Then a kaleidoscope of images beset the King's vision. Conflict and battle were fought soundlessly before him. At various intervals, the Arbiters arose and walked to their chosen pictures. Flammel, Leonid and Fabian attended to the tree, violently agitating at various branches until all the leaves had parted company, whilst the other picture was dealt with by Kirsten, Gregor and Perceval, who all took turns at restoring the rose to its former glory.

Both visions and Arbiters passed Arthur by in a blur. He was being assailed on all sides by memories long suppressed, dubious acts long buried and great deeds long forgotten. Despite this visual maelstrom, he understood what was occurring and every now and again would glance nervously over his shoulder at the two images on the wall behind him.

To the left of the door the tree stood, appearing somehow huddled against the grasping hands that continually disturbed it. There remained only three branches that contained any foliage. Arthur had long realised that for every deed perceived wrong and amoral by the Arbiters, a branch would be shaken and the tree would wither. He could only guess at what would occur should the tree become totally free of greenery.

His demeanour brightened somewhat when he switched his stare to the rose and saw that it was, at the most, one or two petals short of being in full bloom. He had definitely tried to live his life as a good man and a good king and he felt that that was being borne out by the vibrancy of the rose, because for every deed perceived right and just, a petal was added to the bloom.

Chewing thoughtfully on his lip, Arthur tried with all his might to second-guess what the next event replayed before him would be. It turned out to be the field of Camlann where he so nearly succumbed to death all those years ago.

The picture in front of him leapt to life so vividly that as soon as it appeared, he remembered what had happened. For that reason, he did not watch the duel between himself and Mordred. Instead, he watched the Arbiters intently for a sign as to which one would rise and visit their allocated picture.

To his delight, it was the beauteous Kirsten, arising like an angel and saving him from a fall from grace. She strode purposefully over to the rose and attached another petal to it. Arthur could clearly see that there remained room for only one more petal then the flower would be complete and he would be walking through the door into paradise.

His gaze was drawn back to the duel just at the moment that Mordred's sword slid into him, coming within an ace of being a killing stroke. Wincing, the limited movement of his hands was just enough that he could brush tenderly the scar that would be with him until the day he died.

In a detached way, he watched himself desperately swing at Mordred, decapitating him. Then Merlin was there, casting his spell and vanishing them both back to his chambers. He stared at the Arbiters, expecting one of the tree's branches to be shaken as a penance for the murder of his nephew but all seven remained unmoved.

It was only when the next scene appeared showing him and Merlin in the magician's apartments that any of the septet got up. Disconcertingly, it was Raemund, who had remained seated throughout the entire proceedings that left his chair. He cleared his throat and announced in a most pompous voice, "Each Arbiter presides over the judgement process for the span of one day. It falls to me to seal Arthur Pendragon's fate as, on this day, I am the one seated on the cusp of right and wrong."

With that said, he emerged from behind the table.

Arthur heaved a huge sigh of relief. If Raemund was to have the final say, then there could only be one outcome, for the flower was bereft of but one petal whereas the tree still held leaves on three of its extremities.

Raemund stood in front of the massive door through which Arthur and the Arbiters had entered the magnificent room. He closed his eyes and in turn bowed towards each one of his fellow judges, he murmured, "It is agreed then."

A commotion at the table caused Arthur to twist around momentarily. He noted that Kirsten, Fabian and Perceval looked highly aggrieved. Intrigued by this, he turned back just as Raemund began talking once more. "As this is a special case and as I am the presiding Arbiter, my judgement is that the

215

majority vote carries the day." To Arthur's horror, instead of walking to the picture of the rose, Raemund stood by the image of the tree.

"Arthur Pendragon," he intoned, "you have been called to account and you have been found wanting. You caused much grief among your friends and peers by maintaining the pretence that you had passed on." The first branch of the three was shaken. "You then decided to pursue longevity for no other reason than your vanity." The second branch was shaken. "You then, along with Merlin the magician, committed the greatest crime of all, you drank the potion that artificially elongated your life. The life you live now is not yours to live, Arthur Pendragon. You are an effrontery to us all and as such deserve the destiny that is finally coming to you."

Holding Arthur's gaze, Raemund's hand closed around the final branch and shook it with great deliberation.

As the last leaf touched the ground, Arthur snapped out of his daze and snarled, "What manner of justice is this? Who are you to determine what is right and what is wrong? You have watched incidents of my life and interpreted them in your own way. You know nothing of the real truth behind my actions. Mine and Merlin's pursuit of longevity was designed to thwart an evil magician and his dire machinations and nothing more. You condemn me without having all the facts at your disposal."

Raemund stood unmoved by the gale of Arthur's wrath. "Nonetheless, Arthur Pendragon, the verdict has been pronounced. The balance of your life is such that the evil deeds outweigh the good. Therefore, there can be no alternative but to usher you through to the beyond that your errant behaviour has doomed you to." Raemund nodded towards the table. Leonid and Gregor stood up and began to walk over to the enchained King.

Arthur struggled manfully against his bonds. "When you ushered Montagu through the door, did you not repeat this selfsame process? Did you not see what heinous acts he had perpetrated? He is the reason that I partook of the potion. He is the reason I chose the loneliness and isolation of long life. Because of him, I have seen innumerable friends despatched to the Halls. I have outlived all whom I love, save one." A racking sigh shuddered through his body. "Have I not been punished enough?" he moaned.

Raemund looked thoughtful for a moment. He closed his eyes and the Arbiters communed. After his outburst a drained Arthur had hung his head and mentally prepared himself for his fate, fearing that no amount of reasoning or flowery speeches would sway the seven who judged him. Ever since he had drunk the potion, he reflected, his life had been one of hardship and ill fortune. The faces that he had seen throughout the narrative of his life had stirred a multitude of memories. Jeremy, his squire, skewered by one of Montagu's soldiers upon the field of Camlann. His cuckolder, Sir Lancelot

Du Lac, dismissed when an offer of help would have, indeed, should have been welcomed with open arms. Could he have swallowed his pride and accepted Lancelot's proposition? Could anyone have done so? He was only human and he had always been a man who wore his heart upon his sleeve, he was unable to turn his emotions on and off in the manner of some. It was part of what made him the King he was. It was an injustice that the humanity which had made him such a well-respected monarch was the thing that had condemned him to such an ignominious end.

When his mind broke free of this chain of thought, he resurfaced back into reality and was surprised to find that Leonid and Gregor remained where they were and had still not removed him from the chamber. Instead they stood, as immobile as statues, still taking part in the communion.

Abruptly, Raemund opened his eyes and stalked over to the table. "Arthur Pendragon," he intoned, lifting a small gavel in the air, "I hereby sentence you..."

A bell tolled, cutting him off in mid-flow. It was not loud in the room but Arthur found himself all too easily imagining the thunderous echo that would be reverberating around the massive cavern that housed the souls of the dead.

Kirsten jumped from her seat and deftly manoeuvred the gavel from Raemund's grip. She fixed her fellow judge with a dazzling smile which in no way extended to her eyes and said, "Once again your time has passed, Raemund. Please take your rightful seat at the table and accede to the presiding Arbiter's judgement."

Raemund was so taken aback that he was rendered speechless whilst Gregor and Leonid stood uncertainly, not sure how to react, "Enough of this foolishness, Kirsten. I have made the judgement, the decision is final." Raemund finally sniffed pompously when he had regained his voice.

The only female Arbiter regarded her colleague with eyes as cold as ice. "Choose your words carefully, Raemund. I believe that *we* made the judgement and I also believe that *we* were not all as enthusiastic about it as some were," she flashed the icy look at Flammel, Leonid and Gregor, "now, as you were so keen to point out to Gregor when he was on the brink of striking the one who stands before us, he must be judged and judged properly according to our rules. "And," Kirsten preened and turned to Arthur with eyes alight and full of purpose, "according to the rules, the judgement is not sealed until the hammer has been struck."

Momentarily forgetting the Arbiters ability to communicate mentally, Raemund shouted, "This is a chance to halve our problems. This is the chance we have waited upon for centuries."

217

Arthur noticed how expressive Kirsten's eyes became, for they blazed with such severity that the King found himself flinching away from them.

"You would risk our honour, our integrity, our incorruptibility, simply because all is not well in the Halls?" she hissed. "To make the decision on that basis is to spit on every single verdict that we have pronounced since we began our duty. How may we sit in judgement of others if we are found wanting ourselves? No, Raemund, this will be done correctly and fairly, otherwise we may as well walk through the flaming door ourselves." She smoothed down her robe and jerked her head towards the seat she had so recently vacated. "Now, as I asked you to do before, please assume your correct seat and I will assume mine."

For a moment, Raemund looked as if he was about to offer some sort of resistance but, at the last, he scuttled from the centre of the table and took his seat.

With a deep breath, Kirsten now turned her gaze to Arthur. "Arthur Pendragon, you attest that you imbibed the longevity potion for the sole reason of foiling this Montagu's plans, yes."

With a huge sigh, Arthur nodded, "Yes, my lady," he bowed floridly.

One or two of the Arbiters rolled their eyes but they said nothing.

"You also state that you believe we have made our decision without possession of all the facts."

Again, Arthur nodded.

"As my colleague pointed out, this is a special case and, as I am now the presiding Arbiter, I think that we should examine the life you have led since the potion has flowed through your veins."

In unison the Arbiters eyes all snapped shut. *"Have you lost your mind, Kirsten? How can we accept that which should not be? You know as well as I do that he should have perished at Camlann. That sword punctured his heart,"* Gregor sneered.

"Do you sit at this table with your eyes and ears shut?" Kirsten snapped back. *"Have you not noticed the frequency with which the name Montagu is being heard in these Halls? He has been responsible for more deaths in the last few decades than all the plagues in the world. He is a cancer upon the earth and perhaps this Pendragon has it within him to cease his virulence."*

"So now we come to the crux of the matter," Raemund snarled. *"Your sympathy for humanity is deeply touching. Remind me again what you were saying about not making decisions to satisfy our own ends?"*

Kirsten sighed, *"All I ask is that Pendragon be given a chance to prove his case. There can be no secrets from us. If we witness the life that he should not have lived and he is still found wanting, then I will push him through the door myself."*

"What does it matter? Good or evil have no place in this room. We can only judge what we see," Leonid put in.

"Precisely my point. Let us see then let us judge," Kirsten nodded.

The communion broke off and Raemund snorted, "This is farcical."

Kirsten ignored him and waved her hand. "Let us proceed."

The air in front of Arthur shimmered into the screen once again.

This time, the judgement was much easier. Arthur was seen protecting little Montagu's mother, then ensuring she was given a proper burial after the hideous rites that Montagu had committed upon her body.

His slaughter of the Vikings earned him a few shaken branches, but his instant remorse and offer of help to the injured Norsemen helped redress the balance a little.

In very quick time the rose was in full bloom and Arthur knew that the verdict would count in his favour. In a way though, he reflected, it left him no better off for, whichever afterlife he was pitched into, he would still be unable to aid Merlin. He found little joy in the decision that he knew Kirsten was compelled to give because he had still failed in his quest and failed in his vow to protect his friend. As the Arbiter banged the gavel and pronounced that his good deeds outweighed his bad deeds, instead of euphoria, he felt a cloud of melancholia settle upon his shoulders.

"Arthur Pendragon, attend to my words," Kirsten said.

The King shook his head to try and free it of its despondency and stared at the beautiful woman who had saved him from the burning fires of hell.

"From what we have seen and heard, it is clear that you did indeed speak the truth regarding your reasons for flouting the laws of mortality. Such a flagrant disregard is not to be taken lightly and we find ourselves torn between which course of action to take. However, it is also clear that you are a man of the deepest integrity and honour. Therefore that is why we have reached the decision to tell you what I tell you now. Before I do so, I must make it clear that what is vouchsafed to you in this place does not leave this place. Do I have your word?"

Arthur nodded with as much eagerness as he could muster. The other Arbiters were not so keen however and all eyes snapped shut once again. All eyes except Kirsten's, that is.

Six brows furrowed then Raemund's eyes shot open and with outrage dripping from every pore, he pointed at Kirsten. "You refuse to join the communion?" he gasped incredulously.

She turned to him and hissed, "This is too important, Raemund. What needs to be said needs to be said out in the open where Arthur Pendragon is privy to it. You spoke earlier of re-establishing equilibrium. Perhaps this is the chance we have been waiting for. He is the second of the four to have passed

219

through here. The first one had a valid right to be here for he had lived his legitimate life and also lived his second life. This one is different, he still lives his second life."

Raemund looked highly dubious. "I feel this is wrong. How can we trust him? He is human, what we have seen just goes to prove how volatile humanity's whims can be."

Kirsten looked upon her fellow Arbiter with something akin to pity. "Do you not remember when we too were human? We were subject to the same impulses and emotions yet when we walked the Halls we were deemed worthy of attaining the office of Arbiter, were we not?"

The pinched mouth remained on Raemund's face but a softening around the eyes indicated that Kirsten's reasoning had carried the day. "That is true, yes." Raemund sighed, his eyes misting in reminiscence.

The female Arbiter turned back to the King, "Your word?"

Bowing his head, he rumbled, "You have my oath as man and King."

Nodding, Kirsten began to speak. "The reasons that we have to take the rules of mortality so seriously are manifold, however, they all come down to the same indisputable truth. Everyone has their own time allocated to them from the second they are born. Simply put, people do not live past their allotted span of years. It is impossible," she paused, "or rather it should be impossible. However, as you are standing before us, living and breathing, it is clear that the rules do not seem to apply in your instance," She sighed, a plaintive sound that wrenched at Arthur's heart. "Arthur Pendragon, yours and the others' longevity is destroying the Halls."

The King's eyes widened at this but he held his counsel.

Kirsten continued, "The green slime that even now drips down the walls and pools on the floor of these Halls did not exist until you and your companion drank the potion. But now it grows like a deadly parasite, rotten and unstoppable. When we first became aware of it, we did not apprehend its source. Then we consulted our records and saw that there was a gap. A gap that should not have been. It was you, Arthur Pendragon. By all rights and by all the rules that had gone before, you should have died upon the corpse-strewn field of Camlann."

Once again, Kirsten's disclosure struck Arthur dumb.

"However, you did not. Your magician concocted a potion that somehow cheated us or at least delayed your meeting with us. From that moment on, the parasite grew until it began to affect the men and women who came to stand before us. Some were so caked in it that we were unable to administer our justice upon them for we were unable to perceive them in their rightful state. We started to make errors in our verdicts. Good men and women were being consumed by the fire whilst tainted ones found themselves on the path to paradise. This only accelerated the parasite's growth. We also then learned of two others that had taken a similar potion. This Montagu you speak of and Mordred, who has since passed through our hands into the beyond. Make no mistake, if this hideous bacterium is not halted, then the Halls will crumble to dust and dead souls will have nowhere to find peace. They will walk the earth forever tormented, forever yearning for an end that will not come."

Finally, Arthur found his voice. "So what would you have me do, my lady?" he croaked.

Kirsten's eyes pinned Arthur to the spot. "There can only be one solution to the problem, Arthur Pendragon. The growth of the parasite will not cease until its cause has been eradicated. We are already a quarter of the way towards that goal, for the death of Mordred has slowed down the spread of it somewhat. However, the longer you and your fellow partners in crime live lives that should not be then the worse the infection will get." Her words blew through Arthur like the bitterest of winter breezes and froze his heart. "There is only one way forward from this, Arthur Pendragon. You must find Merlin and Montagu and you must kill them. And then, Arthur Pendragon..."

The King knew the words that were coming but that did not make them any more palatable.

"...you must kill yourself."

The King dropped to his knees. "I did not know any of this. I am truly sorry for what has occurred in this place, but is there no other way that the blight can be halted?"

Kirsten's eyes grew hard. "It matters not that you had no knowledge of the repercussions of your actions. You were aware that there would be some sort of consequence to your deed, your reluctance to drink the potion made that clear. From the moment the liquid first touched your lips, though, the damage was done. There is no other way, Arthur Pendragon. This is how things must be."

The King's mind was in chaos. He now had to murder his best friend, a friend with whom he had walked the earth for nearly three centuries or take the responsibility for turning the world into a wasteland of lost souls, wailing and pleading for an end to their suffering.

When he thought back to the reasons which Merlin had used to cajole him into drinking the potion, he wanted to laugh and cry in equal measure. If his acts did indeed turn the planet into a haunted nightmare then that would surely be a way to ensure that his name was remembered for all time.

He was yanked from his thoughts by Kirsten's voice. "Think yourself fortunate. You have now been granted a third life. No-one has ever walked from the Halls of Reckoning and returned to the earth alive. You are indeed privileged." She banged the gavel on the table. "Arthur Pendragon is to be returned to the body from whence he came, charged with the following task. He must rid the Halls of the corruption that eats away at the bedrock. He must deliver both himself and the two who still elude us into our judgement. Only then will he know peace."

A tiny warning bell that had been ringing in the back of Arthur's mind and had hitherto been drowned out by the thunderous enormity of what he had been asked to do suddenly increased tenfold in volume. "Please, my lady, you state that I am the second of the quartet to have come under your scrutiny?" he asked urgently.

Kirsten nodded.

"The first one being Mordred, yes?"

Slightly irritated, Kirsten nodded again. "Do not seek to delay your task, Arthur Pendragon," she warned.

"Then Montagu still lives," he gaped.

Kirsten's face screwed up in disgust at the mention of the black magician's name but nonetheless nodded again. "Yes, that is correct. We have not yet had the dubious pleasure of meeting him, although we do seem to have heard his name mentioned on far too many occasions in recent times."

"He still lives," Arthur whispered, oblivious to all that was being said to him.

"Go now, Arthur Pendragon. You know what you must do. Remember, if you fail in your task or if you disclose anything of this to anyone, then when you do finally stand before us to be judged, you will have no need for a trial for your actions will condemn you immediately to the fiery pit."

"He still lives," Arthur repeated, "he still lives."

Chapter 14

The shore of the Grail Lake

King Arthur's eyes fluttered open and he found himself staring up into the face of his long-lived friend.

Slowly looking around, he saw that he was lying once again upon the cold stone of the shoreline, head resting in the magician's lap. Merlin, for his part, was sitting with his eyes clamped shut, presumably still engaged in searching the lake for the Grail.

'The Grail!' The words blazed in his head. Perhaps the wondrous vessel of Jesus would have the means of solving the predicament he found himself in. Perhaps the Grail would be able to combat the creeping fungus that was infecting the Halls and remove the need for him to kill his companion.

Sensing the movement in his stricken friend, Merlin's eyes opened and were immediately dragged down to where Arthur lay. For a long moment, he was speechless, gaping ridiculously at the King as if he was seeing him for the first time.

The King was equally quiet, his sense of elation at being back at the side of his confidante tempered by the cold knowledge in his soul that there could be a time when he would have to put him to the sword.

"Well met, sire," the magician finally spluttered.

"Likewise, my friend. Likewise." Arthur forced a smile onto his face. Heaving a huge sigh, he stood up, stretching and twisting to relieve his aching joints, for though his spirit had been active whilst he was in the Halls, his body had remained in a comatose state.

Merlin joined him on his feet and regarded the King strangely. Then, in a move that took Arthur completely by surprise, the normally reserved magician nearly ran forward and engulfed him in a rib-snapping bear-hug. "By God, Arthur, it's good to see you."

The King was too choked to respond, both due to the roughness of the embrace and the fear that if he spoke, he would break down in tears. How could he murder Merlin? It would be like slaying his own brother. No, there was only one thing for it, they would have to find the Grail and use it to right all the wrongs that their quest had caused.

Ultimately, he knew the Grail was the key to all that they endeavoured to do. It was one of the catalysts for the quest and therefore one of the causes of the infection of the Halls.

Right there and then, Arthur decided that it could be the cure as well as the disease.

Merlin slapped his hand on Arthur's shoulder. "I had thought you lost. Where did you bide? I know that I managed to halt your plunge into the deathly fires of the pit but after that I could not detect you or commune with you."

Arthur chewed upon his lip. Exactly how much should he impart to the wizard? Kirsten's warning of the need for secrecy still loomed large in his mind, but what of the rest of his journey? She had not said he could not disclose what had happened outwith the judgement chamber. He was sure that Merlin would be all too well aware that something extraordinary had gone on for him to have re-emerged from the Halls still alive. Thinking quickly, he blurted, "I know not where I was. It was a dark eerie place, a cave of sorts, I think. The dimensions were so massive and the light so feeble that I could not get a clear idea of it."

Immediately the King saw the scepticism apparent in the mage's face. He yearned to tell Merlin what he had seen, what he had found out and when he thought of the danger they were in with Montagu still at large, his blood ran cold. He looked at Merlin sombrely, feeling as if he was being ripped in two by his responsibility to his friend and his responsibility to the Arbiters.

Merlin returned the stare with equal gravity. "Arthur, before you came to, you were murmuring something in your sleep."

The monarch's eyes hooded instantly. Perhaps Merlin had not been so intent on scouring the lake as it had seemed when Arthur had woken. "Was I?" he replied with painfully false casualness.

Merlin nodded. "You kept repeating that someone still lived. You must have said it half a dozen times."

"The ramblings of a delirious man," he shrugged half-heartedly.

Merlin's eyes grew cold and where there had been warmth before now only the usual cool arrogance dwelt. "Come now, sire. Your brow was not fevered, nor your pulse irregular." The magician leant into him and pierced him with a fearsome gaze. "Who still lives?" he hissed.

The King spun on his heel and stood at the edge of the lake, staring out across the glittering moonlit expanse of water. There was nothing for it, he had to tell Merlin. He had pleaded for his life on the fact that this quest was nothing to do with his vanity or to save his own skin and yet here he was, prevaricating over whether to disclose the secrets of the Arbiters chamber in order to cheat his destiny. Could he really stand by and see Merlin perish in a surprise attack by Montagu? After all, Merlin was convinced that he had slain Montagu aboard the Viking longship, so even an unexpected appearance by the dark magician could be enough to tempt Merlin into recklessness and making a fatal error of judgement.

"I am sorry to have to say this, old friend, but I was talking of Montagu. Montagu still lives," Arthur sighed. As if prompted by the mention of the evil wizard's name, a chill wind rippled over the lake and both men shivered. Merlin stepped away from the King and threw his head back with laughter. "Now that is the ramblings of a delirious man," he snorted.

King Arthur shook his head at the not unexpected response to his revelation. He stepped forward and placed a hand upon the magician's shoulder. "It is true. As God is my witness, I swear it."

Merlin ceased his laughter and stared at the King with a discomforting intensity. After a few seconds, he slapped away his hand and stalked over to where a small indentation in the shore indicated one of his favourite spots for sitting and searching the water. "That is nonsensical, Arthur. I killed him myself. I stood over him until the lifeblood seeped from his ears and he breathed no more. He is dead, Arthur, dead."

Arthur was distraught to see his friend's reaction. Merlin had now begun stalking the beach in a frenzy, screeching imprecations at the sky. Deciding to let Merlin work through his rage alone, the King took himself off to the shore of the lake once again. He gazed unseeing at the flat surface wondering whether the treasure at the bottom of it would be enough to save him from the inferno or whether he had condemned himself to an early grave mere minutes after being saved from it. He was so wrapped up in his ponderings that he did not hear Merlin approach until the wizard was practically upon him. He turned round quickly, fearful of the countenance that would greet him.

The magician held his hands up apologetically. "I am sorry, sire. I rather lost my composure there," he smiled ruefully. "Perhaps now you are back in the land of the living, these delusional nightmares will cease."

Arthur snorted derisively. "Merlin, I was not deranged. I know that you find it hard to accept but Montagu is still walking the earth. I know that for a fact."

The ice returned to Merlin's stare and he spat on the stones at the King's feet. "Excuse my doubting you, my liege," he sniffed sarcastically, "but I fail to see how that can be true. You were not there aboard the ship, you did not see me put that bastard through the agony of a thousand hells, you did not see me melt the very skin from his body, you did not see him beg for mercy as I crushed his spirit, his soul and his life." The magician leant into Arthur again and hissed, "You did not see. So do not presume to stand there and tell me that you know Montagu lives, for I know that Montagu is dead." With that said, Merlin turned away as his robe swirled behind him in a dark circle.

Despite understanding Merlin's reaction, the King was still taken aback by the vehemence of Merlin's diatribe. He knew how shocked he felt when he had unmasked Mordred in the Halls and tried to guess how shocked he would be if Mordred were to walk over the hills right now. After all, if a man began to doubt his own eyes, then what was he to believe?

Arthur gathered himself and prepared to seal his own fate, knowing that his next words would condemn him to a life in hell. "Merlin," he said.

To the King's chagrin, Merlin refused to turn round and folded his arms like a recalcitrant child.

Irked by this, Arthur sighed but refused to stoop to the man's level so he carried on regardless of whether the wizard was listening to him or not. "Merlin, I do know where I was when my body lay in its deep sleep. I was walking the Halls of Reckoning. I have stood in front of the Arbiters. They were the ones who told me of Montagu's continued existence. That is why I was so sure of myself when I told you what I did. They are incorruptible, incapable of lies. I am truly sorry, my friend." Arthur hung his head. "I do not know whether your destruction of Montagu was a cunningly staged ruse or he clouded your mind in some way but you cannot have seen what you thought you saw."

Merlin grabbed hold of the King's tunic and yanked him to the ground, seating himself opposite. "Tell me. Tell me all."

Arthur smoothed his rumpled clothes down and began to recount what had happened from the moment that the stranger had appeared in the scrubland on the hill.

When he had finished, Merlin sat across from him, agape and dumbstruck.

It was Arthur who broke the supercharged silence first. "One can only presume that the mystery man who tried to kill us was Montagu, for it was certainly not Mordred."

The court magician sat as still as a statue, obviously preoccupied with the knowledge that Arthur had imparted. "What? Mmm, yes I suppose so." He suddenly looked up with a rather disturbing light in his eyes. "Mordred is definitely dead?"

Arthur nodded strongly. "Definitely," he replied.

Merlin smacked his hands together. "Well, that is one less thing to worry about anyway." He got up, took a huge lungful of air and exhaled. "Shall we resume our search then, my liege?"

The transformation of Merlin was incredible and Arthur found his mouth opening and shutting like a hooked fish, so unexpected was his friend's attitude.

"Perhaps we should redouble our efforts if the evil one is still at large, eh?" Merlin suggested.

King Arthur stared at his companion's back as the magician squatted down upon the irregular rocks and stones that littered the shores of the lake. "Perhaps so," he murmured.

Later on that night, Arthur yanked the two flaps of his cowl tightly around himself in an attempt to create some warmth in his body. It was a spectacularly clear night and he found himself staring in awe at the millions of pinpricks that punctured the blackened sky. Merlin had been mentally dredging the lake for nearly two hours and the King found himself alone once again.

Off to the right, an owl hooted and occasional flutters of movement across the silver shafts of moonlight indicated that a colony of bats must have been in residency somewhere close at hand.

The King stamped his feet and followed the progress of the white clouds of breath as they dwindled into nothingness in front of him. He turned round abruptly at the sound of movement on the shore but it was only his companion regaining his feet. Merlin walked over to Arthur unsteadily, rubbing at various pressure points on his legs to relieve the pain of where particularly sharp pebbles had dug into them.

"No luck?" he asked.

The magician regarded him coolly. "Yes, sire. I found the Grail a long time ago, but I find it so refreshing to sit on a cold stony beach that I just cannot seem to let a day go by without doing it again."

Arthur coloured and in a fit of pettiness decided to respond in such a way as to hit Merlin where it hurt the most. Ever since he had returned from the Halls although he had seemed outwardly pleased to see him, there had been an undercurrent of mockery in some of the comments coming from the magician that had begun to grate on the King. "No, please allow me to apologise," he said ingratiatingly, "It was a stupid question, especially as you have so much on your mind at the moment, what with the continuing survival of Montagu after you thought you had killed him."

Much to his surprise, his attempt to prick Merlin's ego had the opposite effect on the magician's demeanour because, rather than a scowl forming on Merlin's face, it split with an impish smile at the mention of his arch-enemy's name.

Exasperated that his attempted insult had failed to have the desired effect, Arthur took himself off to the shore once again, ostensibly to gaze at the play of moonbeams on the flat surface of the lake.

After a time he felt a hand upon his shoulder. He turned round slowly, childishly refusing to look the magician in the eye.

"Arthur, I apologise," Merlin said in a murmur. "My words were borne of frustration at myself, not you. We have been combing the dregs of this god-forsaken pond for nearly two and a half years and it has brought naught but trouble. With the powers at my disposal, I should have located the Grail by now." He glanced at the lake. "As you well know, failure does not sit well with me and unfortunately, aside from you, I have no other targets to lash out at."

The King acknowledged the apology with a slight incline of his head. "I too am sorry. It was an incredibly stupid question, truth be told. Believe me, I am just as frustrated as you by our inability to find it when it appears close enough to grasp." He looked pensive for a moment. "Would you permit me another imbecilic question?"

Merlin nodded with a twinkle in his eye. "I will try not to snap my answer back at you, but I cannot promise, after all, I do not know how imbecilic the question is?"

Arthur was unsure whether Merlin was laughing with him or at him, but decided to assume it was the former. "Well, I can think of only two reasons why your powers have not been able to locate the Grail."

"And they are?" Merlin interjected.

Arthur shrugged. "Well, the most obvious one is that it is not actually here. What I mean is, well..."

"Come on, Arthur. Out with it." Merlin tutted.

"Well, this is definitely the right lake, is it? I mean it was a long time ago since you stood with Galahad upon the cliffs and a lake is not exactly the most recognisable of geographical features, is it," he blurted, half expecting an eruption of anger from the man opposite him.

Merlin looked up into the darkness in the vague direction of the bluff where he had saved Galahad from suicide. "That is a fair question. And it would explain our lack of success were it not for the fact that this place is indelibly branded upon my memory for all time. I know the Grail is here. I can practically taste it."

The King held Merlin's gaze for some time, discomfited by the zeal contained within the magician's deep blue eyes. "Then there can only be one other reason why it remains beyond your sight," he said.

Merlin raised his eyebrows in anticipation of the answer.

"It is masking itself from you."

The magician's eyes swivelled in their sockets, "Nonsense. I have handled it before and it did not react to my touch then. Why should it mask itself now?"

Arthur prayed that the suspicion he was feeling towards his companion's motives was not in any way visible in his expression. He shrugged. "I do not know. Your intentions have always been good. I have known you too long to think otherwise."

The spellweaver's face screwed itself up in distaste. "I sense there is a 'but' approaching this conversation," he muttered.

Arthur chuckled, "I am unable to hide anything from you, my old friend." Then his expression turned grave once more. "Merlin, we are both all too well aware of the power that the Grail is imbued with. We also both know that it has properties that we are unaware of and perhaps will never unravel. Now, I am not saying that you are consciously seeking it out as a source of absolute power, but could it be possible that the Grail itself is wary of the forces that you already have at your disposal? Could it be possible that the Grail is afeared of what it will become should it fall into such a powerful magician's hands?" The King finished, then held his breath and not for the first time wondered at what was occurring within the labyrinthine pathways of Merlin's brilliant mind.

"You talk of the Grail as if it is a living creature, Arthur. It is an object of metal, without doubt infused with great potential and great capabilities, but an object nonetheless. It cannot think, it cannot distinguish between the one who wields it for good or evil," Merlin protested.

"Perhaps not. It was just a thought." Arthur paced up and down the shoreline. "Yet it accepted Galahad's stewardship, did it not? It did not change in appearance or manner at any time when you were alone with it in the banqueting hall at Camelot. It only reacted when Galahad was present."

Merlin's teeth ground together and he spun round with a demented flourish. "Then what in the nine circles of hell are we supposed to do?" he shrieked, sending a procession of fireballs thundering into the scrubland upon the hill and setting it ablaze.

King Arthur leapt forward and grabbed hold of Merlin's arms, dragging them downwards away from the conflagration on the slope. "Dammit, get a hold of yourself, man. Do you wish to announce our presence to everyone within a hundred miles of where we stand?"

The wizard's eyes blazed at Arthur and the King stepped back hurriedly for, though it had only been present for a second, the level of hate present within Merlin's eyes had been shocking to behold. "I..." Merlin seethed before closing his eyes and taking several deep breaths. When he opened them again, he extinguished the fire upon the hill with a flick of his wrist. "You are, as ever, the voice of reason, sire. I am sorry for my outburst but I am so frustrated at the thought that we have spent so long tediously searching for something that does not wish to be found. You truly think the Grail is concealing itself from my sight?"

Arthur tried to forget the look in Merlin's eyes but found it difficult. "As you are so sure that this is the place where it was lost then I can think of no other explanation," he said shakily.

Merlin threw his head back and stared at the star-pocked sky. "Then we are undone. All the endeavour that we have ploughed into our quest has been for nothing."

Arthur shook his head. "No, Merlin, I will not accept that. The Grail must be resurrected, it must be found, especially now it emerges that Montagu is still corrupting the earth with his presence."

The mention of Montagu's name ignited the flame of hatred again in Merlin's eyes and the King had to use all his resolve simply to stand his ground.

"There must be a way, Merlin," Arthur insisted, shifting some pebbles with his foot. "What is it?" he said as he looked up and found himself under the intense scrutiny of the magician once more.

Merlin's face creased into a smile. "Perhaps there is a way?" he murmured enigmatically.

Arthur opened his mouth to ask what he meant when suddenly Merlin pitched forward, flinging him to the ground. A mere second after that, an incandescent ball of flame sliced over their heads and landed barely feet away from them. It was so close that Arthur felt his eyebrows singe as the whoomph of superheated air washed over them both.

The pair ignored the torrent of pebbles and rock that showered them but they had barely made it to their feet when the next barrage came.

As another fireball flew at them from halfway down the cliff side, they heard the air above them ripped in two by what sounded like a massive pair of wings. As they stumbled about the beach trying to locate the exact source of the danger and produce some sort of response, they perceived a deeper darkness in the sky above.

Suddenly there was brightness so intense that it left the two of them staggering blindly about the shore, completely bereft of any sort of night vision.

Hissing clouds of steam began wafting into the cool night air as gush after gush of flame hit the water of the lake. All the while, comets of fire were being dispatched from the hill forcing Merlin and Arthur further from the shore.

Merlin tripped over and took Arthur's legs from under him and the two hit the ground in a tangle of limbs.

"Dragon," Merlin coughed painfully, his lungs and throat rebelling against the acrid smoke.

"Fireball," Arthur pointed to the cliff as another guttering ball of flame barrelled towards them.

Grabbing Merlin by the back of his robe, the King practically lifted the magician to his feet single-handedly and threw him to the left, only dodging the impact himself by mere inches.

"Do you need any more evidence of Montagu's continuing existence, Merlin?" Arthur bellowed.

The magician's expression looked positively infernal as it flickered between the darkness of the night and the brightness of the flame but as he leant in to Arthur, it changed to a look of iron determination. "I find it intriguing that the dragon does not seek to attack us." He shouted above the blood-curdling screech of the huge lizard and the concussions of the fireballs. "I sense a diversionary tactic here. The projectiles are meant to distract us from the real reason for this attack. I believe he seeks to drain the lake. Perhaps he is as vulnerable to water as the both of us and so he seeks to remove that which stands between him and the Grail. Do you see, Arthur, it matters not who wields the Grail, be they good or evil. I know it and that bastard magician on the hill knows it."

Another fireball landed in close proximity but not near enough to cause a break in the conversation.

"Do you really think that is what he plans?" Arthur asked.

Fixing the King with a gaze that turned his spine to ice, Merlin nodded. "Yes, I do, my liege, for that was the plan that had begun to sprout in my head as well."

Arthur nodded curtly. "How are we to thwart him then?"

"I am sorry to have to do this to you, Arthur, truly I am but dragons are impervious to my powers so I would be next to useless if I were to take the beast on. You must slay the dragon whilst I deal with the scum upon the hill."

Merlin wheeled away, running surprisingly quickly for one of his age towards the origin of the fiery missiles, leaving the King alone and afraid on the beach.

Behind him, the lake was bubbling and broiling with the strength of heat emanating from the dragon's maw. The vegetation that was liberally dotted about the surface of the lake was all ablaze, giving the impression of tiny volcanic islands in an ocean of boiling water. It did however afford Arthur his first real view of the massive creature laying waste to the lake.

The creature used its thirty foot long thick scaly tail for balance as it reared up on gargantuan hind legs and spat its fire. The flame issued from a mouth lined with three frightening rows of vicious teeth, each razor-sharp and able to rend anything in their path to shreds. The eyes were yellow with malevolent black pupils slicing them down the middle. A huge rubbery neck

231

of fully twenty feet attached the head to the ungainly body that had, by now, resumed its huddled position on the shore.

Whilst the animal had appeared incredibly graceful in the air with the only sound of its passage being the swish of its wings, its immensity left it uncomfortable upon the ground and Arthur immediately seized upon that as something that could possibly work in his favour. Stopping it getting airborne was the key. He began to circle the mammoth creature, keeping a wary eye upon the tail as it swished back and forth.

The unseen enemy on the hill must have seen Arthur move towards the dragon because a ball of flame came crashing down within a few feet of where he walked. This time, the right half of his beard was singed and his hand flew to his cheek in pain. He risked the briefest of glances back towards the cliff and was gratified to see a torpedo of fire sent back in response from Merlin. He could not afford to worry about what was occurring behind him, he had to stop the dragon in its tracks because if it was victorious and enabled Montagu to obtain the Grail, then their quest would be all for naught anyway. What he did need to worry about however was that the fireball must have come into contact with the dragon's tail for the creature had lumbered round to see what had stung it.

The King was frozen to the spot. He knew what he should be doing. He should be unsheathing Excalibur and setting about the dragon. Unfortunately though, his body would not respond and the only thought that occupied his mind was simply that he was going to die whether he had drunk a special potion or not. He knew that theoretically the only thing that could kill him was water, sunlight or having his heart ripped out, but as he stared up at the massive face with eyes as big as the moon, he was so overwhelmed by his powerlessness that he knew for a certainty that this was his time, this was his final curtain, this was his last night upon the earth.

He closed his eyes and prepared himself for the eternal sleep of death. Seconds later, he opened them again in puzzlement. The dragon had turned back to the lake and begun flaming again.

What he did not know was that, though they were by and large nocturnal creatures, the dragon's eyesight was poor, even in daylight. Their favoured method of hunting was to sniff out their prey with their keen noses then lay waste the area with their flame, causing their quarry to either flee from cover or perish in the fire.

As Arthur had become petrified in fear, the dragon had actually not even seen him because he was standing amidst a multitude of dull hues from the rocks and pebbles of the beach. That, coupled with the cloying stench of smoke from the dragon's own flame meant that, as far as the creature was concerned, Arthur was invisible.

The King's knees sagged beneath him in relief and he took a few moments to compose himself. Trying to mask his steps under the noise of all the mayhem that was occurring around and about him, King Arthur tiptoed to within touching distance of the fire-breathing monster. He gingerly reached out and felt one of the creature's scales. It was leathery to the touch and looked about a foot thick.

For a long moment, Arthur stood, hands on hips, wondering how on earth he was to best a creature of this magnitude. He knew he would only get one chance to land a killing blow but how could one blow possibly be enough to kill something so gigantic.

The battle on the hill seemed to be reaching its climax. The frequency of missiles was becoming more frenzied and concentrated but just as it reached its peak, Merlin popped into existence on Arthur's left, causing him to nearly drop Excalibur in fright.

"How goes it, Arthur?" he breathed heavily, just as the dragon reared up in preparation for another gust of flame.

The King whined. "How do I kill such a creature with such a small blade? It would take me ten strokes to hack through one scale."

Merlin's eyes spoke volumes about the King's wheedling tones but his voice remained businesslike. "All creatures possess a weakness and dragons are no different. There is a point on a dragon's head near the crown, the fontanelle, I believe it is called. Basically, it is a hole in the skull, a hole straight through to the brain. All animals are born with it but on most, it heals over. However, with dragons it is different for some reason and it never mends. That is where you must strike it." The mage glanced down at the lake. "See, already the water level has diminished by a half. Hurry, Arthur, you must strike the moment you are able."

A ball of flame landed a few yards to the left of where they stood, once again nearly hitting the dragon. "I must finish what I have started upon the bluff. May Excalibur strike clean and true." With that, Merlin winked out of existence again.

"That piece of information might have been slightly more useful if you had told me it before," Arthur murmured. He took a deep breath to steel himself then began ascending the dragon's back, using the high ridges lining its spine as handholds.

If the giant lizard was aware of the King's climb, then it showed no sign. On more than one occasion though, it nearly inadvertently dislodged him when it rose upon its hind legs to engulf the water in its flame.

After what seemed like hours but was in reality only a matter of minutes, Arthur found himself balancing with outstretched arms upon the creature's nape. As he neared his target, he wondered whether he should ready

Excalibur for its gory task. However that would mean only having one hand available to maintain his grip on the beast. It was a calculated risk he knew, but one that he realised he would have to take. He reasoned that he may have gone undetected so far but surely the creature would notice his presence when he reached its head in which case he would have to deliver the killing stroke as quickly as possible. With that decision made, he unsheathed his blade and continued moving upwards.

As it was, the decision was taken out of his hands by the animal elevating itself again. The sudden movement lifted the King from his feet and he began to slide down the dragon's back.

As Arthur had often found when he was faced with great danger, gut instinct took over. He could have made a grab with his free hand and it probably would have halted his plunge towards the rocks below but as it was without a second's thought, he brought Excalibur round in an agricultural hack and stabbed down into one of the scales on the dragon's neck.

Immediately the beast ceased flaming and its head reared up at the sudden discomfort on its back. The massive equine face whipped round surprisingly quickly and tried to focus on the tiny figure that was clinging for dear life atop its shoulder blade. A deep grunt emanated from the dragon's throat along with a foul-smelling cloud of smoke, which caused Arthur to gag and his eyes to tear. An immense talon reached round and raked down in an attempt to rid itself of the bothersome irritation.

The King's eyes widened as the colossal claw descended towards him. He wrenched Excalibur clear of the beast's hide and threw himself to the right, winding himself in the process but still meaning he was able to grab hold of one of the pitted ridges on its back. Scrambling for some purchase, he hid behind the enormous triangle of bone, not willing to risk even a quick glance backwards at the huge head as it sought him out. Knowing that he had now been seen, a rush of adrenaline coursed through him and he practically ran up the creature's spinal column, returning to his previous position at the base of the dragon's neck. Breathing hard but knowing that he could not afford to stop, the King plunged on, stumbling over the improbably smooth scales as they became more tightly packed at the top of the monster's neck.

As he gained the summit of the head, he felt as if he was staring at a dried river-bed. The scales that criss-crossed the flat top of the beast's skull were almost perfect squares and as Arthur gazed at them, he realised that there was no obvious sign as to where the fontanelle was.

As he stepped forward, a gust of wind blew him from his feet. He looked up and saw it had been one of the ears flicking at him. However he realised that it meant he was not far from being located again and the need to complete his task became even more pressing than before.

234

He struck out across the head, desperately searching for a weak spot. A pained whine rent the air and a huge claw swooped over him, coming within inches of knocking him clear of the head and down to a bloody death on the stones below.

This time Arthur managed to insert his fingers in the small channel between two of the scales on the skull. He used it to lever himself to his feet and, as the claw ripped through the air on its return journey, he steadied himself and launched a brutal two-handed stab at it with all his might.

Although the dragon was an immense creature, its front legs were little more than balancing tools and did not have much in the way of power within them. Excalibur's sharpened edge sliced through the meaty flesh of the wrist, causing the dragon to scream a bellow that echoed across the darkness, sending a chill down Arthur's spine.

Frantically he withdrew the blade from the dragon's limb, although not before enduring a jarring concussion with one of the creature's bones. He switched his sword to his unfavoured left hand as the contact with the creature's skeleton had left his right hand numbed. Fighting for balance, he staggered across the beast's head once more, weeping in frustration, vainly attempting to find the vulnerable point.

The dragon was now wheeling about in agony at its injury. So unused were the imposing beasts to any sort of harm being inflicted upon them that the pain itself was magnified tenfold from the shock.

Arthur lost his footing once again due to the dragon's thrashing and he fell forward towards its face. He tumbled end over end, past the ears and nearly to the lumpy brow of the animal's forehead. In desperation, he lashed out with his sword, hoping to stab it into the creature's skin once more and arrest his tumble. On this occasion though, rather than stabbing down, Excalibur sliced across which opened up two huge flaps of skin that flapped obscenely atop the dragon's head.

Mercifully it slowed his momentum enough that he was momentarily able to take stock of the situation, because the dragon was fussing and licking at its wounded arm, the cut upon its head being a mere inconvenience compared to the white-hot pain of its wrist.

Arthur gaped in horror as the huge leathery wings started to unfold themselves. The dragon had decided that enough was enough and the indignity of having its blood spilt was simply too much to bear.

The King knew that if the beast took off, he was lost. He would plummet to the ground within seconds. To his eternal relief, he saw that the cut he had sheared across the dragon's skull had exposed a gaping hole under the two flaps of skin. That must be it, he guessed, and leapt like a salmon forcing its way upstream. He reached desperately for the hole, slashing down with his

235

sword, expecting to hit the spongy yielding fabric of the dragon's brain. Instead, he hit nothing and fell forward into the gap.

The reason that he had hit nothing but thin air was that the dragon's brain rested a few feet beneath the fontanelle and he ended up landing on it rather than stabbing it. However, now that the flaps of skin were free of Arthur's attentions, they returned to their usual resting place and he was plunged into darkness.

In a second, the dragon's wings stopped expanding and the creature's front claws clamped on either side of its head as wave upon wave of excruciating torment wracked its body.

The King fought to wrestle Excalibur free from the cloying sticky substance of brain tissue but it had been swallowed to the hilt and he could not. Panicking, he simply began tearing and ripping at the fabric of the brain, separating chunks from the mass and flinging them aside.

The dragon shrieked and staggered into the boiling lake, engulfing itself in searing hot water and causing new waves of acid torture to ripple through its abused body.

Still Arthur continued on his berserk rampage.

The dragon could no longer keep its feet and it slumped forwards, reduced to a gibbering vegetable by Arthur's frenzy, but the King did not notice, he simply continued destroying all he could of the creature's brain.

Eventually the cessation of movement and primeval screams of agony seeped into Arthur's consciousness and he stopped his fevered assault. His garments were caked in the animal's blood and brains and for the first time he became aware of the hideous smell that had erupted from the wounds he had inflicted during his attack. Gagging at the gore before him, he steeled himself and wrenched the blade free.

Unsteadily he got to his feet. Luckily, one of the flaps of skin had fallen aside and he could make his way out by the light of the many fires that still blazed in the night.

Grimacing in distaste, he pushed away the other flap of skin and emerged, white-faced and nauseous, from the dragon's head. Immediately he saw that the gargantuan creature's head had come to rest in the shallow water at the edge of the lake. The water lapped at the slit and Arthur shrank back from it, well remembering the pain that had burned up and down his legs for the first few months of their residence at the lake when he had stupidly run into the lake.

Without any obvious means of escape, he simply stood silently, trying to think of a way to get to the shore but also listening for sounds of battle from the headland. He peered at the lightening horizon, tinged with pink, as the occasional zip and sizzle told him that the conflict still continued. Cursing at his inability to aid his comrade in his fight and also his inability to extricate himself from the dragon's head, Arthur gingerly placed his finger in the lake. At first, he thought that the effects of the longevity potion had worn off because the initial contact was painless. However when he withdrew it from the lake and peered at it in the dawn light, he felt it begin to burn. "Dammit," he hissed as he tried to relieve the pain by sucking at his finger. "This is ridiculous," he whispered to himself. "There must be a way."

With a snarl of rage, he grabbed hold of the loose flap of thick skin which flopped over his vantage point and after a few minutes of brutal scything, hacked it off with Excalibur. Reaching up, he tried to pull himself out of the brain cavity so that he might flee over the corpse of the slaughtered lizard, mindful of the fact that if he slipped, he would fall backwards into the water and an acid world of hurt.

His fingertips managed to brush against one of the dragon's ears but not to the extent that he could grip it with any certainty. Frustrated by this, he hunkered down in the beast's head and pondered his next move. Perhaps all he should do was wait, wait until Merlin returned and fished him out. But what if Merlin did not return, Arthur thought with a chill running down his spine, what if Montagu overcame him and, after killing the magician, came down to the shore to investigate the demise of his gigantic ally?

No, he had to get out and he had to get out now. He decided to attempt to pull himself upwards and outwards again. Grunting with exertion, he managed to get his torso out but he was well aware that his handhold felt as if it was on the brink of detaching itself from the dragon's hide. Besides, the effort had left his arms with very little strength in them anyway, certainly not enough to pull himself totally free. He was about to slide back into the hole when, with an audible snap, the scale came away, leaving the King grasping at thin air and fighting a losing battle with gravity. Gritting his teeth in preparation for the horrendous agony that awaited him, the King finally lost his balance and hit the surface of the lake.

And there was nothing. No pain, no wetness. Breathlessly, Arthur peered out of the corner of his eye wondering what had caused this miracle. He nearly wept with relief when he realised he was lying on the wedge of skin that he had carved away from the dragon's head. The King could feel it bobbing up and down in unison with the water's movement. With great care he twisted round to get a better look at his impromptu raft. It was not just their invulnerability to magic that made them unique among the fauna of Britain then, he thought manically. The surge of adrenaline that had coursed through his veins when he had thought he was about to be engulfed by the water had heightened his senses and he found himself marvelling at the intricacies of the dragon's skin.

Now he was completely free of the dragon's cavernous skull, he could see that the nearest area of shoreline was not very far away. "Come on, man," he said to himself encouragingly, "that should be easy enough to get to." For a second he forgot himself and nearly plunged his hands into the water but stopped himself just in time. For a moment he fingered the jacinth-laden hilt of Excalibur before deciding he was not prepared to subject his blade to the indignity of being used as an oar. Suddenly, he hit upon an idea. He began worrying at the raw wound left by his haphazard surgery upon the dragon. Soon he had sliced off another two hunks of flesh, wrapped them around his hands the best he could and, after taking a deep breath, slowly placed them in the water, steeling himself for the roar of pain that he felt sure was to follow, but instead the plan worked and he began propelling himself towards the pebbles. Within minutes he was standing proudly upon the beach, dry and unharmed, feeling a swell of pride as, for the first time, he was able to fully appreciate how impressive the successful conclusion to his task had been.

He had fought many adversaries before, but none as large or deadly as this. It gave him a feeling of invincibility and he felt as if he could take on anything or anyone and emerge victorious. It lessened the fear of what was ahead of him and he found himself relishing the final confrontation with Montagu that he felt sure was now upon the horizon.

The thought of Merlin's struggle jarred him back to reality and he looked up towards the bluff.

Apart from the dying embers of a plethora of small fires, all was still and silent.

He was about to begin advancing towards the pockets of flame on the promontory, trying to remember the exact position of where the last exchange had been, when a glint in the water caught his eye. At first he thought it a reflection of the rapidly rising sun or one of the numerous blazes thereabouts, but the more he looked, the more he fancied there were other colours writhing and swirling within the midst of the oranges and yellows, fighting each other for dominance.

He felt torn, knowing that he should be worrying over the wellbeing of his companion but the peculiar glistening in the lake appeared to be calling to him, beckoning him towards it.

With a last longing look up at the cliff, Arthur tiptoed towards the water's edge, making sure he stood clear of the lapping fringe of foam. Without once taking his eyes off the ethereal glow, he reached down and grasped the two pieces of dragon hide that he had used to protect his hands. Hissing in pain, he dropped one to the sandy floor. He had grabbed the side that had been in contact with the water and it was still wet. He cursed profusely as he sucked at his fingers. Concentrating now on not hurting himself rather than the light beneath the water, he wrapped his hands in the hide and used them to paddle himself out to the area of water where he had first noticed the radiance, once again using the large lump of flesh that he had cut away as a makeshift raft.

As he bobbed to a halt in the gentle current, he slowly stretched himself out full length across the animal hide and stared intently over the side.

Thus it was that Merlin found him as he popped into existence at the side of the lake where Arthur had just been standing. He stared at the dragon's corpse for a moment, then shielding his eyes from the low dawn sun, sought out his travelling companion. "Come, Arthur, I have injured him, we must harry him or..." the magician's urgent words trailed into silence as he took in the scene before him, "what in hell are you doing, man?" he snapped. "If we keep after him we might be able to kill him once and for all." Merlin shouted, exasperated by the lack of response. "Arthur!" he bellowed.

"Can you not see it?" the King breathed huskily, unwilling to speak loudly lest it spoilt the awesome spectacle that he was witnessing below the waterline.

"See what?" Merlin's neck craned to see past the foot-thick lump of skin that Arthur had prostrated himself on. "You're raving, sire. The heady heights of your triumph over this winged fiend have addled your brain. There is nothing to see."

"But there is, Merlin, there is," the King half-turned to face his companion but found his vision inexorably drawn back to the display under the water. To the King it seemed as if a rainbow had been projected onto the silt-laden ground at the bottom of the lake. That, coupled with the brightness of the new sun, lent the array a beauty and vividness that stole the breath from his throat.

The magician nearly stamped his foot at his associate's lack of activity. "Dammit, Arthur, if we leave it much longer, he will be lost to us again. We must strike whilst we have the upper hand."

The King finally made eye contact with his impatient companion. "You do not wish to take possession of the Holy Grail then?" he said calmly, trying with little success to keep a stupid grin from splitting his face.

"I..." Merlin's mouth hung open. "What?" he spluttered.

With a jerk of his head, Arthur indicated the patch of water where he had been looking so intently just moments before, "The Cup of Christ. It rests mere feet from where I am lying," he whispered.

If he was honest, some of the humour in his grin was from the fact that he had been the one to find the vessel. Though it was a surprisingly petty thought to have at such a momentous juncture, he found himself rather enjoying the deflation of the wizard's ego.

Merlin did not seem overly worried by the fact that he had searched for nearly two and a half years to no avail but Arthur had found the Grail in just over an hour, he merely became so excited that he nearly forgot himself and came within an ace of splashing into the water. Instead, he stopped just short of the water's edge and began hopping agitatedly from foot to foot. "Where is it," he babbled, "I cannot see."

Arthur snorted. "What nonsense is this? It is as if the spectrum itself has been planted and is growing like algae in the water."

Merlin nearly wept with frustration. "I swear to you, my liege, I see nothing."

"Then perhaps it is as I suspected and it is masking itself from you for I can see it as clearly as I can see you capering on the shore," the King muttered.

At that rather unflattering description of his behaviour, Merlin ceased his display, feeling it was inappropriate for one of his gravitas. Inside though, his heart continued to do cartwheels. He smoothed down his robe and said in as dignified a voice as he could muster, "Even if I cannot see it, you can, so let us not tarry any further, extricate it from the water and let us be away. With the Grail in our hands, that bastard will not stand a chance."

"Therein lies the problem, my friend," Arthur sighed. "It may be a few feet away from my grasp, but it might as well be a thousand miles. I cannot reach it from here without immersing myself in the water."

Merlin pulled irritably at his beard. "Perhaps I can elevate it from the lake's bed then." The magician closed his eyes and began muttering arcane words of magic that sent shivers down Arthur's spine, their unpleasant sibilance intimating at origins best not investigated.

After a few minutes, Merlin threw his hands up in frustration. "I can perceive nothing. The blasted thing must still be hiding itself from my sight."

"Could you teach me the spell?" Arthur asked pleadingly. Though he found the utterances unsettling, he resolved that he would not let something as trifling as that stand in the way of the Grail's retrieval.

Merlin looked slightly shifty as he shook his head. "It would probably be best if you did not. You have to prepare your mind in exactly the right way to perform magic, lest your brain dribble from your ears. It is not something that can be taught in a matter of moments." Once again the wizard pulled at his beard as he pondered the problem. "Sadly," he sighed, "I can see no other option."

"What do you..." the King began but was cut short by a flick of Merlin's wrist.

The hunk of dragon hide flipped over violently, sending Arthur sprawling into the water below. Agony seared him from head to toe. The pain was so severe that he did not even have the wherewithal to curse Merlin. The only thought that occupied his brain was achieving an end to the hideous torture that rippled up and down his body.

Merlin watched dispassionately from the shore, chewing his lip feverishly and hoping against hope that the healing powers of the Grail would salve the wounds that Arthur would be swathed in when he emerged from the lake.

The King continued to thrash about uncontrollably in the water. He was seconds away from lapsing into shock when his fingers closed about the half-buried goblet resting on the lake's bottom.

Immediately, where the heat had been like the flame of a thousand suns, it became no more uncomfortable than the pleasant temperature of a normal summer's day.

As the pain diminished, the blindness that had been triggered by the extreme pain disappeared and he watched in wonder as his blistered skin repaired itself before his very eyes. Sighing in relief, he struck out for the surface, grabbing hold of the square of flesh and hauling himself aboard it. For a few moments he lay on his back on the leathery hide, oblivious to everything other than the warming breeze upon his skin and the metal vessel that nestled in his left hand. Lifting it unsteadily, he gazed upon it, reverence in his eyes, as he followed the play of light that danced across its golden surface.

"Did you retrieve it?" an anxious voice asked from the edge of the lake.

A large part of Arthur's mind wondered why he did not fly into a killing rage and set about Merlin with Excalibur when he heard the wheedling question, but one look at the goblet was enough to give him an answer. What would have been the point? For better or worse, Merlin's impetuous action had resulted in Arthur holding the greatest treasure that had ever been seen upon God's earth in his hand. He even wondered if he should extend his gratitude to Merlin for providing the push he needed to conclude the search. Staring at his companion of over three centuries, he balanced the Grail on the palm of his hand and held it up for inspection.

The smile upon Merlin's face crazed slightly as he looked at what, to him, appeared to be nothing more than the King holding up his empty hand.

"Do you still not see it?" Arthur's brow creased in confusion.

Merlin shook his head dumbly.

The King spluttered. "But I am holding it here in my hand. Can you not see the aurora that shines from its crown? Can you not see the golden glow that emanates from its surface?"

The spellweaver stood on the brink of tears once more. "I see nothing, Arthur. Not a damned thing. Surely, after all our years of searching, the glory of our discovery is not to be denied to me. Surely, if there was any justice in the world, I too would be able to gaze upon its resplendence," he whined.

241

The King was at a loss for words. The power that he could feel issuing from the Grail was such that he felt sure everyone for miles around would be able to bask in its incandescence. Yet it was glaringly clear that Merlin could not. His joy at locating the cup became tempered somewhat by Merlin's despair. The goblet was such a magnificent spectacle that it did indeed seem hugely unfair that his companion remained blinded to it. After all, were it not for the superhuman efforts of Merlin with his awesome command of magic and his sympathetic companionship then the King would never have found himself in such an exalted position in the first place.

An idea formed in Arthur's head. "Perhaps Montagu formulated some sort of hex on it, rendering it invisible to anyone of magical talent. He was, after all, the last one to lay hands on it before it plummeted into the depths of the lake."

The doubt was plain to see on Merlin's face at that presumption. "I think not, sire," he said.

Arthur rested the Grail upon the dragon-hide and propelled himself to the shore, using the holy vessel once again to heal himself when he had gained the pebbles. He determined that he would try to use it as little as possible from then on in case there was some sort of limit to its power.

Once he was back on dry land, he held the Grail up again this time mere inches from Merlin's face.

Shaking his head, the mage snaked out a hand to see if he could at least touch it.

As Arthur watched breathlessly, Merlin's slim fingers passed through the solid metal as if it was smoke and though he clenched his fist around where Arthur could see the stem of the goblet was, he still felt nothing. "Damn it to hell," he snarled.

To take Merlin's mind off his frustrations with the Grail, Arthur changed the subject. "What happened upon the cliffs? You say you inflicted injury upon the fiend?"

Camelot's magician made one last futile grab at the air just above Arthur's hand before shaking his head and giving up. Muttering a foul curse under his breath, he caught Arthur's eye, "Aye, that I did, sire. I sent him packing with his forked tail between his legs." He stared longingly up at the cliff where some fires still guttered, the clouds of smoke they were giving off rising heavenwards in the early morning sun. "I just hope he has not had time to recover sufficiently to thwart us once again."

As if on cue, a terrible screech rent the air. The two men swung about, peering at the skies in search of its origin. All too soon the answer became clear. Over the cliff where Merlin and Montagu had fought, another dragon appeared. It hovered momentarily, squinting at the devastation below it both

242

on the cliff and by the lakeside. Upon seeing the fallen dragon lying in the water, it screeched again, although this time, to the King's and Merlin's ears, the noise had a poignant edge to it that had not been present in the first cry.

"Come, we must flee before it sees us." Merlin grabbed a handful of Arthur's cloak and yanked him towards a fairly large thicket that had miraculously escaped the conflagration.

Unfortunately for the pair of them, the movement of their flight was enough for the dragon to spot them and with a thunderous thump of its wings, it swooped over the highest point of the headland and hurtled towards them.

Risking a glance over his shoulder, Arthur found, as he had before in moments of great peril, that his mind focussed on small inconsequences that he might not have noticed in the normal course of events. He found himself thinking that a creature of that size should be making some sort of noise as it made its headlong progress towards them. Instead, the silence seemed to add an even greater sense of hopelessness to their escape attempt. It seemed to say that they could run as fast as a lightning bolt, but the dragon would still catch them and destroy them.

With a suddenness that nearly jerked Merlin from his feet, King Arthur stopped in his tracks. He knew that there was no hope of escape, but for some inexplicable reason, he also felt that there was no need for them to try to escape. Despite the massive beast slicing through the air towards him, he found that he had never felt more protected and safe.

Merlin tried to pull the King into the dubious safety of the thicket but he may as well have tried to move the dead dragon instead. Arthur had planted his feet firmly in the pebbles that laced the shore and was holding the Grail in the air, in much the same way as he had wielded Excalibur so many times before. If the dragon was perturbed by this, it showed no sign, for it continued its relentless approach. In seconds it was upon them, rearing magnificently into the air and expanding its lungs, in preparation to unleash a fatal tsunami of fire.

Merlin, realising that Arthur was not going to move any further, hunkered down behind him and covered his head with his hands, knowing that his powers were useless against the gargantuan beast.

Arthur grimly looked into the huge lizard's gaping maw, ready for the first indication of a flame.

He did not have long to wait. The orange and yellow billowed powerfully from the dragon's mouth, swamping the two men in an inferno.

Arthur felt no heat upon him although, in an abstract way, he knew that he should. Almost dreamily, he waved the Grail in front of him as if trying to erase a charcoal smudge from a piece of parchment.

Sure enough, wherever the Grail touched, the fire sputtered and died until the entire flame had been extinguished.

An almost quizzical grunt escaped the dragon's lips as it struggled to understand why its tried and tested method of hunting had failed. It flamed again and Arthur repeated his defensive actions.

This time the failure enraged the dragon and it slumped to the ground, the concussion knocking them both from their feet. The monstrous beast loomed over them and tried to crush them with its massive claws.

Merlin and Arthur were frantically trying to regain their feet so they could get clear of the ungainly rampage. They managed to duck under the dragon's leg as it swiped at them and ended up behind it, each keeping one wary eye on the massive body of the beast and the other eye on the huge tail that was swishing insanely as the creature started to turn.

This brought them enough time for Merlin to incant the spell for flight and just as the immense tail crashed onto the rocks on the shore, they were away into the air.

Arthur clung to the Grail for dear life, clasping it to his chest and whispering a prayer of thanks for allowing the pair of them to escape the dragon's attentions.

It soon became clear that the cup of Christ would soon be in employment once more though, because the dragon had launched itself into the air after them.

Arthur turned to look at his companion. Whether Merlin was aware of the dragon's pursuit or not, he could not tell, for the court magician was only intent on the horizon before him, eyes set in an expression of ferocious intensity. With a final look at the dragon which was lagging behind them due to its bulk, Arthur turned from it and also began scrutinising their path forward.

"Where are we going, Merlin?" he shouted above the quickening wind. "We have the Grail but we are still woefully ignorant of the knowledge to make it work."

Merlin spared the King a glance. "We head back to Lindisfarne, for there is an unexpected surprise waiting for us there." He grinned, using some sort of magic to enable his normal speaking voice to be heard by Arthur.

"Surprise? What surprise?" The King demanded.

"You will see, Arthur. You will see."

Infuriated by his companion's penchant for evasiveness, Arthur asked twice more but Merlin ignored him, merely responding with an enigmatic smile.

They flew on in silence which left Arthur ample time to remind himself why they had not utilised the flying spell on more than a couple of occasions. Aside from the need to disguise themselves from their enemies, Arthur was so discomfited by the lack of solidity beneath his feet that he had made Merlin swear to only use the spell as a last resort. His tear-blinded eyes tried to focus on the greenish blur whipping underneath him when an unsympathetic chuckle sounded in his ears. "How many times have I told you, Arthur?" Merlin chortled. "Looking at the ground will only disorientate you, your senses will try and keep pace with the features passing below us. Keep your eyes on the horizon and your nausea will diminish."

Much to the King's disgust, the smug wizard's advice proved correct and almost immediately the lurching in his stomach settled down as he dragged his stare to the middle distance.

The threat from the dragon at the lake had come to nothing, as they had left it wallowing in the wake of their rapid departure and the journey had, so far, been fairly pleasant.

Unfortunately for the two Grail bearers, all that changed as a murder of crows erupted from the trees below them. There were fully a hundred of the raucous birds and they chose the moment of Merlin and Arthur's fly-past to take wing.

Suddenly, the two men were swamped in a flapping cloud of chaos. To make matters worse, some of the birds had been thrown into a state of panic by the unexpected appearance of the pair and began to attack them in a whirlwind of talon and beak.

The sharp stabs and scratches were enough to cause a faltering in the effectiveness of Merlin's conjuration and as a consequence the two of them were thrown into an uncontrolled descent into the canopy of the woods.

The last that the King saw of Merlin was the magician disappearing into the branches of a huge oak tree. At that point, he too came into contact with the branches of the trees and lost sight of him. Arthur crossed his arms to try and ward off any major damage to himself but the branches and boughs thrashed into him until he bled.

In horror he watched helplessly as he careered towards a ten-inch thick wooden limb. The branch smacked him right across the nose, snapping his head back and rendering him immediately unconscious.

Chapter 15

Kieran's Wood

"Arthur."

The word echoed distantly on the borders of the King's consciousness.

"Arthur."

This time, his eyes fluttered open and for a brief second he found himself looking into the grey face of his companion, then the brightness of the day knifed into his head and he was forced to close them again.

"Arthur."

Though the King kept his eyes clamped tightly shut, he was fully alert and waved an irritable hand in the general direction of the familiar voice. "I am awake, Merlin. There is no need to keep calling my name." He tried to sit up but the movement caused an onrush of agony to explode in his head and he slumped back to the cooling embrace of the leaf litter.

"Arthur."

If the former monarch of Britain had not been in so much pain, he may have picked up the subtle nuance that was evident in the magician's voice. However, his head felt like it was clamped in a vice and he was in no position to recognise the strained quality that permeated it. "Dammit, man, are you deaf? I said I am awake," he roared in anger before instantly wishing he had not. The words that he had just spat seemed to pound on either side of his head, leaving a ringing in his ears and a throbbing like a hammer pounding against his temple.

Gingerly he opened his eyes as far as he could. His contact with the branch had left him with two grotesquely swollen black eyes that he could barely see through. After the initial stab of pain from the light, the discomfort settled down into a dull ache that was just about bearable. Slowly he sat up, quickly grasping a handful of Merlin's robe to steady himself, "Satisfied now that you have roused me?" he sniped sarcastically.

"I..." Merlin began.

Cutting him off, Arthur was suddenly assailed by a massive panic as the realisation that he no longer held the Grail in his hand hit him. "Where is it?" he wailed.

The blurred figure of Merlin faced him and whispered gravely. "Have a care with your words, Arthur. We are surrounded by bandits and they have bound my hands. I could probably defeat some of them but their weapons would be slicing through my stomach before I could beat them all."

Gradually the shapes behind the po-faced magician changed from being mere blobs of colour and began to resolve themselves into human figures.

Merlin continued to speak, his words chosen with precision and care. "Fortunately, these gentlemen are looking after us now," he spoke more loudly this time for the benefit of his captors.

One of the shadows detached itself from the crowd and moved into Arthur's vision. "My my, you did catch yourself a hefty fall, did you not," the voice drawled.

Trying in vain to focus on the man's features as they swum across his vision, Arthur snapped back, "Yes, I did, did I not" in a reasonable impersonation of the man's brogue.

There appeared to be a metaphorical drop in temperature as the newcomer chewed over his heated words. Merlin leant in and whispered urgently into Arthur's ear. "Do you wish to be skewered like a boar on a spit? Hold your tongue else we will be dead before we have a chance to draw breath."

The villain who had felt the sting of the King's sarcastic tongue whistled between his teeth. "Hardly a fitting way to talk to one who has nursed you back to wakefulness after such a headlong plummet. Perhaps old Kieran should have left you for the crows to pick clean, yes?"

Tenderly caressing the swellings that temporarily disfigured his face, Arthur held up his hand in a conciliatory fashion. "I apologise for my quick temper, sir. It is the pain that sharpens my tongue and blunts my manners. Please accept my thanks for your ministrations."

Kieran bowed floridly. "Such pretty words fair do bring a tear to my eye, laddie."

There was an unpleasant sniggering that seemed to come from all sides. It was the first indication Arthur had had of the full number that surrounded the pair of questers and it caused him no little unease.

Arthur found that his vision was slowly beginning to clear and it soon became obvious to him why Kieran's sarcasm had met with such a sycophantic response.

The chief bandit was approximately six feet tall and very well muscled. An unruly mop of sandy hair nestled atop his head, giving way to an extremely lived-in face. There were deep creases all over it, though whether they were due to age or the ravages of a life lived permanently under the sun and moon was unclear. His most striking feature was the jet-black patch that sat over his left eye. It had jewels garlanding it which gave it the impression of a star-kissed area of the sky on a clear night.

The other eye was ice-blue and had about it a hardness that belied the playful twinkle that was shining from it at that precise moment.

When the King's gaze had completed its tour of the man's face, it stopped at the right eye and followed its trajectory. The eye had swivelled downwards and Arthur's eyes did likewise.

There in the bandit's right hand was Excalibur.

Futilely the King's hand toyed with the empty scabbard that hung uselessly by his side.

Kieran fixed Arthur with a penetrating gaze as he twisted Excalibur this way and that, catching the bright morning sun every now and again on the keen blade. "This is a mighty fine sword for two journeymen to be carrying. I'll wager that there is a fine tale behind how the pair of you came by it."

At that moment, a beam of light caught the blade and it lanced into the King's squinting eyes, causing a resurgence of the agony in his head. "It is mine, good sir. I thank you for taking stewardship of it whilst I was incapacitated, however, now that I am recovered, perhaps I may have it back." Arthur stumbled to his feet and staggered drunkenly towards the head of the bandit troop.

The brigand held up his hands to his cohorts, some of whom had become restive when the King had begun to approach him. Easily side-stepping the clumsy advance, Kieran pushed him in the back, sending the King sprawling to the floor in an ungainly heap. In two huge strides, he was at Arthur's side. "I think not," he rasped. "See, you can barely put one foot in front of the other. No, I think it would be best if I held onto it for a little longer." Slowly he brought the sword round until the tip rested on Arthur's Adam's apple, "Any objections?"

The King gritted his teeth, biting back the reply that he so wished to snarl at the unkempt brigand.

A gap-toothed grin suddenly split Kieran's face and he withdrew the sword and offered his hand to his stricken captive. Arthur pushed it away and struggled to his feet under his own power.

Swaying painfully, he looked around the clearing. Fully thirty unknown faces were weighing him up and a chill flew down his spine. He realised that what he had thought was Merlin's unnecessary pessimism was in fact a healthy dose of realism.

There was a slim chance that they would be able to extricate themselves from their predicament if Excalibur had been to hand, but the magician had been correct in his surmising that he would be gutted like a fish before he had a chance to despatch them all.

And, of course, the one thing that could be of possible aid was now lost once more in the forest. The sense of injustice at that was what hurt Arthur the most, even more so than the tattoo of torment caroming around his skull. He had overcome a dragon to hold the Grail in his hand, a dragon for God's sake, yet here he was mere hours later bereft of it once more and fighting for his life.

Frustration began to bubble inside him, slowly at first but, as he thought about the events that had just passed, the rage began to multiply tenfold then a hundredfold. Somewhere in the volcanic turmoil, a single word began to repeat itself again and again, in perfect rhythm with the throb in his temples. Montagu, Montagu, Montagu.

As his eyes swivelled madly in their sockets, it seemed to Arthur that whichever face he looked at, the sneering supercilious smirk of the dark magician leered back at him. Even as he beheld Merlin, the wizard's all too familiar face seemed to take on a distressing darkness and an aura of evil seemed to descend on the clearing in which they stood.

The pain inside the King's head seemed to be building into a crescendo of torture and he clutched at his temples, screaming in agony. He screamed and screamed until he felt his lungs would burst.

Against all reason, this cathartic outpouring of anguish seemed to clear his head momentarily and the scene that he now found himself staring at was now as clear as day. Both the bandits and Merlin stood transfixed, the shriek unsettling them to the extent that they were petrified in horror by the heart-freezing sound.

Arthur knew that there would not be another chance to escape the clutches of the robbers and he leapt forward, bowling Kieran from his feet and knocking Excalibur from his grasp.

The sudden movement snapped everyone out of their trance and all hell broke loose within the glade.

Kieran gasped as he tried to recover the wind that had been knocked from him by Arthur's opportunistic move. He desperately snaked out a hand to try and retrieve the blade but he was too late.

Excalibur was back in the hands of its rightful owner and the blade sang joyously as it cut a swathe amongst the banditry. Five men were down before the bandit leader had gained his feet. A look of complete awe illuminated the grizzled thief's face as he watched Arthur continue his bloody work. Before his eyes he saw his complement of men halved within minutes, such was the prowess of the King as he wielded his newly regained weapon.

The barbarity of Arthur's swordplay was such that the remaining bandits were circling him fearfully, half sure that their numbers would still prevail but unwilling to step within the diameter of Excalibur's murderous sweep.

The King, momentarily robbed of an opponent, snarled like a caged animal. His efforts had caused sweat to cascade from his greasy mop of greying hair, but he still held the robbers' gazes unfalteringly.

Relieved at his companion's intervention, Merlin forgot himself and ran in between two of the marauders into the circle of devastation that surrounded the berserk King. Sensing the movement and expecting a renewed assault,

Arthur swept his sword round in a vicious backhand sweep. In unison, both men's eyes widened in alarm as they realised what was to happen.

The next few seconds appeared to happen in slow motion. The instant he registered who was approaching, he tried to stop the momentum of the stroke but to no avail.

As soon as Merlin saw the unstoppable blade glinting in the rarefied air of the killing ground, he tried to turn tail and avoid its bite but, as his hands were still tied behind his back, his attempt to evade the stroke was hopelessly unbalanced and he could not move quickly enough.

Excalibur sliced through the magician's neck as if it was made of air. The stroke had such power within it that the blade was fully halfway across Merlin's throat before its movement ceased.

The mage slid off the sword with a sigh and crumpled to the leaf-strewn floor.

The turmoil that Arthur had been feeling returned with a heart-stopping vengeance but it was now of a very different nature. Oceans of guilt, grief and shame threatened to swamp him. What had he done? What had he done?

The remaining bandits had, by now, fled the maniac who they had captured, reasoning that they had been extremely lucky to avoid an appointment with the Grim Reaper but knowing if they did not flee they would soon be making his acquaintance anyway.

Arthur collapsed to his knees, weeping incoherently and cradling his fallen friend's lolling head in his lap, ignoring the gush of blood that drenched his cloak and leggings.

He was jerked from his apoplexy by an unexpected shadow falling across him. Looking up, he found himself staring into the pitted face of Kieran, the head bandit. The look upon his face was one of a man who had seen the depths of hell and would be forever haunted by them. He pointed at the body in Arthur's arms and whispered hoarsely. "He lives!"

Arthur blinked at the words and gaped at Kieran blankly.

The bandit dropped to his haunches and drew a muscular arm across his sweating brow. "He lives!" he repeated.

Arthur still did not move, appearing not to understand what the footpad was saying, however he did follow the direction of Kieran's finger.

Staring up at him with a look of shock and anger painted in stark relief upon his face was Merlin. His breathing was ragged and shallow but the longevity spell was still potent enough to resist an injury as horrific and gory as this.

"Merlin, I am so sorry, I…"

The wizard cut him off with an anguished snarl and painfully manoeuvred himself from Arthur's lap, leaving a growing stain of blood pooling on Arthur's clothing. He fell forward and began grunting furiously at Kieran, allowing what little room for movement his bonds allowed him to indicate that he wished them cut.

Arthur stepped forward with Excalibur at the ready. However, another strangled squeal from the magician made it clear that he did not want Arthur anywhere near him.

Kieran knelt by Merlin's side as if in a trance and drew a wicked looking blade from his belt. He slowly cut through the ropes binding the gravely wounded man, unable to take his eyes from the gaping gash that still pumped sweet-smelling blood onto the soil.

Once he was freed of his shackles, Merlin stood up with as much dignity as possible then stared sombrely at Kieran and pointed a slim finger towards him.

The elderly thief peered in confusion as the gratitude in Merlin's eyes transformed into a hideous mask of hatred. His bewildered look transferred from Merlin's face to his own arms. They were being pulled behind him by an invisible force. Try though he might he could not halt their inexorable progress behind his back and he soon found himself in the same position that Merlin had been, although his wrists were not bonded in any way visible to the human eye.

Sadly for Kieran, they did not stop there. His discomfort at being bound in such a way began to give way to intense pain as his arms continued their tortuous journey behind his back. His shoulders began to send waves of pain down his spine and with audible cracks they both dislocated within seconds of each other. The searing agony was not quite enough for Kieran to pass out and he watched in strangely blissful serenity as the final tendons gave way in his shoulders and his arms tore themselves free of his torso in a torrential gush of blood. The armless man collapsed face down in the leaf litter.

King Arthur's jaw was hanging agape. This was cruelty beyond anything he had seen Merlin perpetrate before. The fact that the wizard had done this to the bandit rather than himself only served to make the brutality of the death more shocking. "Why, Merlin?" he wept, "It was I who injured you so grievously."

Merlin spun round, his head at a disquieting angle and tried to speak. No sound issued forth. Rightly guessing that Arthur's sword stroke had cut through his vocal cords, he extended the index finger of his right hand and began to write words in the air.

"Had he not chosen to bind me, he would have lived."

Arthur's gaze travelled across the ornate writing hovering in the air. "But surely to have killed him in such a way was not necessary?" he responded.

251

A dangerous glint in Merlin's eye caused the King to take a step back. **"You dare talk to me as if I am in the wrong when you damned near took my head from my shoulders?"** The magician replied, the anger in his words causing them to burn red for a moment.

Arthur held up a placating hand. "I am sorry, Merlin. I do not know what came over me," he said hoarsely, hanging his head.

"Enough of your whining, man. Just think yourself lucky that it is not you lying face down in the soil."

Arthur coloured slightly at the threat but he knew that the magician must be exercising a massive amount of restraint to be as civil as this in the face of Arthur's ill-advised swing.

"I must away to repair the damage you have wrought upon me with your too-quick temper and your too-slow brain. I was going to tell you on the way to our destination but I have not yet had a chance. During my skirmish with Montagu by the Grail Lake, when his defences were momentarily befuddled by my spells, I saw into his mind. It appears that the Gospels are still in existence though I know not how. However, I now know where they are secreted. Once you have retrieved the Grail, you will meet me there and together we will unlock its secrets."

"Where are they?" Arthur exclaimed shrilly, his excitement at such news partially masking his guilt at his wounding of Merlin. The elation soon began to disappear however when another thought struck him. "What of Montagu though? Surely he will spirit away the Gospels to another secret place?"

"I do not believe he knows that I am aware of their location. I wounded him nearly as seriously as you have wounded me. But we must act quickly. If he suspects that we know of their continued existence then he will do as you say and remove them from their sanctuary. Speak of this to no-one. I will heal myself as quickly as I may but for now your task must be to relocate the Grail for, without it, we are undone. Find it, Arthur. Find it as quickly as you can because the longer we tarry, the better chance Montagu has of concealing the Gospels from us again and denying us our ultimate goal."

Arthur nodded at this. Feeling buoyed by the news, he decided to risk a bit of sarcasm at his long-lived friend's expense, "Ever the evasive enigma, Merlin. You still did not tell me where we are supposed to rendezvous."

Merlin eyed the King coldly but conceded the point. **"Believe me, I hope to be with you before you arrive there, but it is possible that I may still be incapacitated, so you may be unaccompanied for the entire journey."**

"Entire journey where, Merlin?" Arthur asked, sighing with frustration at his companion's continued dodging of the question.

With an imperious swish of his robe, Merlin wrote one last message before disappearing and left it hanging in the air for Arthur to contemplate. **"That is the surprise that I alluded to when we fled the dragon. I had thought to keep the location of the Gospels from you until we were upon them and they were safe in our hands in case we were separated in such a manner as this but now there is no help for it. I must repair the damage you have inflicted upon me as soon as I can for this wound hurts like the devil.
The Gospels are at the end of a road which we have walked before, sire. Montagu may be a cruel and heartless fiend but he is also a devilishly clever one. The minute we left there after I thought I had killed him, he must have gone back, presumably thinking that it would not occur to us to look in a ruin for something so magnificent."**

The King stared at the final sentence and found his breath stolen from him by the audacity of their foe. Shaking his head, he fled the clearing like a man possessed to begin his task, for there was now an ultimate destination before him, a light at the end of the tunnel, perhaps even an end to his quest, although with the multitude of setbacks they had experienced, he found himself shying away from that idea.
As he left the glade, the words began to dissipate in the air.

"The Gospels are housed in the sanctum at Lindisfarne Abbey."

*

Montagu stared through one of the holes that had formed in the ceiling of the Abbey in the years since the Viking rampage. The vast majority of rooms were too far gone to rack and ruin for him to bother with reparation. He could have restored them to their former glory had he chosen to, but he did not have the desire nor the inclination. He strode purposefully up the damp corridor until he arrived at the one wholly undamaged room in the Abbey.

He knew that he had read the text over a thousand times but he found that he could not resist another glance at them. His aquiline fingers grasped the side of the Gospels and peeled them open. He saw that he was on a page that was so familiar he could recite it verbatim with his eyes shut. Peering at the elaborate script but not really taking in its contents, he let a lazy smile touch his lips. He knew that he would soon hold the Grail in his hands for, just as a spider can sense the vibrations in its web when an unfortunate insect becomes entwined, he could sense the footsteps of destiny approaching.

His fingers tingled in anticipation of possessing the key to such power. He had read the Gospels many times over and was sure that he could master the Cup of Christ and its energies. He could not apprehend all of its magics but he was certain that he knew enough. Enough to wipe his enemies from the face of the earth. Enough for him to become the master of the world.

*

Arthur fluttered his cloak about him in an attempt to allow some air to circulate his sweat-sodden body. Pausing for a moment to regain his breath, he peered towards the midday sun, beating down so mercilessly upon him. He had been searching for the Grail for approximately three hours, ever since Merlin had disappeared into the ether. The words of the magician were echoing around his head and he knew that he dare not relent in his efforts to relocate that which he had lost.

When he had held the Grail in his hands, the feeling of warmth and goodness that had flowed through his blistered body was so pure and calming that the thought of it being lost from the world yet again was too frightening to contemplate.

Mopping the moisture from his brow, he decided on a change of tactic. So far his physical exertions had come to naught and the area of woodland still to be searched was so huge that the prospect of combing every twig, branch and bough was daunting, to say the least. Instead, he simply stood in the sun-kissed glade and closed his eyes, sending his consciousness forth into the air.

He knew in his heart that he was incapable of magic in the way that Merlin utilised it, but his experiences with the Grail made him feel that perhaps it was beyond the mysticism that Merlin commanded.

To Arthur's way of thinking, in the world of magic, the Grail was an object that would forever remain untouchable over the horizon. It was the pot of gold at the end of the rainbow that would always be just around the corner and never within reach. That was why Merlin could not see it and that was why he had not bothered to join Arthur in the search. However, to one who had held it in their hands, to one who had felt the healing power and the immaculate completeness of the Grail's energy coursing through their veins, well, perhaps they could be the one to detect the holy vessel in ways beyond the worldly.

Capturing the soothing feeling of the Grail in his mind once again, Arthur projected it into the air and searched the forest with his senses to see if there was anything he could detect which bore even the slightest resemblance.

Through the soughing trees and pitted branches, his consciousness flew. Among thickets and spinneys, around gnarled trunks and piled leaves, searching, ever searching for the treasure beyond imagining.

He stood statuesque for what could have been minutes but could just as well have been hours, frozen as a sculpture, his physical presence rooted to the ground but his mental presence soaring and swooping through the woodland.

Suddenly his eyes snapped open. He knew where the Grail rested. In his mind's eye, he now had an indelible image of where he needed to be. Spinning on his heel, he set off at a run, the adrenaline of discovery banishing the discomfort of his sweat-drenched clothing from his mind.

The picture that had flashed into his hindbrain was that of a mighty oak tree, standing many feet above its surrounding brethren, shadowing them with its magnificence, stifling their growth with its domination of the sunlight that shone upon the glade. There was the Grail, lodged at the conjoining of two of the peripheral branches that sprouted from the gargantuan trunk.

Sprinting athletically for a man of his advancing years, Arthur paid little heed to where his feet fell, instead concentrating on the foliage that crowded him on all sides. With each powerful stride, however, his confidence began to wane. He was, after all, in a wood and whilst the stupendous nature of the tree had caused it to rampage to the forefront of his vision, here in the true light of day, he started to doubt whether he would be able to distinguish it so readily.

Despite his best efforts to maintain the pace of his search, he found himself forced to cease his progress momentarily to catch his breath.

Once again he stretched and cuffed the droplets of sweat from his forehead. A wind picked up high in the canopy and he found his eyes drawn to the chaos of leaves above his head. Surely only a trick of the wind, but Arthur felt that there was a hint of mockery to be heard in the sinister susurration that swept around the branches.

Immediately the sneering face of Montagu reared into his mind. What limits were there to his power? Arthur had seen the astonishing feats that Merlin had performed yet Montagu appeared to be overcoming him at every turn.

Could the evil magician change the weather? Could the wind that sniggered irritatingly through the leaves above be the product of the dark magician's evil spellcasting? Chewing on his bottom lip, another thought occurred to the King. Perhaps the crows that had taken flight to such devastating effect were compelled to do so by Montagu's monstrous arts. Could he hold sway over the minds of animals? After all he had commanded many men to do his bidding and the human mind was surely a more complex puzzle to unravel. He must certainly have had some sort of influence over the dragon for why else would the beast have seen fit to act in such a way?

Did he now have to count the birds in the sky as his foe as well?

Trying to dismiss such pessimism from his mind, he shook his head and tried to recall the aura of the Grail to his memory once more. After a few minutes, he found he was sufficiently becalmed to do so and so he resumed the hunt.

He had barely taken one step when the silken sound of a sword being unsheathed from its scabbard reached his ears. Wheeling around, he saw three of Kieran's men approaching. Something about their manner and stance suggested that they would not be so easily persuaded to take flight this time.

"We saw what you did, you whoreson. We saw it all," one of the men shouted, drawing a grubby sleeve across his dirt-smeared face and snivelling, "Kieran may have been a thief but he didn't deserve to die like that. No-one deserves to die like that."

Arthur eyed their approach warily but said nothing.

The one in the centre of the trio drew a wicked looking cutlass from his belt and jabbed it in Arthur's direction. "Old Kieran was like a father to us. He took us in, fed us, clothed us, he looked after us, he did and then after he saves you and your mate's bleedin' lives, you both snap him in half like a bloody wishbone. Oh no, my lad, we can't let that go." The bandit finished, his two mean eyes gleaming brightly like two diamonds in a dirt-rich mine.

"He bound my friend, he threatened me, he should not have..." Arthur stammered but it was clear even to the three bandits that his heart was not really in the protest of innocence.

Hawking a huge gobbet of spit onto the floor, the man in the centre gestured his friends forward and the trio continued to advance. "Lawrence, he's only standing there trying to bloody justify himself," he gasped.

Lawrence, the one who had spoken previously, looked up at his companion who stood a good foot taller than him and tutted, "Seems to me that makes him as guilty as him what actually did the deed then, don't it you, Martin?"

The third member of the trio who had been silent hitherto merely rumbled his assent to this verdict.

"In that case, I feel we owe it to old Kieran to repay him the compliment and remove his arms from his body as well." Lawrence stated jovially. However the face he turned on Arthur was anything but. There was a horrifying bleakness to the way Lawrence spoke as he stared at the King. "We will not flee this time, my friend. By the time this is over, either you will lie dead or the three of us will. We have seen your swordsmanship and it stands amongst the best in the land but, though it may be the death of us, we will go to our graves happy if we bleed you."

The trio began to space out and encircle the guilt-ridden King.

In a sudden flashback Arthur found himself remembering Lindisfarne Abbey, ringed by the trio of Vikings and in desperate danger. This time however there was no Kelson to even up the odds.

Breathing evenly, he backed into the nearest tree trunk, all the while eyeing his assailants. He found himself reflecting on the other major difference between his confrontation with the Vikings and the one he now found himself in. When he and the massive hound had overcome the three Norsemen, there had not been a hint of remorse. There had been no quarter asked for and no quarter given. That was how the Vikings had always fought. In this situation however, Arthur could not help but feel a huge sense of pity for the ragged band that stood before him.

He also knew that there was no way on earth he could justify Merlin's extermination of the head thief. Perhaps he could rationalise the killing spree that he had embarked upon before his fateful stroke upon Merlin's neck, after all, the brigands that he had killed had all approached him with nothing but murder in their eyes but what had happened to Kieran was an unnecessary barbarity that seemed to taint the nobility of the quest.

Chancing a quick look left and right, Arthur straightened up from his battle stance and pointed Excalibur towards the ground. "Please, I wish to see no harm come to you. I can understand your horror at the fate of your friend and I will not insult you by trying to excuse it. But I beg of you, turn around and walk away from this. Attacking me will not bring back Kieran, nor will it avenge his death. I would explain further but if I did, you would think me lying, mad or both. I have no desire to kill you but if you remain on this path then I will have no choice but to respond in kind."

To Arthur's despair, the three thieves simply ignored him and continued their flanking movement. Sighing deeply, he brought up the point of Excalibur to defend himself. He had decided that, depending on the skills of his adversaries, he would simply try to disarm them or only inflict minor wounds upon them. He would stop them hurting him but he would try his utmost to refrain from hurting them as well.

The first to attack was Lawrence. Luckily for Arthur his lack of height meant that he could not get close enough to the King to strike effectively and the stroke was easily avoided.

The next assault was simultaneous and it came from the lumbering untalkative Martin and the unnamed one who had stood between them. The hulking brute was not very quick but his slash had a good deal of power behind it and Arthur struggled to bring his sword up in time to thwart the other man's thrust.

Nodding acknowledgment at the near success of the stratagem, Arthur decided to go on the offensive and try and buy himself some time. First he feinted then snaked out a quick thrust that Martin turned awkwardly aside. Taking advantage of the larger man's step backwards, Arthur skipped lightly onto one of the massive roots that erupted from the base of the tree, threw his left hand up onto a thick branch that was now within his reach and with an impressive show of strength, swung himself up and over, landing heavily astride it.

With frustrated cries, the three bandits began attempting to scale the tree as well, but were easily held back by the potent threat of Excalibur mere feet away. The trio prowled around the base of the huge trunk, spitting threats and promising vile tortures once they got hold of Arthur.

"You cannot stay up there forever, you murdering bastard. Or do you intend to sprout wings and fly away?" Lawrence sneered, raising cackles of laughter from the other two.

The King paid little heed to the posturing below. He knew that, for now, he was safe. He held the high ground and was able to fend off any hostile sorties from below, but for how long? He had to sleep and as it was, he stood outnumbered three to one. He glimpsed the afternoon sun through the branches that spider-webbed across the sky and was shocked to see how low it had fallen. Had this skirmish really lasted that long? He realised that it would not be too long before the light had fled the wood and then the trio would be upon him ensuring that his breath fled his body. He had to move, but how?

The question nearly became immaterial because, during his introspection, Martin had gained a foothold on one of the gnarled roots below him. The thief swung his blade at Arthur and the King threw himself backwards, coming within an ace of losing his balance. Acting on instinct, he began to slice downwards with Excalibur.

Martin's swooping attack had left his weapon well and truly lodged in the trunk of the tree and, unfortunately for him, he decided to try and free his blade rather than flee the situation.

Arthur's famed blade continued on its way down but, at the last second, he saw that his assailant was unarmed. In desperation, he checked his stroke, mindful of both his promise to himself when the trio first threatened him and also the reasons for their hostility in the first place. Unfortunately, that only changed a killing blow into a maiming blow.

Martin toppled off the base of the tree in horror as he surveyed the spurting stump that was where his hand should have been. In a state of blind panic, he cast about for his missing extremity, finally spotting it a good ten feet away from where he had fallen. After a few seconds however, the shock of his wound overwhelmed him and he fainted, falling face down on the ground as if he was one of the massive trees that shadowed the clearing and had been felled by an axe.

Meanwhile, Arthur found himself having to contend with another flanking attempt. Lawrence circled around to where Martin had stood moments before. The other bandit positioned himself almost directly under the branch where the King perched, using the thick bough as protection from Arthur's harassment but still darting out every now and again to bring his own weapon into play.

Despite the odds being slightly better now, Arthur knew that flight was rapidly becoming his only option because whilst Martin had been lumbering and ponderous, these two were as quick and nimble as ferrets.

Lawrence lunged at the King, who had overbalanced whilst defending himself and was ecstatic to hear Arthur gasp as he felt the flick of metal snake across his left cheek.

Feeling a thin trickle of blood mingle with his unkempt beard, the King hissed. "There. You have your wish. You have bled me. Now I beg of you, leave me in peace." He knew the words were futile, for when Lawrence had seen the scarlet stream flowing, an obscene light had flared in his eyes and he had licked his lips hungrily, but he felt he had to say them. Though there was no-one to corroborate it if he were ever needed to justify his actions, he knew now that he had satisfied himself in his own mind that he had given his assailants every chance to escape.

His sword sliced down to his right leg as he saw the other thief's cutlass thrusting up towards him out of the corner of his eye. Then with surprising speed and the element of surprise, he leapt onto one of the numerous branches that were scalable and began to climb the tree.

Foul-mouthed curses followed him up the trunk but sounded far enough away for him to stop the initial burst of ascension and take stock. Peering down as best he could, he was struck by how dark the forest floor seemed from his elevated position and, despite his best efforts, found that he was unable to locate the two who harried him.

He stared intently at the base of the tree and the lower branches for what seemed like an age until he was certain that his pursuers were absent from the scene. Perhaps they had given up, although their words and actions had certainly seemed passionate enough when they had come upon him. However, they were thieves and such people were seldom as good as their word.

Gingerly he brought his sweating hand up to his cheek, wincing as the perspiration stung the cut. Taking one last look below him, he went to descend the tree for he felt acutely vulnerable in his current position. He looked to his right to make sure he gained a safe handhold and stopped.

His mouth gaped open stupidly as he beheld the view before him.

From his lofty perch he could see a great deal more of the sky than was perceptible from the ground. Where the ocean of blue had been, a huge roiling maelstrom of cloud was banking up in the heavens. It fluctuated and billowed with such force that Arthur was amazed it did not make a sound. With a suddenness that nearly sent him crashing fatally to the ground his cloak whipped up, haunted by a gale force wind which buffeted him into the main trunk of the tree. He tried to grasp one of the branches that jerked madly around him but their movements were too frenzied for him to gain a grip. The wind pressed him against the trunk of the tree and pinned him like a butterfly, unable to move, rooted to the spot by a pressure that threatened to squeeze the very life from him.

He wanted to scream but the wind was so powerful he could not find the breath to. Instead a low moan escaped his lips as the thunderhead before him sent a bolt of lightning into the forest sparking an almost instant inferno. First one, then two, then a third, all stabbing down viciously into the greenery, scorching it to a crisp in seconds.

Then it stopped. As suddenly as it began, it stopped. Arthur, who had been fighting with all his might against the hurricane, fell forward onto the branch. Fortunately he still had enough presence of mind to wrap his arms and legs around it and fought to regain control of his breath, hoping that the hammering of his heart would soon calm down lest it dislodge him from his treacherous perch.

He lay there for a few moments, head bowed, thanking God that he had survived.

Unexpectedly the trees began to sway again and an icy chill swept over him. Desperately not wanting to but feeling compelled to do so, Arthur lifted his head from its pillow of bark and looked up. The greyness of the sky was absolute. It stretched from horizon to horizon without stint. Except for...

Arthur's thought screamed to a halt as his eyes readjusted to the panorama and he registered exactly what he was seeing.

There had been many a day on the ramparts of Camelot, after Guinevere had taken flight with her ill-gotten beau, that Arthur had found himself disturbed by a depthless depression and had taken to walking in the topmost towers alone, staring out across the lands he commanded, sometimes marvelling at the wonders of God's creation but mainly despairing at how much he possessed yet how little it mattered when the one thing he wanted to possess more than anything else was beyond his reach.

It was on days such as these that he had taken to blindly staring towards the clouds that scudded across his vision, astonished at how one moment they were nothing but shapeless blobs yet in the blink of an eye when viewed from a slightly different perspective, they became figures in battle or wild horses or any number of fantastic sights.

Right here, right now, he remembered a beauteous summer's day when he had been engaged in one of these walks. He had, in actual fact, been on his way to one of his usual viewing places when he happened to glance through one of the slim windows dotted liberally up the side of the tower.

The sky had been as blue then as it was grey now, but there had been one small wisp of purest white up there. At first his eye had been drawn to it because of its bizarre isolation from any other cloud, but as he stared at it, it gradually resolved itself into a face. A face that had lit up every single day but now haunted every single night. His Guinevere.

As he stared, enraptured by this miracle, the face seemed to change from a benign smile to a painfully sad frown. Tears had risen unbidden in the King's eyes as his love's face appeared to turn from him and disappear.

From that day onwards when he had found himself within Camelot's walls, at that exact time of day, he had returned religiously to that window, hoping against hope that he would see her again. He never did.

But now her image dominated the sky.

Arthur's gaze roamed every exquisite inch of her face from the gentle curve of her delicate chin to the irregular line where her hair cascaded halfway down over her forehead. Her nose was as perfect as he remembered and his breath quickened as he gazed upon her luscious mouth but it was the eyes that brought a lump to his throat. They were the cells that had imprisoned his heart all those years ago and even now, centuries later, they still possessed the ability to reduce him to a speechless statue.

Against all reason, the lips began to move and a warm wind kissed his ear. "Come to me, my love", it seemed to say, "come to me."

The King's senses were screaming at him that this was wrong, that what he was seeing could not be real, but the vision of his long lost love was so all-consuming that he paid them no heed. He began to walk haltingly towards the end of the branch.

"Come to me, my love. Come to me."

In his mind, the happiness of his life with Guinevere and his pride at having such a beautiful wife was replaying itself over and over again.

"Come to me, my love. Come to me."

The bough was beginning to thin out under the King's feet and he was but scant yards away from walking straight out of the tree, so entranced was he by the vision before him.

"Come to me, my Lancelot. Come to me."

Arthur blinked as his heart skipped a beat. What cruelty was this? "Guinny?" he whimpered. "Please...please," he sank to his knees, balancing precariously on the insubstantial branch. He looked up in agony as his wife's eyes, the eyes that he had lost himself in for so long, the eyes that had bested him with one look, grew hard and unforgiving. A callous laugh echoed all around Arthur, rushing into his ears and searing into his brain. Before his very eyes, his beloved's face changed into someone else.

Montagu's merciless grin bestrode the sky. "Know the pain that you have visited upon me, Arthur."

"Dear God, no," Arthur rocked back and forth on the slim branch, staring straight through Montagu's smirk, into the past. A past that Arthur had thought drowned in tears of betrayal, a past that the King had, up until now, successfully smothered but no more. It had all been brought crashing down upon his shoulders, bringing him to his knees and he was not sure that he would ever regain his feet.

Thinking that Arthur was still looking at him, Montagu continued to crow, "You will not defeat me. You cannot defeat me. I can see into your mind, Arthur. I can snap your brain in half should I so choose."

Arthur's head slumped down in absolute despair. So this was it, he thought. Montagu has defeated me by ripping out my heart and he did not have to lift a finger.

"Mind you," the evil one said conversationally, "I can see why you fell so far for this Guinevere. The memories that you have of her are very, erm, vivid, shall we say."

Arthur was not listening. The pain had reached a zenith and he felt himself to be on the brink, staring into a bottomless abyss.

"She certainly did not act like royalty in the bedchamber, did she?" snorted the dark magician.

Arthur froze, the innuendo in Montagu's voice beginning to drown out the shrieking agony he felt at the dredged-up memories that now sat so starkly at the forefront of his mind.

"Perhaps you were unable to sate her lusts sufficiently," the wizard sniggered. "Perhaps that is why she fell so readily into the arms of another."

The former King of England gained his feet like an avenging angel. "Enough!" he bellowed. The bitter anguish he had felt at seeing his sweetheart again had been replaced by a diamond-hard rage at the violation of his mind and his memories. Drawing Excalibur, he pointed it directly between Montagu's eyes. "Know this. It is *you* who will not stop me. It is *you* who will experience pain such as the pain I feel now but magnified tenfold. Kill me and I will descend from heaven to stamp you into the ground. Bury me and I will rise up from the soil and thrust Excalibur up your demonic backside. It is *you* who will not defeat me."

Montagu raised an eyebrow at this outburst, "Very impressive, Arthur. I had thought that my strategy would tip you over the edge," he tutted irritably, "I do so hate having a plan fail, don't you?"

Arthur turned his back upon the titanic face in the sky. "Begone, fiend. Begone from my sight." He spun around on his heel and walked back towards him, jabbing Excalibur forward to make his point. "Enjoy your little games, Montagu. Once myself and Merlin rendezvous at Lindisfarne, we will wipe that smirk off your face."

"Lindisfarne, you say?" Montagu inquired innocently.

The King gaped stupidly for a moment then closed his eyes, ashamed at himself for being so easily tricked.

"I look forward to it, your majesty," Montagu drawled sarcastically.

Then, just as clouds can sometimes resolve themselves into faces in the blink of an eye or vice versa, the dark one's face transformed into an irregular mass of grey, pregnant with freezing rain.

Arthur sat down despondently upon the branch, oblivious to the cold water that hammered down upon him from the granite sky above. Once again his heart had overruled his head. The obvious impossibility of Guinevere appearing in such a way only served to heap further humiliation upon him. Intellectually, he knew he should have spotted the ruse but, once again, Montagu had pinpointed exactly where his weakness was and exploited it ruthlessly.

He did not even hear the two strangled screams beneath him and it was not until a hoarse voice emanated up from below the tree that he even knew that he was no longer alone. "Arthur?" it called.

The shame rose like bile in his throat. It was Merlin. He had grievously wounded him scant hours previously and now he had done the one thing that the magician had stressed he must not do and revealed the location of their proposed assignation. For a brief moment, he felt like letting the magician walk by his hiding place and remaining there in his private ignominy forever. Sighing deeply, he shouted down. "I am here, Merlin."

He could vaguely make out the figure that stalked around beneath the tree, seeing it stop and look up. It was but a few seconds before he found himself sharing the upper branches with the magician.

"What on earth are you skulking about up here for, man? You are highly vulnerable. Did you know that there were two fellows on the ground below about to take axes to this tree?"

The King shook his head. So Lawrence and his cohort had come back after all. Merlin peered at him strangely as if he was trying to get some sort of handle on the King's mood. "Well, it was the work of but a moment to dispatch them so it is of no matter," he sniffed. "Tell me, what are you doing up here, quivering in this godforsaken weather when there is ample shelter to be had on the forest floor below?"

Arthur's eyes narrowed at the casual way in which Merlin described his latest victims. "May I say that if anyone were in pursuit of us, they would have little trouble finding our location because all they would need to do would be wade through the oceans of blood that you seem intent on creating."

"Your meaning?" Merlin's eyes blazed dangerously.

Arthur knew that he was lashing out mainly because of anger at his own foolishness but Merlin's blasé dismissal of two human lives only served to enrage him further, "Meaning that recently you do not seem to be particularly shy about using your powers to kill."

The magician coloured at this blatantly aggressive response and was about to shoot back an equally belligerent point when Arthur stood up and stared beyond him over his right shoulder. He bit back his retort and turned around to see what had engrossed the King.

"Do you see it, Merlin?" Arthur whispered.

Rolling his eyes, Merlin got to his feet. "See what? The sky is darker than your mood, if that were possible," he added sarcastically.

"You do not see the aurora?"

"With this downpour, I can barely see my hand in front of my face." Merlin hissed, cringing as a large droplet from one of the few branches that still overhung their vertiginous perch deposited itself down his back.

Arthur laughed and, at first, Merlin felt that the laugh had more than a hint of madness about it but the sound soon resolved itself into one of pure unbridled joy.

The King capered like a jester on the precarious branch causing it to shake and Merlin to nearly lose his balance.

"What are you doing, you fool?" he sneered.

"A rainbow that only I can see?" Arthur asked. "Merlin, it is the Grail. All you need to do is fly us in the direction I give you and it will be ours once more."

An unseemly glint gleamed in the magician's suddenly beady eyes as Arthur's aggressive comments were forgotten in the light of the discovery. "Then tell me. Tell me where to take you so we can away to Lindisfarne before Montagu catches wind of what we plan."

The joy on the former monarch's face dissolved causing Merlin to freeze in apprehension. "What concerns you, Arthur? Is this not the scheme we discussed?"

The King's shoulders hunched over and his face, when he eventually brought it up to face the magician of Camelot, was one of abject misery. "He knows, Merlin, he knows already." Arthur whispered.

"And how is this?" There was no discernable change in the wizard's face but his voice was as chill as an Arctic gale.

Shaking his head, King Arthur recounted what had occurred scant minutes before Merlin's return.

The magician listened impassively and when Arthur had finished the only indication that Merlin had even heard what he had said was a slight reddening of his cheeks and a sense of huge, barely suppressed, rage being restrained only by the tightest of leashes. "Where is the rainbow, Arthur?" Merlin asked after taking a huge deep breath.

For a brief moment the King's mouth hung open, for he was nonplussed by the lack of reaction to his tale.

Merlin grabbed him by the front of his tunic and yanked him across the space between them until their noses were no more than six inches apart. "No rush, your majesty," he hissed. "You have only told our foe what we plan to do once we retrieve the Grail. It is nothing to upset yourself about," he continued, sarcasm dripping from every word like blood from a fresh wound, "only now we will probably have to fight him every step of the damned way whilst he searches for a new place to hide the Gospels. Gods, man, is there no end to your idiocy?"

Arthur knew that he should not have been taken aback by the wizard's reaction, indeed he should think himself lucky that it had been as controlled as it was, but the shock of actually being manhandled still jolted him uncomfortably.

"You look surprised?" Merlin pressed remorselessly. "To be honest with you Arthur, that was my only plan anyway. I had no other stratagem to fall back on. That has now been ruined by your gullibility, but we have had that obstacle in our way during the whole journey, have we not?" the mage smiled witheringly.

Arthur broke free from his grip. "Have you never loved, Merlin? Have you never felt that all-consuming feeling overwhelm your heart?"

In the dim light, Arthur fancied that a slight flicker of pain briefly lit the magician's eyes, but it came and went in a second. "What has that to do with anything? If Montagu is allowed to accomplish his plans then there will be no more love. Dammit, there will be no more life." He took a step towards the King, long finger jabbing the air. "Do not seek to deflect any guilt from yourself, Arthur. Montagu tricked you far too easily and no amount of wheedling on your part will change that fact," Merlin sighed and wheeled around in the direction of where Arthur indicated the Grail was then extended his hand behind him for the King to take. "Come, we have wasted enough time already. The Gospels could be halfway around the world by now."

The two men took to the air in an atmosphere as cold as the wind that whipped and tore at their cloaks. The King directed Merlin to the Grail with simple one-word directions, not trusting himself to engage the magician in any conversation for he felt sure it would only create more friction between them.

After they had retrieved the cup from its eyrie in the branches of the regal oak, they were off once more, speeding across the land.

The countryside accelerated along underneath them at a nauseating rate though they only saw brief snatches of it, because a fog, tenuous at first but thickening the further north they travelled, began to obscure the fields and woods far below them. The pace that Merlin had set was such that his advice of looking toward the horizon rather than at the ground did very little to settle the churning in the King's stomach.

At what seemed like regular intervals, they came under the frightening scrutiny of massive dragons but, due to their lack of speed and manoeuvrability, Merlin considered them to be more of an irritation than any great threat so there was no need for any undue concern. In any case, against the ponderous bulk of the monsters, speed was their greatest ally and they had that in abundance so it was easy enough for them to leave the massive beasts floundering in their wake far behind.

After about an hour of flying, Arthur decided to test the water and see if Merlin's temper had cooled any. He sought a neutral subject and said, "My, those dragons are awesome beasts. Where do they hail from? They cannot be native to these lands because we would surely have come upon them before now?"

Arthur was not sure if Merlin had not heard his question or was simply still ignoring him but, just as the King was about to resume his scrutiny of the horizon, the magician of Camelot began to speak, his voice set at a clear enough pitch that he did not have to shout.

"They are creatures sired by yet also invulnerable to magic. As to where they came from," the magician shrugged, "the myriad texts on the subject are unclear. Some say they dwell in the centre of the earth, feeding on the gargantuan fires that burn there, hence their ability to breathe flame. But then, on the other hand, some say they are formed when the clouds in the sky are struck by lightning."

Arthur was about to scoff at that until he thought about the day when the solitary cloud had morphed so vividly into Guinevere's beauteous face. How many times had he stared up at the sky or at a roiling thunderhead and seen images held within it? Faces and figures, human and animal and, yes, now he considered it, he had sometimes beheld the imperious outline of one of the massive lizard-like beasts rearing into the heavens, seemingly poised to rain down searing death upon an unseen victim.

Whilst he was contemplating that, Merlin continued to speak, "Though they are winged, I think it more likely that they dwell under the earth though and am more inclined to believe the first hypothesis."

"Have you had any experience of them before now?" Arthur asked, pleased that the magician seemed to have gotten over his ire at Montagu duping him so effortlessly.

Merlin shook his head. "No, and I will be honest, though at this precise moment it chokes me to say it, I was mightily impressed with the way you vanquished the heinous beast by the lake, given its size and agility."

Inwardly Arthur was grateful for the compliment but chose not to dwell on it, given his ignominious behaviour since. His brows wrinkled. "Have you not? I am sure I have heard you talking about... what was the name...Vortigern," he snapped his fingers, "before you came to Camelot, something about a fort continually collapsing because of two duelling dragons under the earth."

The magician looked blank for a moment then rolled his eyes in remembrance. "That was a mere ruse to salve the mood of an intemperate King. The monarch in question was trying to build a fort on ground that would not support it but he would not heed his advisers when they told him so. Therefore I came up with the tale of the red and white dragons so that he could change his mind without losing face with his councillors." He cast a scornful glance towards his flying companion. "I do not need to tell you how stubborn monarchs can be when they receive counsel they do not wish to hear."

Arthur ignored the comment and returned to the subject of dragons. "So, beyond a few texts which you have read, you know little about the creatures, yes?"

Merlin, who Arthur knew baulked at admitting his ignorance on any subject, was surprisingly diffident in his response, "Yes, my liege, you are correct. I have never had any first-hand experience of dragons before yesterday."

The King cast a nervous glance over his shoulder but any pursuit had long since fallen away. He turned back and said, "Well, happily the chance to study them up close again has diminished somewhat. Having been so close to one, I have no wish to find out anything more about them unless it is in a book or manuscript."

Merlin smiled. "They are quite formidable, are they not?"

Arthur returned the smirk. "Aye, they..."

He was cut off in mid-sentence by two huge equine heads which had reared up simultaneously at them out of the fog. They were forced to ascend vertically through the uncomfortably moist blanket of cloud rather than simply flying past. Below them, they had watched a patch of the impenetrable mist bloom into vivid orange as one of the beasts had discharged its flame in a vain attempt to bring the two of them down.

They had rocketed upwards and Arthur felt the air begin to get thinner. "Merlin..." he slurred as he felt his grip begin to loosen.

"I wish to show you something, Arthur. Hush now, it will not be long," the wizard said.

For a moment in his giddy state, the King thought that Merlin had gone mad and was leading them into the maw of another dragon, for the fog above them was becoming bright yellow. However, the two unlikely fliers burst through the cloud cover and were instantly bathed in the raw incandescence by the rays of an uninhibited sun.

They found themselves peering over what seemed to be range upon range of snow capped mountains stretching away into infinity. "Wondrous, is it not?" The mage smiled knowingly. "I have gazed upon this sight so many times yet its magnificence never fails to steal my breath away."

Arthur could only nod dumbly. He yearned to cast his cloak aside and enjoy the full benefit of the sun upon his pallid body, but he knew that the effects of the longevity spell were such that to do so would be suicide. In all the years that he and Merlin roamed the land, he had not given the matter much thought, merely, after the initial incredulity at not being able to enjoy the daylight properly, accepting the fact that it was for the greater good if he were to deny himself the pleasure. However, when he gazed upon such an awesome panorama, he found that instead of enjoying it as he should, he actually resented it for the fact that it was forever denied to him.

"May we go, Merlin? I have seen enough," he mumbled dispiritedly.

Shrugging, the magician murmured a few words and they were off again, their passage through the clouds causing a turmoil that suggested they were moving at such speed, it was creating a trail of smoke behind them.

"I merely thought that it would provide a momentary diversion from the weightiness of what will face us when we arrive at Lindisfarne." Merlin sniffed sulkily as they descended once more into the slate-grey cloud and chaotic sheets of rain.

Arthur turned to face the wizard with an unseemly scowl upon his face, though it was more to do with his own misery rather than any antipathy towards his travelling companion. Mindful of their new-found détente Arthur proceeded to explain his expression of disgust. "I am sorry, Merlin. I was afraid that the beauty of the scene would have seduced me into doffing my cloak. I did not appreciate that the sight of such unadulterated beauty would stir such intense feelings within me. I never realised how much I hated the fact that my life is and forever will be starved of such warmth and serenity."

Merlin's eyes swivelled in their sockets but he said nothing.

They flew on in silence for a few more seconds until a thought that had been gnawing away at the King finally found its voice. "You had your cowl about your shoulders, did you not?" Arthur asked pointedly.

The magician shook his head but did not look at the King, he merely intensified his concentration as he scrutinised the horizon.

"You did, Merlin. How is that possible?" the King gasped. "I remember you squinting in the sunshine. It was shining directly on your face yet you did not burn. How is this miracle possible, Merlin?" Arthur hissed, his confusion rising in exact conjunction with the volume of his voice.

The mage pretended to ignore the question, yanking the hood of his cowl over his head, but it was clear to the King that he had heard every word. "Dammit, man, tell me." Arthur reached through the crisp cold air between them and grasped a handful of the wizard's black robe. "Answer me," he bellowed.

"I…" the spellweaver began before pausing and turning his explanation into a strangled yelp. "Dragons!" he yelled, smacking away Arthur's hand and pointing urgently towards a range of green hills whose summits peeped through the mists before them.

Over the peaks they came, fully twenty of them, some red, some white, some black and one or two of a golden hue that sparkled even in the dullness of the overcast. The air was shredded by their grating screeches and the two men paused in their flight, desperately searching for somewhere they could shelter whilst always keeping one eye on the approaching horde of winged death that drew ever closer.

With rising despair, they dropped through the clouds only to find themselves staring at a flat featureless landscape beneath them, landscape that provided them with nothing but the scantest cover. They were surrounded by tilled fields, all stripped clean by the farmers of anything that occupied land fit for crops. The flat expanse stretched to all four points of the compass, the only slight break in the monotony being some straggly hedgerows used to mark the border between the farmsteads and the odd tree sprouting incongruously atop some of the lower hills.

The pair of questers watched grimly as the dragons' obscured shadows grew ever thicker in perfect parallel with the actual beasts in the sky above. "Will they see us if we stay still?" Arthur whispered urgently.

"We will not know that until they are upon us and, if they can, by then it will be too late to elude them." He turned to the King with hatred in his eyes. "This is your doing, you simpleton," he spat. "No doubt this is the first of many diversions sent to prevent us reaching Lindisfarne. I do not know why you did not just pass the Grail into Montagu's possession and have done with it. It would have been so much easier," he sneered.

The King's jaw dropped open. "How can these beasts be under Montagu's enchantment? You said that such creatures were impervious to magic," he bit back, "Or did you actually mean they are impervious to *your* magic?" he snarled.

Merlin's eyes widened and his face reddened. However instead of the heated words and vengeful magic that he expected, the magician jumped forward and pushed him back with both hands.

Spinning in an uncontrollable nosedive, Arthur plunged, end over end, flailing his arms about in a vain attempt to gain some sort of control over his plummet. This proved impossible for there was nothing to even enable him to change direction, let alone halt his inexorable progress towards the ground. He happened to be looking at Merlin when the magician cast his spell. With a gentle wafting gesture, the magician swung his left arm across his body.

Immediately Arthur felt himself wrenched onto a horizontal plane. Again, he was left twisting end over end vainly trying to arrest his momentum. With mounting horror he saw a tree directly in his path. Tensing himself for the impact, he tried to scrunch himself up as best he could in the foetal position. A sense of deceleration tempted him enough to open his eyes, just as he came to rest in the blessedly smooth branches. He ended up slouched across three tightly bunched boughs in a huge state of relief.

Several blood-curdling shrieks above him drew his mind back to the predicament from which he had just escaped. With a horrified gaze, he saw the first of the dragons reach his airborne companion. A ball of flame erupted from its mouth but it narrowly missed its target.

Arthur propped himself up as best he could upon the branches where he had come to rest, but he knew he was helpless to aid his friend. Without really thinking of the consequences, he began hollering and waving frantically at the dragons, trying to distract them from Merlin.

A couple of the nearest creatures detached themselves from the group assailing the magician and began to swoop down towards the tree in which Arthur stood.

Then, with a suddenness that caused Arthur to lose his footing, Merlin appeared before him. "Come," he said.

As he was picked up from the tree's branches, the King made a grab for the magician's robe. He thought he had hold of it but inexplicably his fingers passed through it as if it was as insubstantial as a cobweb. Even more confusingly, instead of plummeting to the ground, he now found himself flying horizontally across the land, again with little or no control. The wind buffeted him and sent him spiralling head over heels until the dizziness nearly caused him to pass out.

The object that kept him conscious was the object that had sustained him through every single one of the long, long years he had walked the earth. He clasped the Grail to his breast and tried to pray but the words were lost in the tornado of wind that tore at him unceasingly. Instead he merely recited the Lord's Prayer in his mind, finding a mental comfort that was denied to his physical body.

For how long he prayed he did not know because the landscape passed below him in a blur and he could not judge his speed.

At length he began to slow down. For a little while, he had been able to discern the sea to his right. As his pace decelerated, the unmistakable smell of the salt came to his nose and the raucous screech of seagulls came to his ears. During the journey, he had found that he could manoeuvre himself to a certain extent. Therefore he now tried to spin his body round so he could see what his destination would be. As he had suspected, the ruins of Lindisfarne Abbey came to his sight and he found himself marvelling anew at his companion's command of the mystical arts. To think that Merlin had been able to materialise and then transport him all this way whilst being attacked by a horde of dragons. It was a hugely impressive feat and Arthur could not help but be awestruck by it.

The amazed look on his face slowly disappeared and a rictus of fear replaced it. Perhaps his companion's mastery of magic was not quite as omnipotent as he had thought, for it soon became clear that although the King was definitely slowing down, he would not be able to stop completely before he entered the Abbey.

271

Once again Arthur attempted to curl his body into the foetal position but the wind that wrenched and pawed at him prevented him from doing so.

Suddenly the daylight disappeared and Arthur was under the ceiling of one of the abbey's numerous rooms. He had flown through a window and was now tumbling uncontrollably in an acrobatic roll across the rubble strewn floor.

His momentum was stopped with sickening abruptness by a wall. Luckily he had managed to bring his arms up just in time to partially shield his face. He fell to the floor in agony, his body ripped to shreds by innumerable cuts and passed into unconsciousness.

Chapter 16

Lindisfarne Abbey

Arthur's left hand fell to the floor and he heard the metallic tinkle of the Grail as he relinquished his grip on it. That caused a body-wide eruption of pain and he nearly fainted from it. Instead his head lolled to the side and he watched the Cup of Christ come to a spiralling halt on the floor. He knew he had to regain possession of it and so he hauled himself agonisingly onto all fours and crawled across the cold flagstones to it.

He grabbed it in both hands with tears starting from his eyes. He had done it. Finally. He had brought the Grail to Lindisfarne Abbey. To the Gospels. It was at an end. All that had to be done now was for Merlin to... his train of thought crashed to a halt. Merlin! The speed of his passage and the giddiness of finishing the quest had pushed the fate of his companion from his mind. What chance was there that he had survived the dragons?

Arthur began to weep. He was at a loss as to what he should do. He did not presume to be able to activate the Grail without Merlin's help and now the magician and all his knowledge was lost.

"How can this be?" he whispered, staring intently at the Grail.

As he did so, a tear fell from his face and landed in the bowl of the Grail. He stared at it as if hypnotised, for colours had begun to emanate from it, pulsing gently before his eyes. Without knowing why, he reached into the cup and pushed at the teardrop with his bloodied fingers.

The pain disappeared. The aches, the bruises, the throbbing, it was all gone. Then a song sounded in his ears. A song that filled him with such wonder that he thought his heart would burst.

Then, a light. A light that bathed him in the purest peace he had ever known and left him breathless with awe. Without knowing how, he had done it. He had activated the Grail. He had needed no help from anyone. He had fulfilled his destiny. He was the one destined to wield the Cup of Christ. He was the chosen one.

King Arthur Pendragon held the Holy Grail aloft with an almost obscene look of triumph on his face. So many years, decades, centuries spent traversing the land all dissolved into the forgotten past as he felt the energy of the holy antiquity pulse through his veins. He knew with unshakeable certainty that that which he wielded was possessed with an awesome power, yet the feeling that enveloped him was one of great gentleness and serenity.

He let his eyes trace the beatific glow that bathed the far wall in its glorious phosphoresence. All was light and all was clear and although the former

King of The Britons found himself in a glare as bright as a thousand suns, it caused him no discomfort.

A vague feeling of disquiet began prodding at the edges of Arthur's ecstasy, but the culmination of relief that his quest was finally at an end coupled with the rapture he now found himself experiencing overrode the unease that crept over him.

Then a shadow whipped across the coruscating display, momentarily blackening its glow. Arthur turned quickly and saw that it was a man flying through the gap in an exceedingly more elegant way than he had moments before. Arthur stowed the Grail in his cloak and the light, though it still glowed inside his clothing was muted at last. He blinked his eyes until they had adjusted to the dull gloom of the day outside. He did not need to see the face of the newcomer though because the walk was so familiar.

"Merlin!" he addressed his companion of more years than he cared to count. "You survived the dragons!"

The magician rolled his eyes at such an obvious observation but said nothing. Arthur ignored the rudeness, so excited was he by his inadvertent success. "Thank goodness you are now able to gaze upon this beauteous display." He yanked the Grail free of his clothing once more and held it before him. "Is this not the most wondrous spectacle that you have ever witnessed?"

Merlin turned a jaundiced eye at the rainbow of brilliance and shrugged.

The former monarch was slightly nonplussed by his friend's reaction but could not stop himself enthusing further. "We have done it, my trusty companion. We have found the Grail." Once again, he held it aloft, captivated by the play of light upon its shiny veneer.

Merlin's fist cannoned into the side of Arthur's head, sending him sprawling to the cold, hard floor and causing the brightness to wink out of existence.

The blow was delivered with such force that it took Arthur a full minute to recover. As he shook his head to regain his senses, he saw the blurred figure of his attacker stooping to retrieve the holy goblet from the corner of the room where it had come to rest.

"What are you doing?" Arthur spat. He licked his lips and tasted the unmistakable tang of blood upon his tongue. "What are..." he began, but lapsed into silence as the answer to his unfinished question became apparent before his very eyes.

The magician's features were writhing frantically upon his face. The bones moved in such a way that they appeared liquid and the rippling became so frenzied that the King was forced to avert his gaze from the horror before him.

Merlin, for his part, stood unmoved even though he must have been in agony at the rearrangement of his facial features. The only indication that he felt anything at all was the whiteness of his knuckles as they gripped the stem of the Grail tightly. Gradually, the activity on his face slowed then halted, leaving a quite different face for Arthur to gaze upon.

Montagu smiled lazily at the King's expression.

Arthur sat dumbfounded. Every one of his senses was screaming that the man who stood before him was an impossibility made flesh. One minute before, Merlin had beheld him, now it was the cruel, sickening face of Montagu that stared at him. "God, no," he breathed. How could this be? Had the concussion of the blow befuddled his mind?

The figure stood silently, twisting the Grail around in his hand, staring at the King with eyebrows raised, awaiting some sort of response.

The smug, arrogant look upon the man's face was all the confirmation Arthur needed. This man was here and he had just handed the Grail to him as if it was a birthday gift. As the enormity of that realisation registered fully in Arthur's mind, he retched violently and vomited.

"Oh, really?" Montagu chided. "Must you?" He tutted then held the Grail up to the rays of watery sunlight that began to ooze through the openings in the age-ravaged roof. "Nice little trinket, is it not," he murmured conversationally. "Bit tacky for my usual taste, but never mind. Never judge a book by its cover and all that," he drawled, turning back to the grey-faced monarch who lay, propped up on his elbows, still staring at the wizard in disbelief.

Montagu took a few steps towards him and waved a slim-fingered hand in front of the King's unblinking eyes. Tutting at the lack of response, he kicked Arthur's boot. "I hardly feel it comely for a monarch, dethroned or otherwise, to stare so." He rolled his eyes theatrically.

The contact jerked Arthur out of his catatonia. "How can this be?" he whispered hoarsely. "How can this be?"

The black magician smirked obscenely. "Do not believe everything you hear, my liege." Montagu closed his eyes and when he spoke again his voice was the exact replica of Merlin's. "Yes, Arthur. I killed the bastard. I have single-handedly removed the obstacle that stood between us and the Grail, leaving us over two hundred years to search for it, unharried and unharassed." His voice returned to its usual rich timbre. "Sound familiar?" he asked with a raised eyebrow.

Once again, the shock at the manner of Montagu's appearance overwhelmed the King and he disgorged the remaining contents of his stomach.

Ignoring this, Montagu continued walking back and forth across the cold damp floor. "Enough of this," he barked with a dismissive wave of his hand. He turned his back on the King and eyed the goblet in his hand lustfully. "I have read the Gospels of Lindisfarne from front to back on so many occasions that the script is emblazoned upon my mind forever."

A sharp intake of breath prompted the magician to peer over his shoulder. He snorted incredulously, "Surely you did not think them destroyed? Have you not figured it out yet, Arthur?"

The King just stared numbly at the magician of the dark arts.

"Merlin did not defeat me aboard the Skarvlang, I defeated him. It was I who departed Lindisfarne with you, not him. It was I who helped bury that irritating bloody hound. It was I who was trawling the lake for the last two and a half years."

Arthur nearly fainted at that revelation. "No, I would have known if..." his voice trailed into silence, then returned with the force of one trying to justify the mother of all mistakes. "It is not possible."

"Well, you would have thought so, would you not?" Montagu smirked, giving the metaphorical knife another twist. "Perhaps you did not know Merlin quite as well as you thought you did?"

No matter how much Montagu told him of what had occurred aboard the Viking longship, Arthur still found that he could not cope with the reality of the situation. He staggered to his feet drunkenly and stumbled towards the gloating wizard.

"Ah, ah, ah!" Montagu waved a warning finger as the King weaved closer. "Do not even think about pointing that glorified dagger at me." The glow of triumph returned instantly to his face. "I could snuff your life out with a click of my fingers, yet I cannot help but feel indebted to you, for without your aid, there is no way on God's green earth that I ever would have laid my hands on this."

Again, the Grail was thrust heavenwards in all its glory.

"How dare you sully the name of Our Lord by spewing it from your filthy mouth," Arthur raged.

Montagu feigned a look of injury. "Is that any way to talk to your companion-at-arms?" he simpered.

If Arthur was honest with himself, the anger that coursed through every fibre of his body was just as much directed at himself as the boastful braggart in front of him. Every word that was spoken was like Excalibur being thrust into his guts then twisted gleefully by the man before him.

The thought of his blade made up his mind. He knew it was a futile gesture, he knew it was doomed, he knew that it would probably cost him his life, but he had to try and stop the fiend. His right hand closed around the pommel of his blade and he withdrew it from its sheath.

The weapon barely made it free from its scabbard.

With an impatient huff and roll of his eyes, Montagu held his hand out, palm facing the King and within a split second, Arthur was rendered immobile. The only part of his body that was still able to move was his eyes and they swivelled, blinked and teared as he fought with every muscle and sinew he possessed to be free of Montagu's hex.

The black magician strode around the living statue of the former King with an impish smile creasing his aquiline features. He leant in and whispered in Arthur's ear. "Do you know who spared me from Merlin's wrath?"

A wheeze of effort escaped Arthur's lips, but even had he wanted to, he could not respond.

"You would not believe me anyway." He ceased whispering and rested his elbow on Arthur's frozen shoulder. "Who is the most unlikely person that comes to mind? Who would be the last man on earth whom you would think able to snatch me from the jaws of death at the hands of Merlin?" he asked. "For make no mistake, I was lost. The reaper's arms were outstretched and beckoning me into their cold embrace."

By this time, Arthur had stopped struggling and was actually paying attention to what Montagu was saying.

"It was Mordred, that odious little tick Mordred."

At the mention of his treacherous nephew's name, Arthur renewed his efforts to free himself from his magical prison.

"I know, it is most vexing, is it not." The black magician nodded. "Montagu, the mighty magician rescued from his doom by Mordred, the misshapen maggot."

Arthur's endeavours had become so strenuous that grunts of exertion were issuing more and more frequently from his lips.

Montagu snapped out of his memories for a moment and regarded the King with rising amusement. Finally he could contain himself no longer and burst out laughing at the strange noises coming from Arthur's direction. "I have to say that I am very glad you are no longer atop the throne of this land, if those are the sort of contributions you make towards the conversation." He wiped his eyes and drew a finger across Arthur's neck.

For a frightening moment, Arthur thought that Montagu was magically decapitating him. "No," he squealed, his voice still strangulated by the wizard's spell. The only effect of the gesture, however, was that Arthur's head and neck were now mobile and his vocal cords were capable of speech once more. After a second or so, he regained his voice. "What rubbish is this? My loathsome nephew could not best Merlin in a thousand years."

Montagu held up his hands. "Believe me, Arthur, I was as surprised as you are," the wizard shrugged, "Although, perhaps I should qualify that achievement a little." He stopped pacing for a moment and stared into the depths of the Grail, passing the vessel around and around in his hand. When he turned back to the King, Arthur gasped at how haunted he looked.

"As I said, I was lost. My ego had swelled because of my success at locating the Gospels and I thought myself invincible." His gaze found itself drawn back to the Grail and Arthur gazed in wonder at the aurora of colours flickering over the magician's face. "It is in your holy writ, is it not? Pride comes before a fall or some such cliché?" he sighed. "The trouble is clichés become clichés because they are proved true so often." With a shake of the head, he turned back to Arthur. "My complacency allowed Merlin to surprise me in my cabin." He closed his eyes and sighed once more. "I can still see him towering over me, hands raised, beard bristling and his eyes, dear God, his eyes, so cold and ruthless." With a shudder, he stared directly at the King, "Mordred must have sensed something was amiss because he came rushing headlong into my quarters." Montagu chuckled bitterly at the reminiscence. "He thrust open the door and knocked Merlin into the wall, rendering him unconscious."

Arthur gaped stupidly as the realisation that Montagu had duped him for centuries hit him again with redoubled vigour.

The magician continued speaking, seemingly just as much to himself as to Arthur. "So after I had tortured Merlin, I took on his persona and have walked the land at your side ever since we left this abbey all those years ago. Without you, I would not now hold the Grail in my hands." He bowed with an exaggerated flourish. "I am forever in your debt, my liege. In respect of that fact, I will spare your life when I hold dominion over the world of men."

The King managed to spit in Montagu's general direction. "Please do not worry on my account," he snarled before once again wrestling with the spell that bound him. "Free me from this trickery and fight me like a man."

The mage shook his head. "I think not, Arthur. In fact," he stood, pondering the King's face for a while, "yes, in fact I might leave you here, still as a statue, frozen to the spot, seeing your days out as a living gargoyle." He made to walk away from Arthur. "I will look in from time to time to ensure that you are still enjoying our hospitality. You see, I do have a habit of leaving people imprisoned and helpless. I did it to Merlin, you know. I did actually promise that I would bring you to see him for one last reunion before I slaughtered you both but that over-eager idiot Mordred put paid to that idea."

The King's brows creased in confusion.

Seeing this, Montagu found himself unable to resist tormenting Arthur even further. "After Mordred had knocked Merlin out, I chained him to the wall of my cabin so that I might have something to play with on the Skarvlang's long journey back across the sea."

Arthur's breathing quickened and he gritted his teeth as he waited for the full horrific explanation of how Montagu had dispatched his nemesis.

"Relax. By the time I had finished with him, he could not feel much anyway. Well, that is to say, physically he could not feel much. It knocked him insensible, you see, the door that is. It ruined his mind. He was a gibbering wreck when he finally came round. To be honest with you, the fact that he could not experience the full power of my ministrations was hugely galling. Still, no matter. As I said, I had left him to go and find you and the Grail. Whilst I was on the shores of the lake searching for it, I took the opportunity from time to time to go and check on him and the Gospels. On one such occasion, I went back to the Skarvlang only to find that, according to Mordred, without my attentions, Merlin had died." There was a gentle sigh from Montagu and the look he bestowed on Arthur was, surprisingly, full of a poignancy that the King never thought he would see on the evil one's face. "Believe it or not, I did have a deep admiration for the old fool and it was a shame that he met his end in such ignominious circumstances but..." His voice trailed off for a moment before returning with its more customary sarcastic drawl, "Mordred, damnable cretin that he was, thinking that I would be pleased with his initiative, took it upon himself to give Merlin a burial at sea and threw him overboard." A cruel smile settled upon the wizard's lips. "Still, he regretted it as soon as he told me what he had done. In fact, I believe you bumped into him on your tour of the Halls, did you not? I hope you passed on my best wishes before I killed him."

The remembrance of Mordred's demise had haunted Arthur for many nights since it had happened, and now, to see the perpetrator of such a crime standing before him, talking about it as if it was of little or no consequence, reignited the flames of his anger and he began writhing in struggle once more, fighting ineffectually against the binding spell.

"Do you wish your death to come in the same manner, Arthur? It is of no moment to me. You have served your purpose, you have flung open the doors and allowed me ingress into the Grail's depths. You are now as important to me as a fly buzzing round a pile of cow dung." Montagu waggled his fingers and sent a searing bolt of fire past Arthur's ear, singeing his hair and burning the lobe.

The anger that tore through Arthur died aborning as it gave way to despair and dread. Montagu was in possession of the Grail, Merlin was dead and he was in no position to do anything about it other than die at Montagu's whim. His head drooped as far as the spell would allow and his tears began to disturb the dust of centuries that carpeted the ancient flagstones.

Then, one last flicker of hope illuminated Arthur's doom-laden thoughts. A voice, a familiar god-like voice sounded in his head. "Fear not, my liege, revenge will be ours," it said.

"Merlin?" he breathed as his eyes widened in wonderment.

Montagu ceased his stride towards the door. "What?" he hissed, his voice as flat and emotionless as death itself.

Arthur ignored the question, straining his neck this way and that to try and locate the source of the voice, the voice that fell on his ears like a choir of angels serenading the ranks of heaven.

A thundering fist wrenched him from his reverie. "What did you say, Pendragon?" Montagu snarled. "Tell me!" he shrieked when no answer was forthcoming. "Tell me or so help me, I will visit pain upon you unlike any you have felt before."

Through the bright lights that pinwheeled across his vision, Arthur smiled. He felt the salty tang of blood in his mouth once more but still he smiled. "It seems I am not the only one who has been duped these past two hundred years," he smirked. "Have you not asked yourself, Montagu, who sent the dragons?" Arthur chuckled. "Who sent the fireballs?" He bit his lip as the painful memory came back to him. "Who fooled me with the vision of Guinevere?" he finished quietly.

"Oh, Arthur, Arthur, Arthur," Montagu shook his head and laughed, much to the chagrin of the King. "I did not want it to seem too easy, did I?"

The King's brow wrinkled. "What?" he asked bemusedly.

"What did you tell me when you returned from the Halls? You told me that you knew Montagu was not dead, yes?" The magician began to circle the frozen man once more. "I could see in your eyes that there was some sort of doubt beginning to insinuate its way into your head, for though I count disguise as one of my masteries, I do not doubt that some of my impersonation of Merlin would have been slightly off-kilter. What better way to get you to trust me once again than to save your life from 'the evil one' that you had just told me was not dead?"

"But the dragons?" Arthur whined.

"I was impressed by you killing their king, I must say. To be honest, I expected you to prevaricate long enough for it to drain the lake and fly away rather than actually kill it. That was my plan after all. I did tell you that, did I not?"

The King nearly wept in defeat as Montagu tore his last hope to shreds before his eyes.

"It did get a bit hairy when I had to explain to the other dragons that their King was dead but when his successor arrived, I managed to smooth it over with them. Come now," he looked at Arthur, "you saw them, you did not think I could really best that many of the beasts without some help, did you?" Arthur played his final card. "Guinevere?" was all he said.

Montagu advanced on him, jabbing a thin finger whilst he did. "What was the one thing I told you not to do after you had injured me in the clearing?" Arthur rolled his eyes in remembrance.

"Yes, exactly," Montagu nodded. "I told you not to reveal our destination to 'the evil one' should he try and obtain it. And what did you do within hours of my disappearance?"

"Only because I was tricked," Arthur sobbed, "only because I was crazed with grief at my Guinny's hateful words."

"Yes, I was pleased with that impersonation, I must say."

Arthur's eyes became filled with tears of anguish. "But why?" he wailed.

Montagu continued to speak conversationally. "Two reasons. One," he held up his index finger, "to make you feel mortified and confuse your mind so it did not find itself mulling over your suspicions as to my true identity and two," another finger came up, "I just wanted to see how far I could push you until your mind snapped."

"But his voice, I just heard his voice," Arthur cried, "it was so vivid, it was him, I know it."

The look on Arthur's face was so sincere that Montagu found himself searching the former King's face for signs of artifice. "You really believe that, don't you?"

The hatred in Arthur's eyes was such that Montagu actually took a step back from it.

"He said we will have our revenge, you bastard."

"Your mind has snapped, Pendragon. Do not seek to distract me any further."

As he said this, a fey wind erupted and blew through the room, soughing mournfully through the ruins and raising the dust into unpleasant and unsettling shapes.

A look of alarm raced onto Montagu's face and he spun round, as if expecting an assault from his long absent foe at any moment.

For long seconds they both stood, a frozen tableau, hardly daring to breathe, as still as death itself.

When nothing materialised, Montagu slowly turned back to the King. For his part, Arthur, who upon hearing his friend's voice had also assumed that an attack was imminent, looked slightly less sure of himself.

"Now who is spouting rubbish, Pendragon?" Montagu sneered. "I used my powers to scan Merlin's brain when he was suspended from my cabin wall. It was ruined beyond repair. He is dead, Arthur, and he is not coming back."

281

The King shook his head. The voice had been Merlin's, of that he was certain. Perhaps it was his desperate need to believe that there was still hope and the soothing words that had run through his mind had been no more than figments of his imagination.

The black hearted magician laughed uneasily, amused by Arthur's distress, but also slightly wary of an unexpected assault. The arch-mage ceased his scrutiny of the King for a moment and perched himself on a dusty pew that had somehow remained intact despite the relentless onslaught of the elements and the damage wrought by the Vikings when they had pillaged the holy building so utterly all those years ago. He twisted the Grail round in his hand, peering with a frightening intensity that belied the forced casualness in his voice. He took a huge breath and muttered, "I cannot wait any longer. I must know whether the Lindisfarne Gospels are indeed a true recounting of deeds and tales from the time of the Nazarene or the piffling ramblings of charlatans, preying on the gullible and weak of mind."

With that said he closed his eyes and began a sibilant chanting that unsettled King Arthur in a manner that he could not pinpoint. He found his gaze drawn to the threadbare tapestries that were draped untidily on the walls of this long abandoned house of God and noted that what little colour they still possessed appeared washed-out and wan. Even the grey stone of the walls and floor appeared muted and lifeless in a way that he could not understand. He tried to send out a mental plea for the voice of Merlin to return to him and supply some sort of comfort but when that last forlorn request remained unanswered, instead of falling into a pit of despair, an abiding sense of calm descended upon the former monarch. He pondered why his first thought had been to find succour from Merlin and not from the place where he had been finding it for most of his adult life.

Arthur Pendragon closed his eyes and began to pray.

Montagu ceased his unsettling mantra and opened his eyes slowly, placed the Grail on the seat next to him and fixed it with narrowed eyes. He had seen his future written in the heavens for more years than he could remember. All the sins that he had committed, all the crimes he had perpetrated and all the heinous things that he had done in his life had been building towards this moment.

In the darker days, when the taint of slaughter had been slow to disperse from his nostrils and the blood clung to his hands like some sort of hideous glue, he had questioned himself, his faith, his very being, but always the aphrodisiac of absolute power had been enough to override his doubts.

He clapped his hands together. This is what it had all been about, now it was time to see if his endeavours had been worthwhile or whether they had all been for naught. Slowly, closing his eyes once more, he began to read from the scripture emblazoned on his mind. As he tripped over a complicated passage of text, his eyes snapped open and he stalked over to where Arthur stood, head upturned towards heaven, his face a study of peace.

"Cease that infernal muttering or I will strike you dead where you stand," He snapped.

Montagu's fury multiplied still further when his threat produced no reaction. If anything, the King's expression seemed to exude more calmness than before.

"Damn you, Pendragon, you leave me no choice," the black magician spat. He raised his hands and began to bring them down, fingers splayed and pointing in Arthur's direction.

A crackling line of fire exploded from the tips wrapping Arthur in a seething, roiling mass of flame. For all the effect it had on the King though, it might as well have been a swatch of satin, for Arthur continued in his prayer.

More than a little discomfited by this, Montagu screamed at him. "Why do you persist in your beseeching? I have won. Can you not see? If your God does exist, would he have permitted me to prevail? Would he have allowed one such as me to possess so much raw power?"

Arthur appeared to pay no heed to the apoplectic sorcerer, but a slight faltering in the rhythm and tone of his prayer suggested that he was not as ignorant of Montagu as he was pretending to be.

"Damn it, Arthur. I know you can hear me. Can you answer me?"

When he was ignored once again, he tried another tack. "I thought not," he snorted. "You try to present yourself as royalty, King and master of all you survey when, in reality, rather than facing evil yourself, you hide behind an intangibility and bleat like a lamb." He leant in close and hissed. "Lambs are not leaders, Arthur, they are followers." He stepped back. "You are nothing, Arthur. A non-entity, just like your so-called God." The magician of the dark arts looked Arthur up and down. "You sicken me," he said simply. "I refuse to waste my breath on you any longer."

He thrust his hands out again but this time, rather than splaying his fingers, he placed them together, concentrating the searing blast at Arthur's brain rather than all over his body.

The King screamed in agony and Montagu laughed. "Where is your God now, Pendragon?"

"ENOUGH!" roared a voice of earth-shattering volume.

The whole building shook from roof to floor and Montagu collapsed to the cold flagstones in horror. "Wh...what manner of magic is this?" he gibbered, staring at Arthur through narrowed suspicious eyes.

The voice continued, "Remove your craven hide from the floor of my sanctified home and fall to your knees in the presence of your God."

The evil magician's head whipped round left and right, up and down, searching for the origin of the voice that seemed to surround him, echoing through the derelict windows, reverberating from the ruined ceiling, ascending from the cold stones beneath him. In his terror, he despatched fireballs hither and thither, destroying sections of the pitted walls and obliterating what remained of the pews.

The voice continued relentlessly. "Kneel!" it bellowed.

The last word was snapped out like a whip and Montagu's whole body sagged to its knees.

The King's mouth hung open in astonishment. He had prayed for salvation, prayed for succour but he had not expected such a display of outright power. It was a full minute before he realised he had full use of his body once more. He walked slowly towards the sobbing practitioner of the dark arts, wallowing in his enemy's fear.

Montagu caught his eye and whimpered. "Please, I beg of you. Call him off. Make it stop."

Arthur's face wrinkled in disgust. "You talk of Him as if He was some sort of dog, attendant at my beck and call. He is master, I am servant, not vice versa."

Facing Montagu, Arthur dropped to one knee. "My Lord, do with me what you will. I have been cruelly duped by the one who cowers before you but I do not offer that as an excuse. I have failed you and I am fully prepared to accept whatever your punishment may be."

For a moment the voice was silent but when it returned, it was imbued with warmth and stripped of hostility. "Come, come, Arthur. Arise and be proud of your efforts. You stuck to the task appointed to you and, were it not for the machinations of this hell-spawn, you would even now be feted throughout the kingdom as the saviour of the Grail."

The King slowly got to his feet but still could not bring himself to gaze skyward. So, with head bowed, he accepted the platitudes.

"I have but one more task to ask of you, Arthur Pendragon," the voice went on.

"Name it, my Lord and I will endeavour to…"

"Yes, yes," the voice snapped impatiently. "You know the task already. If you had had the chance to accomplish it when you first thought of it, then I would have no need to ask it of you now."

Arthur's brow creased in confusion.

"Not a few minutes hence. It was the thought that filled your head, screaming at you to fulfil it. You know to what I refer."

"I…" the King remained nonplussed.

"Kill him, Arthur. Slay the evil one who cringes before you."

Though the King had suspected that this would be the request and he could not deny that the thought had loomed hugely in his brain moments ago, he was unsure if he could bring himself to send the gibbering wreck of a mage back to the world of damnation that had birthed him when he lay powerless and weaponless.

"My Lord, I..." he began.

"Arthur," the voice carried on with the same warmth but was also pervaded with an undercurrent that suggested that the warmth could disappear rather quickly. "I have asked for this to be done by your hand of your own free will. Do not make me order you to do it."

King Arthur found his gaze drawn to Montagu's. The dark one stared back at the King, with mouth unmoving but eyes full of pathos. For his part, Arthur remained where he was, torn between a reluctance to commit cold-blooded murder and a reluctance to defy his God.

"Would you stand in my house and disobey my request?" the voice boomed with warmth noticeably absent and coolness painfully apparent.

Montagu hissed urgently. "This is not your God, Arthur, I know not who it is but..." the wizard's words were cut off as his body spasmed in paroxysms of agony. "It is not him, Arthur," he shrieked. "Stay your hand, it is not your God."

In shock, Arthur stared down at his right arm for it had suddenly become possessed. It snaked down and wrenched Excalibur free, flourishing the royal blade manically.

His instinct took over and he tried with all his might to resist but he had no more control over his actions than a salmon responding to nature's call and returning to its spawning ground.

In horror, he watched as his blade swung down, shearing through Montagu's skull as if it were made of paper. The tortured cries of the tormentor turned tormented ceased abruptly as the dark wizard's brain was sundered.

Still with his blood-drenched weapon in his hand, Arthur turned away, knowing that he had been coerced into the deed, but still hating himself for his weakness in not preventing it.

Soundlessly, Montagu's hideously wounded body slid off the weapon and slumped to the ground. Through pitying eyes, Arthur winced as the magician's body fitted and convulsed, kept alive by the longevity potion, but nothing more. Such ruination to the man's brain had transformed Montagu from near omnipotence to a hollow shell of organs.

The King stared dumbly at his right hand, slowly realising that he had control over its actions once again. He dropped his sword to the floor as if it was a red-hot poker and it fell with a clatter to the floor.

"Why... why did you force me into committing such a foul execution?" Arthur whimpered. "I perpetrated this vile act in your name, oh Lord, so why can I only think about the wrongness of it?"

"You dare question me?" roared the huge voice. "That thing lying at your feet is responsible for suffering beyond your wildest dreams," it continued, contempt dripping from every word. "It is fitting that he should live out his remaining years in such a manner."

Arthur shuddered. "You cannot leave him like this, surely? It is inhuman."

Once again, the voice reverberated around the abbey, "Why not? That is how he left me," it said.

Arthur bowed his head in despair. "How can you justify..." his voice trailed off into silence as his brain caught up with his ears, "What did you say?" he asked flatly.

"I said," came a far more normal voice over his shoulder, "that is how he left me."

King Arthur Pendragon, former monarch of the Britons, sunk to the floor in shock. He watched frozen as Merlin stalked across the room to his fallen enemy and loomed over him, studying what remained of his face. He then moved to Montagu's hand which still held the Grail in a vicelike grip.

He attempted to prise apart the wizard's fingers but found them solid and immovable. Without a second's thought, he brought his boot down upon the clenched fist, breaking a couple of fingers and loosening the grip. The bones cracked with a hideous report and Arthur shuddered once more. Finally he managed to find his voice. "How..." he began.

Merlin held up his hand and once again Arthur found himself struck dumb. The former magician of Camelot turned around, stared for a moment at the King and then began to speak. "As I said, that is how Montagu left me, slowly dying, my life gradually draining away between the cracks in the floor. However, unlike what I have done to him, he made sure that I was fully aware of my helplessness. He made sure that a part of my brain still remembered. Remembered both what I had been and what I had been reduced to. You see, Arthur, as I said, my suffering was beyond your wildest dreams. You may have walked the earth for as long as I have, but in terms of experience, you are but a mere pup."

The wizard smiled quickly at the flash of annoyance that blazed in the King's eyes.

Arthur tried to mouth something back to him but he could make no sound.

Merlin sighed deeply. "Ah, if only I had thought of doing that decades ago, it would have saved my ears from your monotonous bleating." He advanced on the stricken monarch. "Perhaps now you will listen to me rather to your own vainglorious wittering."

Arthur ground his teeth together and mouthed a few choice obscenities in the magician's direction. Oblivious to this, Merlin continued. "I was left unable to perform even the simplest tasks with my physical body but acutely aware of the situation in my mind."

The King noted the anguished haunted look that settled on Merlin's face and, setting aside the man's towering arrogance for a moment, considered what that must have been like for one such as Merlin, possessed as he was with such power and ego.

"Ye gods, they were dark days," the magician whispered hoarsely. His gaze left the painful reminiscences of memory lane and focussed back on the present. He bestowed a hate-filled glare upon the twitching Montagu. "He kept me alive for sport. He chained me to the wall of his cabin like a living trophy, taunting me as I soiled myself, beating me whenever I began to show any hint of coherence. I know not how long I was imprisoned. It may have been a matter of hours, it may have been days or even months. All I can think of is his sneering face and mocking laughter." He spat upon the body then kicked the fallen man so hard that his whole frame lifted off the ground for a moment. "Where is your laughter now, bastard?" Merlin shrieked, bending over the prostrate body.

When he straightened up and resumed his story, Arthur found his eyes following the flecks of spittle as they left Merlin's mouth and came to rest in his beard. With a growing horror, he realised that something had broken within his friend's mind. The wizard was stalking around the chamber like a madman, flailing his arms and laughing insanely. Suddenly in the constant stream of words that flooded out like a diatribe of acid from Merlin's mouth, a name caught his ears and dragged his attention back to what the wizard was actually saying. "I only wish your cretinous nephew Mordred was here to see what his omnipotent master has been reduced to."

Arthur opened his mouth to impart the tidings of Mordred's demise then remembered the incantation that had left him dumbstruck. Instead, he waited until Merlin held his gaze then drew a finger across his throat.

Merlin stopped in his tracks. "You mean Mordred is dead?" he breathed.

Arthur nodded.

The magician grabbed him by the front of his tunic, "Where? How? Give me details?" he hissed.

The King gestured at his throat and pulled a face.

Tutting impatiently, Merlin snapped his long fingers and the King's rich timbre filled the room once more.

"Yes, he is dead." Arthur croaked, massaging his throat. "I mortally wounded him then his master finished the job."

A huge sigh issued from Merlin's mouth and for a moment he seemed lost in his own world.

"So how did you escape, Merlin?" Arthur asked intently. "Montagu claimed that he had defeated you and Mordred had thrown you overboard when you had died."

The ecstatic look on Merlin's face dissolved into confusion. "I know not why he would say that. It is true that he bested me and imprisoned me but I did not die." Pensiveness overtook him and he murmured, "A stranger. A stranger saved me," he shrugged. "That is all I remember of that time, three faces, Montagu, Mordred and the stranger."

"And what did he look like, this stranger?" the King asked but even as he said it, he was not sure that Merlin was even aware that he was there, let alone listening to him.

"He came to me one evening after yet another bout of indignity and mockery. Montagu said he was going to find you and slit your throat before me and claim the Grail for his own. I probably passed out again because the next thing I remember is the stranger simply walking into the cabin, placing a hand upon my head and muttering a few words. Suddenly I was lucid again but he departed as swiftly as he came and I was not able to speak with him any further," Merlin shrugged again. "I have not seen him since so I can tell you no more."

"You can remember nothing more of your saviour then?" Arthur asked, a strange set to his features.

"He was everyman. Were I to see him in a crowd, I would have to look straight at him before I could give a definite identification for there was nothing that marked him as outstanding," he said, eyes moving shiftily from side to side. "I just remember a great…" the wizard hesitated, making movements with his hands as if he was trying to mould the words that he so desperately sought, "…a great sureness of action as if he were totally confident in both word and deed." Merlin was staring into the middle distance in wonderment, still deeply affected by the brief encounter that had happened nearly five years ago.

Arthur bowed his head. "I think I know of whom you speak, Merlin. I also think I know of a way by which you could thank him."

Some of the arrogance that had momentarily deserted the magician returned and he replied haughtily, "Oh really?"

"Yes, I do. Fall to your knees and pray, Merlin." Arthur stated calmly. "You said it yourself. He was your saviour. Your description of the one who rescued you is too similar to the description of one who strove to rescue all of us to be coincidence."

"What rubbish." Merlin sneered, all shred of humility banished.

288

"Well," Arthur responded hotly, "your remembrance of the event makes it sound like a miracle to me. Can you explain it away as anything other, Merlin?"

The magician opened his mouth to respond but bit back his rejoinder.

The pair stood in uncomfortable silence for a moment until Arthur said, "What happened after your salvation, Merlin? You have been gone for nearly five years. I walked with that travesty and treated him like a brother when in actual fact, he was my greatest enemy. I feel so violated."

Chewing his lip, Merlin resumed his tale. "I am ashamed to admit it, Arthur, but the experience of hovering on the cusp of life and death for so long and the ease with which Montagu had bested me yet again, scared the living hell out of me." He hung his head and went on. "I hid," he shrugged simply. "Me, Merlin the magician, adviser to royalty, the power behind the throne, foremost practitioner of the mystic arts within the kingdom, hid. I cowered like a craven dog in my chambers, wary of the slightest sound, frightened of my own shadow. For years I was frozen in abject terror, no longer interested in the quest for the Grail, no longer interested in the world." Shaking his head, he sighed once more. "Eventually though, when the foreboding began to recede and the darkness began to lighten, a new resolution began to build within me for the thought of avenging myself upon Montagu had never truly left me despite the utter helplessness under which I laboured. One day the fire within that Montagu had quashed so effectively, sputtered and flamed back to life and I re-emerged, blinking in the brightness of a new day, determined to revenge my humiliation."

At this point the magician ceased his speech and hung his head, cheeks flaming red with embarassment. "I am ashamed to say though that my previous encounters with Montagu tainted my response. I had neither the confidence nor the will to confront him face to face. Instead I opted for a strategy of cunning and stealth, undermining his actions from a distance rather than by means of direct conflict."

"I am astounded," Arthur stammered. "You are both as treacherous and deceitful as each other and you have treated me with the lowest contempt imaginable." He pierced Merlin with a stare composed half of distress and half of naked rage. "Could you not have told me? Could you not have let me know by some means or other? For three tedious years I patrolled the shores of that lake, guarding that charlatan as he roamed the water with his mind. I could have struck him dead in the blink of an eye had I known his true identity."

Merlin answered with a firm shake of his head. "He would have seen the truth reflected in your eyes in a second."

"But..." the King protested.

"Believe me, Arthur, I debated long and hard with myself before embarking on this course. It was with heavy heart that I kept you ignorant of my continued life, but I had to. Do you not see?" he asked beseechingly.

The King turned away from his former confidante, not trusting himself to provide a civil response. His eyes roamed the room, not settling on any one thing, whilst his mind feverishly pondered the multitude of questions thrown up by the miraculous reappearance of the two wizards.

Eventually it came to rest on Montagu's convulsing remains. "Dear God, Merlin, can you not put him out of his misery and end this once and for all?" Arthur hissed, for despite the hurt and pain that Montagu had caused him over the centuries, he still found that he could not bear to see another human being suffer so much, even one as black of heart as the fallen mage.

Merlin blanched at the request. "But what he put me through..."

"Is done with," Arthur stared at his former court magician. "I will kill him, if needs be. Just free me and I will dispatch him."

Merlin looked from Arthur to his gravely injured foe then shrugged, waving his hand almost lazily towards the King to free him of the spell's effects.

"Thank you," Arthur nodded. He then withdrew Excalibur slowly from its scabbard and stared pityingly at the ruined husk of a man wriggling on the flagstones, surrounded in a pool of blood.

Suddenly his expression froze, locked in a state of petrified indignation. His breathing quickened and his heart turned to ice as the painful memory of the lake came flooding back. "It was you," he snarled.

Merlin's eyes shifted guiltily from left to right. "What was me?" he asked warily.

The King sprang at him, lifting him from his feet and sending the two of them sprawling to the floor in a tangle of limbs. "At the lake," Arthur shrieked, "you were the one, the one who attacked. The cowled stranger who appeared from nowhere and damned near sent me to my grave. Were it not for..." The boiling rage hit an icy pool of calm and the anger evaporated.

Merlin lay underneath the King, immobile and nonplussed both by the sudden start and the abrupt end of the assault. "Arthur, I am not...I have never...I know not to what you refer but I can assure you that I have never harmed a hair on your head, let alone sent you to the brink of death."

The King did not heed the wizard's babbling, instead he was left mentally reeling by the revelation that had just come to him. "Montagu saved my life. The fire would have claimed me, had not Montagu...' Arthur refocused on Merlin. "He must be allowed to finish his final journey. Do not try to stop me. I am a man of honour and that includes my debts. On the shore of the lake he stopped you killing me. Moments later, he arrested my plummet into the fiery depths and sent me to another place. In that other place, he diverted

Mordred's attention long enough for me to apply a fatal wound and thus put me in a position to escape that hellish dominion. Now I have the chance to maintain that equilibrium." With eyes as cold and hard as diamonds, the King stared at the magician then without a word spun round and strode over to Montagu's ruined body, knelt beside it and using Excalibur with the delicacy of a needle, cut his heart free from his body.

For a brief second, clarity alighted in Montagu's eyes and Arthur fancied there was the tiniest hint of gratitude twinkling in them. Then he was gone.

Arthur breathed out hugely and found himself staring at the bloodied organ, still vivid and scarlet, that rested in his hand. "Why did you spare me?" he whispered.

Merlin's measured tones invaded the King's consciousness. "I know why, my liege," he sniffed. "First though, let me reiterate that I have no idea what you are talking about regarding the lake's shore."

Arthur kept his face carefully neutral and gestured for Merlin to continue.

"As soon as I was sufficiently recovered, it is true that I watched you both many times at the lake but something happened recently that caused me to adopt a new plan of attack." He raised his hands to fend off the questions that he knew would be coming his way. "Please, let me finish. It was I who masked the Grail from Montagu, you see, physically and magically he may have bested me, but mentally I am and always will be his superior." He glanced over his shoulder and drawled. "Especially now," he chuckled before continuing. "I found you both by the lake and immediately realised why you were there, for I recalled the spot where I found Galahad on the brink of suicide after his valiant injuring of Montagu in his daemon form. Whether good fortune it was or not, Montagu had yet to locate the Grail with his mind's eye. I on the other hand perceived it instantly. At that point however, I sensed an increase in his alertness and my courage failed me once more so I withdrew my consciousness immediately for fear of discovery. I merely contented myself with the subtlest of masking spells that hid the trinket from his probing mind. Long did I ponder my next move, sitting for weeks, gently observing Montagu's pursuit in case he happened upon my magickry. Then I began to notice that sometimes, as he sat, statuesque and frozen upon the beach, his mind did not swim in the water, it soared through the air travelling to who knew where. One day, I know not why, my courage returned and I flew with him, determined to find out the destination to which his mind soared. Thus I found the Gospels in this very chamber where we now stand. I was so caught up in the euphoria of discovery that I very nearly showed myself to him. However, something distracted him. I watched him from the shadows as his face grew afeared and he disappeared in the blink of an eye. With my bravery having received another boost, I did not follow him back to the lakeside. I took the opportunity to study the Gospels and the secrets therein. When I returned to the lake, you were gravely injured with Montagu cradling your head in his lap, spitting out curses in an evil, ancient tongue. Having now read the Gospels, I realised what the fiend was planning and I decided that more direct action was required."

The King looked at the wizard sceptically. "All very interesting but it still does not explain why he strived so hard to save my life."

"Have patience, Arthur, it will," Merlin said patiently, "as I said, I felt more direct action was needed, so to that end, I sought out the King of Dragons."

The anger that had been ebbing away slowly from Arthur's mind returned at frightening speed. "You sent..." Arthur's brows creased in confusion, "but Montagu said that..."

Merlin spread his hands and smiled lazily. "A mere bit of mental legerdemain on my part, I am afraid. I planted that idea in his brain as I did the one regarding the fireballs."

"What?" Arthur spluttered. "You sent them as well? Some of them nearly roasted me to ashes."

"My apologies, sire. I knew I had to thwart him somehow but I did not want to risk Montagu realising it was me, so I took advantage of the chaos to tweak his memory somewhat."

"Dragons are impervious to magic though, are they not? How did you make them do your bidding?" Arthur gasped.

"Magic that seeks to harm them, certainly. Anyway I did the one thing that Montagu would never thought to have done."

Arthur raised his eyebrows.

"I went to the King and asked him. I explained the quest, requesting from him a favour which, after much deliberation, he granted. You see, I knew that Montagu could overcome me, but not if I was protected by an unbreakable shield." Merlin sighed. "After I told him what the Grail was capable of and what its salvation could mean to a rapidly diminishing species, he was only too eager to accommodate me."

"You made promises to him? Promises that were not yours to make, I would wager." Arthur jabbed an accusing finger into his chest.

Ignoring this, Merlin continued, "I showed him where the Grail lay. Whilst he searched the lake, I sent the fireballs over to distract you both. Unfortunately, the moment slipped away and chaos reigned. I had no inkling that you would perform as heroically as you did. No man has ever slain the King of The Dragons in battle before. I thought you would flee not fight," he breathed heavily.

292

"Then how little you know me, magician," Arthur sneered. "I suppose it was your twisted mind that conjured up the image of my Guinevere as well, was it?"

"No," Merlin shook his head sadly and, to Arthur, there did seem to be a genuine misery in his eyes. "No, that was Montagu. I would never do that to you, sire. I know the pain you went through when she left you the first time." He shook his head. "No, I would not do that to you."

"Yet you would still see me incinerated by dragon's breath or a misdirected fireball?" Arthur snarled but Merlin's eyes had glazed again and he returned to his story without really hearing Arthur's barbed comment.

"The dragon's killing was such a setback to me that my old fears and insecurities resurfaced, overwhelming and unmanning me." Again, the haunted look returned to the wizard's face. "That night, Montagu nearly killed me yet again and I retreated back into my shell."

"Enough of this flim-flam, Merlin. You said you knew why Montagu spared me. Are you going to tell me or will it take so long that the Grail will have tarnished and rusted away before you enlighten me?" Arthur snorted.

"Bear with me, sire, the answer draws ever closer. I could sense now that the Grail was on the move and I knew you must have found it and somehow rescued it from the lake's depths. Although I knew that I would now have the dragons hunting me down to avenge the loss of their king, I went forth again, desperate to wrest the goblet from Montagu's clutches. Then when I saw that he had been waylaid by the lizards, I could not believe my luck and sent you here. After everything I had tried, the flock of birds, the dragon, the bandits in the wood, something totally out of my control had arrived to stop Montagu in his tracks. I was about to show myself to you, when he appeared out of the mists to snatch the Grail from you in your greatest hour. You see, *that* is why he needed you, Arthur. *That* is why he saved your life. You are the key to the Grail and everything within it. Without you, Montagu's plans would have come to naught for your deeds are writ large in the Gospel texts." The magician began to recite,

The Crownless King who walks for years
Will wield the cup of blood and tears
He is the key that unlocks the door
Which once ajar will shut no more

"It is you, sire. You are the Crownless King. You are the key," he breathed, his booming tones suddenly dropping to an urgent whisper.

Arthur stood dumbstruck. The scripture of the Gospels had been penned over five centuries before he had even been conceived. It was now nearly six hundred years since the four foremost disciples of Jesus Christ had foreseen him, known him and fated him to be the Grailbearer. The enormity of the explanation left him reeling and he physically staggered at the huge responsibility that had suddenly been thrust upon his shoulders even though, unbeknownst to him, he had carried it since the day he was born.

"So there you have it, Arthur. Your quest is at an end, your destiny is fulfilled," Merlin beamed, sidling towards him.

The King's gaze swept the room, halting on Merlin's guileless smile. Ever since he had released the Grail from its dormancy and Montagu had been vanquished, a choir of angels had been exulting in his head, their words providing a clear, constant note in the maelstrom of emotions that he had experienced in the last few moments. They recited the verse that Merlin had just recounted from the Gospels, but now the final line seemed to contain a jarring discordance that grated urgently at the King's attention.

'Which once ajar will shut no more'

Arthur stared at Merlin again and saw that the joy apparently contained within his smile overlaid a harsh twisted smirk. With every repeat of the rhyme in the King's head, the shadowy smirk emerged further from behind the sunshine of the smile.

The monarch's eyes widened in realisation and he made a desperate grab for the goblet.

With a startled cry, Merlin saw it knocked from his hand and it skittered loudly across the flagstones.

"What is this?" His brows bristled and any semblance of friendliness disappeared as he gripped a handful of Arthur's cloak as the King tried to follow its path across the floor.

The two of them wrestled viciously on the frigid flagstones. Merlin, striving to prevent the stronger man reaching the Cup of Christ and denying him his triumph and Arthur desperately trying to stop his adversary using his magic to cast him into oblivion.

Over and over they rolled, gouging and tearing, scratching and punching, each unable to gain the upper hand. Decades-old dust wafted up in choking clouds, shrouding the room in a man-made fog as tapestries and pews were uprooted and disrupted.

Eventually Merlin wrenched himself free of Arthur's grip, courtesy of a brutal elbow that cannoned into the King's stomach, winding him and bending him double. However, instead of casting a spell, he ran to the Grail to claim it, taunting his former leader. "It is a pity, Arthur. I had great plans for us. You as the figurehead, me as the power that guided your leadership in the right direction," he giggled insanely. "It will be lonely at the summit of the world without you, but I am sure my omnipotence will gain me many new friends in due course." Again the shrill laughter echoed through the draughty abbey. Arthur hissed through gritted teeth, "How long has this monstrous treachery been stalking through your mind, wizard?" He straightened up painfully, massaging his abused stomach. "Have you ever counted me as a friend or have I never been anything other than a means to an end to you?"

The magician peered at Arthur out of the corner of his eye. It was not long however before his gaze was drawn irresistibly back to the golden cup. With a sigh, he answered. "Perhaps once, when you ruled Camelot, perhaps then I deemed you comrade and equal, but that ceased the moment Galahad entered the castle with the Grail." This time Merlin concentrated his full attention on the King. "You see, I have always known of your destiny. From the day of your birth I have watched over you, nurturing your upbringing, shaping you into the man you are today."

If Arthur had felt sickened by the duplicity of Montagu, then there were no words on earth that described the feeling of disgust that permeated his being at this precise moment. "So I have been your puppet since I first drew breath," he croaked. "Never a king, merely a pawn," he sighed, trying to dislodge the unbearable ache that seized his heart. "My whole life has been a travesty." With that said he lapsed into a brooding silence and merely gazed intensely at the Grail.

At that last statement, Merlin sniggered, "Harsh words, my liege," he gestured at the cup and brought it under his scrutiny, marvelling again at the myriad lights that danced before his sight. "Look what you have achieved. You have solved the conundrum that has defeated the greatest magicians in the world. The Grail and all its potential would be lost forever, were it not for your intervention." He grinned manically at the King, eyes widened with ecstasy and tinged with insanity. "How many men can say that they were put on the earth to accomplish one specific deed and when called upon to perform it, were not found wanting? You are the stuff of legends, man. My spell may not have been able to bestow immortality upon you, but your actions this day have ensured that your name will live on forever in the legends of men."

A thousand emotions were raging in Arthur's mind, each one vying for supremacy and causing such turmoil that the King paid no heed to Merlin's words. In a daze, he leant down and picked Excalibur from the floor, staring at his trusty blade as if he was seeing it for the first time. "Was my monarchy ever legitimate or was my extrication of Excalibur from its stone prison naught but a charade?"

Merlin regarded him for a long moment. "Your reign was legitimate, yes."

Arthur sighed at that small crumb of comfort.

"To all those who witnessed it," he finished.

The King had only experienced this level of anger once before and it had been in this selfsame building. This time however, instead of the red mist descending and the uncontrollable savagery of the berserker enveloping him, he felt his insides freeze as if encased by ice. "Then let the object that started all this be the one to end it." With that said, he flicked his wrist effortlessly and in a split second, Excalibur had embedded itself in the far wall.

Arthur looked up and the icy grip upon his emotions melted away in the heat of the flame of faith that had rekindled in his breast, for his weapon's flight must have been blessed.

Merlin stared wordlessly at the gleaming handle that protruded from his chest. Mere inches behind him, occupying the space between the wizard's blood-sodden back and the scarlet drenched wall, his still fluttering heart pumped out its last gush of blood and beat no more.

The Grail tumbled from the magician's lifeless fingers and fell to the ground, creating a thunderous crash in the sudden silence.

Dispassionately, Arthur regarded the spinning goblet until it came to rest on the ancient flagstones. He surveyed the carnage that besmirched the remainder of the room, Montagu's heinously maimed corpse, Merlin's lifeless cadaver held in place by his royal blade, the overturned pews and clouds of dust still floating in the air.

Suddenly, a wave of giddiness claimed him and he slumped to the floor unable to support himself. He felt corrupted and tainted. Every decision he had ever made, every thought he had ever had, every memory in his head no longer belonged to him. Every deed and achievement of his life now found itself darkened by Merlin's brooding shadow.

The black thoughts that engulfed him conjured up a picture of the Arbiters in his mind. Even in the only place where he had been free from the machinations of the two mages, he had wound up being used by others for their own ends. Every step he had ever taken had been at the behest of others.

Never had the King felt so low. Despair had not been a stranger to him on the quest for the Grail and there had been many a time when he had found himself questioning whether he had done the right thing all those years ago by acquiescing to Merlin's wishes and drinking the longevity potion.

As he looked at his former companion's empty eyes, it was all too obvious that it had been the wrong choice but, at the time, his vanity had demanded that he take up the challenge laid before him. It had seemed so simple in Merlin's chamber. Then he had no concept of Montagu's capacity for evil or

Merlin's capacity for treachery. He had been the hero, born for this moment, born to search out the Grail, born to save the world from evil.

"Look at yourself now, Arthur," he reflected bitterly. Some hero, firmly rooted in the depths of despair, a puppet with all its strings slashed.

He remained on the floor, hollow in both mind and body, neither knowing or really caring what his mockery of a life held next. One thought did briefly alight in the numbness of his mind, but again it would mean dancing to someone else's tune. It would, however, bring an end to it all. Or would it? Even suicide would deliver him into the hands of the Arbiters. Would they be satisfied with his deed or would there always be one more task to complete before he was allowed to go to his rest?

He was well aware of the Arbiters' reputation for unquestioned incorruptibility yet he had walked away from their judgement still vital because of the task they had set him. Could it be that they had ulterior motives as yet undisclosed? Could it even be that the power of the Grail was so seductive and absolute that it had tainted even the purest of the pure?

The thoughts that were beginning to filter through the barriers of anguish in the King's mind began to awaken some frightening new possibilities. He caught himself staring at the Cup of Christ as he had done so many times before, but this time he found it no longer projected serenity and peace, but instead there appeared to be an intangible sense of urgency within the pulsing rainbow of colours swimming in its depths.

Could the Grail have been the catalyst for all that had gone before?

A cacophony of thoughts began to clamour for attention in the King's mind. He clamped his hands over his ears and moaned, trying in vain to drown out the voices, the voices of all who had been slain in the name of the Grail, the hundreds and hundreds of voices. He tried to forget the hundreds of deaths as well, be they at the hands of Montagu, Merlin or the King himself, all caught up in the battle to unleash its power.

He staggered to his feet and stumbled across the room, tripping over Montagu's outstretched boot. He fell, landing heavily on the floor and facing the magician's ruined features. Could one man really be capable of such evil were his hand free from interference? Everything that Arthur had seen or experienced told him no. It was true that man could be capable of the most shocking acts of brutality but on such a wide scale?

The King shook his head. No, he must have been possessed by something, something urging him on to perpetrate such foul deeds.

Crawling onwards, he came upon the limp form of Merlin, still upright, pinned into place by Excalibur like a butterfly on the page of a collector's album.

Again, analysis of the wizard Arthur knew before the quest had begun and his behaviour afterwards led the King to an inescapable conclusion. Something had guided Merlin onto the path of perfidy and deception. Following the train of thought to its logical conclusion, Arthur realised that the Arbiters were next, if they had not been lost already.

A certainty settled in his mind. So many had been lost already to the goblet lying on the floor scant yards away. He decided there and then that Merlin would be its final victim.

The knowledge that he had strived for nearly three centuries to unearth something that had the capacity to turn brother against brother, friend against friend and honest men into liars lent the King's arm a rage-fuelled strength and he wrenched Excalibur free from the wall.

Merlin slid from the blade with an unpleasant sucking noise and collapsed to the floor.

Arthur stepped forward and in one massive sweep brought the weapon down in an unstoppable stroke, aimed at the stem of the Grail. "No more!" he shrieked as he braced himself for the contact of metal upon metal and stone.

He screeched in agony as the sword was clamped in a vice-like grip. It hovered but a few agonising inches over the holy vessel but no matter how hard he tried Arthur could not complete the stroke.

"You may not destroy my cup, my son," came a voice, gentle as the breeze, yet underlain with tangible authority.

Slowly, Arthur became aware of a light, a bright incandescence that emblazoned his silhouette in stark relief upon the wall before him. Awestruck, he turned, squinting into the vivid luminescence that suddenly flooded the room. A figure emerged from it, gracefully making his way towards the frozen statue that was Britain's former king.

With the breath stuck in his throat, Arthur beheld the face of the new arrival.

"Do not torture yourself over the misdeeds of others, Arthur Pendragon. The quest you embarked upon was for the noblest of reasons and your successful completion of it is the greatest testament possible to your honour, valour and courage. Unfortunately, the betrayal by your closest companion has clouded your thinking. You esteem that it is the Grail itself that is evil, yet it does not appear to have tainted you and you above all are the one who is most inextricably entwined with it, bar none but myself. For indeed, Merlin was truthful in his words, you were the key in the lock, Arthur. Without you, this beacon of light in the darkness would still be cloaked in the night and I would have been unable to walk the earth again as prophesied in the Gospels. Do not let the logic of the head overrule the emotions of the heart. Look at the Grail then look inside yourself. In your heart, do you really

298

believe that the Grail is culpable for all the evil you have witnessed these centuries past?"

For a long moment, the King stood in a petrified tableau, gaze darting from the Grail to the newcomer's eyes and back again. Eventually he sighed as if a great weight had been lifted from his shoulders and dropped to his knees. "No my Lord, I do not."

The bearded face broke from its sombre solemnity and lit up with a benign smile. "I am glad you have taken the counsel of your heart, my son."

At this simple benediction, Arthur broke down, sobbing painfully, "Forgive me, Lord, I did not mean to doubt you or your actions."

The man placed his hands on the King's elbow and gently ushered him to his feet. "There is no need for apologies, my son. The trials you have endured are beyond that of any mortal man. You would not have been human, had you not been affected by them."

The King smiled thankfully upon the face of Jesus Christ and sighed. "What will you do with the Grail now it has been returned to you?"

The figure nodded. "Your anguished surmising was correct, Arthur Pendragon. This goblet has indeed caused much suffering despite its sanctity and holiness. I feel that I erred when I entrusted it to Joseph of Arimathea all those years ago. Indeed, though it pains me deeply to say it, Montagu was also correct. The Grail does have the capacity for both good and evil, dependent on its wielder. As that is the case, I cannot allow it to remain upon the earth. I will ascend with it so that it may adorn my Father's table in Heaven."

Quickly the figure stooped and placed the Grail within the folds of his loose-fitting robe. "Fare thee well. I know of your bargain with the Arbiters, Steward of the Grail. The last task I would ask of you is that you honour it and follow me on my journey skyward so you may take a seat at my table, there to break bread and drink the sweetest wine for all eternity."

A shrill keening sound began to permeate the room and the figure in front of Arthur appeared to dissolve, fragmenting into a thick ray of light that suddenly flew upwards into the ceiling and onwards through it into the granite-grey sky.

The joy at such an unexpected resolution to his quest had been jarred slightly by the messiah's final wish, but the King had long ago accepted that, one way or another, once the Grail's power had been released and set into motion, his too-long life would be at an end.

With a resigned air of inevitability, Arthur wedged Excalibur, point upwards, between a wrecked pew and some fallen statuary. With careful deliberation, he ensured that it was firmly braced and stepped back to take a last look at the earth through mortal eyes. Sweat ran down his face for he knew that he had to skewer his heart and separate it from his body, lest he would remain alive like a stuck pig, in horrible pain, until the longevity potion wore off and he passed over naturally.

He solemnly drew back his cloak, feeling around his chest for his heartbeat, the better to pinpoint exactly where Excalibur would need to enter him. That done, he knelt down, leaning forward until the point of his weapon pricked the skin above his heart.

Through tears of pain and joy, he was not sure which, he looked at the fallen form of Merlin for the final time, finding himself wondering what hand fate had dealt the wizard. Surely his treachery had condemned him to hell along with Montagu and Mordred. He was his oldest...he wanted to call him friend, but the final minutes of Merlin's life had put paid to that epithet, yet despite the massive duplicity committed upon him by the magician he could not bring himself to condemn the man completely. He was merely a victim of his ego, corrupted by the thought of so much power, yet arrogant enough to believe it would not change him.

King Arthur breathed a huge sigh and contemplated meeting his old companions again. Galahad, the first Knight of the Round Table to be named Steward of the Grail, Gawain the Green, jovial hearty Bors, Sir Bedivere, he reeled off the names in his memory with a grin creasing his features. All long gone but all still instantly memorable in Arthur's heart.

With that thought warming him, Arthur Pendragon, former King of the Britons, thrust himself forward, impaling his body on Excalibur with such force that his heart was punched through his ribs and erupted out of his back.

Arthur's final sight was of the figure, sunlit and peaceful, carved into the base of the lectern on which had stood the Lindisfarne Gospels and with a gurgling sigh, the quest for the Holy Grail ceased to concern the world of mortal men.

Chapter 17

The Chamber of the Arbiters

King Arthur emerged, blinking furiously in the golden brightness of the Arbiter's chamber and though he had seen it previously, the sheer magnificence of the room still took his breath away.

A clipped female voice jarred him from his appreciation. "The final piece of the puzzle has arrived to complete the picture," pronounced Kirsten. "Finally we can pass judgement upon those before us, so that we may mend the damage that has been wrought on the Halls."

For a short time then the Arbiters deliberated, employing their communal mind.

The King turned round to return to his examination of the tapestries and intricate carvings that adorned the walls but instead, he found himself staring into the blanched faces of Montagu and Merlin, whom he had not perceived when he first entered.

They both gazed at him with unfettered hatred in their eyes but said nothing.

At length, Montagu was called before the seven. He attempted to feign indifference to his plight but his eyes continually darted back and forth between the Arbiters and the differing doors on either side of them. Behind him the leaves were being shaken from their branches with unusual vigour by Flammel and Leonid and the soft patter as they landed put all who heard it in mind of a heavy rainfall.

Unsurprisingly, Montagu's fate was sealed in double-quick time. However, the magician of the dark arts went to face the horrors behind the door with unexpected dignity. Arthur had been bracing himself for filth-ridden imprecations to be hurled at him or Merlin or even the septet of judges, but instead Montagu simply strode purposefully towards the darkened wood. He stood there for a second then raised his boot and kicked the door so hard that one of the hinges came away from the wall.

With a final contemptuous look at all who remained in the room, Montagu walked into hell and was consumed almost immediately by the flames that were now licking and flashing into the Arbiters' chamber through the ruined door.

It all seemed a huge anticlimax to Arthur as Montagu walked into the inferno. He felt that there should have been some sort of penance inflicted upon the black magician in return for all the agonies and cruelty he had brought into the world.

A movement at his right shoulder ceased his contemplation of the broken door. Head bowed, Merlin shuffled forward to face judgement.

Arthur was assailed by ambivalence at the abject state his erstwhile companion had been reduced to. It seemed to the King that every shred of ego and arrogance had deserted Merlin and here, for the first time in a long time, was the true mage of Camelot, as Arthur had known him when he had ascended the throne.

Merlin did not look any of the Arbiters in the eye, even when they addressed him directly. He simply stood, staring at the floor, letting the details of his life wash over him.

The King fancied that, every now and again, the wizard's head gave the slightest of turns toward him whenever his name was mentioned, although he still did not make eye contact with the man that he had betrayed in such a breathtaking fashion.

Shaking his head, Arthur turned to look at the tree and the flower, the two symbols by which his fate would be decided. To his shock, the tree had but a few denuded branches, whilst the flower was filling up rapidly with petals of an exquisite shade of azure.

The sense of injustice that Arthur had felt at Montagu's subdued exit was now compounded by the apparent possibility that Merlin would be judged worthy of a place in paradise despite his monstrous treachery. His mouth dropped open and he stared dumbly at the scene unfolding before him. His eyes whipped from Arbiter to Arbiter, but his stare was not returned for the seven bent their full concentration on the one who stood before their judgement.

Wild thoughts began careering through Arthur's brain. Had Merlin engineered some sort of deal with the septet of supposedly incorruptible judges? The King shook his head and dismissed the thought as quickly as it had appeared, for if Merlin was able to taint the Arbiters' deliberations in his favour then surely the same ruse would have been used by Montagu.

As yet another petal burst forth from the ripe bud on the flower on the wall, Arthur could restrain himself no longer. "This is outrageous," he snarled, "He is bewitching you. I know not how but you are under his spell. He is twisting your minds."

The seven broke off from their monotone recounting of Merlin's deeds and cast contemptuous looks upon the former monarch of Britain.

Raemund leaned forward and pointed at Arthur, stabbing his finger viciously through the air, as if wielding it like a weapon. "You of all people, you who have stood before us once already in your evilly enchanted long-lived life, you should know that we are beyond reproach. We are..."

The Arbiter stopped in amazement as Merlin snapped round like a whip and looked Arthur fully in the eye for the first time since he had entered the room. "You...you have been here before?" he exclaimed, choking out the words as if they were ashes in his mouth. "Yet you still live," he breathed gaping stupidly at the noble face before him.

King Arthur nodded his head grimly. "After your attack on the beach, Montagu managed to transport me to the Halls, whence I ended up here, being judged as you are now for spilling Mordred's blood in this sanctified place. My life was spared on one condition. I was to despatch all who partook of the longevity potion, so that they would meet their final judgement before the Arbiters and face up to the fate that they had cheated for so long."

Merlin drew himself up to his full impressive height. "Now who stands guilty of duplicity?"

Arthur's face froze. He strode forward, hand flying down to his left side, poised to unsheath Excalibur and allow it to repeat its bloody deed. A puzzled sound escaped his throat as he found himself groping empty air for both scabbard and sword were missing from his belt.

The sonorous voice of Gregor filled the chamber. "Violence will avail you nothing, Arthur Pendragon. You have already violated the Halls with the stuff of life. Do not dare to pollute our chamber with it lest we forgo a trial and despatch you through whichever door we see fit."

The King stood, frustrated and helpless. He was torn asunder by his fury at Merlin and his rage at the Arbiters. He opted to face down the Arbiters first. "Not a minute hence you were wallowing in your supposed impartiality, yet now you say if I spill this liar's blood, I will be sentenced without trial?" He spat on the floor. "Suddenly the stench of untruth and dishonesty assails my nostrils. If you were truly just, then my smiting of Merlin would be no more than another fallen branch from my tree."

The Arbiters sat in shocked silence at the accusation that was being levelled at them. "We spared your life," Raemund stuttered.

"Aye, and for what reason? So you could use me to clean up a mess that you could not resolve yourselves. Now though your little errand boy has served his purpose and is dispensable once more. Is that not about the size of it?"

Mustering as much dignity as he could gather, Raemund shrugged. "Think what you will, Pendragon, but rest assured, Merlin, court magician of Camelot is subject to the same rules and laws that have governed proceedings in this chamber for years uncountable."

Arthur ground his teeth together, painfully aware that he could argue until the earth stood still with the seven judges but it would still gain him nothing. With a shake of his head and a snarl of frustration, he began to vent his fury at Merlin. "And you, you dare stand there and accuse me of treachery after your deeds?" He spun away in disgust. "I wish I had never set eyes upon you, you contemptible charlatan."

The air continued to crackle between Arthur and the Arbiters but no more was said. Merlin, however, muttered something under his breath.

"At least have the courage to speak your lies out loud," Arthur snapped. With a shuddering breath, Merlin faced him again. "To what end? You will not believe me. As I told you before, the attack by the lake that you keep alluding to, the attack that so very nearly killed you," he held out his hands placatingly, "It was not me."

The King affected disdain for the wizard's plea but, as he stared into those mesmerising eyes, he could not detect anything other than honesty, "If not you, then who?" he sneered.

"I know not, Arthur." His eyes widened as a thought struck him. He quickly turned to the Arbiters. "Were I to have attacked Arthur by the lakeside, would it not be listed in the misdemeanours that would render my tree bereft of leaves?" he asked eagerly.

"It would," Raemund confirmed.

Merlin turned back to Arthur with a smug look upon his face. "Then we shall see, shall we not," the magician smiled as a measure of confidence hitherto missing from his time in the chamber asserted itself in his voice.

Intrigued, Arthur merely nodded, repeating his last statement but this time with a modicum of uncertainty, "If not you, then who?"

With that, Merlin's trial resumed and, when they reached the point when the longevity potion had been concocted and supped, the leaves began to fall like rain from Merlin's tree.

Arthur shuffled uncomfortably under the stern gazes of the Arbiters, for they stared at him pointedly, as if challenging him to find fault with them.

As the room reverberated to the soporific reading voice of Leonid, Arthur waited with baited breath as the events detailed began to approach the time of the near fatal battle upon the shore of the Grail Lake.

In Arthur's mind, it had become hugely important to him whether Merlin was lying or if, in this instance, the magician's pleading was a single green shoot of honesty in an otherwise barren field of lies. It would somehow soften the blow of his being manipulated so completely and utterly.

And suddenly there it was.

The tale was told and, sure enough, at the time of the attack, Merlin had indeed been studying the Lindisfarne Gospels and had been nowhere near the scene.

With a sigh made up in equal parts of relief and puzzlement, King Arthur turned to face his court magician. "I apologise for my mistrust," he murmured, "but in the current circumstances, I am finding it very hard to believe anything that anyone tells me."

Merlin, for his part, simply wore a look of injured innocence and ignored him.

The King then turned to the seven magistrates of the ultimate. Bowing low, he said, "I would also like to offer my apologies to you, most noble judges. I did not mean to question your integrity. It is just that, as I said to the one who stands before you, I have seen that my whole life has been one of fallacy and deceit and I am finding trust a precious commodity that I am no longer prepared to give away very easily."

Sniffing dismissively, Leonid, who had been chairing Merlin's trial, waved away Arthur's grovelling apology and resumed the litany of the magician's life.

Despite the outcome being far less clear-cut than Arthur had thought, Merlin was finally sentenced to walk the same path so recently trodden by his nemesis. Before he departed, he rounded on the King. "I know that you now look upon me with hatred rather than the fondness and respect that you used to, but know this, Arthur. As I told you before, your destiny and mine were both written across the stars before you took your first breath."

The King rolled his eyes and nodded, pointedly yawning at the repeated story.

Merlin's eyes flashed in anger but he continued nonetheless. "Well, that was the one thing that I did not lie about. You were ever the one who would solve the conundrum of the Grail's untapped power."

Arthur brought his face to within inches of the magician's. "Only to have it stolen from me by a common thief masquerading as a friend," he hissed.

The wizard threw his hands up in despair. "Damn it, man. Hold your tongue and engage your brain for once. That was your destiny. It was my destiny to wield it after your sterling efforts in unravelling its riddles."

The former King of England snorted derisively. "Did your destiny mention this?" he flourished his arm in an all-encompassing sweep. "After you fulfilled your destiny and wielded the Grail, did it foretell you being skewered like a pig on Excalibur's blade and condemned to the dank pits of Satan's dominion for evermore?"

Merlin shrunk back as if Arthur had landed a physical blow upon him and his imposing frame seemed to shrink. Now before the King stood an old man wizened by age and circumstance, to be pitied not bullied.

With a dry chuckle, Merlin shook his head. "Beyond my wielding of the Grail, I could not pierce the future's veil. Had I known of this then perhaps I would have woven my webs differently." He peered pensively at the exquisite mosaic decorating the floor of the chamber. "Yet I suspect the knowledge would not have diverted me from my path. I suspect that I would have convinced myself that, with the energy of the Grail engorging my veins, I would have been able to overcome any obstacle laid before me, so perhaps we would have been standing here regardless anyway," he shrugged. "My self-belief and pride were always both my best features and my worst faults." Arthur was at a loss as to how to respond. He watched in a daze as the man whom he had known longer than any other trudged slowly towards his doom.

At the last, just as Merlin reached forward to push open the magically renewed door to damnation, he spun round with eyes twinkling. "When you held it, Arthur, when you clasped the golden stem of the Grail in your hand, did you not feel the power, did you not yearn to utilise such forces for your own ends?" he asked, almost pleading for an answer in the affirmative, so that he might have some indication that the King could, whilst not actually sympathise, at least begin to understand what had seduced his companion into such a complex and twisted betrayal.

Arthur replied quietly. "All I felt was a serenity beyond anything I had ever experienced and a warmth that comforted me to the very core of my being," he breathed, enraptured once more by the memory of his all-too-brief encounter with the power of the Grail, "And the light, oh Merlin, the light. Bright enough to banish all the shadows from the world yet not too harsh that it could not be gazed upon and enjoyed in all its glory," his eyes refocused on the present and fixed upon Merlin's contorted features. "Any power that I did feel was benign and subtle, not to be used to coerce like a sword but instead to persuade like a reasoned argument or stirring oration."

As he stood on the threshold, Merlin stared in wonder at the King. The response had engendered a new level of respect for Arthur in his heart, yet always below the calm surface, the arrogance and ego bubbled seeking an outlet through which to burst. He wanted to acknowledge Arthur's strength and fortitude in forgoing such an opportunity but he could not, for his conceit would not let him. The one vision that dominated his mind as he looked at the King was that this man had denied him the Grail.

For, as it was with Arthur, the memory of the few seconds spent holding the Grail engulfed his mind and his thoughts. There though the similarity ended because the potency that Merlin had felt when brandishing the vessel was that of a white-hot whirlwind whipping through his being, a tsunami of unstoppable force. There had been nothing benign or subtle about it, it was simply power, it was simply dominion.

All his senses had been stretched to their utmost in those few seconds but then, as the thrill of remembrance reached its height, the violent dislocation of Arthur's killing stroke hoved into his mind, cleaving his memory into smithereens and filling his whole being with the unbearable loss once more. With that anguished memory consuming his soul in raw agony, Merlin stared upon King Arthur for the final time. "Might I gaze upon it once more?" he pleaded, "My magic is torn from me and I bear no weapon. I do not seek to wrest it from you, for I have neither the means nor the spirit anymore. All I ask is to see my destiny and my downfall one last time before the fires of hell claim me."

Arthur peered intently at the mystic's eyes but, as before, he could discern no deceit within them. Pain and anguish certainly, maybe even sorrow, but no sign of artifice. Still though, the King shied away from total belief of the mage's motives. For a moment, he toyed with the idea of deceiving the magician by claiming possession of it about his person but refusing to bring it forth but that, he felt, would be lowering himself to Merlin's level. Would he want his final act towards Merlin to be one of falsity and sham? No, he decided, he would not.

"I no longer possess it," he stated matter-of-factly.

To his surprise, there were sharp intakes of breath from the Arbiters as well as the magician.

Merlin stepped away from the door to Hell and advanced threateningly upon the King. Fabian and Flammel swiftly moved between them counselling the wizard against any further retreat from the dread portal. "What do you mean?" Merlin bellowed. "Where is it then, God damn you?" His maniacal eyes swept away from Arthur and scoured the faces of the Arbiters. "It is you, is it not?" he screamed. "You have poisoned his susceptible mind and tricked him into passing stewardship over to you!"

He lunged at Flammel, who was standing to his right. However, despite being the tallest man in Camelot, he was no match for the massively built Arbiter, who easily resisted the attack and now grappled the mage into an arm-breaking hold that was inescapable, no matter how fiercely the fury inside Merlin made him struggle.

"Calm yourself, Merlin," Arthur said. "The Arbiters do not possess it. It has found its way full circle into the hands of its rightful owner, whom we have now both had the privilege to gaze upon." the King pronounced solemnly, trying not to smile at the memory of Christ's presence.

"Gullible imbecile," Merlin blurted. "You would not willingly yield it to one whom you have known for centuries, yet you hand over the most potent weapon on earth to one who you have seen for a mere few minutes!"

"Yes," Arthur responded hotly, "its rightful owner. The one who saved your life, if you remember."

Flammel released him from his iron grip as Merlin held up resigned hands. "May I be permitted to use my arts if they cause no physical harm to any here present?" he asked in an apparently calm voice.

For long moments, the Arbiters communed mentally. All the while, Merlin paced the length of the room, muttering under his breath and occasionally casting hate-filled looks towards Arthur.

Finally Leonid, who was the current holder of the central chair at the table, spoke. "You are permitted but only if you are good to your word and no harm is done to any here."

Smiling evilly, Merlin faced King Arthur across the room.

Catching the expression, the pompous tones of Raemund rang out. "Know this, Merlin the magician, if any injury is sustained then you will be cast into the pit before you can blink. In addition to this, the one whom you wound will be restored to full health for, although never used, ever have the seven had the power to restore life should they so choose."

Merlin bowed low. "Your provisos are duly noted. Know that I only wish to show this naïve cretin the limits of his brain."

Arthur coloured at the insult, especially as it provoked flickers of amusement on a couple of the Arbiters' faces.

"Proceed then, for though it will have no bearing on our final judgement, we are intrigued as to where this holy artifact that you find so quarrelsome has disappeared to," Leonid intoned.

Merlin's eyebrows creased. "Disappeared, you say?"

"Yes," answered Kirsten, "we have long followed its path through the ages ever since it was bestowed upon Joseph of Arimathea by Jesus Christ the Nazarene. We have always been aware of its potential for good or ill. Indeed, once the quartet of which you are but one half drunk of the potion which has wreaked so much havoc in our realm, we entertained thoughts of direct intervention but, at the last, it was concluded that that would have caused still more chaos, for our impartiality would have been forever tainted." She paused. "However, just before Arthur Pendragon fell upon his sword and honoured his promise to us, the Grail was obscured from our sight. We would hear more of an object so powerful that it can mask itself even from our omniscience."

At this point, Arthur re-entered the conversation. "It was the saviour. I felt the same warmth as I felt when I held the Grail. That is how I know I did right in yielding ownership to Him," he said forcefully.

Merlin began to make mystical passes with his hands, hiding his face from everyone's view. "Tell me, did your saviour look anything like this?" With the question hanging in the air, Merlin dropped his hands to his sides.

Arthur found himself gaping stupidly at the perfect facsimile of the face of the one who had come to him in the ruins of the abbey. "Yes," he stammered in shock before recovering himself and rallying, "you cannot recreate the all-pervasive essence of tranquillity that emanated from him though, can you." He sneered.

"Believe me..." Merlin began to say.

"No, but I can," a booming voice reverberated around the golden sanctum. All within turned to face the voice. Rich in timbre and confident in tone, it commanded itself to be heard. Standing in the frame of the door that gave entrance to the Arbiters chamber from the Halls of Reckoning stood the man Merlin recognised as the one who had been his salvation from the living hell aboard the Skarvlang.

To Arthur's eyes, it was the saviour made flesh. Once again, he found himself lost in the soothing serenity that seemed to transmit itself to the four corners of the room.

To the Arbiters, it was the face of death and the end. The end of all they knew. Never had one been able to come and go at will about their realm. All who dwelt within the Halls were subject to their bidding, subject to the rules of time and order. Yet here was one who had entered their chamber utterly undetected and with minimum effort.

As the seven stared into the piercing blue eyes, all they saw was doom. They saw armies of hideous evil, marching through time, burning, crucifying, raping, torturing. Armies of brainwashed zombies, infused with a hateful zeal, perpetrating acts of heinous barbarity and brutality, killing for the sake of killing, murdering for the sake of murder, all masked by a smokescreen of righteousness and sanctimony.

The septet quailed before him. With a horrified rictus, Raemund turned to Arthur and hissed, "All is lost. You have doomed us all."

The newcomer snorted at the Arbiter as he pathetically pawed at the King's cloak.

For his part, Arthur stood perplexed, for he had neither the skill nor the wit to penetrate the new arrival's guise. All he could see was the Son of God before him. He pushed Raemund away in disgust. "Do not be afraid. This is the saviour unto whom I delivered the Grail. He means you no harm."

That was too much for Merlin. He launched himself at Arthur, grabbing his throat and throttling him, for his magic had now pierced the man's façade and he could see the pure malignance that emanated from him.

The fury within Merlin was too much for Arthur to withstand and he was unable to break the stranglehold. As he began to slip from consciousness, his head lolled to the side and he beheld the messiah.

The lack of oxygen to his brain heightened his senses and finally, with a gasp of consternation, he saw what everyone else in the room could see. He saw what really lurked beneath the calm visage. He saw the twisted wreck of a man who hid behind the beautiful mask. He saw and he knew. Knew what he had done. The final manipulation of his existence would be the one that would end his life. The one that would end all life. His eyes fluttered and he was about to lapse into unconsciousness when the newcomer flung out his right arm.

Merlin was catapulted into the wall so violently that a fine layer of dust cascaded down from the ceiling. The man began to stride lazily forward, "Hmm!" he murmured. "Such a dilemma. Do I spare the life of one who once saved mine?" He sauntered over to where Merlin writhed, agonisingly pinned to the wall by an unseen blade, gasping for breath through his torn lungs, shredded as they had been by the shards of his shattered ribs.

Despite the incandescent pain searing every inch of his body, the words caused Merlin to cease his squirming and stare intently at the one who had bested him without a second's thought.

The King would not have believed that Merlin's pallor could become any greyer but, as the light of realisation bloomed in his eyes, he saw what colour there was drain from his cheeks as quickly as the tide of blood that now ran from Merlin's back down the wall, pooling obscenely at the new man's feet.

"You!" Merlin gasped.

The man merely nodded.

To everyone's surprise, Merlin choked out a gurgling laugh. "So the stars were not lying. I was to have been killed by a cruel and terrible wizard named Montagu."

The man raised an eyebrow. "Indeed," he said.

With a rattling sigh, Merlin, court magician of Camelot, died for the second and final time.

Dismissively, as he turned away from the ruined corpse, he gestured towards the door that led to Paradise. In an instant, Merlin's broken remains were catapulted through it, reducing it to a cloud of splinters. Shrugging, he murmured. "It is the least I could do. He did save my life after all."

At the sound of the voice addressing him, Arthur wrenched his horrified gaze from the ruined door and stared open-mouthed at the reality of what had come to pass.

The manner of Merlin's demise had left him in no doubt that the gnarled thing he had seen behind the vision of Christ had not been a trick of the light. The man leant into him and removed the final remnants of his disguise with a practised flick of the wrist.

Arthur could not help but recoil at the sight of him.

"Look at me," he screamed, the strength in his voice belying the feebleness of his true form.

He was no more than five feet tall. His legs were twisted and misshapen, knees meeting in the middle but feet splayed at different angles. The trunk of his body was swollen and fat with a distended gut drooping grossly over his waist. Bizarrely, his arms seemed to be well-muscled and in proportion with each other. However, they looked out of place on the malformed body that stood before the King. Atop the body lay a grotesque bulbous head. The mouth was twained with a harelip and the nose was smeared across the face, flat and squatting. The visage was completed by two gargantuan brows that overhung the eyes like the awning of a tent.

By far though, the most striking aspect was the eyes. They shone with an inner fire so bright that the King felt that he would still be able to see them even if all the lights in the chamber were dimmed.

"Who…who are you?" he managed to stammer.

The man regarded him coolly. "Did you not hear Merlin's last utterance?" he asked.

Arthur nodded. "I took it to be the raving of a man seconds from death. All in this room saw Montagu walk through the door of Hell." He gestured at the Arbiters, all seven of whom were cowering behind their chairs.

"And you think that my bastard father was the only soul accursed with that name?" the newcomer spat.

A flashback hit Arthur's memory so hard that he actually gasped at the reminiscence. A flashback to a barn in a far-off hamlet called Bakerstown, of Merlin ministering to a seemingly dead child, of Merlin feeding it his blood to restore its life.

"Recognition has dawned at last, I see," Montagu drawled.

A further memory erupted to the forefront of the King's mind. Of a lakeside, of a headlong plummet toward an infernal blaze, of a timeless torture within the Halls of Reckoning. Arthur's eyes widened but he could not bring himself to speak.

"Yes, that was me," Montagu chuckled.

"Why?" Arthur managed to choke.

"Had you been unfortunate enough to live my life, you would have no need to ask the question. Wrenched from the breast by my soulless demon father who then proceeded to use my blood in the rites that murdered my mother." For a brief moment, his left hand moved to his right arm and stroked the livid scar that had escaped Arthur's notice upon his first look at Montagu's son. "Not long after that, when my father realised I was malformed and would grow into this travesty of a man, he cast me out, for if I was to be a worthy heir to him then I would have to be perfect and it soon became all too clear that I was not."

In a sudden move that startled Arthur, he thrust out his right arm, finger extended and bellowed. "Be still!"

311

The Arbiters, who were surreptitiously making their way towards the door to the Halls, froze in various skulking attitudes and despite their best efforts, could not move an inch further.

"He left me in a cave," Montagu continued, "a mere babe of two years, he left me to fend for myself or die." For a split second, the agony of the memory dampened down the volcanic flame that raged within Montagu's eyes. "It was then, when I realised he was not coming back, that the magic surfaced within me for, though I was too young to know it, the blood of two of the most powerful mages ever to have walked the earth pumped in my veins. All I knew was that, if I willed it, the beasts of the ground and the birds of the air would do as I bid, bringing me food and providing me with warmth as and when I required it. For years, I know not how many, I dwelt in that cave, ashamed of my appearance and content with the company I was keeping. I had no need for human contact and I did not wish it."

As Montagu brought his head up to face the King again, the light rekindled, dancing hypnotically and entrancing Arthur completely and utterly.

"Yet every now and again, a discomfort came upon me and I felt the edges of something teasing my consciousness, something calling me forth into the world, a stirring in my blood. Often I would stand in the mouth of the cave, sending my senses forth to roam the land, unaware of what I was searching for, yet certain of recognising it the moment I happened upon it."

The sensual lull of Montagu's voice bewitched the King and he found himself pleading for the squat ugly man to continue.

Smiling pompously at Arthur's pathetically wheedling expression, Montagu went on. "One morning I awoke to find the pull irresistible. I did not wait to break my fast, I had to know what it was that disturbed me like an unscratchable itch.

For the first time since my father took me into that cave, for the first time in years, decades even, I walked fully into the daylight. At first, my pale skin could not take the heat of the sun and within seconds it began to redden and throb, forcing me to retire back into the shadows. But I would not be stayed. I surmise that I used what you would call magic to solve the problem, but that was a word outside my knowledge at that time.

Mentally I soothed my skin and went out into the world. I walked for many days and nights, marvelling at the beauty of the countryside by day and awestruck by the millions of stars that adorned the sky at night. Finally, however, I came upon the source of my irritation. The discomfiture that I was feeling was a resonance from my ancestry. It was my father, you see. Every time he employed his dark arts, I felt the ripples and snuffed the stench of it." Montagu hung his head and muttered. "I knew not what to do. I had lost count of the number of years that we had been estranged. When I laid eyes

312

upon him again, it shocked me to my very bones. I wanted to slaughter him there and then, just as he had my mother all those years ago, yet I could not. I was scared of what would happen and I could not face him. So I fled, fled like a craven coward back to my cave.

For days I sat, my mind awhirl with hatred and fear in equal measure. Every once in a while, the feeling of his magic would creep up on me once again and I would venture out into the sunlight, determined to make him pay for what he did to my mother and me but, at the last, my spirit would waver and I would skulk back into the darkness, weeping at my impotence."

Suddenly, as if Montagu's face had been touched by the summer sun, the twisted features softened and there was a hint of joy present in his eyes. "Then my mother came to me in a waking dream. She sat with me, held me, spoke to me," he sighed and blinked away tears, "she completed me."

The catch in Montagu's voice was too much for Arthur and he had to look away. On more than one occasion, he had woken in the night, awash with sweat as the awful vision of the discovery of the young woman in Bakerstown reared its ugliness in his mind.

Montagu cleared his throat and buried a thumb and forefinger into his moistened eyes, as if he was trying to grind away the pain. When he withdrew them, the steely purpose and depthless hatred had returned. "Then she was gone from me again," his voice dropped to a barely audible whisper, "and the emptiness, dear God, the emptiness." He stared at the ceiling in despair.

The two men remained where they were for some time, each alone with their thoughts, each unwilling to break the poignant silence.

Montagu was the first to move as a shuddering sigh escaped his lips. "That was what served to inspire me from my apathy. It was the spur that I needed to face my demon sire. I left the cave that day, never to return, determined to do right by my mother and slay the fiend that had robbed her of her life. However, I was not about to charge recklessly and blindly into my father's ever grasping clutches, so I found a village, for I knew I would need to study human behaviour, so I could better approach the task before me. It did not take me long to realise that I had gifts beyond normalcy amongst men. I quickly removed myself from the villagers' scrutiny for they were all distrustful of me, pointing at me and calling me cursed," and here his voice took on a faraway quality and it seemed to Arthur that he was talking to himself rather than addressing anyone in the chamber, "perhaps I am cursed, cursed for being the progeny of such a foul father."

Blinking, he returned to the present. "I began to live my old hermit life once more but this time, the days were not wasted. I trained myself, exploring my abilities and forever testing their limits until they were working at their

313

utmost power. The first few days drained me to the point of exhaustion for I had tapped into a well of enormous potential that I never knew dwelt within me. In those early days, I was nearly lost, drowned in an overwhelming ocean of energy but always, at the last, I broke the surface until I learnt to hone my skills, ride the wave, catch the lightning and break down the walls within. I know not which day it was, nor which month or year, but one cold winter's morning, I awoke and I knew. I knew I was ready to face him and I knew I was ready to kill him."

King Arthur let out an explosive gasp as the pieces of the puzzle finally clicked into place. "It was you. That is why you studied his face for so long and that is why you took such violent exception to me saving him."

The wizard broke into a sarcastic round of applause. "And so we finally get there. Yes, it would have been over. The hellspawn would have been headless and lifeless were it not for your trusty Excalibur," he spat.

The King shrank back from the venom directed towards him. "But I did not know it was your father. As far as I knew, it was Merlin I guarded. If I had known whom I protected then rest assured, my weapon would have remained firmly in its sheath when you struck."

A strange look passed over the misshapen face and for the first time since he entered the Arbiters chamber, Montagu looked slightly unsure of himself. After a moment, he nodded. "Never let it be said that I am above mistakes. What you have to understand is that my father's mask did not work on me. I could see his true identity and simply assumed that he had bewitched you into his support."

Arthur's hand instinctively caressed his neck where the younger Montagu's boot had planted itself when he had lain stricken upon the rocky shore of the Grail Lake.

"From then on," Montagu continued, "I became even more wary for had I not fallen over your body, my father's fireball would have killed me. So I retreated again and watched you, all three of you, Merlin included, and I saw it all. The locating of the Grail, the dragon slaying, all of it and like a thunderclap it hit me and I knew what I had to do, how I could right the wrongs done to me and my mother."

Arthur stared blankly at him. Montagu rolled his eyes and sighed. "It is clear that the only thing that kept your crown atop your head was your ears, for obviously nothing exists between them. The Grail, you dullard. The so-called holy Cup of Christ. The instant I laid eyes upon it, I knew what possibilities lay before me, were I to possess it. To anyone with the merest modicum of magical talent, it is clearly a vessel with power beyond imagining." Once again, the expressive eyes lit up with an obscene zeal. "My plan was to wait until my father was convinced of his triumph, then simply snatch it from him,

314

make him plead for his life then snuff him out like the flame of a candle." He jabbed a bulbous finger at the King. "You robbed me of the chance to kill him but I am nothing if not magnanimous in victory, so you will not be punished for it. With the Grail in my hand, in time I imagine I shall be able to call him back from the dead and kill him myself again and again and again." Montagu began to pace around the room. "I must say though, Merlin's trick voice did take me unawares for a moment. However, once I regained my wits, I could see what his lust for the Grail had done to him and he was not so vigilant as perhaps he should have been in such circumstances." He ceased his stride and spun round to face Arthur. "I would wager that you did not expect Excalibur to fly so straight and true, did you?"

All the King could do was shake his head dumbly. There was still a tinge of regret at his slaying of Merlin and Montagu's crowing was not helping him forget it.

"Well, are you not going to thank me for guiding it like an arrow?" Montagu asked.

Arthur eyes widened then his whole body sagged as realisation hit him. "Has nothing in my life been achieved without trickery or deception? Dear God, what have I done to be condemned to live like this, doing the foul deeds of others whilst under the illusion that my choices were driven by my own hand," he wailed.

Montagu shrugged. "We are all subject to the whims of destiny, Arthur. Know though, that of everyone caught up in this centuries old pursuit, you are the one who has played his part to the fullest. Of all who have fallen under the Grail's witchery, you are the only one who has been uncorrupted by its seduction."

The fallen monarch eyed Montagu distastefully and muttered, "That is of scant consolation." He drew himself up to his full height and tried to gather the last remnants of his dignity together. "Do not however try to sweeten the bitter pill by laying the blame upon the Grail. I have been dragged through my life at the behest of Merlin, your father and now you, not the Grail," he sneered, "a pox on all wizards and their filthy underhand ways."

At this, Montagu's eyes blazed. Suddenly, the tall muscular man that had nearly sent Arthur to his death at the lakeside loomed large over him, somehow unfolding seamlessly from the dwarflike figure of the real magician. A powerful arm was thrust forward and the fingers closed around the King's throat. Montagu lifted Arthur a full foot off the ground and held him there, dangling uselessly, choking and gagging, fighting feebly to try and loosen the death grip.

"What in hell do you think the Grail is, you simpleton? The Grail is wizardry. It *is* magic. The Grail is the fount of all the supernatural power in

315

the world. Your precious Nazarene was the first wizard to walk the earth. What were his miracles if not sleight of hand and mystical illusion? Why did his sermons attract so many believers when in those times you could not walk the streets without being assailed by preachers and proselytes on every corner?" Montagu raged.

The King tried to say something but could not. With his free hand, Montagu gestured and allowed him to speak, albeit with a painfully strangulated voice. "His miracles were the work of His Father, The Lord God and his sermons attracted so many listeners because their message was one of love not hate, one of tolerance, not enmity."

The wizard stared open-mouthed at the King. "Even after all you have been through, you still cling to your blind faith like a newborn babe to its mother's teat. Why do you think my father and Merlin went to such lengths to obtain it? They knew all along what it was and they also knew all along that you were the only one who could unleash its power. That is why Merlin groomed you from birth, watched over you and ensured no harm came to you."

"What about Camlann?" Arthur challenged. "Mordred came within an ace of killing me."

Montagu raised an eyebrow.

"Or so Merlin said…" The King's voice trailed off.

"And who has been your only counsel for nearly three hundred years? Either Merlin or my father, yes?"

"But why me?" Arthur whispered hoarsely.

"Blood, Arthur. It all comes down to your blood. Magic is in the blood, you see. It was in the blood of your so-called messiah. The Holy Grail was the only vessel in which the stuff of pure magic and the stuff of pure life ever mingled. The tears that fell from his eyes and the blood that pumped from his veins. Never was a more potent mixture concocted. That is what infuses the Grail. Not love, not peace, simply pure unadulterated magic and power."

Lights began to dance in front of Arthur's eyes as the pressure of Montagu's grip upon his windpipe began to tell, but he still persisted, "Why me?" he slurred.

"You are the last surviving descendant of Christ. His blood, though somewhat diluted, runs through your veins. That is what the key to unlocking the Grail was. Your tears and your blood."

Arthur's face had begun to turn purple and his eyes were starting from his head, yet he managed to blurt, "What of the Judas Cup? That was what your father ultimately sought."

Shaking his head, Montagu laughed, "Judas Cup? Poor gullible little man. That is naught but a title bestowed upon the trinket that you so kindly delivered to me by my father. He thought it unseemly that one of his persuasion should be actively pursuing something named the Holy Grail. He felt the Judas Cup was a more appropriate title for it."

With an absolute darkness rapidly approaching and nothing left in the world except the pain of Montagu's grip, Arthur's final words were, "Why was Merlin so afeared of it, if...if..." The King's eyes rolled back in his head and his tongue lolled.

Montagu dropped him to the floor and bent over him, placing two fingers upon the King's wrist. Not a flicker met his feather-light touch. "Oh no, Pendragon, your agony does not end that easily," he drawled. He made a few passes over the King's brow then slapped his face.

Coughing violently, the King began breathing once more. With a wide-eyed look at his tormentor, he tried to back away but, like the Arbiters, he was frozen to the spot. "Oh yes, Arthur, your gift has given me power even over life and death. But, in answer to your unfinished question, have you really not puzzled it out yet? Are you really that naïve?"

The implication rebounded around the King's head. His haunted eyes travelled from Montagu's flawless face to the ravaged remains of the door to Paradise. "No, no, that is not possible. I well remember the fear and horror in Merlin's eyes as he described the Cup and what damage it could cause were it to fall into your father's hands."

The magus loomed over the King. "And what devastation do you think would have occurred if the Grail had fallen under my father's influence? Make no mistake, Arthur, the fear you saw in your companion's eyes was naught but fear of a double cross. My father and Merlin were and always had been in cahoots, unfortunately for them though, it was a marriage of mistrust and suspicion. Each entered into the relationship with a view to seizing the spoils for themselves, yet outwardly they spoke of a dominion of duality, a double seated throne from which both could command."

Arthur laughed hysterically even though he knew his mockery would certainly cost him his life. "What rubbish you spout, Montagu." With a suicidal determination the King returned his captor's steely gaze with one of equal strength. "You certainly have your father's capacity for lies and misinformation."

It was as if someone had lit a fire within the magician. His face coloured to scarlet and his eyes glowed with a rage barely held in check. His hand snapped out like a whip and lifted Arthur from the ground once again, leaving the King striving frantically for a breath that was beyond him.

"I am nothing like my father!" he screeched, "Nothing!" The pressure increased and the longest-lived member of the human race stared into the face of death once again.

"Believe me or not, you sanctimonious moron, but I speak the truth. Why do you think Merlin took you to Lindisfarne Abbey? He expected Montagu to be there with the Gospels for he passed on to my father the ancient secrets that allowed him to rout the monks. What he did not envisage was that my father would renege on the bargain and steal the tome, stowing it aboard the longship. That is why he flew into such a rage and acted so recklessly in his pursuit."

With a final desperate effort, the King wrenched himself clear of the wizard's reach, knowing that he was merely delaying the inevitable but determined to say his piece nonetheless. "No," he croaked, "that cannot be true. Who saved him then, Montagu? How did he escape your father's clutches? Who pulled him back from the Reaper's embrace?" He jabbed an accusing finger. "In fact, how do you even know all of this?" Exhausted by his predicament, Arthur staggered to the nearest wall and tried to stand but his legs would not support him.

"The Grail," Montagu replied simply, "as the prophecy says, once it is unlocked it can never be closed. It yielded the information to me in a matter of minutes once I apprehended its workings. Such power," he breathed sensually, "such power." He shook his head and returned to the first of the King's questions. "As to who saved him, well, that would be your oh-so-holy friend, the Nazarene."

King Arthur wanted to laugh, wanted to pour scorn on Montagu's revelations, but the enormity of this statement rendered him speechless. He did, however, cross himself much to the amusement of his tormentor.

"Yes, that is right," Montagu chuckled sarcastically, "the holy of holies." Striding forward with a youthful vigour, Montagu poked Arthur in the shoulder. "And do you know why he provided Merlin with salvation?"

Numbly, Arthur shook his head.

"He knew that Merlin was the only one who could manipulate you into activating the Grail. He could see what the future held and he guessed that either Montagu or Merlin would end up as ultimate steward of it but he favoured Merlin because of his connection to you and also because of my father's previous deeds." Montagu grabbed the King by the front of his cloak and hauled him upright. "Never mind that he could perceive Merlin's all-consuming lust for the Grail, never mind that he could see that Merlin had previously joined forces with the devil incarnate, never mind that he could see that Merlin had betrayed the Grail monks. Your so-called messiah picked sides because he believed Merlin's motives and actions would remain a secret for all eternity and he would prove a fitting ambassador alongside you as you continued the legacy of the Grail."

Such a monstrous blasphemy could not go unanswered and finally Arthur regained his voice. "Absurdity!" he blurted. "You would have me believe that the saviour of all would allow such a traitorous cur to dominate his vessel, even though he knew of his complicity with Montagu?"

The wizard smiled languidly. "Uncomfortable, is it not, when everything that you believe in proves itself false," he purred.

"Proved!" Arthur managed to conjure a laugh from the pit of despair that had opened within him, although inwardly it sounded rather hollow even to him, for the seed of doubt that Montagu had planted began to take flower. "You have proved nothing!" he spat.

Exasperated, Montagu delved within his flowing robes. "Choose not to believe me at your peril, Pendragon. Tell me though, would you doubt the evidence of your own eyes?" he snarled. With a flourish, he produced the Holy Grail from beneath his garments.

As it was brought forth, the light that had enveloped Arthur so blissfully when he had first released it blazed anew. Despite his situation and his close proximity to one who wished him dead, he could not help but smile and sigh blissfully at the wonder of it.

Montagu, in stark contrast to his father's reaction of disinterest, stared all around and about him as the light cascaded over everything, giving the gilded hall an even brighter lustre. "Raw magic," he chuckled then stood in the middle of the room, drawing in huge lungfuls of breath, as if he was on a beach snuffing up the salty tang of the sea. "Exhilarating, is it not?" he asked Arthur.

The King was too wrapped up in his own awestruck thoughts to respond. Chagrined by this, Montagu muttered words to the Grail and the inspiring display winked out of existence in an instant.

Stalking over to the Arbiters table, Montagu swept his arm across it, sending goblets and manuscripts tumbling to the floor. He placed the Grail down in its centre and retreated a couple of steps. "Show," he commanded, the order barked out with fierce venom.

"How do I know this is not simply another ruse to try and convince me, or perhaps even yourself, that the ends you have achieved were justified by the means by which you attained them?" Arthur questioned.

The mage shrugged. "You do not. I do not even have to show you this, Pendragon. I only do so to prove my words right and to demonstrate to you what a tremendous idiot you have been. How Merlin tricked you into drinking the potion simply so he could keep you alive. He had no thought for your welfare, he merely wished to buy himself more time so he could weasel his way into a position where he could use you to untie the ropes that bound the Grail's powers. Now cease your interminable whining and witness it for yourself. Whether you choose to believe it or not is no concern of mine. I certainly do not need approval from an empty headed fool such as yourself." Turning back to the Grail, he repeated, "Show."

As it had when it had first sprung into life at Camelot, a colourless smoke bloomed into the air directly above the Grail then froze. Suddenly, it resolved into a smooth flat screen. After a moment, two figures appeared seated at a table. The table itself was bare save for two untouched goblets of wine. With a nausea hurtling from his stomach to his throat, Arthur could clearly make out the faces of Montagu and Merlin. "I..." he began to say.

Without moving his eyes from the pair, Montagu flicked a hand out and struck Arthur dumb.

The King jumped as, all of a sudden, the voices of the two archmages reached his ears. The rich tones of both were startlingly similar but there was something in Merlin's voice that marked it out as separate from Montagu's. Guilt, perhaps? Arthur pondered.

With a heavy heart, he realised that the difference was the urgency in his voice that was not normally there. Arthur did not doubt that it was the product of his greed for glory and power.

"So it would seem that the corridor has been walked and the door is finally in view?" Montagu drawled.

Merlin nodded. "Indeed. The only unfortunate circumstance in this is that it was that insufferable prig, Galahad, who found it. I did not think it possible for that pious bastard to become more sanctimonious than he already is, but now he perches himself upon the Siege Perilous like he has touched hands with God." The magician hawked and spat.

Montagu's face twisted in amusement at Merlin's sneer. "Calm yourself. The main thing is that it is found. Galahad can pray to it or worship it or even piss in it until he is blue in the face but both you and I know it will do him no good. Only your master can unravel its mysteries."

"I call no man master!" Merlin snapped.

"How should I describe him then? Your pet?" he grinned.

After a moment, the sternness left Merlin's face and he grinned back. "That is preferable, yes," he chortled. Taking a sip from his goblet, he cleared his throat and his face took on a serious look once again. "So it is agreed then. I will draw the King out of Camelot to face yourself and Mordred at Camlann. Whilst we are there, in the ensuing melee, you will uplift the Grail from Galahad on the battlefield and bring it to the abbey. I will then bring Arthur to Lindisfarne, claiming to be in pursuit of you. Once we are together, we can use him to activate it. To think one droplet of Christ's blood and Christ's tears is enough. Truly it must have been an age of wonder to have walked the earth with him."

A derisive snort erupted from Montagu's side of the table. "Spare me, Merlin. You are beginning to sound like one of those tiresome Christians. Setting that aside, in answer to your question, yes it is agreed. It must be done in secret, though, for if any suspect, we could fail. How will you do it? How will you magic away the King without arousing suspicion?"

"That is of no moment. Rest assured, it will be done. Just ensure you are there at Lindisfarne to meet me and Arthur." He stabbed out a long finger inches from Montagu's face. "Do not think of betrayal for, without the King, the Grail is nothing more than a rather ornate drinking vessel."

Montagu feigned a look of injured innocence. "Such disservice you do me," he sighed then shrugged, "to the Judas Cup," he said as he raised his goblet.

Merlin raised his drink in return. "To the Holy Grail," he replied. "Judas Cup?" he asked questioningly with a hint of mirth playing around his lips.

Montagu shrugged again. "I deem it a more suitable name. For some reason, the word holy seems to stick in my throat."

Merlin stood up, "Until the abbey then."

Montagu said nothing, merely nodding as Merlin took his leave.

Gradually the screen went black.

Even had he not still been dumbstruck by Montagu's spell, King Arthur would have been unable to find any words to accurately sum up his feelings towards the scene he had just witnessed.

Montagu smirked. "The story is only half told, Arthur. There are other things that you must see, other things that you count as lies because they have come from my lips. Let us see what the Grail can tell us about them, shall we?" He waved his hand vigorously across the insubstantial screen. "Show," he commanded once more.

The blackness turned grey and froze once more. Gradually, a room began to swim into focus. A man was hanging limply from two chains secured to the planking of the wall. His head was bowed and his hair was matted with blood and sweat. A thin line of drool hung from the slack-jawed mouth and an incoherent mumble issued from it, providing a constant undercurrent to the background noise. Arthur could make out occasional shouts from others beyond the Grail's sight, but their words were no clearer than the continuous muttering of the prisoner. As the King watched, the room seemed to sway gently and there were numerous creaks from the wood that made up the wall. As if Arthur needed telling, Montagu explained bluntly, "Aboard the Skarvlang." After that little statement, he lapsed back into silence.

The King looked over in surprise at the magician for he had turned sharply so as not to face the screen. Arthur's brows knitted in confusion until he became aware of the other figure that had just entered the cabin.

Clearly, he still had trouble facing his evil sire for any length of time.

321

Arthur peered at the screen as Montagu, clothed in Viking garb, strode over to his captive and yanked his head up.

With a gasp, Arthur gazed upon the emaciated features of Merlin. The face had been pummelled remorselessly for both eyes were swollen and bulbous to the extent that it was unlikely that the magician could see anything clearly. His nose had been broken and was caked with blood and mucus. Some of the blood had flowed into his unkempt beard which was now sticking out in clumps at varying crazy angles. To complete the picture, the lips were both cracked and scarlet and fresh blood oozed from between them.

"Hello, Merlin," Montagu screamed in the man's ear. Despite the noise, no reaction was forthcoming. Montagu looked his victim up and down, shaking his head and tutting, "Messed yourself again. Poor Mordred has only just cleaned you up. He won't be pleased, you know." The magician of the dark arts regarded his broken ally dispassionately. "Look at you, you're a disgrace."

Arthur turned away from the screen as Montagu brought his fist back, cannoning into Merlin's face with a sickening thud.

The younger Montagu, seeing Arthur turn from the carnage, strode over to him and wrenched his head round by the hair so that he was forced to watch the vicious beating being inflicted.

The King watched in horror as the elder Montagu broke off his violent assault, shaking his hands to restore the blood flow. He then began to pace up and down in front of Merlin, hands clasped behind his back. "I just came down to let you know that I soon intend to depart with your oh-so-obliging majesty to find that which we both coveted. Once I am in possession of it, I think I shall bring it back here, so you can watch me slit his throat over it and take possession of all its power. Will you enjoy that, do you think? Seeing me become the most powerful wizard in the world right under your nose. I know you can hear me, Merlin, and I know you can see me. It will be such a pleasure to see your pride crumble and hear your ego burst." He leant into the lifeless man and whispered in his ear and though Arthur could not see the lips move, he could hear the words as vividly as if they were being spoken over his shoulder. "You dared to think you could outwit me. You dared to think that you were my better. Sad arrogant fool. To think I had to treat you as my equal in order to trick you into bringing Arthur to me. Did you really think you would get a share of the spoils and I would allow someone as pathetic and feeble as you to rule alongside me? Did you really think I would allow you to come between me and absolute power?" He withdrew from his position at Merlin's ear and when he spoke again, the sibilant murmuring that had seduced so many minds to its will became an oaken booming voice of frightening power, one that had battered many minds to its command.

"There is only one that can deny me now. Only one whose veins thicken with the blood of the purest of the pure. Only he or his progeny may thwart my designs."

At this point, Montagu turned away from the still catatonic Merlin and, to the King, it seemed that he was staring directly at him from across the years, from across the divide between life and death. Montagu continued. "But he is and always will be ignorant of it and will be so until I prise the Grail from his cold dead hands."

Arthur gasped as, inexplicably, he felt the full weight of loathing and hatred that Montagu held for him. Open mouthed he watched, frozen in terror as Montagu's face began its bone-crushing transformation into that of Merlin's. "I shall return with cup and key and you will witness my triumph then kneel before me and die."

Then, in the blink of an eye, he was gone.

In the Arbiters' chamber, Arthur let out an explosive sigh and turned to the son of his nemesis with pleading eyes, begging for an end to the voyeuristic display of Merlin's degradation, but a brief shake of the head indicated that there was more to be seen.

For long moments, nothing changed, save for the barely audible but constant moaning that escaped from the tortured mage's mouth. Then, as had happened in the abbey when Arthur wielded the Grail for the last time, a placid serene light began to emanate from all around the cabin, filling the screen with a light so bright that Arthur and Montagu had to avert their eyes.

After Montagu's departure from the scene, Merlin's head had flopped down to face the floor once more and so the light did not elicit a response from him.

When the incandescence became so unbearable that it hurt even closed eyes, it winked out into nothingness. Frantically trying to blink away the green and red after-images that danced manically across his vision, Arthur found himself staring upon a familiar figure.

The benign countenance of Jesus Christ of Nazareth stared fixedly at the pathetic specimen before him. A slight hint of distaste flitted across his features as his nostrils were assailed by the stench of Merlin's soiled garments. He advanced towards the comatose magician with his right hand extended.

Merlin's head suddenly jerked up as if it was hanging on the end of a newly-tautened string.

As the King stared, it was as if the bewilderment and confusion that clouded Merlin's face was being gently stripped away until, suddenly, the man who had held sway over all things magical in the confines of Camelot and far beyond, was back in the land of the living, squinting confusedly at the figure before him.

Jesus smiled unto him and laid a hand in the middle of his forehead. Slowly at first, then with more rapidity, the brutal injuries inflicted upon the mage healed into nothingness and he slumped forward as the chains that bound him to the cabin wall relinquished their grip upon his wrists.

The Son of God caught him as he fell, manhandling him over to the single table that stood in the room and steadying him upon it.

"Montagu? Where is Montagu?" Merlin bleated, the blind panic and spine-freezing fear all too evident in his voice.

Jesus held up his hands and made soothing motions towards the agitated man. "He has left the boat and will not trouble you again for a long time."

This seemed to soothe Merlin's fear a little and for the first time he took a long look at his rescuer. "You!" he exclaimed, his voice filled with an equal measure of shock and curiosity. He blinked owlishly and got to his feet. Walking on unsteady legs, he described a circle around his saviour, peering at him as if he was a sculpture on display.

Jesus smiled slightly at Merlin's pointed scrutiny. "Pray seat yourself again, magician. I fear your legs will not support you much longer if you attempt too much too soon after your incarceration."

There was no hint of coercion in the voice yet, before he had even thought about it, Merlin had resumed his perch upon the edge of the table.

Jesus began to speak. "My time here is short, so I must avail you of my purpose without delay. Only you and the one whom imprisoned you know the truth of the Holy Grail. It is my legacy to all who followed and all who continue to follow my teachings. I cannot allow it to fall into the hands of one such as Montagu. He is evil beyond evil. His soul is a black hole of sin and iniquity. He is the nadir of all that is base and low." Jesus took a deep breath. "Know that I hesitate to approach one who so readily entered into a partnership with him but I realise that you intend to rob him of possession of the Grail should the unthinkable happen and he gains a hold over it."

For a moment, Jesus stopped and held Merlin's glare. When he spoke again, the strain and tension in his voice was all too obvious to Arthur. "I warn you now, Merlin. If you pursue that course of action, you will fail. Like it or not, he is too strong for you. He will snuff out your life in the blink of an eye. There is only one who can thwart him."

The magician's face was unreadable as the man whom millions called messiah continued, "You know of whom I speak. The one whom you have played false for all these years, the one whom you cajoled into drinking the longevity potion. He is the only one who can stop the dark one's relentless march toward supremacy over all whom live and die."

Merlin's face screwed itself into an attitude of revulsion as he contemplated what Jesus said.

324

"I know you think of him as a musclebound simpleton with little or no intellect to speak of, but he is mankind's only hope. His heart is stouter than any in the land and his courage second to none." Jesus waved a finger of warning in the magician's face. "I beseech you, wizard of Camelot. Put aside your own plans for domination and aid your King in his quest."

Merlin shook his head from side to side. "But I cannot allow the indignities visited upon me to go unavenged. Did your omniscience allow you to see the treatment I have been subjected to?"

"Have you heard nothing?" Jesus barked back. "If you challenge Montagu to a duel of magic and sorcery, then you write your own death warrant."

"Nonetheless, it is what I must do," Merlin hissed.

"No," the messiah advanced upon him, causing the mage to shrink back in fear. "What you must do is help Arthur defeat that travesty." He raised his hand as if to strike the wizard.

For long seconds the two of them stood, petrified in place, Jesus Christ towering over Merlin and the mage's arm raised in front of his face in a vain attempt to ward off the holy man's wrath. Then with a huge sigh, Jesus backed away. For a while, he said nothing then in a hoarse whisper, he muttered. "I cannot compel you. I can only plead with you once more. Do not challenge the hell-spawn for he will kill you."

"Not if I possess the Grail," Merlin answered, recovering his composure but not quite keeping the tell-tale quiver of fear out of his voice.

"Curse your pig-headedness and cloth ears, wizard," Jesus spat with vitriol. "You cannot possess the Grail without Arthur Pendragon. You know he is the key. He is the only one alive who can animate the Grail and defeat the monster's ambitions of misrule and tyranny."

The magician stood up and began to stalk around the cabin, waving his arms about in a frustrated flourish. "Why that imbecile? Why is the destiny of the most powerful magical artifact in the history of the world inextricably linked to that untalented fool?"

Christ laughed at the over-dramatic display. "There you are mistaken, Merlin."

He ceased his circuit of the damp room and stared intently at his saviour. "What?" he said in a flat voice.

"I said..." and here the voice of Jesus Christ filled both rooms, not just the cabin but also the Arbiters' chamber as well, "Arthur Pendragon is my last living descendant. The blood that courses through his veins is the blood that coursed through mine. The stuff of pure magic. He has the potential within him to end this once and for all. He merely has to look deep within himself."

Suddenly the face of Jesus filled the screen that hovered above the Grail. "Look deep inside yourself, Arthur and tap into the well of potency that has ever dwelt within you."

Time seemed to grind into slow motion.

The King was suddenly acutely aware of all in the room. He could sense the confusion in Montagu's mind as well as the sheer naked terror screaming through the collective consciousness of the Arbiters. He felt as if a flower had bloomed within him, a flower that had heightened his senses to their utmost and opened a door that led to a place inside him that he had never been before.

And he understood.

The magic that had been shackled within him for untold centuries erupted irresistibly through his body and he was catapulted into the air, arms flung out to his sides as if he was pinned to an invisible crucifix.

An eerie light began to surround him and emanated to all four corners of the room. As he stared at the stark shadows cast upon the walls, he sensed the bewilderment in Montagu turn to rage, yet he found that he did not fear it.

Turning casually towards the wizard, he sneered dismissively. "Do your worst, scum. You cannot hurt me any more."

This only served to anger Montagu even further and he sent a volley of fireballs in Arthur's direction.

With a barely perceptible flick of his hand, all but one of them deflected harmlessly away. The one that was not hovered mere inches above the surface of the palm of Arthur's right hand, spewing and spitting relentlessly, yet causing the King no discomfort.

He stared down his nose at Montagu as the sorcerer bellowed imprecations, sending forth all manner of violent spells towards the King. It availed him naught.

Arthur Pendragon, former King of the Britons and newest addition to the realm of magical practitioners that walked the land, began to laugh. The sound echoed around the chamber, booming in the ears of all who heard it. Slowly, a sense of hysteria began to pervade it and Arthur found it hard to catch his breath. The euphoria was beginning to overwhelm him and he tried desperately to keep his emotions in check.

For the very first time in his life, he was in control. He had the power to determine what would happen to him and he was beholden to no other. He tapped into the well of unspent magic inside him and sent it hurtling in all directions around the room.

The Arbiters screamed as magical fire consumed them but he heeded them not.

Montagu's body convulsed and writhed as agony upon agony ripped through it, tearing it to pieces in a bloody explosion, yet still Arthur laughed. Eventually the chaos subsided and the insanity that had overcome him dissipated and he was able to survey the absolute ruin he had wrought.

He stared at the seven piles of ash that were all that was left of the Arbiters.

His gaze then fell upon the remains of the blackened, smoking corpse of Montagu, twisted and unrecognisable.

His eyes then sought out the Grail. The Cup of Christ. The goblet from which He had sipped at the Last Supper in Gethsemane and which had also captured His blood as it spurted from the wound inflicted by the Roman legionary Longinus all those centuries ago.

As he looked at it, he glanced at the figure upon the screen which still fixed him with a piercing look but it was not long before he found his stare drawn irresistibly back to the holy vessel. He floated back to the mosaic-laden floor without taking his eyes from the goblet.

As he did so, Jesus Christ, Son of God, spoke to him. "You have finally come into your birthright, Arthur Pendragon. You have finally embraced your destimy. I knew all along that of those destined to wield the Grail, only you would be able to take it and all it stands for forwards into the next century and beyond." A wry smile creased his features. "I must say that Montagu's son was an unknown quantity, but it soon became clear that he was enveloped by an all-consuming desire to kill his father and so was tainted from the very beginning. But you, Arthur, you were always the paragon of virtue, the purest of the pure. You were always the figurehead destined to carry the Grail forward into the future." Jesus Christ of Nazareth spread his arms in a benevolent gesture. "Come, take up the vessel and walk with me into the age of glory and wonder that stands before us."

Arthur had not moved during the compelling speech. A million thoughts were rebounding around his mind and he found it difficult to concentrate on the praise being heaped upon him whilst Montagu's charred body still smouldered scant yards away from him.

"Please, Lord, there are many things I would ask of you," he began haltingly. "So much of this is beyond my comprehension."

Jesus smiled benignly. "You have all the time in the world now, Arthur. Ask on," he said.

"If Merlin was really in league with the dark one," Arthur stammered, unwilling to say Montagu's name any more now he had killed both father and son, "why did it take nearly a century and a half for him to convince me to go to Lindisfarne? If he had wanted to, he could have taken me there immediately after my false funeral had ended."

Jesus stroked his beard and replied. "He hid himself from Montagu's sight, hoping that Montagu would come to look for him and leave the Gospels unguarded so that he could steal them without him realising and then return to the Grail Lake with you. That is why he did not want to risk using magic whilst you trudged the land. He had been pondering various ways by which to obtain the book of my disciples by underhand means, but all his plans were foiled by Montagu taking the book away from the Abbey's confines."

The King nodded, still shaken by the depth of treachery that Merlin had stooped to.

He looked back towards the awfully maimed cadaver of Montagu. "What of him? Why did he despise me so much? I did nothing to him?" Arthur asked.

Jesus laughed heartily. "You prevented him from slaying his father. You blocked his fireball with Excalibur on the shores of the Grail Lake. You then compounded that by actually doing the deed and killing his father thus robbing him of his revenge, unless he could make the Grail his own. Then he would have had the power to bring his father back to life so he could torture and murder him again and again and again. The only person who could possibly have stood in his way was you, the last of my bloodline. Though you and I would not view it as such, your actions, even your very presence, were reason enough for him to kill you."

Arthur shook his head. "Why then did he not just kill me where I stood? Why show me what happened aboard the Skarvlang if he knew what the consequences would be?"

Jesus waved a dismissive hand, "A slight manipulation on my part. Up until now, Montagu had not seen the full conversation that I had with Merlin. Though I could not intervene directly, I used my affinity with the Grail to mask some of what went on aboard the longship. I ensured that Montagu knew of your bloodline but not of your power." Once again, the gaze held Arthur in its spell. "Believe me, Arthur, had I not done so, your life would have been taken immediately and the chance would have been lost. I had to fool Montagu into showing you this so that I could use the Grail to communicate with you, to inspire you, to allow you to take your place atop the pedestal of humanity, standing shoulder to shoulder with me on our journey to enlighten the world. To show everyone how to live life as it should be lived, free from oppression, free from tyranny and full of hope and joy."

Arthur nodded thoughtfully at the messiah's words. He was slightly stunned from the exhilaration of using his power for the first time, but instead of the uplifting thrill it should have been, he found himself feeling drained and empty. "Has the magic always been inside me?" he found himself asking.

"Yes, Arthur," Jesus intoned. "My blood is infused with it and it is present in you also."

"All those lives wasted," the King sighed, "all those undeserving souls sent to the Halls before their time because of this," he gestured towards the Grail, "because of me, because of Merlin, because of Montagu and his son. And all that time I had the potential in me to stop it, to stop all the bloodshed."

The more he thought about it, the angrier he became. "Why did you not come to me before now and tell me who I was, tell me what power I had at my disposal?" He jabbed an accusing finger towards Jesus. "I came into contact with the Grail when Galahad first found it. I could have utilised it then to lance the boil before it swelled, to cure the cancer before it had time to spread and ruin so many lives," he snarled.

The Son of God shook his head. "You were not ready then. You were still too far under the influence of Merlin, to the extent that he would have warped your good intentions to his own twisted ends. You had to be free of his persuasions before you could grow into your own skin."

Arthur advanced on the screen. "Do not preach to me. I am perfectly aware of what is right and what is wrong. If Merlin's designs had been anything other than just then I would not have acceded to them."

Jesus tried to keep his face neutral, but a flicker in his eyes indicated to the King that he was sceptical of his confidence in his own ability.

The lack of response or apology riled Arthur still further. "So you did not think me able to cope with Merlin's insinuating distractions, yet you seem quite well disposed to begin telling me what we are going to do now we have the Grail before I have even caught my breath." He hissed.

Still the messiah said nothing, but his brows tightened in a way that suggested the conversation was not progressing in the way he would have wished it to.

Arthur had begun to pace the chamber, no longer talking directly to Jesus. "All my life I have been pushed and pulled according to the whims of others and still it goes on. Still I am not free to live my life, to walk my own path." He shook his head and lapsed into a brooding silence.

Jesus was at a loss for words. "You have a gift now. You can repair what has gone before if it haunts you so," he blurted. "You can show all how it should be. You can show all how to live the ideals of Christian life."

"No," Arthur snapped. "What if they choose not to? What then? Am I to punish them or place them under a spell that compels them to follow?"

Baffled, Jesus said, "Why would they not want to live like that? Why would they not wish to gain entrance into my Father's kingdom?"

Arthur sighed and stared at the ceiling. "That is surely the point. Why is there a need to impel anyone? If your words are so just and right then why is there a need for coercion?" He countered.

"Some will always seek to undermine all that is good in the world," Jesus pointed out.

Arthur breathed deeply, pondering the argument. "That is true, I suppose," he murmured, almost to himself. Inside him a titanic conflict was underway. He could do so much good back in the land of the living but he knew it would all be false, it would be due to intimidation and domination and, worst of all, fear. He did not wish to be feared as a leader. When he had ruled Camelot, his enemies had indeed feared him but it had been a healthy fear borne of respect for his nobility and courage, not because he could snuff out their lives when the mood took him. "No, this is wrong," he muttered. "This is not how it should be. This is not how it should end." Tears welled in his eyes as the final brick in the foundation of his faith disintegrated. He stared at the man in whose name he had walked the earth for many lifetimes, the man who he had worshipped, the man who he had killed for. And that was what finally decided him on his course of action. Stripped of his powers and unable to bring to bear anything other than the force of his words, Jesus Christ, the messiah, the saviour of all, revealed himself to be just that. A man. A man seeking to manipulate Arthur to further his own ends, his own ambitions, just as so many had done before. Both Montagus, Merlin. Now, in Arthur's eyes, the man who stood before him was no different from them.

Fixing a sorrowful gaze upon Jesus, the King stalked over to the Grail and snatched it from its perch upon the Arbiters table.

The image of Christ wavered, rippled and began to fade.

"What are you doing?" the reedy voice wailed distantly.

"It is at an end. The quest is fulfilled. I have seized the Grail and prevented it falling into the hands of evil." He paused. "But at what cost? The Arbiters told me what had been started by myself, Montagu, Merlin and Mordred. If it is true, and of all whom I have encountered the Arbiters are the only ones whose words I count as trustworthy, then my conscience will not allow me to follow my own needs and yearnings."

The presence of Jesus Christ was now no more than a whisper in the air, yet still it sounded clearly in Arthur's ear. "What are you saying?" it asked.

"I must repair the damage done," Arthur said simply. "I will use the Grail to heal the ruin visited upon the Halls and then, as my magic has robbed the Halls of its judges, I will remain here with the Grail, for if there is anything within this realm or within the land of men that is incorruptible, then it is that." He walked round and sat on the chair in the centre of the Arbiters table. "Each soul will take sup from it and the Grail will determine their final path."

"No, you cannot." Jesus' wail dissolved into nothingness. With a tired flick of his hand, Arthur obliterated the remnants of the silver screen above the Grail. He stared for a time at the goblet, tracing the line of the filigree carving that ran along its base then travelling up the untarnished stem and eventually alighting on the brilliance of the jewels as they glittered in the light of the chamber. "Such potential," he sighed to himself. "But where there is potential for such good, then there is also potential for great evil. I could not live with myself if my stewardship were to be remembered only as a precursor to the death of freedom and the birth of tyranny."

He looked about the chamber, at the piles of rubble and the numerous small fires that dotted the devastated room. With a wave of his hand, he restored it to its former glory. "Still, as prisons go, this is not the worst by any means," he smiled slightly.

Picking up the Grail, he placed it in the exact centre of the table. Looking towards the door that led out into the deadness of the Halls, he said to it, "Come, let us begin to repair the havoc that we have instigated."

A white light blazed into the room, throwing everything into sharp relief for a second then a woman stood before him, looking dazed and confused.

Arthur beckoned her over, "Please be seated."

The woman stumbled to the table and sat upon the chair that Arthur had set in place, directly opposite where he sat.

"Drink," he said, indicating the Grail.

Her hand reached out to the ornate goblet and she took a long draught. "What happens now?" she asked once she had swallowed the sweet liquid.

"Justice," said Arthur Pendragon.

THE END

Lightning Source UK Ltd.
Milton Keynes UK
UKOW030646200512

192931UK00001B/1/P